# The Family

# THE FAMILY

## NAOMI KRUPITSKY

**WHEELER PUBLISHING**
A part of Gale, a Cengage Company

Wheeler Publishing Large Print Hardcover.
The text of this Large Print edition is unabridged.
Other aspects of the book may vary from the original edition.
Set in 16 pt. Plantin.

LIBRARY OF CONGRESS CIP DATA ON FILE.
CATALOGUING IN PUBLICATION FOR THIS BOOK
IS AVAILABLE FROM THE LIBRARY OF CONGRESS.

ISBN-13: 978-1-4328-9555-6 (hardcover alk. paper)

Published in 2022 by arrangement with G.P. Putnam's Sons, an imprint
of Penguin Publishing Group, a division of Penguin Random House LLC.

Printed in Mexico
Print Number: 01          Print Year: 2022

For Lil and Marty Krupitsky,
who never got to read this book,
but always knew I could write it.
And for New York City.

# PROLOGUE

## [JULY 1948]

Shooting a gun is like jumping into cold water.

You stand there, poised on the edge, muscles coiled to leap, and at every moment until the last, there is the possibility of not doing it. You are filled with power: not as you jump, but just before. And the longer you stand there, the more power you have, so that by the time you jump the whole world is waiting.

But the moment you leap, you are lost: at the mercy of the wind and gravity and the decision you made moments before. You can do nothing but watch helplessly as the water looms closer and closer and then there you are, submerged and soaking, ice gripping your torso with its hands, breath caught at the back of your throat.

So a gun unfired holds its power. In the moments before trigger clicks and bullet is unleashed, beyond your grasp, out of your control. As thunder crashes in the distant wet clouds and the electric air raises the small hairs on your arms. As you stand, feet planted like your papa taught you *just in case,* shoulder flexed against the recoil.

As you decide and decide again.

*Fire.*

■ ■ ■ ■

# Book One

1928–1937

■ ■ ■ ■

Sofia Colicchio is a dark-eyed animal, a quick runner, a loud shouter. She is best friends with Antonia Russo, who lives next door.

They live in Brooklyn, in a neighborhood called Red Hook, which is bordered by the neighborhood that will become Carroll Gardens and Cobble Hill. Red Hook is younger than Lower Manhattan, but older than Canarsie and Harlem, those wild outskirts where almost anything goes. Many of the buildings are low wooden lean-tos near the river, but the rooftops climb higher away from the waterfront, toward still-low but more permanent brick townhouses, everything a dark gray from the wind and the rain and the soot in the air.

Sofia's and Antonia's families moved to Red Hook on the instructions of their fathers' boss, Tommy Fianzo. Tommy lives in Manhattan, but he needs help managing

11

his operations in Brooklyn. When their neighbors ask Carlo and Joey what they do, Carlo and Joey say, *this and that.* They say, *importing and exporting.* Sometimes they say, *we're in the business of helping people.* Then their new neighbors understand and do not ask any more questions. They communicate via snapped-shut window shade, and by telling their children, *it's none of our concern,* loudly, in the hallway.

The other people in the neighborhood are Italian and Irish; they work the docks; they build the skyscrapers sprouting like beanstalks from the Manhattan landscape. Though the violence has abated since the adults in this neighborhood were children, it is still there, hovering in the spaces between streetlamp circles.

Sofia and Antonia know that they are to tell a grown-up before going to one another's houses, but not why. Their world consists of the walk to and from the park in the summers, the clang and hiss of winter radiators, and all year round, the faraway splash and echo of men working the docks. They know certain things absolutely, and do not know that there is anything they do not know; rather, the world comes into focus as they grow. *That's an elm tree,* Antonia says one

12

morning, and Sofia realizes there is a tree in front of her building. *Uncle Billy is coming for dinner tonight,* says Sofia, and Antonia suddenly knows that she hates Uncle Billy: his pointed nose, the shine of his shoes, the stink of cigars and sweat he leaves in his wake. *Cross the street or you'll wake the maga,* they remind each other, giving a wide berth to the smallest building on the block, where everyone knows — but how do they know? — that a witch lives on the third floor.

Sofia and Antonia know that Uncle Billy is not their real Uncle, but he is Family anyway. They know they are to call him Uncle Billy, like Uncle Tommy, and that they have to play nicely with Uncle Tommy's children at Sunday dinner. They know there will be no discussion in this regard.

They know that Family is everything.

Sofia lives in an apartment with three bedrooms and a wide window in the kitchen, which looks out onto the no-backyard-access backyard. The landlord sits out there in the summer with no shirt on and falls asleep with cigarettes dangling from his thick fingers. The midday heat burns the places his body is exposed to the sun, leaving the underside of his round belly and arms lily-white. Sofia and Antonia are not supposed to stare. In Sofia's room there is a bed with a new bedspread, which is red flannel; there are three dolls with porcelain faces lined up on the shelf; there is a plush rug she likes to sink her toes into.

Down the hall from her bedroom there is her parents' room, where she is not supposed to go unless it's an emergency. *Cara mia,* her papa says, *there have to be some things just for Mamma and Papa, no? No,* she responds, and he makes claws of his hands and chases her down the hall to tickle her, and she shrieks and runs. And then there is an empty room with a small cradle from when Sofia was a baby, which is no one's. Her mamma goes in there sometimes and folds very small clothes. Her papa says, *come on, let's not do this. Come on,* and leads her mamma out.

Sofia has just started to notice that people are afraid of her father.

At the deli or the café, he is served first. *Signore,* the waiters say. *So nice to see you again. Here — on the house. It's a specialty. Prego.* Sofia holds him by the hand like a mushroom growing from the base of a tree. He is her shade; her nourishment; her foundation. *And this must be Sofia,* they say. Her cheeks are squeezed; her hair is ruffled.

Sofia pays only a glancing attention to other adults. She notices when they enter her father's gravitational field, and when the warmth of his attention skips from one to another. She notices that her father always seems to be the tallest in the room. She accepts the offerings of jellied candies and biscotti handed down by men who, even Sofia can tell, are more concerned with currying her father's favor.

After his meetings Sofia's papa takes her for gelato; they sit at the counter on Smith Street and he sips thick black espresso while she tries not to drip stracciatella down the front of her shirt. Sofia's papa smokes long thin cigarettes and tells her about his meetings. *We're in the business of helping people,* he tells Sofia. *For that, they pay us a little bit, here and there.* So Sofia learns: you can help people, even if they are afraid of you.

She is his girl, she knows that. His favorite. He sees himself in her. Sofia can smell the danger on her father like a dog smells a storm coming: an earthy quickening in his wake. A taste like rust. She knows that means he would do anything for her.

Sofia can feel the pulse of the universe thrumming through her at every moment. She is so alive she cannot separate herself from anything around her. She is a ball of fire and at any moment she might consume her apartment, the street outside, the park where she goes with Antonia, the church and the streets her papa drives on for work, and the tall Manhattan buildings across the water. It is all tinder.

Instead of burning the whole world Sofia contents herself with asking why, *Papa, why, what is that.*

Antonia Russo lives in an apartment with two bedrooms, one that is hers and one that is her parents'. Her mamma and papa leave the door to their room open and Antonia sleeps best when she can hear the cresting waves of her papa snoring. Her kitchen has no window and a small round wooden table instead of the square dining table Sofia's family has. Her mamma scrubs and scrubs the floor and then sighs and says, *there is nothing to be done about this.* In the living room there are pictures on all the walls, the grayish-brown old-fashioned kind where everyone looks upset. The pictures are of Antonia's grandparents, before they left *the-oldcountry.* Sometimes her mamma looks at them and kisses the necklace around her neck and shuts her eyes tightly, just for a moment.

Antonia finds that though she is expected

to stay inside her own body, she often feels like she is in Sofia's body, or her mamma's body, or the body of the princess in a story. It is easy for her to slip away, spread out, and exist in the whole universe instead of within the confines of her own skin.

In the mornings, Antonia lines up her stuffed animals and names them. She makes her bed without being asked.

Sofia often appears in the doorway of Antonia's home with unbrushed hair and dirt under her fingernails; she possesses the effortless light of the sun, sure she will rise, confident that she can wake everyone up. Antonia is both attracted and repelled: fascinated in the way a child will circle a dead bird, admire a lone feather, build a shrine to it. She is scrupulous about her own appearance. She wants to drink Sofia, to fill herself with her friend's addictive magic.

Sofia and Antonia spend all of their time together, because they are young, and they live next door to one another, and their parents encourage their friendship. It is convenient for parents when your child can always be found with someone else's.

The texture of Sofia's walk is as familiar to Antonia as the heft and rhythm of her own; her reflection in Sofia's brown eyes is more grounding than the reflection of a mirror. Sofia, for her part, recognizes Antonia by way of a smell of powder and lilies, left in her room long after her friend has gone home for dinner; by the perfectly stacked tower of blocks on her shelf; in the wave of her favorite doll's neatly brushed hair.

Sofia and Antonia do not realize that their friendship is undisturbed by other children.

Sofia and Antonia close their eyes and make the world. Together, they go on safari, narrowly escaping bloody death in the teeth of a lion. They travel in airplanes, to Sicilia, where their families are from, and to Japan, and to Panama. They survive in the wilderness with only two sticks and a tin of Christmas cookies to sustain them; they escape quicksand and locusts. They marry princes, who ride down bedraggled Red Hook avenues on horseback. Sofia and Antonia straddle their own horses. They lean forward and whisper into their horses' ears. They shout, *fly like the wind!* and are *hushed* by their mammas. *Go play somewhere else,* the mammas say. Sofia and Antonia play on the moon.

Antonia feels free next to Sofia, who is lit by an internal flame that Antonia can warm her hands and face next to. Antonia catches herself just watching Sofia sometimes; staring at the place her dress tugs between her shoulders as she hunches over a table, or forgetting to rinse her hands as they wash up side by side in the bathroom before dinner. *If I can see you, I must be here.* Antonia feels that without Sofia she might float away, disintegrate into the night air. And Sofia, comfortable in the spotlight of her friend's undivided attention, feels herself growing brighter as it shines. *If you can see me, I must be here.*

Antonia and Sofia live, mostly, with their mothers, and with each other. Their fathers are often gone, though Sofia's father comes home for supper often enough that she can feel his presence like bookends to her days: filling the house with the smell of brilliantine and espresso in the morning; rumbling around the kitchen just before she goes to bed at night. Sometimes, the click of the front door and his retreating footsteps just as she falls into sleep: leaving again.

Antonia has no idea that her father's absence two or three nights a week is unusual compared with other fathers in her neighborhood, or that her mother once broke down crying in the butcher, overcome with a deep, existential exhaustion from planning meals "for two *or* three," or that deep in the belly of the night when her father comes home, he tiptoes into Antonia's room and cups her forehead in his palm and shuts his eyes in prayer. Antonia doesn't know what he does, only that it is work with Uncle Billy or Uncle Tommy. *He has meetings,* Sofia once told her. *Meetings about helping people.* But something about that seems insubstantial and incomplete to Antonia. Here is what she knows: she knows that while he is gone her mother is never the right size and shape — either larger than life, trailing a cloud of matter and chaos around as she obsessively cleans, arranges, fixes, fusses; or small, skeletal, a shadow of her usual self. And Antonia, five years old, depends upon her mother the way the ocean depends on the moon: she grows and shrinks accordingly.

She imagines her father sitting in a small room. Uncle Billy smokes cigars and swivels back and forth in his chair and gesticulates fiercely and shouts into a telephone. Uncle Tommy stands in a corner and watches over them; he is the boss. Her father sits quietly, with pen and paper. Antonia puts him at a desk and gives him an expression of deep concentration. He stares out the window, and occasionally drops his gaze to scribble something on his paper. He stays out of the fray.

Antonia thinks she can make the world up if she shuts her eyes.

At night, when her mother has put her to bed, Antonia can feel the apartment straining up away from its foundation. The weight of herself and her mother is not enough to keep it attached to the earth, and so it bucks and floats and Antonia shuts her eyes and builds foundation brick by brick until she drifts into sleep.

In the next room, her mother reads, or, more than once, slips on shoes and goes next door to drink three fingers of wine with Sofia's mother, Rosa. The two women are subdued, weighted down by the knowledge that their husbands are out doing *God-knows-what, God-knows-where.* They are both twenty-seven; by day, each of them can conjure the blinding glow of youth, but by lamplight, maps of concern crease each of their faces; some pockets of skin darken with exhaustion while others thin over the bone. They, like so many women before them, are made older by worry, and stretched taut by the ticking seconds, which they swear pass slower at night than during the light of day.

Antonia's mamma, Lina, has a nervous

constitution. As a child Lina stayed in to read when the other children played rough outside. She looked back and forth five or six times before crossing streets. She startled easily. Lina's mother often looked at her sternly, shook her head, sighed. Lina will always be able to picture this. Look; shake; sigh. Marrying Carlo Russo did not make her less nervous.

Every time Antonia's papa, Carlo, leaves the house, fear whittles away at Lina's person until he is home again. And when Tommy Fianzo decides he needs Carlo to spend nights picking up and transporting crates of Canadian liquor, fear grips Lina around the throat and will not let her sleep at all.

So Lina develops a system: she doesn't worry until the sun comes up. When she is awakened by the pulled-taffy air stretched between herself and Carlo, by the knowledge that he is elsewhere and has taken the most vulnerable part of her with him, Lina slips out of bed and alights on the floor lightly, like a bird. She pads down the steps of her building and up into the Colicchio apartment next door. She uses her spare key, and she sits on the couch with Rosa until she can bear the silence of her own apartment.

Just before dawn, Lina knows a key will turn in the front door. Carlo will move quietly into the apartment. And it, and she, will settle back down into the earth where they belong.

Sofia's mamma, Rosa, remembers her own father working nights. Rosa stayed at home with her mother, who spent her days finishing the buttonholes of men's shirts, making small stitches and worrying about Rosa's father, spinning yarns for her children about her childhood before the boat ride to America, shouting at them to finish their homework, for God's sake, to study, to sit up straight, to be careful, to make something of themselves, her babies. Rosa's mother, with her raw fingertips from sewing, slicing onions for dinner and never wincing, but shutting her mouth, quiet for once, which is how Rosa and her siblings knew she was in pain. This all made sense to Rosa: the building of community and home no matter how, no matter where, no matter what the cost.

So when she met tall and striking Joey Colicchio, who had accepted a job from her father's associate Tommy Fianzo Sr., Rosa knew what it would take to build her own house.

■ ■ ■ ■

Antonia and Sofia do not always go to sleep when their mammas tell them to. They pass many hours pressing messages to one another through the wall between their bedrooms. They doze fitfully. Sleep is not as finite for them as it is for adults: there is no reason they cannot continue their conversation in a dream. They tell each other, *your mamma is here tonight,* because of course they know. And the mammas sit pressed together in one kitchen or another, sipping their wine and laughing, sometimes, and crying, others, and of course, they know when their daughters fall asleep, because they can still feel the shapes of those daughters turning against the insides of their bellies.

They remember being pregnant at the same time: tender to the touch, humming with potential. That, more than their husbands' shared work, is what bonded them.

When they were pregnant is when Rosa and Lina took to whispered late-night conversations in one another's apartments. There, by low light, they laid themselves open. They talked about the future, which always means talking about the past: about Rosa's father and mother, their buzzing, bustling house, and about how Rosa wanted a bustling house of her own. *But no needles,* Rosa always said, *no thread.* No raw-pricked fingers. Her children would want for nothing. Lina, whose future had always felt like a vise tightening, was just relieved to love the baby growing inside of her more often than she was afraid of it. She thought of her own childhood, where there was no room for want in the face of the fight for survival. *No have-to's,* she told Rosa. *No musts.* Her children would have a full world of choice. She would teach them to read.

*It looks like a boy,* the other Family ladies told Rosa at the butcher, at the park. *It looks like twins,* they told Lina, who was big, big, big, and could no longer fit in her usual shoes, and could not see her feet anyway, and who thought, *of course, I will not be good at this either.* The ladies reached out their hands to pinch Rosa's and Lina's faces and pat the domes of their stomachs. Rosa and Lina interlocked elbows and hobbled down the street. They realized that their babies would not have a blank slate: that they would be born into a world that expects them to be the right size, shape. *If it's a boy,* they prayed, *let him be good with his hands.*

*If it's a girl, let her be careful with her heart.*
Lina, with her clammy hands and her pinched low back, added, *let this child fear nothing.*

In the fall of 1928, Sofia and Antonia start school together, and the world gets exponentially bigger with each passing day. They race there each morning, tripping over each other's feet and legs. They are fierce and small, and arrive breathless and early. They learn numbers, and letters, and geography.

They learn on the first day that half the kids in their class are Italian, and half are Irish. They learn that Ireland is a small island far away from Italy, but not as far away as America, *where we all are,* says Mr. Monaghan. Sofia and Antonia make friends with Maria Panzini and Clara O'Malley. They are all wearing blue ribbons in their hair. They decide they will also do this tomorrow. They eat lunch together and they hold hands on the way out to their waiting mammas. *Mamma, mamma,* the four of them are ready to call out, but the mammas have dark shades drawn over their faces.

The next day Maria Panzini eats lunch with another table of girls, and Clara eats all the way across the courtyard. *The Irish kids eat over there,* Antonia realizes. *Just stick with Antonia,* Sofia's mamma says later. *Our families are a little different,* Rosa and Lina tell their daughters, and Sofia and Antonia don't know whether that means they are better or worse, but soon they spend lunch alone.

They still love school, because of Mr. Monaghan, who fought in the Great War and has a limp, and who lives by himself in the basement apartment of a run-down brownstone a stone's throw from the ship forge. Mr. Monaghan has a twinkle in his eye. He is long and lanky and lively. He looks at them when they speak.

Every morning they spin a globe and pick a part of the world to learn about. This is how they have come to know about the pyramids, and the Taj Mahal, and Antarctica. No matter where Mr. Monaghan's finger lands, he knows stories about the place, and he has pictures, and he tells them great, animated, nearly too-tall tales that hold twenty children rapt, still as stones in their seats. And today Marco DeLuca has stolen Sofia's turn to spin the globe.

He did it without knowing, which means

when Sofia looks at him with a furrow in her brow and a boiling fury in her chest, he returns her gaze with his own soft, impassive stare, and does not know why she is glaring, and that makes it worse. Inside Sofia's body a heat builds, flushing her face and shaking her fingertips and turning the breath in her body to bile. Later in her life, friends and family will come to recognize the telltale tightening at the mouth and narrowing of the eyes as Sofia sinks into anger. She, too, will come to appreciate the hot, swollen, all-consuming fire of an imminent fight.

Today Sofia does not participate as her classmates look at pictures of sea creatures in old copies of *National Geographic* and Mr. Monaghan's special *Encyclopædia Britannica*. She does not *ooh* and *whoa* with them as Mr. Monaghan draws a to-scale stick figure of a human being on the chalkboard, and next to it a to-scale giant squid, and next to that a blue whale. She stares at Marco, and she waits in vain for Mr. Monaghan to remember that it should have been her turn. She feels the great unfairness of life rippling through every fiber of her being.

Antonia knows something is wrong with Sofia with the sixth sense of someone who does not understand, yet, that human beings think of themselves as separate containers. She participates in the sea creatures lesson, though rumbling around in the crush of children without Sofia makes her nervous. She cranes her neck with everyone else to see the picture of sharks lined up by size, and gasps on cue at the diagram of a shark's many rows of sinister, red-rimmed teeth, but she sits quietly as Mr. Monaghan calls on her classmates to name the seven seas, and doesn't raise her hand even when the rest of the class is stumped on "Indian." She looks down at her shoes, which are very black against the pale of her stockinged legs. For a moment, she imagines being one inch tall. She could live inside her desk then — weave blankets out of torn-up paper, the way the mice she found in her closet had done with tissues; eat crumbs and bits of rice from leftover arancini and the occasional shaving of milk chocolate. She does not notice Sofia narrow her eyes as Marco makes his way back up the row of desks.

It is this moment that Sofia's anger boils and cannot be contained inside her skin anymore. As Marco DeLuca approaches her seat, Sofia clenches her small hands, and extends her leg to catch him across the shins.

Antonia looks up to see Marco DeLuca sobbing as he picks himself up from the floor. In the din that follows, Antonia snatches up images that she will sort out later — Sofia, her leg still lifted into the aisle, her mouth open in shock; Maria Panzini, wailing and clutching the side of her desk in a very good impression of an old lady; Mr. Monaghan, face bare in unmasked shock and horror; and a single, glistening, red-rimmed tooth, lying on its side on the linoleum floor.

And as Antonia watches, she sees a strange expression creep over Sofia's face — a version of the one Sofia's father wears when he smashes a water bug under his shoe, or slits the glistening belly of a fish.

That expression will haunt Antonia for many years. It will come back to her in the moments she is not sure whether to trust Sofia, during the dark and thin parts of their friendship. There is a seed of something volatile in Sofia. Antonia searches herself and cannot find a similar place. She does not know whether or not she is relieved.

Later that evening, Sofia sits in her chair in the kitchen, snapping the ends off of green beans. She understands by the stiffness of her mamma's shoulders and the thick quiet in the kitchen that she is in trouble. Tripping Marco had made her feel giddy, and a little surprised. She hadn't meant to hurt him. But Sofia does not quite feel sorry.

Every Sunday, after Mass, the Russos and the Colicchios pile into one car and drive across the Brooklyn Bridge, to Tommy Fianzo's house for dinner.

Tommy Fianzo lives in a sprawling four-bedroom penthouse close enough to Gramercy Park that everyone who walks by outside his home is dressed head to toe in silk and leather, furs and pearls. He doesn't have a key to the park but can often be heard telling anyone who will listen that he doesn't want one, doesn't care about the things the Americans do, *here, your glass is empty, come, have a drink, have some wine.* The Colicchios and the Russos arrive as one unit in a slow parade of Tommy's employees.

By three o'clock, the usually spacious-seeming Fianzo apartment is stuffed to the brim with the buzzing and spitting of adults, the smell of wine and garlic. In the winter, the windows steam and the house fills with the singed, snowy smell of gloves and scarves drying on radiators; in the summer there is the sharp stench of sweat, and melting buckets of ice for lemonade and white wine on every surface. Antonia and Sofia are quickly forgotten in the maelstrom and fend for themselves with the other Family children, who they see once a week but who they do not know well, because their families are the only ones who live in Red Hook.

Tommy Fianzo has a son, Tommy Jr., who is bigger than Sofia and Antonia and mean, given to vicious pinches and obscene gestures when no adults are looking. Tommy's brother Billy comes, who Sofia and Antonia like even less than Tommy's son. He doesn't have a wife, or children, and he seems to skulk at the edges of rooms like a barnacle on a rock. His eyes are narrow and black, and his teeth crowd into his mouth like commuters on a train platform. He rarely speaks to them, but he watches them with his beady eyes, and Sofia and Antonia avoid him.

At six, Tommy Fianzo and his wife carry the platters of food into the room. *Bellissima,* the guests cheer. They welcome the bowl of pasta, the falling apart lamb, the cold plates of beans and sliced squid drenched in olive oil, the slippery roasted red peppers. The guests kiss their fingers. They beam. *Moltissime grazie,* they moan. *I have never been so full. I have never seen*

33

*food so beautiful.*

For the most part, Sofia and Antonia are ignored: left to their own devices, they play precarious games of tag, racing around the table and between the legs and gesturing elbows of adults. The house fills with pipe tobacco and ladies' perfume; the chaos is friendly, familiar, the burbling high point of a wave. Eventually, their parents fill their plates.

On the way home, Sofia and Antonia are half-asleep, eyes lowered, limbs heavy. Manhattan sparkles through the car windows as they flash over the Brooklyn Bridge. And if they are lucky, Antonia's papa will put a hand to each of their backs and sing to them, low and soft songs that he remembers from his own mamma, from the island where he grew up. He tells them about the red-hot dirt, the whitewashed ancient church, the fragrant shade of gnarled lemon trees, the old woman with long and tangled hair who lived in a hut overlooking the sea.

When they get home, the Colicchios and the Russos unfurl from the car and the grown-ups kiss one another before they go into their respective apartments. Carlo carries Antonia upstairs and Joey takes Sofia by the hand and Rosa and Lina share a lingering look at one another, at their husbands, at their girls.

*Papa,* Antonia says, before she drifts into solid sleep, *you would rather be here all the time instead of going to work, wouldn't you.* It is not a question. *Cara mia,* Carlo whispers. *Of course.*

In the other room, Lina Russo always knows when Carlo gives this answer. She knows when Carlo eases their daughter into sleep. *Cara mia,* and Lina is weighted down at last, balanced and calm. *Of course.*

On Sundays after Sofia is asleep Rosa stands still in her living room and surveys her territory. *Cara mia,* she thinks. Her sleeping daughter, who wants for nothing. Her husband with his raised eyebrows, waiting for her to decide the room can be abandoned for morning. *Of course.*

The next morning Sofia will wake in her bed, and Antonia will wake in hers. The garbage carts come on Monday morning and if the trashmen look up, they sometimes see, in adjoining buildings on a small side street in Red Hook, two little girls in nightgowns, both staring out of their windows as a new week begins.

The summer when Sofia and Antonia are seven, their parents decide they have had enough of the punishing heat, and plan a beach trip.

At the beginning of August, they set out: Antonia's mamma crammed into the tiny backseat with Sofia, Antonia, and the luggage, the other grown-ups in front. They join the throngs of New Yorkers crowding the Long Island Motor Parkway and proceed to inch along, a couple of miles per hour, for the whole afternoon.

The sun beats down on top of the car and inside they sweat into their clothes and seats and try their best not to touch each other. The traffic moves like a full and languid snake across Long Island.

Sofia quickly grows tired of watching the occupants of other cars and falls to counting the spots on her new skirt, but Antonia leans forward around Sofia and watches as a man in a suit picks his nose; as a woman with a white blouse taps her manicured finger idly on the windowsill; as two children push each other in a backseat that looks roomy and clean compared to the one Antonia is stuffed into like an oiled sardine.

Outside, the scenery is increasingly marshy. The trees shrink and curl, bent by a lifetime of Atlantic wind. It is desolate and calm.

Antonia's papa, Carlo, looks at the browning, windblown grasses. He knows the exact moment his life turned in this direction instead of another.

It was the summer of 1908, ten days before his ocean liner docked at Ellis Island. He was sixteen years old, and he was hungry. His mother had stuffed his trunk with sausages and cheese; thick black bread; oranges from the orchard. She had also folded his grandmother's rosary into his fist and held him tightly and sobbed.

Carlo ate like a king for the first two days of his trip. He spent the following week curled in a fetal position around a sloshing, putrid bucket.

It was on that ship that he met Tommy Fianzo, who had crossed the ocean five times. Tommy dragged Carlo out of his seasick stupor and fed him warm water, biscuit crumbs, weak broth. Tommy told Carlo to avoid coughing in the Ellis Island immigration line. Tommy offered Carlo a job.

It started as inexplicable errands. *Stand here on this corner,* Tommy might say, *and watch that man — that one, with the red shirt, sitting at that café. Follow him if he leaves. I'll catch up with you later.* Or, *when a tall man comes out of this door, tell him Mr. Fianzo says hello.* He arrived when he was told and stayed until he was told to leave. He picked up packages and dropped them off. Eventually, he began accompanying Tommy's brother Billy on overnight expeditions to pick up shipments of top-shelf bootleg liquor upstate. For his compliance and for all of the questions he did not ask, Carlo was paid — and handsomely. He sent his mamma packages stuffed with cash.

Carlo woke each morning with New York City drumming through him like a heartbeat. Eventually, he learned to walk quickly down the crowded Manhattan avenues; to see the people around him without really looking at them; to let himself be buoyed along by the rushing pulse of humanity. The summer smell of rotting fruit and charred meat and hot cobblestone was replaced by the damp leaves and roasted nuts of fall, and then muted in winter. Carlo felt taller with each season that passed.

And Tommy Fianzo was a kind and knowledgeable tour guide. Tommy introduced him to men close to his age; one of them, Joey Colicchio, became his best friend. Together, they drank until dawn; they sucked down oysters by the dozen at hole-in-the-wall bars; they felt themselves begin to put out the roots that would bind them to New York City. And Tommy was there when they cried for their mothers as the winter wind sucked at their skin, and when they needed a woman, and when they needed a post office or a telephone installation.

For the first few months, in fact, Carlo didn't know how he would have gotten along without Tommy. Tommy told him where he could go in search of clothing, furniture, tobacco, food; which church basement would become a dance hall filled with eligible Italian girls on a Friday night.

It was several years after he arrived in America, somewhere in the churning innards of one of these dances — the flocking of young men and women back and forth, the display, like birds, of their finest clothes; the turbulent air making them all jittery — that Carlo met Lina, who became his wife on a stormy fall afternoon soon afterward. Carlo despaired about the rain, sputtering as it did in sheets of icy needles with each gust of wind, but Tommy said, *sposa bagnata, sposa fortunata,* and straightened Carlo's tie before the ceremony, and looked at him like a brother.

Tommy encouraged Carlo to befriend a certain *type* of immigrant — one with slicked-back hair and a clean-shaven face. Carlo learned to ask if someone was in the Family, and to keep his distance if the answer was no.

It was many years of work for Tommy before Carlo began to notice himself answering questions with, *"Well, Tommy might not like it if . . ."* or, *"Tommy usually says . . ."* It was years more before he began to catalogue the pieces of the life he had built for himself — apartment, wardrobe, whereabouts — and trace each thread of that life back to Tommy. By the time Carlo was keeping a shaky-handed, shallow-breathed watch outside of rooms where unspeakable acts of violence were doled out for minor infractions against the Fianzo Family, it was too late for him to extract himself.

The week he learned he would be a father, Carlo walked up and down the New York avenues asking for jobs — in Brooklyn, in

Manhattan, in restaurants, in factories, in a printing press, as a doorman, a gardener, a plumber's assistant. He tried to apprentice himself to bricklayers. He walked into a boutique with a *Shopgirl Wanted* sign. Everywhere, he was greeted by eyes that would not meet his. He later learned that the one maître d' who had accepted his handshake turned up with a broken arm and wild eyes three days afterward. Tommy took Carlo to dinner and told him over filettos of veal so tender they dissolved without being chewed that they were family; they were brothers; if there was anything that was upsetting Carlo he could talk about it. "We'll always keep you safe," Tommy had said, earnest face made sinister in the low candlelight of the restaurant. After dinner the two men embraced in the midnight gaslight and Tommy cupped Carlo's neck with his palm and called him brother again. "Business is booming," Tommy said as he walked away.

That night, Carlo couldn't sleep. *We'll always keep you safe,* Tommy said in his head.

As he looks at the browning, windblown grasses, blurred together now as the car speeds up out of the sludgy New York traffic, Carlo Russo feels something soften inside of him. Suddenly, he could be any-one: a schoolteacher, a dentist, a blacksmith. A regular man, on vacation with his family. Carlo leans out the window and feels the hot air on his face and becomes lighter.

Though he has told no one, not even Joey, Carlo has a plan. This is the last year he will work for the Fianzos. Carlo has been saving small bills in a roll under his floorboard. Just pennies, shaved off here and there, from the money he collects for Tommy Fianzo. He has been inquiring — subtly, this time — about other jobs, in other states. There are farms in Iowa; there are fishermen in Maine; in California, he hears, oranges and grapes ripen under a familiar sun. Carlo is building something of his own. He imagines being in a car several months from now, Lina at his side, Antonia sleeping in the backseat. Driving his family due west at the speed of light.

Joey Colicchio taps his fingers on the steering wheel in time with a beat in his head and does not think about work either. He especially does not think about the fact that Carlo — sweet Carlo, family man Carlo, Carlo of the big heart — has brought in less cash than he was assigned for several months, barely, but enough that Tommy Fianzo has noticed, has asked Joey about it, has said *hm,* in a tone that Joey knows belies deep suspicion and danger. He especially does not think of that, because he is with his family, and his wife is smiling for the first time in weeks, and the persistent trail of sweat that leaks down into a puddle at his lower back all summer will feel a sea breeze this weekend. Joey knows that Carlo is dissatisfied. Flighty, Tommy calls it. *Our flighty friend,* he says. Tommy purses his lips; *it can't go on. Commitment is essential in a family.* And in those moments Joey nods and feels like a traitor. He is good at his job. He doesn't feel restless or ambivalent, like Carlo does. Not anymore. Not since he decided he would feel grateful, and accepted, and important instead.

Joey Colicchio had been brought to America by his parents when he was small enough to fit in the crooks of his mamma's elbows. He imagines that he can remember a wooden bunk attached to the floor and ceiling; the boat rocking steadily on its way to somewhere else. The song of his parents' hopes for him as they whispered through the seasick nights.

He does know that his papa insisted on Brooklyn, rather than the small Italian neighborhood in the heart of Manhattan, because he had heard there were still farms there. *We are farming people,* Joey can remember his papa saying. *How do you know which way is up if you can't see the ground?* Joey's father had wanted his children to have a sense of their roots, more than anything. It had caused him physical pain to collect his wife and his son and bundle them onto a boat to a new country, where they would never again feel the warm Sicilian dirt between their toes; where they would lose the ability to tell what time of year it was by the quality of the light, by the melody of the cicadas; where they would forget the old dialect in favor of hybridized American-Italian syntax that would be neither American nor Italian. Joey's father had wanted Joey to know what it felt like to belong somewhere.

Unfortunately, America seemed not to want Joey's family to feel like they belonged. They settled in Bensonhurst, a quickly growing Italian and Jewish settlement so far south in Brooklyn Joey grew up joking it was easier to go down around the South Pole to get to work in Manhattan than it was to fight the traffic on the Brooklyn Bridge. The community was insular; they hardly left; they found themselves unwelcome in any area where the majority population was not Italian. Joey's father took a job on a construction crew that spent more time hanging precariously from ropes in the air than digging in the earth. When they dug, it was to chisel out the landscape, to tame and iron flat the hills of Manhattan and the bigger Brooklyn settlements. Progress in New York was to be industry: buildings covering every square inch of the already-bursting islands.

Joey, though his parents filled his head with their dreams for him — be a doctor, be a scientist, own a business, bring us grandchildren — found that though he had grown up there, America accepted him only under strict conditions. *Stay with your own kind; take the jobs we do not want.* The American dream would have to be gleaned, bought, or stolen.

As soon as he was sixteen, Joey joined his father and a team of other barrel-chested, foul-mouthed, big-hearted Sicilian men who spent their days constructing the city. Joey finished every day caked in brick dust. He walked home with his father through the rows of immigrant homes and each day he could feel the disappointment rising off his father like a fever.

Over the course of those walks home Joey grew into his adult form, which would be tall and broad, with straight shoulders and arms crisscrossed with ropes of hardworking muscle. Joey's nose lengthened and his eyes sharpened. And as they did, he began to evolve out of his little boy's empathy for his father. *You brought us here,* he imagined saying. *This is your fault!*

Joey's ears also began to pick up more sound; he started listening to the hum of rumors that sustained the construction crew as they raised roofs and dug foundations. It was said that there were *organizations* in Manhattan; small hubs of Italian men with real power, who walked where they wanted. Who ate at beautiful restaurants; not just Italian ones, but American steakhouses; small cafés where the owners served delicacies from their own homelands: spiced meats wrapped in pastry, raw fish with gingered dressings. These men did not live in poor facsimiles of the villages back home. They lived in America.

Because Joey was young and shimmering with potential, it was not hard for him to wend his way into the good graces of Tommy Fianzo, who recognized in Joey a combination of determination and canniness that would serve him well in the intestinal New York streets.

And, ignoring his mother's entreaties and

46

his father's stunned silence, and the rumors that as the *organizations* grew bigger, so did the acts of violence they were compelled to commit, and the jail sentences they were compelled to serve, Giuseppe Colicchio strode chest first, eyes blazing, into the new world on his own.

Maybe the difference between Joey and Carlo can be explained like this: When Antonia was born, Carlo wept, and apologized to the silky down on top of her head, for not being able to escape his job before she arrived. When Sofia was born, Joey kissed Rosa, donned his hat, took a car to the Lower East Side, and bought a gun.

In the front seat, next to Joey, Rosa Colicchio is imagining what she will name their next baby, even though she worries it is bad luck. She is thinking of the name Francesca, which was her grandmother's name. Her grandmother, whom Rosa never met, sent each of her children to America with one jar full of tears and another of olive pits, for luck. Rosa Colicchio is in need of some luck. When Sofia was a baby, Rosa imagined surrounding herself with children. Now that Sofia has lengthened — suddenly! — into a little girl, with big hands and feet and fierce eyes and a sharp tongue, Rosa has narrowed her wishes down to just one. One more child. She thinks of Sofia, growing up without siblings. There is Antonia, for whom Rosa is immeasurably grateful. But Rosa's childhood was suffused with an inimitable sense of belonging, and she wants to give that to Sofia. To be surrounded by other people who were made like you. Together, to be a river, rather than a solitary puddle.

Rosa does not have the vocabulary to be disappointed in her body's function, or lack thereof. But something unnameable would feel more full, more complete, better, if she had another child. She would feel good — a good mother, a good wife. Rosa has always wanted to be good. She turns her face away from the window and blinks to clear her eyes and breathes away quick clenching panic.

"The air is starting to smell like ocean," says Joey. They are driving alongside sand and sparse grasses now. Small birds dart riotously across the road.

There is a collective sniff and sigh of appreciation, and then everyone in the car falls back into their own thoughts. By the time they get to the inn, everyone is exhausted and on edge.

Dinner is served on the porch, and the

wind blows lazily at napkins and shirt-sleeves. It is the first time Antonia or Sofia has had lobster, and they try to pinch each other with the claws until they dissolve in a fit of hysterical laughter and Rosa has to say *basta*! in a sharp whisper. But Sofia sees her smile a little, when she looks away.

The ocean stretches out in front of them, endless and roiling, as though there is nothing but water forever in all directions. The sunset turns the sky and the water pink, and then orange and a brilliant, hazy red before the sun slips away. Everyone watches until all they can see are flashes of moon reflected in the peaks of waves.

In the morning, Carlo teaches the girls to wade when the tide is still low and the waves small. Their mammas pick their way down from the sheltered porch and shade their eyes with their hands to watch. "Be careful," Carlo says, "if you see foam on top of a wave. That means it's going to crash." Sofia runs in after him and is soon soaked. Antonia stands in water up to her ankles and lets the tide tug her, toward shore and then away. She feels very small, and tired, as though the whole world is rocking her to sleep. Her feet are buried in sand underwater.

She does not see Sofia waving to her. "Look how far I am, Tonia! Look!" Sofia faces her friend, backlit by morning sun. "Look how deep it's getting!" Neither Antonia nor Sofia notices the wave until it breaks: right at the small of Sofia's back, just surprising enough and strong enough to sweep her under the water.

Antonia shrieks, and yanks her feet out of the sand, and feels the ocean and the earth try to suck her in as she runs toward the spot where Sofia was pulled under. But just as suddenly, Sofia is up again, wiping her eyes and coughing, spitting out brine. Carlo has wrapped his big fingers around Sofia's shoulder, and Antonia is left with a pounding heart and unused adrenaline. She is surprised and comforted to realize that she would have gone in. She would have gone all the way in, if she needed to. She looks back at the mammas, standing on the shore. They are faraway shadows, but Antonia knows they would have gone in too.

Carlo pulls Sofia up by the arms and her legs wrap around his waist. He cups her face in his hands and says something Antonia cannot hear.

When all three of them are onshore again, he says, "Never turn your back on the ocean, girls. She's tricky, and she'll sneak up on you the moment you stop paying attention." His face is creased with worry and Antonia is seized by an urge to say, *it's okay, Papa,* but she doesn't.

Sofia, for her part, can't stop reliving the instant she was somersaulted under the waves. The ocean had been so much bigger and more powerful than she could have imagined. The water had rushed past her face and into her nose and eyes as though it already knew her. And how odd, to be suspended and turned that way. To have up and down made so thoroughly irrelevant.

The rest of the day passes in a slow haze. The girls are absorbed in themselves, and their parents, slightly tipsy and sun-drunk, chalk it up to the laziness of vacation. Supper is fish with boiled potatoes, and afterward, the innkeeper takes, with a wink, a brown bottle out of a locked cabinet. Sofia and Antonia are sent to bed, where they can hear the bones of the inn creak in the evening breeze, and the melody of their parents' murmuring on the porch. So it is that Sofia and Antonia fall into the sound sleep of children at the beach, both feeling strangely powerless, and strangely free.

Carlo Russo is awoken sometime in the middle of the night by a soft knock on the door. It is the innkeeper, who apologizes profusely for disturbing him and tells Carlo he's needed on the telephone.

Carlo pulls a robe around himself. There is only one person who would call him so late at night. Only one person who could summon him at a moment's notice, call him from his sleep and his family.

And there is only one reason Carlo can think of that Tommy Fianzo would call him right now.

"Yes, boss," says Carlo into the hallway telephone. He stands up straight as though Tommy can see him. Inside his body, fear rises. It fills his lungs. Carlo pictures the sea. He is drowning even as he stands in the hallway. *She'll sneak up on you. The moment you stop paying attention.*

"I need you to come outside," says Tommy. "I need you to take a little walk."

And soon it is morning. Lina Russo wakes later than she normally does. She stretches her arms and legs under the covers and rolls over. She remembers she is on vacation, and when she rises she will drink coffee and watch the sun climb higher over the ocean. She thinks she will reach for her husband if Antonia is still sleeping.

But then Lina sees the long rectangle of

white morning sun blazing in through her window. She notices Carlo's empty side of the bed. And she feels, with a terrible force like every skyscraper in New York City has collapsed in unison, like acid has been poured down through the hollow places in her bones, like God himself has descended to tell her, that Carlo is gone.

Antonia is downstairs eating cereal with Sofia when she hears the scream. It is unrecognizable as her mamma until her mamma enters the screened-in porch where they are eating, still keening. The scream rattles the dishes on the tables. It makes the hair on Antonia's neck stand on end.

This is how Antonia feels the loss of her papa: a light connecting her to the rest of the world suddenly goes out. The path forward is shrouded in darkness. Antonia drops her spoon and a long crack like a hair appears on the inside of her cereal bowl. Dread crawls like a thick slug down her throat.

And before Lina has managed to get the words out, Antonia knows that both of her parents are gone.

The day Carlo disappears is a nightmare. It isn't in focus; it feels like it must be happening to someone else, but for the few isolated moments that appear crystal clear, real as sun, as concrete. For the rest of their lives, the girls will know that Lina was convinced to take a draft of hot whiskey with a pill the innkeeper draws from a cabinet, saying, *my wife used to — this will help*. They will remember Joey and Rosa, faces like ice.

There is a moment Sofia and Antonia are alone in the room they shared. They are packing to leave. They are each absorbed in the process of picking up things — a sock, a camisole, a doll — and placing those things into their suitcases. When they make eye contact across the room, they both want to speak. But they cannot hear one another over the roar of the old world as it turns into a new one.

When they get home, Joey kisses Sofia on the top of the head and tells Rosa he has to go out for a meeting. Antonia releases Sofia's sweaty hand and takes Lina's cold one and they walk up the stairs to their own apartment. Rosa makes a thick minestrone that fogs up the kitchen until she opens the window and the steam escapes with a gasp into the evening air. While it simmers she makes meatballs, unable to keep still.

She uses a closely guarded recipe involving beef, veal, pork, and, Rosa swears, and her mother swore before her, a tear from the jar her grandmother filled when she sent her children to America. The meatballs are a cure-all, the centerpiece of christenings and birthdays, but are also applied as a salve for failed tests and broken hearts and the unnameable melancholy of November.

Rosa is no stranger to the risks of the life she was born into, and so as she kneads the meatball mixture she is visited by a memory of her own mamma making dinner, waiting for her papa. Joey puts himself in danger, and Rosa holds the fear that something might happen to him. She holds it for Joey, who has no time to waste on fear, and for

Sofia, who may someday need to hold a family's worth of fear but who for now is spared. Her heart aches for Lina, who always felt fear but never knew how to contain it within herself, to use it as fuel. Rosa does not feel paralyzed in the face of Lina's catastrophe; instead, she feels herself expand to hold every note and tremble of worry. She will protect her family. She will fight for them. She will do this at the cost of everything else.

Rosa watches the carrots and tomatoes and beans as they spin in the boiling broth and feels herself settle. She remembers her mother in the kitchen, wrist-deep in ground meat, humming. Her father out, again, working — God knows where. God knows with whom. For God knows how long.

Joey knows without even asking that he needs to meet with Tommy Fianzo. There is a swirling, nauseous pit where his stomach and heart should be.

Joey knows Carlo would never have left his family. He also knows Tommy Fianzo would do anything to protect his standing as one of the most powerful men in Brooklyn. Carlo's ambivalence had been a weakness.

At the mouth of the Red Hook waterfront

there is a bedraggled concrete building where the Fianzos hold court. As Joey arrives he can smell the sea and has to stop and hold a hand to his chest to control himself. He saw Carlo just last night. Joey knew this was coming, didn't he? Somehow, he knew it would be soon. *You should have warned him,* he tells himself. And in the same moment, *I could never have warned him. I would have ended up just like him.* Sofia's face swims to the forefront of his mind. *He made his own decisions.*

And then, *this is your fault.*

Tommy is standing by the window of his office. When he sees Joey, he wraps him in a hug. He thumps Joey on the back, a clap that reverberates through Joey's heart and lungs. "I'm sorry about all this," he says. Joey can hear Tommy's voice move out around them in waves. It gets swallowed in the concrete walls. Joey fights an urge to sink into the comforting arms of the man who has guided him since he was a teenager.

Tommy pours them both glasses of wine. He gestures to the chair on one side of his desk and sits in the other. "Tension," he says, "does not look good, in a family. Conflict does not look good." He takes a sip of his wine. "It exposes us. It makes us vulnerable. You know Eli Leibovich?"

Joey shakes his head. No.

"You will, soon. He's making a name for himself on the Lower East Side. Jewish. Smart as hell."

Joey is used to the nature of a meeting with Tommy Fianzo. Tommy will get to his point eventually. His power affords him the right to express himself in whatever way he wants to. *Even if he has just disappeared your best friend.*

"I'm responsible for a lot of people, Colicchio. Not just you, and not just our flighty friend. A lot of men, and each of them has a family to take care of. So I look at someone like Carlo, and where you see a man who regrets his choices, who wants something different for himself and his family, I see a man who is endangering not just himself but me, and you, and everyone else in this Family. He was skimming off the top, did you know that?"

Joey did not know that. He knew Carlo was restless, ambivalent. *Flighty.* He didn't know Carlo was reckless. *Stupid.* He pictures Carlo, sliding a dollar out of the billfold. A moth circling the flame of freedom. A body, trailing a spiral of blood in the East River current. His breath hitches up into the back of his throat. Betrayal of trust: the worst possible crime. Unforgivable. "I didn't know, boss," he says.

Tommy continues. "Well, he was." Tommy pauses. A muscle twitches in the side of his neck. Tommy Fianzo is a good cook. He is a gentle father, when he wants to be. He is the most violent man Joey has ever known. To control himself in this moment must be costing Tommy a great deal. "He was stealing, from me. From us. And because it's my job, I'm looking across the river at someone like Eli Leibovich and I'm thinking ahead about how to protect us. I'm thinking about how we can offer up a united front."

Joey, unable to help himself, is caught up in the rise and swirl of Tommy's words. Tommy Fianzo, with his chiseled-out chin and the low boom and swell of his voice, exudes confidence. Righteousness. Power. Joey knows all this. He knows how it works. The transition from knowing how it works to experiencing how it works makes him dizzy.

"I've always hoped you'd be my number two, Colicchio. You're like a brother to me. You're good at this. It's why you understand that it's a good thing Carlo Russo seems to have gone away. You understand how it solves a problem."

Joey does understand, and he does not. Loss is like that. The world shimmers in and out of focus: one moment it is the place you live in, and the next it is utterly foreign, and you cannot even breathe the air.

"I think this loss will affect you, though," continues Tommy. "I worry you won't be able to think of me in the same way. If I'm being honest, I think Carlo's disappearance will make it impossible for us to trust each other. Do you agree?"

Joey hears himself nodding, the whistle of air past his eardrums. He feels like he is floating above his body, but he knows that his fists are clenched, that his breath is ragged, that there is boiling within him a vicious thing like hate or fear and that it is directed at Tommy Fianzo.

"So here's what I'd like to do," Tommy says. "I'd like to give you the promotion I always intended to, but a little earlier than planned. And with some conditions."

Then Tommy pulls a map of Brooklyn from his desk drawer, and he begins to outline a section, including Red Hook and Gowanus and a long rectangle up through Brooklyn Heights. "This," he explains, "will be your area. Minus this office, of course." The Fianzos, he explains, will let Joey operate relatively independently. He won't have to go to meetings with them; they will not eat together each week; Joey can hire who he likes, as long as Tommy Fianzo gets a hefty percentage of Joey's earnings each month. This, Tommy explains, is in the interest of keeping the peace. "War does not look good in a family," he repeats. "Losing two strong young men, when it's possible to lose only one, does not look good." Looking good is something the Family needs to do in front of its enemies, and even, though Tommy does not admit it, in front of the Americans, who think the Family is nothing more than a bunch of petty, mewling gangsters, and who would love nothing more than to watch Tommy's Family tear itself apart from the inside out. The Russo widow, Tommy says, will be left up to Joey. *It's traditional to care for her,* Tommy says. *To make things easier.* Tommy Fianzo is not without honor. He will murder a parent, but he is not without honor. These things coexist.

"It's up to you," says Tommy, as he stands and ushers Joey out into the hallway. "If you'd prefer to move, to start over, you can try the Bronx. You can try Chicago. But it looks best when Family sticks together. And it's hard, just starting out, all on your own. It would be hard." Joey interprets this to mean Tommy would make it hard. He dons his hat. He turns to go.

"Hey, Colicchio," calls Tommy from behind him. Joey turns. "This is a once-in-a-lifetime chance."

Sofia watches Joey come home from her seat at the kitchen table, where she is supposed to be folding napkins. Joey is so big the kitchen is dwarfed by comparison. He hangs his hat on its hook and runs his fingers through his hair along the little streaks of gray and white that line his temples. He sidles up behind Rosa and cups the twin domes of her shoulders with his big hands and buries his face in her hair. She leans her weight into his hands and bends her elbow to hold his fingers with her own. He says, "I dealt with it," and Sofia says, "Dealt with what?" from the table and he says, "Nothing, cara mia."

So Joey Colicchio stands in his kitchen. He watches his wife stir soup and he watches his daughter stare, brow creased and lips pursed, at a stack of wrinkled place mats. He is glued in place.

He feels utterly alone.

Next door, Antonia and Lina Russo are in the silent eye of a hurricane.

Antonia is in her room. She is sitting at

the edge of her neatly made bed, and she is scared.

Everything has turned upside down, inside out. Everything is the quick skipped-heartbeat sick-stomach feeling of being in deep trouble.

*Cara mia,* Antonia imagines her father saying. She longs for the smell of him, for the wide soothing warmth of his hands, for the gravitational pull of her body toward the spot where it fits, curled into his chest.

*Of course.*

As the table is set around her, Sofia chews on a pencil eraser. School starts in a week. Her mamma puts bowls on the table with no tablecloth. Her papa pours deep glasses of wine from a jug at the back of the pantry. Antonia and her mamma come over from next door and the five of them crowd around the table. Lina Russo is always small but tonight she is almost translucent in her chair. She sits the still, calm vigil of someone to whom the worst thing has happened. Her soup steams, untouched in front of her.

At their corner of the table, Sofia and Antonia eat quickly, messily. Sofia is filled with a restless discomfort, and wants simultaneously to break the tension at the table and to sink down and flatten under its weight. Antonia watches her mamma out of the corner of her eye. Lina is not eating. Antonia feels like she has woken up on another planet. She wants to be anywhere else. So when Sofia speaks, she feels relief pour down through her body and she shakes with adrenaline, with dread, with the shock of her old body being thrust so viciously forward through passing time.

"I have new dress-up clothes," Sofia says.

Antonia looks up from her soup. *Thank you.* "What are they?"

"Tonia," says Sofia, who wants to fill the room with anything, even the sound of her own voice, "YOU HAVE TO SEE!" This comes out too loud. She knows immediately.

All three adults look up from their steaming silent bowls and her mother glares and says, "That's *way too loud,*" and her father says, "Why don't you girls go play in your room," and so Sofia and Antonia get up meekly and grit their teeth against the scraping of wooden chair on wooden floor and run down the hall together. The air gets lighter as they go, as if their parents' moods can only dampen a certain radius. Both girls are breathless with escape. How often have they done this, running like wildfire through a meadow, so eager to make something new together.

"We can play adventure," says Sofia, digging through her toy chest for a pair of leather-rimmed goggles.

Antonia ties a scarf around her neck. She is free. She is free. She is going somewhere else. "We're arctic explorers!"

Sofia looks at her disdainfully. "You are wearing a royal gown, *not* an explorer's uniform. You should tie that around your *head,*" but Antonia looks at her with a quiet, wild venom and Sofia acquiesces. "Maybe you are a royal explorer."

"We're arctic explorers," says Antonia, climbing onto Sofia's bed and holding her hand to her brow to shade her eyes as she surveys the terrain, "and we have run out of food."

Sofia jumps up next to Antonia. "We're weak with hunger!"

"We are hunting a polar bear!"

"But it won't come out of its cave!"

"We have written letters to our families to tell them we love them." Antonia is solemn, just barely on the wrong side of the make-believe reckoning with mortality. "They will find our bodies in the springtime." Her voice trembles.

"Maybe we should play something else," says Sofia. She sits on the edge of the bed.

Antonia acts as if she does not hear. "Our

souls will be in Heaven," she says quietly.

"Antonia, I think we should play something else," says Sofia. She twists a corner of the blanket in her fingers.

Antonia turns around, eyes on fire, arms raised. "I am an arctic explorer," she says loudly, towering over Sofia.

"Antonia, this isn't fun," says Sofia.

"I am alone in the wilderness. Everyone has left me. I voted to stay alone because I am a women's sufferer and I can vote. I stayed here and I wanted to be alone."

Sofia says nothing. Antonia is unrecognizable. Her voice is coming from somewhere outside of her body. Suddenly Antonia's calm face cracks down the middle. She melts onto the bed next to Sofia. "I don't want to play anymore," she says.

"Okay," says Sofia. She is uncomfortable and suddenly wishes Antonia would leave.

"I don't want to play!" says Antonia.

"I *heard* you," says Sofia.

Antonia bursts into tears. Sofia stares, silent, desperately wishing her parents would come in.

Antonia wails. She shudders. She sits limp on the edge of Sofia's bed and howls.

Rosa bursts into the room.

Sofia is so relieved she starts crying too.

Rosa is pregnant, and she has not told her

husband. She sits between two wailing girls and hugs them both close and wishes for her own mother. She stares out the window and knows she cannot fall apart.

They have a funeral for Carlo, though there is no body. They bury a silk-lined, dark-brown box in St. John's. For the rest of her life, Antonia will be able to picture the funeral in little pieces, as though a broken film is playing in her head. The day is too warm and she sweats in her black stockings and new dress. There are the bent elbows of men clasping one another around the triceps; the rustling of women stepping through long grass in heeled shoes; the nasal drone of the priest, who keeps having to adjust his eyeglasses and off of whose naked pate the sunshine glints as the afternoon wears on. Again and again, the faces of bent-over adults loom toward her like flesh-colored balloons. There is the queasy discomfort of being kissed and hugged and having to say *thank you, thank you, thank you* over and over again, and as the afternoon grows old the adults' breath becomes worse and worse, soured with dark wine and fat-lined slices of lonza shipped from Rome. Antonia can feel her self separating from this day, retreating. Further and further away so by the time Aunt Rosa kisses her and holds her close at the end of the afternoon Antonia can hear her voice echoing, like there is water between them.

Lina is inconsolable for most of the funeral, reddened and teary and leaking. Carlo's well-wishers are sympathetic, but seem wary of getting too close to such a volatile fountain of animal grief. A wife, everyone knows, should have a wan but clear face at a funeral. She should be holding herself together, in honor of the memory of her husband. So the guests at Carlo's funeral give Lina sympathetic glances from afar, ask each other *how does she seem* without asking her themselves; whisper *such a shame* when they think they are out of Antonia's hearing.

Lina had given everything to the conventions she was told would protect her. *Get a husband,* her mother used to say, *and you will be taken care of.* Along with *get a husband* went *fix your hair when you go out, be polite,* and *don't sob like a broken beast at your husband's funeral.* Lina has been betrayed. She sees no need to continue abiding by anyone's rules.

Near the end of the interminable afternoon, Antonia is sitting on the couch, staring in mute exhaustion, when the crowd in her living room seems to part like a zipper being undone as three tall, gray-suit-clad, slick-haired men with clean faces and very shiny shoes walk in. One of them is her uncle Joey, and the other two look familiar: hard-shouldered, bold-eyed, faces gleaming under close new shaves, looking warily around the room. She recognizes them from Sunday dinners, from the circle of men who hunch together in the living room until the food is served.

They remove their hats in unison.

The crowd in the living room is thick with silence. Suddenly, Lina emerges from where she has been cowering under the weight of her own sorrow and fear in the bedroom. "Get out," she says.

"Lina," says Uncle Joey. "No one is sorrier than I am."

"Get out. Get out of my house," says Lina, whose own voice is strong and clear for the first time in days. "How dare you bring them here. How dare you bring this into my home." Antonia can feel herself swimming toward the surface of this moment. There is something about it that sings with significance.

"Lina, I understand why you're angry," says Joey. "He was my best friend."

"You bastard. You get them out of here right now." Lina gestures at the men flanking Uncle Joey. Antonia cannot place them. She does not understand why her mamma is growling so ferociously at Uncle Joey, who has just come to say he is sorry, like all the other adults in the room. But she is grateful and relieved to see the light of Lina's life shining for the first time in days, like there is still a person under there.

"Lina, please —"

"OUT!" Antonia's mother stands up to her full height of five feet two inches and points a shaking finger at the door.

"Okay," says Uncle Joey, deflating like a popped balloon. He jerks his head. It is subtle, but the two men with him turn and walk away at once. The silent crowd swivels its necks in unison to watch them leave.

"Lina, I'm sorry," says Uncle Joey, twisting a hat between his hands. "I don't know how to do this. I'll call you —" but he stops himself at the hateful face Lina is making. "I'll have Rosa call you," he says. And then Uncle Joey turns to go, and Aunt Rosa clasps him around the arm as he walks past her. Antonia can hear her say, *it's okay. It's okay.*

Lina collapses shaking on the floor. Suddenly, Antonia understands human beings as water droplets, part of a cosmic and liquid whole.

"Mamma," asks Antonia, "why did you make them leave?"

Lina will regret her answer to this question for the rest of her life. She looks up at Antonia and before she realizes what she is saying, blurts out, "It's his fault your father is dead."

As an act of survival, Antonia does not believe this. Having lived with the empty shell of her mother for a full week before this funeral, she knows that if it is Uncle Joey's fault her father is dead, she will have no family left at all.

For many weeks after Carlo disappeared, Lina's mother stayed with her and Antonia, and held Lina's hand when Lina woke wailing, sure the ground had disappeared, sure her face had aged a hundred years, disappointed she had fallen asleep at all. Her mother would hum and stroke Lina's forearm and Lina was okay, because she was a baby again.

And then, as the days grew shorter and colder, Lina's mother packed her bag. "You can't be miserable forever," she said to Lina. "You have a child to take care of."

Lina's mother kissed Antonia, who tended to hover in the corner of every room. And she left.

And then for a while Rosa would come over. And instead of being a baby, Lina would get angry. "Why did we marry these men?" she asked. Rosa did not answer, because there was no answer. She had never considered *not* marrying one of These Men. "Why didn't you stop me, why didn't you say something?" Lina asked Rosa. And eventually Rosa, too, was tired, and she had her own family to take care of, and she was always nauseous in those early days of pregnancy. So Rosa kissed Antonia. She said, "Come over anytime, baby." She went home.

And Lina was so relieved.

She was so relieved to be left alone.

Four weeks after a priest wishes Carlo eternal rest and perpetual light, Lina announces that she will worship no god who has killed her husband. She spends Sunday afternoons and Christmas Eve with works of fiction ("*Other* works of fiction," she says, "than the one you spend your Sundays with!") and long, lovingly dog-eared volumes of poetry. She fills their apartment with stacks of books; no bookshelves, but books lined up along the walls, hidden in cupboards, holding up a lame coffee table, layered between winter scarves in the front closet.

Next, Lina proclaims that she will never attend a Sunday dinner again. She is done with them, she says, done with those people. *You can go,* she tells Antonia. *Go, if you want.* Antonia feels she has been cut in half. Aunt Rosa makes Sunday dinner at her own house now, and it is right next door, and the food is good. Eventually, Antonia starts slipping out of the apartment on Sunday afternoons, spending those evenings in the presence of a real family, the cocoon of familiar Sofia and the warmth of a house actually presided over by adults. When she returns after dinner, laden with leftovers Rosa insists on piling into her arms, she often finds her mamma sleeping on the couch.

During the week, their house is quiet. They read. There are days they do not speak at all.

Lina realizes sometime in the spring that she hasn't paid rent all winter. She imagines herself and Antonia, thrown out, sitting in the black slushy puddles that guard each street corner. She opens her mouth and begins to wail and takes to her bed.

Antonia listens patiently, and when Lina has howled out enough of her predicament, Antonia calls Sofia's house and says, "My mamma needs a job."

The next week like magic, Joey calls and says he has a contact at an industrial laundry that washes the linens from restaurants and the sheets from hotels. "It's not glamorous," he says. "And I'm happy to keep helping — to help you out." Of course, Joey had been paying for their apartment all winter. Lina is trapped. She depends upon her captor to release her, and of course, he will not, because she cannot take care of herself without him. The Family will not free Lina; it will not abandon her. *We'll always keep you safe,* Joey almost says.

"I don't want your fucking blood money," she screams at Joey. "I never want anything to do with it again." Joey lies: he tells her that the laundry has nothing to do with the Family. He promises she can support herself from now on. Lina hangs up the phone and tells Antonia, "We're finally done with them."

But later that week Antonia slips next door for Sunday dinner, where Joey resists the urge to put a hand over her arm and apologize for being alive. And when she leaves, Rosa slips a foil-covered dish of leftovers into her hands.

When it is almost summer Rosa goes away for two days and Rosa's mamma comes to stay with Sofia. Nonna is a small woman with hard edges and she has strict rules about what little girls shouldn't do. No running. No loud voices. Wipe that expression off your face. No fidgeting in church. No elbows on the table. For God's sake keep quiet, keep still. Sofia scuffs her feet across the floor and wishes her parents would come home. She imagines being a boy, but it's no fun: there's a void there, something missing. So Sofia stays a girl, but not a very good one. Her shoelaces are untied and she gets a drop of grease on her lap.

Rosa and Joey come back with Frankie while Sofia is in school. When she arrives home her papa opens the door to the apartment and says *shhhh,* and gestures to the living room, where Rosa is sitting on the couch, her arms around a bundle of blankets. "This is your sister," says Rosa. Sofia's eyes get very big, and she turns around and runs as fast as she can down her stairs, out the door of her building, and up to Antonia's apartment.

"Tonia, Tonia, you have to come," she screeches before the door is even all the way open. Antonia is halfway out of her school uniform. Her apartment smells like unwashed hair, like ghosts.

In Sofia's living room, Sofia and Antonia crowd around the baby, Frankie, and pet the down on her head, examine her fingers and toes. And it is not an exact trade, but both of the girls can feel the world shifting:

someone taken from their life, and someone given.

"Mamma," asks Sofia, "where did she come from?"

Rosa gestures toward her deflating belly. "She lived in here," she says. "Remember? You could see her moving."

Sofia and Antonia look at Rosa, and they look at Frankie. They look back and forth. "But, Mamma," says Sofia, finally, "how did she get in there?"

"And how," asks Antonia, "did she get out?"

Rosa sighs. "You'll learn when you're married," she says. "And until then, you have to be careful." Her answer is not enough for Sofia and Antonia, who make a speechless pact to get to the bottom of this as soon as possible.

It is hours before Rosa rises from the couch and puts sleeping Frankie into the small crib that lives in the spare bedroom in their apartment. Sofia peeks around the corner of the halfway shut door. She tries to imagine that Frankie will live with them forever.

Rosa ventures into the kitchen. It smells like her mamma — soap and rising yeast, rose from her perfume. She finds fresh loaves of bread and a full fridge. She presses a loaf of Nonna's bread and a covered casserole dish into Antonia's hands, and Antonia reluctantly pads down the stairs and back to her own apartment.

Later that night, so late that the deepest secrets can be revealed and the darkness will keep them, Rosa sits on the couch to feed Frankie and weeps. In gratitude, for the child in her arms. In exhaustion, for the work she has done to get the child there. And in a pure, clean sadness, for last time Rosa nursed a child on this couch, Lina was there to help her.

In the weeks that follow, Antonia spends every moment she can at the Colicchio apartment. She learns to bathe Frankie, to change and pin her diaper, to rock her. Sofia is more wary, a little cautious about this new creature who commands all the attention in the room. She is torn between protecting her and competing with her. But Sofia, too, falls for Frankie. She learns to make Frankie laugh.

Sometimes Antonia pretends the baby is hers, and she is older, and she lives in a clean glass-walled house next to the sea, and there is always a fire lit and there is music playing from somewhere. She and

Sofia and the baby dance and sway and celebrate. They listen to the waves crashing. She thinks maybe she won't miss her parents so much, when she is older, when she is a mamma herself. She thinks maybe having a baby will divide her life into before and after, will push her past this sad chapter. For while Sofia's family treats her like one of their own, Antonia still feels a jagged tear in the fabric of herself, and she wants, fervently, to be mended.

Children are resilient, and so it is that Antonia appears to be okay relatively soon after her papa's disappearance, when of course, she is not okay. But the world keeps turning, carrying her along.

All around Sofia and Antonia, the economy rages and sputters like a dying animal. They walk to school via a different route in 1931 and 1932, to avoid the shantytowns that have sprung up in vacant lots, where *anything could happen,* Rosa says, bouncing Frankie on her hip, handing Sofia a sandwich to take to school. *Mamma, nothing will happen,* Sofia says, defiant at nine years old, and fearless, and cocooned in certainty that her family will always take care of her, that she will always take care of herself. Antonia at nine years old has a home that echoes when she speaks. The graveyard of their living room, the empty third chair. *Anything could happen, Sof,* she says, tugging on Sofia's hand. *Come on.*

Sofia and Antonia learn new words. Stock market, breadline. Unemployment. Sofia's father is busier than ever. He has new men working for him. He has less time to tell Sofia about his day, but he sneaks into her bedroom when he gets home with a caramel or a lemon drop and whispers, *don't tell your mamma.* Sofia's mother makes Sunday dinners big enough to feed whole countries and sends everyone home with packages of leftovers. Sofia and Antonia sit and watch as Rosa and Joey make their rounds, talking to the men Joey has hired and their wives, to Rosa's parents when they come, to Rosa's brothers and sisters. There are no more Fianzos at dinner. No more Uncle Tommy, no more Uncle Billy. Thankfully, no more Fianzo children, whose thick, pinching fingers had always been the bane of Sunday. Sofia and Antonia balance Frankie between them on two chairs squeezed next to one another and feed her green beans and torn chunks of bread. They make faces when no one is looking. They play tic-tac-toe on napkins.

Sometimes, especially as they turn ten, and eleven, Sofia leaves Frankie with Antonia and ventures into the clumps of adults strewn about the rooms of her home. She reads the newspaper over men's shoulders and imitates their disdainful sighs about the economy, and listens to their worries that Roosevelt will be no better than Hoover, and their jokes that a new Prohibition would make the Family rich again. They say, *Big Joe, this your girl? You'll have your hands full with this one.* She wends her way into conspiratorial hives of women, who talk about hair salons and grocers as a flimsy shield for what they really want to know about one another. The women whisper their future families into being. Sofia breathes in their perfume. They think she is precocious, fearless, a little uncouth. Soon she is shooed back to Antonia, where she will whisper, *that one's pregnant,* over Frankie's head. *Those want to move to the country, but they need savings.* One week, she comes back with the gleaned details of sex itself, her face alight with shock and excitement. Antonia is horrified to learn about her body's permeability. Adulthood, she worries, will make her feel no more solid than she does now. Antonia is happier with Frankie, where anything can be made up and believed and the stakes are not so high. Where she doesn't have to see how many other adults are moving through the world with so much more force and presence than her own mamma.

Mostly, Sofia and Antonia are still too absorbed in the workings of their own lives to spend much time thinking about the world outside of their homes, outside of their own internal architecture. But the older they get, the more different they realize they are from their classmates. Because of their families, Sofia and Antonia are not included in playground games; they are not welcomed into tight circles of gossiping girls. The Family, they learn at school, are petty criminals. They are bullies. They are giving the rest of us a bad reputation. Sofia and Antonia, as a result of being Family children, are not to be trusted.

Sofia and Antonia, by way of listening at doors, by being out of bed and underfoot, know that Carlo's disappearance had to do with escaping the Family, but the idea of this is like escaping air, or sunlight. Impossible, and incomprehensible. They are too young to think about the Family as bullies and themselves as separate. They are still connected at the root. So Sofia and Antonia turn over the possibility that *they* are criminals; that they are untrustworthy at their core. This doesn't feel true either.

Sofia develops a thicker skin. She cannot think of herself as the villain, nor can she imagine herself as the victim. So pre-teen Sofia convinces herself she chose to be alone. *This is what I wanted.* She is filled with the warm certainty that Joey is helping people, that it is an honor to come from a Family family, that if she is ostracized it is by those who do not understand. When Carlo's disappearance rises inside her mind, she shoves it down.

Antonia retreats into her own skin, into her own mind. She carries a book with her everywhere she goes. She reads under the desk in school when she ought to be solving for x.

And of course, they have each other. So when they are twelve, and Angelo Barone corners Antonia in a dark corner of the schoolyard and tells her he knows how her father died, and Carlo deserved it, Sofia overhears, draws back her fist, and punches him in the jaw. *Puttana,* he spits, at one or both of them. In the bathroom before class, Antonia runs cold water over Sofia's reddened fist. They make eye contact in the mirror. Angelo will not tell on Sofia; he will not admit a girl punched him. Sofia and Antonia draw identical masks of cold steel over their faces and get to class before the final bell rings.

When they are thirteen, and Sofia wants to sneak out to a dance in a nearby church basement, Antonia gamely lies to Lina and goes with her. They spend the evening in alternate cold terror and openmouthed awe, in the sweaty thick of the women's powder room and on the bright liquid dance floor. They are the youngest people there, a fact Antonia cringes away from as Sofia puffs herself up, hoping to pass for fifteen, for sixteen, for just another sure-of-herself young woman with nothing to hide. Their pinkies hook together and their arms swing back and forth as they walk home through darkness they should not be out in. Their shadow looks like one creature lumbering along the Brooklyn streets.

On the exact same morning, Antonia and Sofia wake with blood smeared along their thighs. They do not think they're dying: Antonia too practical, with a diagram for padding her underwear already ripped from a library book and squirreled away in her nightstand for just this moment; Sofia not practical but curious. She revels in the metal and musk, bundles her sheets into the laundry, tells Rosa, who purses her lips and whispers instructions through the bathroom door and says, *you have to protect yourself now.* Sofia takes this to mean she is fragile, but she doesn't feel fragile.

Sofia and Antonia meet outside. They do not have to tell one another what happened. They are both ablaze with change in the icy morning sunlight.

It isn't long until Sofia and Antonia begin to dream of escape.

■ ■ ■ ■

# BOOK TWO

1937–1941

■ ■ ■ ■

Antonia has spent ten minutes sharpening three pencils to the same length. She slips them into their own pocket in her knapsack, presses flat the pages in her new notebook, makes sure the straps of her knapsack are tightened to match one another. Antonia lives fully in these rituals — in the brushing of each tooth so her whole mouth feels smooth, in the knotting of bootlace loops into equal ovals, in the methodical rolling of symmetrical meatballs. These things make her mind feel clear and her body uncomplicated. And so it is not a surprise that on the still-warm August evening before she begins high school, Antonia has organized all of her dresses by color; stacked her books by size; cut two loaves of bread into perfectly even slices.

Antonia is looking forward to the new school, where she hopes the bigger campus will afford her some anonymity. She imagines feeling free of the stories people tell about her — *did you hear her mamma hasn't left the house since he died; did you know he killed five men in Sicily and that's why he had to come here; I heard she wears one of his shirts under her school clothes; I've seen other women calling on her mamma, and they don't look like they're bringing scones to share.*

Antonia examines her line of bangs in the mirror and uses a sewing scissor to trim the ends of a couple errant hairs, carefully, breath held in as she cuts and only let out when the hair in question is determined to be the proper length. She leans away from the mirror to examine the bangs, which Sofia convinced her to cut in the middle of an interminably hot and boring July day. They don't fit her face: they make her features look cramped; they tangle with the prominent line of her brow. They are constantly caught and blown by the wind. Sofia says she likes them, but Antonia will grow them back out, she decides. She finds a bobby pin and sweeps them back from her forehead.

At seven o' clock, she reheats a casserole that Sofia's mamma brought over on Thursday. The smell of tomato and cheese and the warmth of the oven lures her own mamma out from where she has been hiding in the deep folds of her favorite armchair. "It smells wonderful in here," she says.

Antonia is piling bread slices in a bowl but she stops to turn around and kiss her mother on the cheek. "Sofia's mamma brought it," she says.

"She's too good to us," says Lina.

"She makes extra," says Antonia. *Here, honey*, Rosa says, at least twice a week. *Take this one to your mamma. Careful, it's heavy.* Her mother will not call Rosa to thank her. Antonia remembers when Rosa and Lina were close, closer than her and Sofia. The rainfall of their voices together in a different room. How warm the world used to feel. "It'll be ready in two minutes."

"Are you excited for school tomorrow?" asks her mother.

Antonia is surprised that her mother remembers she is starting school. "A little," she says. And then, "I'm nervous, I think."

"You're going to do fine," says her mother.

"You think so?" She is both desperate for her mother's reassurance and not at all convinced by it. There is an exposed, pulsing vein in the body of their relationship that reminds Antonia *you have to take care of her.* She was made by her mother and she is also made, again and again, by herself.

"Don't speak to anyone with slicked-back hair," says Lina, before melting backward through the doorframe. Family men, she means. That telltale swoosh up and back away from the temples. Antonia leans over the open oven door to check on dinner. The heat hits her like a fist.

The next day, Sofia and Antonia get a ride to their new school in one of Joey's cars. Antonia does not tell Lina. They are silent on the five-minute ride and once they arrive, they both stand, staring, at the monolithic gray building in front of them. Students stream in and out of the brass double doors. Sofia and Antonia stand close enough that they could be holding hands. On their way up the steps they are jostled by someone they assume is an adult man — he's bearded! — but who they realize is a student, like they are.

Sofia and Antonia are quickly separated by the crowds in the gymnasium where they register. "Russo" is a different line entirely than "Colicchio." The big room echoes with the screeches of teenagers, the rumble of the pecking order, the shuffle of files on the folding tables where maudlin administrators hand out typewritten schedules to each of the students in turn.

Antonia scratches her thumbnail against the cuticle of her pointer finger until she feels skin begin to peel away from her fingertip. Her own breathing echoes in her head. The dress she chose feels too tight and too short and too childish. She watches the room move around her and tries not to look like she might panic.

Sofia is just as nervous, but takes out a lipstick her mamma disapproves of and applies it, using a sliver of mirror she keeps in her bag. In the mirror, she looks like she's playing dress-up: a child's face with a darkened adult mouth.

"That's a sweet color," says the girl standing behind Sofia. Sofia turns and smiles. She offers her lipstick. The line keeps moving and someone has to say, "It's your turn," to Sofia. "I'm Sofia Colicchio," she says, as she steps forward to get her schedule. The woman who hands it to her looks bored and gray, like the building itself.

The girl Sofia shared her lipstick with is in her homeroom. Sofia learns her name is Peggy. Peggy has three friends named Alice, Margaret, and Donna. They eat lunch together, in a cafeteria that smells like old rubber and old grease, and Sofia cranes her neck for Antonia before they sit down, but does not see her.

At lunch, no one asks Sofia about her family. No one asks her about her religion. No one tells her she has responsibilities, or tells her how she is different from these girls. Instead, they ask which boys she thinks are cute. They ask which classes she likes. They eat their carrot sticks and throw their soggy chicken into the trash and no one tells them not to. They hitch their skirts up another half-inch and tighten their belts in the bathroom mirror and toss their hair.

But Sofia aches for Antonia until the final school bell.

In the car on the way home, Antonia tells Sofia, like she is bursting with it, that she found her way to each of her classes without being late for any of them. That she didn't trip or rip her dress or drop her books in the hall; that she got her locker open on the first try. Antonia tells Sofia about the library, where there are thousands, "Thousands, Sof," of books stacked high on metal shelves that anyone, "Anyone!" can read. The freedom of settling in to a chair and realizing no one is looking at her. On Antonia's first day of high school, she was anonymous, and she was filled with hope that there was a place for her in the world after all.

Antonia does not tell Sofia that she spent

her lunch in that library, skipping the cafeteria hubbub in exchange for a growling stomach and a stack of books, Austen and Whitman. That she started like a frightened deer every time anyone said her name.

And Sofia does not tell Antonia that she missed her. In her recounting of the day there is only dark lipstick and smooth stockings. The admiring glance of a senior boy. The bulletproof armor of a group of girls laughing.

On Sunday after her first week of high school it occurs to Sofia that she should not have to go to church if she does not want to, and like a flashbulb has blinded her she cannot see anything else. When she tells her parents this over breakfast, her mother crosses herself and Sofia says, "You're just being dramatic, Mamma," and Frankie opens her mouth in a sharp little *oh.* Her father does not even respond until Sofia says, "Did you hear me, Papa, I said I am not going," and then he raises one eyebrow and looks at her, his gaze inscrutable, and says, "Eat your breakfast."

Sofia does not know it, but when her father is working and wants to remind someone a debt is owed, he calls and asks to take them out to lunch and does not mention the debt even once. Joey, like his daughter, has a little murky blood running through his veins — he relishes the nervous squirm of his indebted lunch dates. The terrified other man — a restaurateur, the owner of a downtown cinema, the manager at a bar — usually vacillates between a tentative, airy calm and an almost palpable panic. *I swear, it's coming,* they say. *Please, I just need a little more time.* Joey finishes his food. He asks about the other man's wife and children. He mentions their names. He smiles. He walks his lunch companion home, and says, *I'll see you soon.*

When confronted with the steely, stubborn, wall of will that has been built around the skin and bones of his daughter, Joey tries to channel the version of himself who, without speaking a single word, can leave a grown man straining not to wet himself. He searches for his cache of calm facial muscles, subtle hand gestures, implacable and aloof expressions.

Joey Colicchio can load a revolver in six seconds. His wife will still go down on him after sixteen years of marriage. He is the most powerful man in his jagged section of Brooklyn.

But his fourteen-year-old daughter finds him irrelevant and unimpressive. "You can't make me," she says casually, as he gestures furiously toward the front door, where the rest of the family waits. Joey, more than most fathers, is torn between acquiescing to the fierce small woman in front of him and a grand show of machismo — *I'll show you what I can and can't make you do,* he imagines saying. But he tries not to bring his work home with him.

Frankie is small and solemn as they leave, six years old and lost without Sofia. *I want to stay too,* she declares, eyes wide. Sofia feels a small tug at the string between her heart and her gut, asking if she should just go, sit in the pew, kneel with everyone else, spend five minutes running her tongue over the roof of her mouth to clear the doughy remains of the host. It wouldn't be so bad, and Frankie doesn't understand why Sofia is refusing to do this easy thing, this thing she does every week. The reflection of herself in Frankie's eyes makes Sofia feel petty and silly, stubborn and strange. Incapable of doing the regular things everyone else does. But Sofia sets her jaw, refuses to leave, watches Frankie trudge down the hall, notices her papa paint a slow line across her mamma's back with his hand as the three of them walk away. She is alone; she is elated; there is an unfamiliar empty air in the apartment.

That day for the first time Sofia sits at home as Sunday morning ripens. She watches passersby through the living room window and wonders how many people have so much time on Sunday, which in her family has always been marked by rushing: to church, home for dinner, into bed before it's too late to get a good night's rest before Monday. Her apartment feels huge. She wanders into the kitchen, carelessly sliding her hands along countertops and over the backs of chairs. She opens the fridge; dips her finger into the ragu waiting in a bowl for Sunday supper; opens a white paper bakery box and chips a corner off a jam-filled cookie. The sugar blooms against her tongue; it makes her eyes water.

Sofia looks at the apartment where she's lived all her life with new eyes: high school eyes, eyes that have spent the past week in a world inaccessible to her family. Sofia is realizing how very alone she has been for most of her life. Aside from Antonia, Sofia has not been immersed in schoolyard dynamics; she has never been the center of a buzzing crowd of children. Sofia feels like she has come up for air, emerged into sunlight, washed a layer of dirt away. She has unearthed, at the center of her person, a little sprouting seed of something that feels like anger, like jealousy. It is looking at her father, at his job, at the structure within which Sofia has been raised, with new suspicion. *What will I do?*

*Who,* Sofia Colicchio wonders, alone in her apartment, *will I be?*

Sofia cannot picture herself as an adult. She knows she will get married and have children. She cannot remember learning that information, but she knows it is true. Marriage is like clothing one must pull on before leaving the house; to be without it is to walk naked through the streets.

Down the block there is a woman who lives alone. She came from Sicily many years ago to escape a horror, some vague thing no one will say, but everyone's parents understand, *yes, us too,* and it always has something to do with hunger, with being forgotten. She came with one ragged leather suitcase full of herbs, cards that tell the future, and a wooden box, locked shut. It is rumored that women having babies can call her and she will help them burn the cord and dim the lights and make poultices of herbs and flowers and show the mothers how to angle their nipples to feed. It is rumored that if she makes eye contact with you no one will ever fall in love with you. It is known that she can curse you with a word or two, and just like that, your future will be altered, shadowed, darkened. Sofia knows she is a witch, and she and Antonia walk the long way around the unassuming building where the shades are always drawn across the face of the attic apartment. They do this out of habit — because it is what they have done since they were six, walking home from school — but even teenage Sofia is filled with a cold fear, a heart-fluttering kind of panic, when she imagines the witch woman, who is only ever spotted on her way to the grocers, wild hair escaping her hat, gnarled fingers curled around her shopping bags like pea tendrils, reaching until they find something to squeeze. No one looks at her, and the idea of this terrifies Sofia. How empty, to walk through the world under no one's gaze. How impossible, to never be seen. How could anything grow like that.

Sofia also knows that if she needed help, the witch would help her. But she would take something in return. Sofia scans her person and finds nothing she would be willing to part with. But she feels invincible and cannot think of anything that could go wrong. She is on the raging pinnacle of fourteen; she knows nothing about sacrifice.

Sky, earth, someday you will be a mother:

these are the constants. Sofia is interested in boys as purveyors of attention. She is interested in them as adventures. There is a tickling, an urgency in her rib cage and tongue when she thinks of kissing one. She can picture exhaling into an open mouth, creating some new breath that lives only between bodies. But she cannot imagine dragging two children across the street, groceries falling off of one shoulder. She cannot imagine being her own mother, whose hair always seems to stay in place, who has mastered the behind-the-scenes co-ordination necessary for keeping two children and a husband fed and clothed and clean, but who sometimes grips the sink and hunches her shoulders and takes a staggering breath in and out, exhaustion seething in the kitchen air. Her papa looks at her mamma, but is he the only one? Sofia wants to belong to the world.

It is easier for Sofia to imagine being Joey. Her papa strides through the world chest-first. If her mamma is behind the scenes, her papa is the star of the show. He is watched, listened to, talked about. *But I wouldn't do what he does,* Sofia tells herself. She knows what he does. There is something about Joey that makes Sofia angry, prone to gnashing her teeth. He is the reason other families cross the street when they see the Colicchios walking. He is the reason no one was allowed to be friends with her at school. *It's best not to ask questions,* Rosa has told her. Sofia has a feeling she will have to get smaller as she gets older. Fit herself into tighter spaces.

Sofia is just starting to realize that the freedom of this Sunday morning will shrivel into boredom when she sees Antonia, clad in a red dress with smart black buttons and capped sleeves, walk down the street. Sofia presses both of her palms and her nose to the glass and holds her breath so it will not fog and watches Antonia cross at the corner.

Antonia would have told her if she was going to the hair salon, or the grocery store, or the post office — somewhere routine. And Antonia would have invited her to the cinema, and would have asked for advice if she was going somewhere forbidden and scandalous (*midday on a Sunday?*) like Central Park, where they are absolutely not allowed to be alone, or Coney Island, where the air is brackish and foreign, and they can watch men shuffling sheepishly in and out of the freak show.

When her family arrives home, Sofia sits patiently as her father, still in his Sunday best, lectures her on the need to participate in the family and follow direction. She nods as her mamma, fighting back tears, says, *sometimes, Sofia, you just have to do things you don't want to do.* Sofia weighs this. *Do I?*

But Sofia is distracted by a deep, manic curiosity for the rest of the day. It trembles her fingers and causes her to kick her right foot against her left heel until she has a bruise. It drags her to the telephone four times and it makes her dial the number for Antonia's building twice before she hangs up. It chews the pointer fingernail on her left hand to the quick.

Antonia arrives for dinner at five and Sofia manages not to ask her where she has been. Two years ago, Sofia would have asked. She would have pulled Antonia into a closet, sweet-breathed and sticky, and whispered, *what, what was it.* She would have reached her arms out and tickled Antonia between the ribs until Antonia gave up the secret, until it was splayed out on the floor for both of them to examine. But tonight, Sofia is sure that admitting Antonia has a secret would make it worse. Asking her about it would be like collecting all the power in the room into a small glowing golden orb and placing it into Antonia's waiting hands, Sofia left to beg at her feet. Sofia spends supper pushing small pieces of eggplant into a circle orbiting her plate. She stays quiet.

In an act of defiance that feels like a rebellion and a homecoming all at once, Antonia has, for the last several months, snuck away on Sunday mornings. She leaves Lina, with her thin cigarettes and her delicate crossed ankles in their browning house shoes, with her stack of books and her trail of things she has forgotten: comb, cooling cup of tea, light sweater, pile of mail, all left to molder where they sit. She leaves Sofia, who is loud and confident and who gives Antonia energy to go on but who also exhausts her. She leaves all of this, and she goes to Sunday morning Mass, eleven o'clock at the Church of the Sacred Hearts of Jesus and Mary.

She tells herself she goes for the smell. It is a combination of old books and incense and vacant air that has been trapped in the cavernous rafters and is doled out to the parishioners breath by sweet breath. It is sharp and toothy pine in the winter and cool metallic stone in the summer and all year long, the distinctly floral scent of relief.

But of course, it is more than the smell. It is the deeply ingrained order, the clearly defined rules. The familiar rise and fall of the kyrie, the round and regular textures of

Latin words brushing against her skin, the ritual of kneeling, the rhythmic flicker of small candles at the altar, the whisper of incense. It is the ability, for an hour each week, to trust that someone else is in control.

Antonia settles onto her knees. She crosses herself and her future seems to hover in the rafters of the church. *Hi, Papa,* she prays. *I miss you.*

Here, missing is a clear thing. She misses the light in their home, the shuffling of her parents' feet as they danced together in the living room. She misses looking up and always finding Carlo looking down, the open window of love in his face, the certainty of that. Her papa's hand on her back as she floats toward sleep.

And it is here that Antonia has been steadily realizing she wants something different from what she has been offered. That she does not want to end up like her mamma: with nothing but a husband who is no longer there and a child she no longer parents to her name. It is here, in the pauses between breaths, in the raising of her head and opening of her eyes after praying, that Antonia realizes she wants a life of her own design. One where papas do not disappear for no reason and life is not governed by so many immutable, unwritten rules you might be suffocated where you sleep.

Later that night at dinner, Antonia chews slowly, hardly tasting her food. The cacophony of Sunday surrounds her, but Antonia retreats into her chair, making herself as inconspicuous as possible. *So, school tomorrow?* Sofia's papa asks her, but since it is not a real question Antonia gets away with saying, *yes,* and moving her attention back to her plate. Besides the library, where Antonia spends every moment she can, school has been disappointing. Antonia is anonymous, sure. She sees fewer kids from their old school than she would expect. No one has whispered about her father or glanced judgmentally at her mother; no one knows about them. She and Sofia have no classes together, and this has never happened before. Without Sofia, Antonia has been disappointed to discover she is timid, and small, and easily brushed past in the hallway. *Just like Mamma,* she says to herself, disgust like a scrap of food inhaled, stuck below her throat. *She lost her husband,* Antonia says to herself, which is what everyone says about Lina when they are trying to engender sympathy or reason away the parts of her that no longer seem to fit into the rest of the world.

Next door, alone, Lina softens into the couch where she spends her days off and feels the emptiness in her apartment buzzing in her ears. How strange it is, to live in an entirely different world from the people with whom you once spent every day. How improbable, to have the same face you have always had, but an unrecognizable soul.

Sofia lies in bed that night and imagines that Antonia has met a new best friend. In her imagination the other girl is taller than Sofia, and thinner, and has brighter eyes. She is quieter and more contained. She does not lash out; she does not lose her temper; she is more like Antonia. The Antonia in Sofia's imagination is much happier with her new friend. She does not need Sofia anymore. The two of them link arms and share the quiet secrets of confident friendships; they laugh softly; their underarms never smell bitter and rotten. Sofia falls into a restless, untethered sleep, and wakes the next morning feeling like she has forgotten something terrible.

On her second Monday of high school Sofia does not ask Antonia what she did that weekend and Antonia does not know how to tell her bright, beautiful friend that she has been spending her Sundays at Mass. Lately, her papa's features hover just on the edge of her memory, refusing to come into focus.

And so this year Sofia and Antonia keep their first secrets. They separate. And in each of them something wholly new begins to grow.

Lina Russo is not a ghost. She is still a woman. She feels herself living inside skin that, when she looks in the mirror, looks like her skin.

But she is a woman frozen in time. Her life ended on the morning Carlo disappeared. She had spent her entire life up to that point fearing that Carlo would disappear, or, when she was a child, fearing that someone like Carlo would do something like disappear.

Lina has always sensed that if she built a world around herself, it could be taken away.

There is nothing to be done, she knows, after the worst has happened.

But it has been seven years. And Lina has a secret too. It is that in the last months, when Antonia sneaks away — to church,

Lina knows, the smell of the incense as familiar as the smell of her own skin — Lina pulls a shawl over her head and floats as quickly as she can down the block to the very smallest and shabbiest building in the neighborhood. She knocks three times and feels her heart pounding in her chest and in the tips of her fingers and behind her eyes. She enters the home of the neighborhood maga.

She first went to answer a question: *where is my husband.* She did not know where that question appeared from again, years after Carlo's disappearance, with such vehemence. But of course, the maga is not there to answer questions as they are asked: she is there to help her clients find the questions they are not asking. *Are you looking for a love potion?* she had asked. Americans like love potions. They are the maga's bread and butter, so to speak. Lina was unsatisfied, and went away frustrated. *Mamma was right,* she thought. *It is an ancient nonsense.*

The next week, though, Lina found herself on the same doorstep. And she has gone every week since.

There, Lina's fears are pored over by the warm eyes of an old woman who speaks almost no English. The fears are laid out against the drawn cards from the tarocchi and discussed quietly over tea with flowers blooming in it. Lina learns the rhythm of the full moon and carries rustling bodies of fava beans nestled in her pockets. She learns to feel out the four directions by the height of the sun, the length of the shadows, the tilt of the wind. She situates herself on the earth. Seven years after her husband's death, Lina Russo, not a ghost, finds herself resting on the breast of La Vecchia. An older and wilder thing, whose stories and rhythms carry her into a place that feels timelessly, strangely, uncannily like home.

It is the first time in her life Lina has done something because she wanted to, and not because someone told her she should. It is the first time she is choosing something and does not care what anyone thinks. If La Vecchia is a street to be crossed, Lina is striding forward without looking left or right.

And without even realizing, like she did when she was a child, Antonia begins to take heed of Lina's mood, and take up space in their home accordingly. In their apartment a silence descends: the witch and the Catholic girl, eating lasagna.

During their first year in high school Antonia and Sofia spend more time apart than together. It happens slowly and simply, and so by the time they do not walk to school together each morning it feels almost natural.

Antonia takes on hours of studying with the enthusiasm of a thirsty man who finds a clear stream. She is never totally comfortable in the hallway rush, but learns to take solace in the library, in the pages of her textbooks. Antonia studies French and Latin. She reads voraciously. She graphs parabolas and puzzles through the dates of famous battles for American independence. On her way home each day, Antonia quizzes herself. She whispers the quadratic equation. She recites the opening of the *Inferno.*

In the afternoons she washes Lina's dishes, the old teacups with the amber stains and the plates with desiccated toast crusts dangling off the edges. She boils pasta or reheats leftovers or brings home containers of soup from the deli and tries to get Lina to sit at the table, to eat something, to ask Antonia how her day was. She leaves each dinner table for her books, and imagines being Antigone, buried with her principles and her god and her unimaginable loss. Or she feels like she is living on the earth, and scooping shovelfuls of black soil down on top of Lina in her tomb. Antonia is

Penelope, abandoned by more courageous adventurers. She is Circe, with only the ghosts of things she has missed out on for company. In this way, Antonia manages to inhabit every bitter and angry and passionate thing she has denied herself in her real life, where she is too busy trying to survive to think about how it feels.

At night, when she is close to sleep, Antonia shuts her books, closes her eyes, and misses Carlo. She does this carefully, for a few minutes at a time. *Good night, Papa,* she whispers.

Sofia finds a group of red-lipped, coiffed-haired older girls who slip notes to one another when the teacher turns around and linger leaning against their lockers between classes. If they know who her family is, they say nothing. It is possible that they do not care. From her new friends, Sofia learns the power of a jutted hip, a manicured nail. She begins to take a different sort of care when she dresses. She dares show up at the dinner table with her proud straight spine and her lips lined and glossy. She begins to notice the eyes of other students at school following her as she walks down the hall, and most of these encounters make her feel taller, more full of red blood and moxie.

And Sofia, armed in bulletproof popularity, moves again, and again, into every new friendship and obsession she can find. And while it is true that people find Sofia Colicchio *a little unpredictable* (this from her layered and coiffed hallway best friends; this from boys she deigned to go out with, from teachers in whose classes she *didn't live up to her potential*), it is also true that she possesses the same addictive magic her father does, so that people cannot help but want to be around her. And while she is not exactly conscious of the fact, it is true that her rotating cast of friends becomes the stuff of clockwork and legend — a regular shuffling, a rhythmic cycle of heartbreak and infatuation. She picks up and falls in love with girl after girl, and drops each of them down just as suddenly. And they line up to be friends with her anyway, because to spend two weeks, or four, or nine, as the object of Sofia's attention is worth it: to exchange sideways smiles with her, to bask in the laser focus of her sharp dark eyes. Despite the pervasive rumors about her family. Despite the danger that snaps like static in the air around her. Despite the cruelty of Sofia's wandering affections, the quick way she moves on, the sunlight of her attention slipping under the horizon. To be friends with her is worth it. Oh, it's worth it.

Of course, it's worth considering whether it is love or *love* and the truth is that this has never occurred to Sofia: that for some particularly consuming friendships between teenage girls the line is blurred anyway. And it is fair to say that Sofia in particular falls in and out of love and *love* with these girls, but she does not name it.

And so Sofia moves again and again, and each time she leaves someone behind she feels a little more like herself. *I'm not like that, I'm not like that, I'm not that either. I am made of something else.* Always possessed of an inimitable electricity, Sofia begins to wield her power. To test its limits.

Eventually, Antonia mentions to Sofia that she is going to Mass every week, alone. She mentions this offhand, and it is clear she does not care what Sofia thinks the way she used to. Sofia does not ask her why she goes. Antonia hears a rumor that Sofia has let Lucas Fellini, the most boring boy in school, put a hand under her blouse, but dares not confirm it with her, dares not ask her what it was like. *Was his hand cold?* she wonders. *Were you wearing the one with the buttons that stick?*

Sofia and Antonia begin to fill the space

between themselves with stories about the future. Antonia decides during her first year of high school that she will go to college. She has realized that reading, which has always been an escape from her immediate surroundings, could be an escape from her entire life. She will leave Brooklyn, she will leave the Family forever — not the way her mother did, by retreating into her own skin, but by bursting forth, by achieving something altogether new. And then, Antonia decides, she will meet someone who has never heard of the Family. Her children will never know about it. They will never feel isolated at school; their father will never disappear one day, never to be seen again. Antonia the arctic explorer, the knight on horseback, the safari adventurer, will rescue herself and her future family from the untamed landscape she has been marooned in since Carlo died.

In Antonia's daydreams, she buys a house with a wraparound porch. She fills it with children and a husband and Lina comes for holidays and Sofia visits on weekends. No one goes to work. No one talks about the past.

Sofia can sense the sea change that must, must, must be on its way: she will end up on an unpredictable adventure. She will have a life that hasn't been dreamed yet. She will throw off the constraints of woman- hood she can already feel tightening around her future.

It isn't lost on Sofia that, like Rosa, she is using those same constraints to her advan- tage, when she can. Sofia learns a lowered eyelid, an imperturbable stare. She lets Lu- cas Fellini take her out, but of course, the rumor about her unbuttoned blouse, his clammy hand, is untrue.

Sofia does learn, this year, to run her hands over her own body. She stands alone in front of her bedroom mirror and finds a softened place at the center of herself. This must be the thing Rosa tells her to protect. This must be the fragile heart, the thing that makes her breakable. This the cause of wars, the source of life.

It is almost enough.

Antonia and Sofia wave to one another when they pass in the hallways; they sit close together and say *oh how are you* with de- tached warmth at Sunday dinner. It is as if their friendship has been put on hold, frozen, and when they are together they both have to time travel to a place where they can speak the same language. They always have to leave something of their present selves behind. Antonia's plain face reflects the ways Sofia is faking. With her new friends, Sofia never wonders if she needs the new sweater, the perfumed neck. Antonia, with her studiousness and her sensible shoes, makes Sofia feel like a fraud. And where once being with Sofia had made Antonia feel stronger, she now feels gawky and uncomfortable in the edges of Sofia's light, even, if she is honest, faintly judgmental of Sofia's new affect. How destabilizing, to question the motives of someone who has always been your compass. How isolating, to wonder if despite your family ties and the friendship promises and oaths of trust you swore, you are alone after all.

Late at night, when the hours seem not to have names anymore, and Antonia's body is heavy with exhaustion but her mind spins a million miles a minute, she sometimes lays a palm flat against the brick wall that her bedroom and Sofia's share. On the other side of the wall, Sofia sometimes rests the plane of her forehead against the brick. Each of them imagines that the other is there.

Antonia reads the news with a manic obsession. She watches Hitler's men and boys trample through Czechoslovakia and imagines, as the summer burns a little less brightly, that they filter into Poland like a glass of water being poured. She feels evil seethe up through the cracks she's beginning to notice in the world around her.

Each day she spends cooped up with Lina exhausts her, even though Lina is a little different now, busier, less fragile. Lina sees no need to iron out her thoughts so they are intelligible to anyone else and so their days are peppered with lines from songs Lina's mother once sang, with scraps of memories as they pass through Lina's mind. Antonia makes them breakfast and Lina stands up in the middle of it and leaves her untouched plate, exclaiming that she cannot eat room-temperature toast, or else saying nothing, and walking away in inexplicable silence. Lina enters a room and begins to wax on about the things she could have done besides marry Carlo: She would have been a writer, she says. She would have been best friends with Zelda Fitzgerald. She would have been a shopgirl, one of those intimidatingly stylish young women who seem comfortable in every situation, though they stick out like well-dressed, long-boned beacons everywhere they go. *Instead, this,* Lina says, holding up her hands, which are covered in perennial cracks and thick white flats of dry skin from the industrial laundry where she whiles away her days washing linens for mid-range hotels. *Instead, we lost your father.* Antonia thinks of going to Sofia's a thousand times a day but is stopped by some vague sense of pride and fear. There is a gulf between them. Sofia wears the mask of women they used to admire like it was made for her all along. She is powdered and perfect. Even imagining herself going to Sofia for comfort makes Antonia cringe. She has been making plans to go to Wellesley, to become a classics professor, to wrap herself in books and solitude like Emily Dickinson. Even to Antonia, there is something fantastical and flimsy about these layered fantasies. *Out there, people are dying, and you are imagin-*

119

*ing a college degree you cannot afford.* Seeing herself through Sofia's eyes would make
it worse.

So Antonia burrows into herself. *Something's coming,* say the newspaper headlines,
the radio broadcasts, the quibbling pigeons
fighting over scraps on street corners. When
Antonia shuts her eyes she is inundated with
sensation. *Malocchio,* her mother says. The
evil eye. Antonia is sixteen.

The world is unsteady.

Sofia and Antonia suddenly look like two
different women, rather than two interchangeable girls. Sofia has grown tall and
her lips and eyes and shoulders and calves
have become round; she seems to hold
within her body innumerable surprises, as
though at any moment she might laugh or
cry or stretch her arms above her head.
Antonia's hair has darkened and her fingers
and toes have lengthened just enough that
she carries with her an inimitable grace.

Of course, when you are sixteen your body
betrays things that will be true about you
later, but which you cannot feel quite yet:
Antonia only feels heavy and unkempt
inside her graceful limbs and Sofia, more
often than not, is bored to tears, desperate

to move, waiting impatiently for something new.

Frankie is eight now, precocious, and as eagle-eyed as Rosa. *Why don't you come over as much,* she asked Antonia last Sunday, and Antonia felt her stomach flip, like she had been caught doing something forbidden, and then she returned to helping Rosa set up. The two card tables folded and stashed behind the sofa are dusted and arranged end to end so that everyone can fit; there is a long brown leaf that, installed in the dining room table, allows it to seat ten squashed, rather than six spread out.

Each week Sofia and Antonia have small conversations about comfortable things while they set the table, chop the onions, wipe the dust out of the wineglasses. They feel close enough to breathe each other in; it is enough time that they do not have to feel guilty about letting their friendship erode away outside. And, each of them notices, *she seems happy. She seems happy without me.*

Sofia and Antonia stumble out of their junior year of high school as June of 1940 begins to swelter in earnest. The next week, the radio announces that Italy has joined Germany, and Antonia and Sofia find themselves crushed into Sofia's apartment with countless familiar bodies, all of them restless in the early summer heat. Wine is poured, and the room fills with a thick cloud of cigarette smoke. A pile of hats and sweaters and pocketbooks buries Sofia's desk.

"It will be just like the Great War," says Rosa's father. Pop rarely makes an appearance at dinner, but when he does he commands the room: sitting spread-legged in Joey's chair across from the couch, hands crossed over his belly. This gesture of deference on Joey's part serves to ameliorate the natural tension between sons-and fathers-in-law, but it is also how he maintains his status: *look how confident he is,* people think. Joey can give away power without losing any. *Look how honorable.* "We will be pared down to our essential functions. To the necessities."

"But what does that mean for us?" asks Paulie DiCicco.

The room hushes. Five men turn their heads toward Paulie: Joey's newest hire, who should not have spoken out of turn. The women, Sofia and Antonia among them, sense the thin tense air and quiet for a moment.

"The anxiety of youth," says Joey, in apology. The air softens. The women turn back to their circle. Without quite acknowledging it, Sofia and Antonia move closer together. Antonia slides napkins into their rings one by one. Sofia is wiping the tarnish off of a pile of forks. Both of them perk up their ears to listen to the men's side of the room.

"But, Pop," says Uncle Legs, Rosa's oldest brother. "All the Families are solvent right now. It won't be like last time. We're all doing good."

"It won't be like last time because this is not a pointless war," says Joey. There is grumbling in response to this.

The Family cannot decide what to think. As Italians, they want to support Italy with their very breaths and bodies, though that's been a complicated task for years and years of rumors about Mussolini's new world order, and most of them are unsurprised that the economically devastated villages they and their families fled have fallen prey to this new evil. As immigrants, they are wary of war, and not sure whether to believe the whispers of inhumane atrocities committed against anyone not aligned with the objectives of the Third Reich. As Americans, they want badly to turn away from yet another European catastrophe, to disengage from the tangled knot of politics and culture dragging their cross-Atlantic cousin into the mire.

As businessmen, of a fashion, they are intrigued. Post-Prohibition finances have been shaky and uncertain, stumbling along thanks to protection payments from easily bullied restaurateurs and small shop proprietors — a flower shop known for beautiful and expensive wedding bouquets, a rug importer on Atlantic Avenue, a travel agency that plans the summer vacations of slightly lesser Rockefellers — but it's not thriving as things did when wine was worth its weight in gold. War, they know, makes some things scarce. Things that can be procured, of course — if you know the right people, and for the right price. And, they realize, war in Europe means that people will want to leave. They will want to get *somewhere.* And they will need help — especially from a discreet group familiar with all the secret paths and trade routes east of the Mississippi along the Canadian border.

Rosa fills glasses with unfamiliar trepidation. At the end of the last war, Rosa met Joey, and the adrenaline of the whole world propelled them smoothly through their courtship; it filled the room when their conversation lagged; it made starlight and majesty out of the gray buildings that were their horizon. *What could happen this time?* she thinks, looking for Joey in the room. She is not interested in change. Her beautiful girls, her husband: Rosa is settled in.

Across the room, Joey is distracted; he does not meet her eyes. If he saw her, he would smile. He hasn't felt real uncertainty in long enough that he is jolly, clapping backs and toasting. He is focused: it draws him in; it electrifies him. The danger of complacency is that it makes you tired. It makes you dull. It distracts you from the heat as the water around you begins to boil.

Late that evening, when the clocks have started again from zero and the conversations have broken apart into little cells of worry and speculation strewn through the living room and hallways, Antonia and Sofia find themselves alone in Sofia's room.

When the awkward dregs of their friendship are not watered down by the presence of others, the air suddenly seems still, and thick. Antonia has an uncontrollable urge to shuffle her limbs around restlessly, and Sofia cannot look Antonia in the eye.

"Well," says Sofia. "I guess everything will be different now."

"Everything is different all the time," says Antonia, and then wants to swallow the words back in. *Why do you always have to say something like that?* she asks herself.

Sofia rolls her eyes toward the ceiling and says, "That wasn't what I meant," and suddenly they are stuck in a sludgy moment with no words and unbidden hostility and they do not know how to get out.

*How did we get here?* wonders Sofia. She misses Antonia, who is staring glumly into her lap, and who seems not to care for Sofia at all anymore. And to whom Sofia is a total ice queen in response.

"Sorry," Sofia says. "I didn't mean — I just — sorry."

"It's fine," Antonia says. She gets up and walks to look out the window and misses Sofia. "I hear you went out with Lucas Fellini," she says, finally.

Sofia laughs. "I did, unfortunately."

Antonia is suddenly more curious than irritated. "What happened?"

Sofia wants to tell Antonia everything, but she doesn't want to seem too eager. "Can you handle it?"

"Gross," says Antonia. "Probably not." She feels herself quickening toward Sofia, an old instinct. A relief.

"Well," says Sofia, "I didn't . . . handle it . . . either. Much to his disappointment."

Antonia grimaces, but there is a little

126

thread of fear running through her. *Would Sofia consider that?*

Sofia smirks, and pats the bed next to her, and Antonia sits down. "He took me to dinner and he couldn't think of anything to say. And I felt sorry for him, at first, because you know, he has his shirt tucked in too tightly and you can just tell his mother did his hair for him and his father gave him a lecture about behaving like a gentleman, but he didn't ask me *one* question and he ordered plain noodles with butter and we just *sat* there in silence for half the meal!" Antonia is grinning now, picturing luminous Sofia trying to fit into a wooden bench on a trattoria patio, ordering Coca-Cola with a straw. Sofia and Lucas Fellini: the most boring boy in school. Sofia covers Antonia's hand with her own. She leans forward conspiratorially. "And then after? It was like he thought it had gone really well — or something — and he walked me the long way back — you know, *past the park outside school*" — and here Antonia gasps, because the park outside the high school is notorious for being a spot where couples meet, and because at least two girls had ended up pregnant after trysts there last year — "I know," continues Sofia, "and he sort of *looked* at me like *alright, here we go,* and I could only look back and think *here you go by yourself, maybe*" — at which Antonia says, "Sofia, *honestly,*" and Sofia waves a hand — "I know, but tell me you don't think he did when he got home! Anyway, he couldn't even bring himself to lean toward me or ask for a kiss and finally he just turned and walked me home!" Sofia stops to catch her breath. "Oh, Tonia, you should have seen him. Standing there looking at me like a kicked dog. As if that would get me going!" The two of them look at each other for a second and a half of held breath and then collapse laughing on the bed. "He was so boring!" wailed Sofia. "I thought it might be contagious!"

"Imagine catching Fellini's *dullness!*" cries Antonia. Tears leak from the corners of her eyes and her stomach hurts. "D'you think you could get it just from kissing him or would you have to . . . ?"

"I didn't even want to breathe the air near him, much less kiss him!" gasps Sofia. "*Much* less . . . ugh! And I'm sure he's told all his friends we did that and more, and God I almost don't care as long as I don't have to talk to him anymore!" Sofia almost tells Antonia there was a moment where she looked at him and thought, *what if I just did it? What if I undid my buttons and just did it,*

128

*just like that, what would happen then?* and that she was stopped not by a sense that it was wrong, or that she had to protect herself, but by a powerful surge of sadness, the idea that Lucas Fellini would be the one to divide her life into before and after, the idea that if she was changed he would be a part of it. Instead, she had turned to him and told him to walk her home, and she had gone to bed still shaking with the thinness of the boundary between saying yes and saying no. But she would feel naked if she told Antonia, who she is sure never has to wrestle with breaking rules the way Sofia does.

Antonia's stomach hurts from laughing — with relief, with love, with horror at the things Sofia is tempted to do. Sofia rests her head on her stretched-out arm so she can look sideways at Antonia.

"I'm sorry, you know?" says Sofia.

Antonia is tempted to ask *about what* but she knows it would be one of those choices that makes her smaller, that Sofia would roll her eyes and say *you know,* and Antonia does know. So she says, "Me too," and they lie together and listen to the adults in the living room. Occasional coughing; a man's laughter.

"Do you ever think about this?" asks

Sofia. She gesticulates toward the closed bedroom door.

"How do you mean?" asks Antonia.

"I mean, do you ever think about what they're doing in there? Do you think about what our — what my father does?"

"I try not to," says Antonia. But of course she thinks about it: every doffed cap an homage to her papa. Every slick suit a reminder of what was taken from her. She almost tells Sofia that she has been building a house with a wraparound porch, in her mind. She has been entertaining fantasies of college, of independence and escape. Sofia would understand this, she thinks. But Sofia would feel abandoned, too. And Sofia would know Antonia was faking something.

Sofia is silent, and then she says, "I do."

"You do what?"

"I think about it." She doesn't often. But she can't get the image of small Antonia, life permanently scarred by the machinations of men with power and secrets to spare, out of her head. And lately, surrounded by friends who don't call on the weekend or ask how she's doing but who will stand next to her, an army of pleated skirts against all that's unknown, Sofia is sometimes suddenly breathless, caught in a memory of grade-school friendlessness, the throat-ache of walking the halls under pinched, judgmental eyes. And Sofia realizes she harbors no curiosity about what it is her father does to run Brooklyn, but rather, is filled with anger. Anger at all of it.

"What do you think, then?"

"I think it's wrong." As Sofia says this she thinks she believes it. As she says it she is buoyed by a pure, sovereign opinion. She realizes this is Joey's worst fear: that she will see what he does, and that she will hate it. "I think it's wrong, and I think they really hurt people."

"I think it is more complicated than that," says Antonia. Antonia, who never has the privilege of single-mindedness. Who knows viscerally how the Family has destroyed her life, but also how they have maintained it. She feels surprised to think this. A hole punctured in the side of her imaginary future life, the air all draining out. *You'll never abandon your family,* she realizes. She's no better than Lina, who cannot escape Family ties either.

"How?" asks Sofia. She feels that she is right. She feels it catch flame inside of her. "How can *you*" — it is coming out, there's no stopping it — "you, of all people, think it's complicated?"

"Excuse me?" Antonia stands, and suddenly there they are: on the brink of some-thing unspoken. They are giddy and close to tears, still fragile together. They do not want to break apart again, but it would be easy.

The fire consumes Sofia's belly and chest and it comes for her throat. "After what they did to your papa. How can you. How can you think it's complicated."

"They pay my rent, Sof. And yours, in case you forgot." Antonia glares. "Isn't it a little hypocritical to criticize them?"

Sofia is suddenly both sorry and even more angry. Tears form behind her eyes. She feels herself grow hot and knows her face is bright red. Her voice is stuck in the back of her mouth. "I'm sorry," she says. "That wasn't what I meant."

"It's okay," says Antonia, and it is: the relief of having something to fight about somehow better than having nothing to say to one another at all.

Sofia looks at Antonia and opens her mouth to ask a thousand questions. "Aren't you angry?" is what she says. "At them? At us?"

Antonia looks at Sofia. She is standing by the doorway of Sofia's bedroom, backlit by the lamp on Sofia's desk. She has the same face she had when she was five, and nine, and thirteen. "Every moment," is what she says. "But what alternative do I have?"

After Antonia leaves, Sofia turns over her newfound anger in her mind. It's hot as molten metal. She cocks her head toward the rumble of end-of-dinner conversation from the sitting room, but she can't quite hear it. So Sofia slips through her bedroom door in stocking feet. As she gets closer to the living room, the rumble sorts itself out into her papa, talking with her uncle and her grandfather.

Sofia peers through a crack in the nearly shut set of French doors to the living room. Joey is sitting up tall, spine straight, broad shoulders inclined toward Rosa's father. "I don't envy you," Sofia's grandfather is saying. "To start a new business venture, right as a war gets going — it's hard to get people to buy anything during a war."

"We'll have to make sure we're selling something they can't get by without," says Joey. A line appears, north to south on his forehead. Sofia watches his thoughts churn. It's hard to hold on to her anger while she is looking at the familiar face of her papa. Sofia is too stubborn to ask herself whether her anger is a flimsy mask for something deeper and more complicated, but looking at Joey, something in her knows she is not just angry. She's not ready to admit it, but Sofia is wildly curious. This makes her feel like a traitor: to Antonia, who has been hurt so profoundly by the machinations of Family. To her mamma, who only ever wanted for Sofia to be happy with the space carved out for her in the world.

It doesn't make her a traitor to Joey, though. It makes her closer to him than Sofia ever imagined.

In the time it takes Antonia to kiss Rosa, close the door to Sofia's apartment, walk down Sofia's stairs, and walk up into her own building, Antonia lets go of her dream of a college degree in a town where no one knows her name. Without the Family, without her history, and without Sofia, she is an empty shell. She'll never make it on her own. This is what she tells herself, but of course, the truth is more complicated: Antonia is suddenly not sure she wants to make it on her own. There has to be a way, she thinks, to get out from under the Family's thumb without abandoning the people she loves. There has to be a way to get everything she wants.

As night settles over Brooklyn like a silence,

Sofia and Antonia plant their hands against the brick wall between their apartments and they each know the other is there. They know they will not abandon one another. They give in to the strength of the bonds that have made them.

Outside a war is growing. The whole world churning. No one goes to bed on time and the radio stays crackling on until there is nothing but canned music and then static. Still, as the night passes, someone is always hovering near the radio, listening. Waiting for information, or for a reason. For proof the world is not ending. To hear a long-lost relative's voice, or a message from God.

Until the morning broadcast, all there will be is static.

The first time Antonia lays eyes on Paolo Luigio, he is a red-eyed, saggy-shouldered blur on his way into Sofia's building, and she is not looking where she is going. When she crashes into him, a brown paper parcel tumbles out of his arms and spills passports — stiff, red, unused, full of promise and obligations — all over the floor. Paolo and Antonia stand stunned for a moment.

Antonia bends to the ground, sweeps up some of the passports, and hands them to Paolo. "Excuse me," she says, as she nearly runs down the street. And then stops, and turns, and says, "I'm late for school," and feels heat prickle across her cheeks and down her back.

"Morning, miss," he says, and touches the edge of his hat.

It is as simple or as infinitely complicated as that.

It does not occur to Antonia until she is

sitting in her social studies class, sweating through the seams of her starched school dress, to wonder what a man she had never seen before was doing delivering passports to Sofia's apartment.

When she sees him again, two weeks later, she says, "Good morning," and he smiles. She spends the rest of the day squirming each time she remembers their interaction. Her words tumbling, louder and harsher than she meant them, out of her childish lips. His gracious eyes, his nod. Antonia, trembling and suddenly much more uncomfortable than ever in the confines of her body.

Antonia finds herself waiting for the sight of Paolo's hat making its way down the sidewalk each morning. She rarely says more than *hello,* but she thinks she can smell him on her clothes each day. In his presence she is butter melting. She is molten lava. She is a small green plant unfurling toward the light.

Paolo Luigio was born on Elizabeth Street, in the kind of boxy tenement apartment with more walls than it was built with and more inhabitants than it was meant to house. He is the youngest of four brothers, and the first to leave for work in Brooklyn, where his impeccable handwriting and meticulous craftsmanship can be of use forging paperwork — passports, birth certificates, letters of reference — that Jewish refugees need to find legitimate American jobs. He doesn't mind the odd hours or the moral ambiguity of the work; he dreams of wearing a suit as beautifully tailored as the ones his bosses wear; of walking into a room and feeling it hush in his presence. Greatness, that ever-elusive standard by which some boys are born judging their lives, had whispered in his ear early on.

Paolo asks Antonia to lunch as the trees begin to lose their leaves. She tells herself to say no, not to go out with a man who so obviously works for Joey Colicchio, but when she opens her mouth nothing comes out and she finds herself nodding. She cannot focus her eyes, but she is warmed syrup. She is an ice cube in the sun. Antonia thinks Paolo seems to exist in two places at once: here, in the hallway, smiling at her, and also, somehow, somewhere in a future of his own imagining. Neither of them lives entirely on the earth. They go to the corner café and Antonia learns that Paolo is twenty years old. She learns that he loves to read but grew up speaking Italian at home and finds reading in either English or Italian to be more difficult than listening to a conversation. She learns that he likes the work he does for Sofia's father, but not what it is. "You know how it goes," he says, by way of not explaining, and she does. She tells him that her father died when she was young, but not how. "It was just one of those things," she says by way of not explaining, and he nods. She learns that Paolo is afraid of heights, and as he tells her, she watches him fiddle mindlessly with the napkin ring, the butter knife, and though the rest of his body is calm she learns that he is never still. She tells him that she is timid in large groups of people. "I don't think you should be," he says, definitively, and she asks, "Why?" and he says, "Because you're spectacular," and then falls silent, and as Paolo watches Antonia in the midday restaurant air he realizes that though her mind is rarely calm she is nearly always still.

After they have paid, Paolo walks Antonia home, and she feels the omnipresent gaze of the neighborhood ladies through the second-story windows on King Street, and the heat of Paolo's body walking next to hers, and the ripple of traffic as the garbage collectors shout their way down the block.

At the bottom of her stairs, Paolo puts three fingers to the brim of his hat and winks, just barely. For the next hour she cannot stop replaying it: his elbow bent, his goodbye quicker than she had imagined, her hand sliding along the wrought iron railing as she walked up the stairs. Until she sees him again, Antonia will not be able to remember what he looks like.

The fall passes this way: lunch with Paolo, and coffee, and slow walks at the edge of Antonia's neighborhood, where she is less likely to run into anyone she knows. She is nervous: she hadn't expected to fall for someone Joey had hired. She hadn't expected to fall for anyone at all. In Antonia's mind, an alternate future begins building itself. She will marry Paolo. She will escape Lina's house without abandoning her. Antonia wants desperately to be good. And for the first time in her memory, it seems like she might be able to pull it off.

Joey Colicchio is now the coordinator of a grand smuggling empire. Using the contacts he's built with olive oil and cured-meat exporters in Italy, Joey has — without directly implicating himself in any of it — constructed a flawless network from Brindisi to Red Hook. For a hefty price, Jewish families can pay him to be discreetly transported amongst wheels of parmigiana and double bottles of Chianti. Of course, it is not just Jews. There are Catholics, too. There are homosexuals. There is a Romani family who sells generations' worth of family jewelry to buy their passage. Joey doesn't care: If they can pay, he arranges for their transport. If they can pay more, he arranges for their passports, their false histories, the references they need to lease shoddy, crowded apartments.

Business is busier than ever. When the first reports of horror inside Dachau and Buchenwald reach Joey's ears, he raises his prices. (Of course, there is a persistent rumor that he will not turn down women and children who cannot pay. Of course, the entire idea that Joey Colicchio is responsible for any of this is an unfounded rumor in and of itself. There is no paper trail, and hardly anyone along the route even knows Joey's name, and those who do would rather have their eyes cut out of their skulls than give it up.)

By the end of 1940, Joey finds himself in need of an assistant.

Does Sofia feel a warmth, or a tremor, or some kind of deep unlocking inside herself as Saul Grossman disembarks from the ocean liner where he has crouched for two weeks, retching bile into a bucket in the hold along with fifteen other threadbare Jews?

Does she settle down a little, into her preordained spot in the universe?

At exactly eleven o'clock at night, two months after he stumbled out of the hold of the SS *Hermes* into American sunlight, Saul Grossman arrives at the deli where he makes sandwiches for hungry, nocturnal New Yorkers. The icy winter air forces streams of liquid from his eyes and nose, which he wipes with a sleeve as he hurries up the block. He shimmies through the post-theater crowd building outside, lifts the grate on Ludlow, and stomps his feet on the way down to scatter the rats. He is no longer surprised at how many people in New York expect to eat at any time they please.

"I can always hear you comin', Saul," says Lenny. "You sound like you weighs four hundred pounds!" Lenny, a three-hundred-pound fixture at the deli, has a slow Brooklyn drawl and a smile that unfolds across his whole face. He exudes a protective gentleness, a slow-to-anger loyalty, a moral compass with a diamond tip. He kept Saul standing and eating when Saul first stumbled into the deli, homesick and haggard.

"We need some cats, Lenny," says Saul. "I just scared a rat the size of a side of pastrami."

"Hogwash," says Lenny. "We got you to keep 'em in line!"

Lenny grins as Saul squeezes past him in the dark basement. In the half-light, he looks maniacal. "Hey, Saul?" he asks.

Saul turns.

"It's good to see you doin' a little better," says Lenny.

"Thanks," says Saul. "I've been trying. I had a letter from home this week."

"Well now, that's the stuff," says Lenny. "Good news?"

Saul shakes his head. "It's my mother, so she lies. She says everything is fine, that she has been given a job sweeping rubbish from the streets. I'm sure it's much worse than she admits." Four years of study in grammar school and months of full immersion had rendered his English nearly perfect, but the German clip of his consonants sneaks in, especially when he is upset.

"She'll make her way out, Saul."

Saul nods and walks to the back of the basement. He is exhausted from imagining everything that could have happened to his mother, to his country. He finds an apron and a hat, and leaves his coat on a hook in the staff room. He washes his hands, dries them on his apron, looks in the mirror and blinks the sleep from his eyes before ascending the stairs to the deli floor.

It's already packed, and the straining crowd outside fogs the windows with its hungry breath. "Get to work, Grossman!" barks Carol. Saul is sure he hadn't paused for more than half a breath, but he nods at Carol and shuffles behind the row of other sandwich makers to his station.

Saul stacks roast beef in precarious towers; he layers steaming chunks of turkey on rye; he spears slices of brisket and ladles their drippings on top. His hands deftly manipulate loaves of bread, slabs of meat, spoonfuls of gravy and dressing, mustard and mayonnaise. The world narrows down to the thumping, hissing, beating of a busy deli. Thoughts of his mother and his country are subsumed into the squeak of rubber shoes on floor, the sizzle of melting cheese, the clang of empty metal trays being exchanged for new ones, the happy burble and chatter of chair-screeching, finger-sucking customers. Down the counter at the pickle station Lenny has emerged from doing the books in the basement to shout, "One sour, one sour, two half, pickles, pickles, dill pickles, how many, ma'am, yes, three sour, enjoy!"

"Hey, kid!"

Saul turns toward the counter, wondering what he has forgotten. Pastrami on rye, two pickles — he can't imagine. "What can I do for you?"

The man who spoke to him is tall and dark-featured like Saul, but with the broad chest, the chiseled-out cheekbones, and the smoothed-back hair he has learned to associate with Italians, rather than Jews. "You make a damn good sandwich," he says.

"Thank you, sir," says Saul. He can feel Carol's watchful eye burning a hole through his apron. "Well —" and he moves to take a ticket from the next customer in line. It's not in his cache of muscle memory to stand still when the deli is this loud and bustling.

"Hey!" says the tall man. Saul turns back around. "Look, kid," says the tall man, balancing his sandwich in one hand and bringing a pickle to his mouth with the other, "you make a damn good sandwich, I was saying — holy Father, that's a good pickle — but you seem like a smart guy."

"I do?" says Saul.

"You do. And I'm in the business of smart guys." The man finishes his pickle and looks for somewhere to wipe his hands; finding

145

none, he brushes his thumb and forefinger along the cuff of the sleeve of his opposite hand and winks.

"Thank you, sir," says Saul, "but I really should get back to work."

"Okay, okay, I get it, you're in the middle of things here. I'll cut to the chase." The tall man puts his hand over the counter to shake Saul's and says, "I'm Joey Colicchio, and I'd like to give you a promotion." The truth is, Joey Colicchio knows that Saul studied English for years before fleeing, and has been watching him for weeks. He's young, strong, and spends all of his time outside of work alone. He's a perfect candidate for a delicate position.

Standing still, delicatessen spinning around him, looking at the Italian man who has just offered him a job for no reason he can discern, Saul is stretched between curiosity and fear. *Trust no one,* his mother had said. But also, *make me proud.*

"Grossman!" erupts Carol's militant growl. Saul looks up, drops Joey Colicchio's hand, says, "I've really got to get back to work," and turns back to his station, where at least ten tickets are lined up in a row at the edge of the counter. "Turkey on white," Saul repeats to himself, refocusing. "Pastrami on rye, turkey on rye, tongue with mustard."

"I'll be back, kid," comes Joey Colicchio's voice from behind him. And then, "Damn, this is a good sandwich."

Seven hours later, Saul is standing on Houston Street watching the early morning traffic thunder by. The sky is pink and periwinkle and streaked with the first yellow light from the sun, which has risen over the bridges connecting Manhattan to Brooklyn by gossamer strings. As it does every clear, cold morning, the overwhelming stench and noise of work seems like a dream.

Back in Brooklyn, Joey Colicchio kisses his sleeping wife's forehead and inhales the familiar dust and detergent of his bedroom. He pauses at the window to look out over the still-sleeping buildings of South Brooklyn before drawing the shade against the bright morning sun. He disrobes, leaving his suspenders clipped to his trousers in a puddle on the floor and his socks in small white balls. Without looking down, he knows his body shows the unmistakable signs of middle age — his legs have lost some of their tone and his torso is more barrel-shaped than it used to be; his skin hangs more softly on his muscles; his muscles don't cling to the bone the way they once did. The mat of curled hair across his chest is flecked with gray and plastered across thinning skin. He climbs into bed next to his wife and moves the bulk of his body against the pliable curves of hers. She leans back against him, and her smell, unearthed from its cavern of sheets, fills the air of their bedroom. Outside there are jobs unfinished — a young man not yet hired; plans not put into place; debts to be paid.

Joey had had several meetings to keep after his conversation with Saul. In the middle of the night, in a moment of cold, calculating determination, he had drawn back his fist and punched a man in the face. Joey is particularly adept at punching a man in the face. Done haphazardly, the bones in the hand can snap like breadsticks. But without even thinking about it, Joey Colicchio can land a devastating blow: fingers curled tightly, thumb on the outside, wrist cocked so the meat of the other man's cheek meets the strong place between Joey's index and middle knuckle. There is no swing; rather, a short sharp forceful jab; a direct path from Joey's fist to the soft tissue of Giancarlo Rubio's cheek. There is some adrenaline. Some unmentionable, addictive satisfaction. *We don't fuck around when you owe us,* Joey had hissed. *And you know, you're lucky I'm here.* Joey wiped his hand on his handkerchief. *You're lucky I came tonight, and not one of my guys. They're not as nice as I am.* Giancarlo Rubio had held the split fruit of his mouth with one hand and said, *I know, I know, it's coming.* Giancarlo owns a restaurant in the growing Italian section of Carroll Gardens. Joey's associates make sure his olive oil, his prosciutto, his wine, get to him on time. Undamaged. Giancarlo has a wife and five children. The children will be sleeping in their narrow bunks when he limps home, but his wife will pour him a glass of wine. She will hold ice against Giancarlo's swollen blackened eye, will put pressure on the gash in his face until Giancarlo stops spitting thick mouthfuls of blood. *Your children eat or mine do,* Joey sometimes thinks of saying. But he cannot admit, or does not believe, that he has no choice. He no longer knows what part of his job is a system from which it is worth breaking free, and what part of it is an inheritance, a heart, the fertile earth out of which he grows.

The Jewish boy will take the job, Joey is sure. He can see something of himself in the young man. Lenny at the deli says he's more timely than a grandfather clock and kind, cool, calm, even when the place is packed and the customers are foaming around the mouth with hunger and impatience. Joey trusts Lenny's judgment — Lenny has been on the Colicchio payroll for years; he's an invaluable asset in what's otherwise Eli Leibovich's territory. Joey can see that Saul will have a knack for the work, and that he will appreciate the benefit of a job that feels eerily like family. It is a good job for someone who has lost his roots. As Joey knows from personal experience.

Joey moves his head onto his wife's pillow and buries his nose in the mane of her hair. *An hour more,* he hopes, as her breathing lengthens and she seems closer to consciousness. *Stay an hour more.*

Sofia is awake. She has been awake since the darkest hour of the night, when it is inconceivable that it will ever get light. When just opening your eyes and looking through the crack in your curtains feels like you are staring at the naked body of the world, all vulnerable folds and soft corners. Sofia does not know what woke her up, only that it was a restlessness with no name, who would not let her soften back into sleep.

Sofia's eyes smart as her room goes gray and lightens, and her limbs ache. Soon her alarm will ring and she will reach a hand out and press the chrome knob to shut it off, automatic. It is the first day of her last term of high school.

The new year dawns frigid and violent, war like a coat the world pulls over its shoulders. Antonia reads the news even after Lina banishes the *Times* from the house. She listens to the radio with her eyes squeezed shut. People are dying in London at incomprehensible rates. They are dying in Eritrea. In Bucharest. Antonia feels each of these losses like a prickle along her spine. The clock speeds up every day: it seems there is no time to waste. It seems human beings are more fragile than Antonia ever could have imagined. She throws herself into her relationship with Paolo. The war rearranges her priorities. It tells her she'd better put down roots, or risk missing her chance. It tells her the world will not iron out its flaws and instabilities for her, so she'd better make do with what she is given. Paolo takes her seriously. He makes her feel safe. They decide on three children: less chaos than

Paolo's upbringing; less silence than Antonia's. The war encourages them to have this conversation. People continue to die. Antonia puts all her energy into constructing a future that will endure the chaos of the world around her. She believes, most days, that she can do this without escaping the Family after all.

Sofia dreams in Technicolor. Her attention wanders, but she lives fully in the present at every moment, so her life is an ever-changing tapestry of friendships and activities, of schoolwork not concentrated on and of meetings she is late for. She feels unsettled and fearful at the thought of graduation. The train is about to run out of tracks, and bold Sofia Colicchio has not figured out what she wants to do. And the war makes it all the more obvious.

Every day, it seems, Joey shuts the parlor doors for another evening meeting and Rosa wrings a dishtowel to shreds before making a platter of coffee and cake for Joey's associates, Frankie comes home from school and tells the rest of them that Donny Giordano said his brother's enlisting and anyone who doesn't is an America-hating, Nazi-loving, kraut-slurping coward, and the room goes silent because Joey employs a raft of able-bodied young men who are already fighting a war of sorts, but they don't talk about it at the supper table, and later Rosa leaves a pair of knitting needles conspicuously on Sofia's bed because they won't have her working in a factory like the other women but they'll be damned if she doesn't participate at all, and there are socks to be sent off in the army care packages. Every day the war circles closer and it tells Sofia, *you decide to do something useful, or I'll decide for you.*

*I don't know what to do,* she tells it, desperately. She hangs out her bedroom window like limp linen, she drapes herself over furniture all over the house. Sofia lying half-comatose on the sofa, sideways in an armchair, sprawled out in the kitchen so Rosa almost trips over her. *I don't know what I want.*

Antonia has shrunk away from Sofia's field of vision. A piece of Antonia — a piece Sofia has almost always been able to scent, to feel out — is missing. Or rather, it is somewhere Sofia has no access to. As the last months of high school tick away, Sofia considers the options laid out before her: marriage, university and then marriage, secretarial school and then marriage. None of them feel like a life she wants to step into. With only herself for company, Sofia feels violently confronted by that which she has not figured out, and expresses it by picking fights with her mother, by losing her temper with Frankie. *You've been a real pill lately,* nine-year-old Frankie tells Sofia, in the same infuriatingly matter-of-fact tone she talks to everyone with, child or adult, Family or grandparent. Where Sofia always wanted to be the center of attention, Frankie has managed to be simply comfortable in any situation. She follows the men's discussions of politics and finances at Sunday dinner. She never burns food when asked to mind a pot. The rules seem slackened for her, as if Rosa and Joey were tired out by raising Sofia and now if Frankie doesn't want to brush her hair one morning, she doesn't have to; if Frankie wants to go to a movie with a friend and no parents, she is allowed to. No one ever says, *Frankie, you don't fit here.* And Frankie manages to do whatever she wants anyway.

*You're always a pill,* Sofia snaps back at her, and then storms into her bedroom and feels like a monstrous, awkward thing.

When Paolo invites Antonia to supper at his family's house, she arrives five minutes early and climbs the creaking stairs slowly, listening to the percussion and melody of the families behind their peeling apartment doors. Paolo's apartment has four rooms stretched out along a narrow hall. The graying walls give off a faint aroma of simmering tomatoes and dusty paint and the sweat of four sons. The wooden floors are scratched by gravel and work boots and thirty years' worth of rearranging furniture and boys running back and forth down the lengths of boards. It is an apartment that would tell stories about its occupants, even if they weren't there. It does its best to contain Paolo's family — to soak up the smells of their cooking and the steam from their showers and the tears from their fights. Paolo shares a room with one brother, two older brothers sandwich into a second room, his parents sleep in a third, and the six of them cook, drink, eat, fight, laugh, cry, and breathe together in the final room. They seem to coexist in their small apartment by moving so quickly they are hard to keep track of. Antonia, sitting at the kitchen table folding napkins, feels like she is on a carousel: slightly dizzy, a little exhilarated, trying fruitlessly to keep track of the ever-changing view. His family is loud and affectionate. His mother: small, wide, exclamatory, kisses Antonia on both cheeks, holds her face and looks into her eyes and says,

"So this is the beautiful girl keeping our Paolo on the other side of the river so often lately?" and Antonia tries to smile but because Paolo's mother is still holding her cheeks, she ends up grimacing oddly. Paolo's father is tall, with long limbs like an octopus and thick black spectacles, and cries, "Basta, Viviana, give the poor boy a chance!" and Paolo's mother swats him with a dishtowel and turns back to the stove. Paolo's brothers pay Antonia no mind, engaged as they are in a loud argument about whether to enlist in the army. "I'll cut off your feet in your sleep before I see you go to war," warns Viviana, gesticulating with her butcher knife, and the boys duck out of the way just in case she means to do it now.

Paolo wants Antonia to marry him. Antonia can feel her desire to say yes beating like a drum on the inside of her chest. She thinks, often, of Sofia: the relief it must be to do what you want, when you want.

But Antonia has told no one about Paolo, and she cannot marry him until she does. She worries that if she tells her mamma, or Sofia, her reasons for loving him will be revealed as flimsy. She is worried that he will be rendered smaller, or less important, in the act of telling her larger-than-life best friend. Sofia never means to belittle Antonia, and perhaps Antonia lets herself be made small too easily, but she still fears the quizzical rise of Sofia's brow; her cherry lips rounding in shock and maybe laughter, a little derision sneaking into the *really, you?* and the *well who is he?* I've *never heard of him.* Antonia's carefully constructed relationship will come crashing down. She knows her mamma will be furious and disappointed that she loves a man who works for the Family. Her mamma might collapse under the weight of Antonia's inadvertent but encompassing betrayal. *Don't speak to anyone with slicked-back hair.* Paolo's is brown, but so dark it's almost black, and it moves toward the back of his head on its own, in a cresting wave that frames his face.

And his job is a good one. Good, in that it is enough to rescue Antonia from her own graveyard home. Good, in that it will pay for their future children to be fed, and it will buy them clothes and books. Good, in that by marrying Paolo, Antonia will buy herself time, and space. No wraparound porch, but an apartment with multiple rooms. A safety net for her children. Antonia, a child of loss, can build with anything she is given. She can see her life unrolling before her like an infinite carpet. Antonia and Paolo, in perpetuity, construct a home from the ground up. They do not carry anything that holds them back.

She wants to tell her mother about him first. She wants to tell Sofia. The secret has started waking her in the night, twisting its fingers through her hair and holding her down. But the words are locked somewhere below her lungs and she cannot find the key.

New York City straddles the mid-Atlantic coast. It is part swamp in the summer; part empty northern wasteland in the winter. And the city creates weather, like a mountain range: in the summer, the pavement and the buildings trap and heat the air; in the winter, wind screams down the long avenues, nature itself whirling through the concrete jungle.

Some years, in the fall, New Yorkers can already tell the winter will be long. Those years there is a patience to the biting wind and the monochrome gray of pre-snowy days. There is a sadistic brilliance even in the blue skies — clear days serve to highlight the leafless trees, to augment the stark lifelessness of the landscape.

Winter hushes the traffic and stops the clocks. It seems as though it has always been cold. New Yorkers know this in their bodies before they consciously accept what they are in for; their shoulders hunch in anticipation; their gaits are measured and slower, pushing through drifts of phantom snow.

Saul Grossman is no stranger to winter, having grown up in Berlin, where on the darkest days the sun doesn't rise until late morning and begins to set again as soon as it has crested the horizon; where a man's toes can turn black in the course of one day's work in badly insulated boots; where the darkness and the cold brew in the belly to produce a hunger that can't be satisfied, even in the most prosperous years and with the most succulent foods. As a child, he relished the first snow angels, the rush of sledding down the unshoveled sidewalks, and the way the heat of his apartment stung before it softened his frozen cheeks; the fleeting *whoosh* of warmth escaping from the opening and closing doors of pubs and bakeries. He longed for the winter break from school, when his mother would take him to work with her, and Saul would spend the morning reading on the floors of grand houses as his mother scrubbed bathroom tiles and swept out fireplaces. In the afternoons, she bought him treats from street carts. Cider and gingerbread sliding down his throat in warm gulps as his nose ran freely and his mother pulled his scarf tighter around his neck. When it snowed, Saul was the first one out the door in his apartment building, soon followed by a passel of bundled-up children, hands stuffed into woolen mittens, sleds under their arms. Even later, after Nuremberg, there were snowy days he remembers feeling carefree and invincible.

But this year, Saul faces the onslaught of winter with a persistent and chilling despair.

If one's soul is warm with love and one's house is full of family and beloved trinkets and fragrant smells and one's work is satisfying; if one sleeps well at night and eats well during the day and the muscles in one's hands and feet do not cramp up, winter can be a welcome means by which to narrow the world down to the most important parts. But Saul, alone in a new country and desperately worried about his old one, has nothing to warm him up or weigh him down. He alternates between certainty that his life in Germany was a dream, and distrust that his feet have really touched earth since he crawled shaking out of the ship's hold three months ago. He feels torn in jagged halves and faces winter in America with nothing outside of his fallible body and a bare room in a Lower East Side boardinghouse to cushion his bones against the cold.

Saul spends the first bitterly cold weeks of 1941 trekking against the wind to the deli and then against the wind home in the dawn; somehow, it manages to shriek down whichever street he walks on. Little bits of news from Europe begin to filter through Saul's meager network. The fragmented stories are guessed at by holding tattered letters up to the light, and whispered so softly from the mouths of still-seasick refugees that they come out as prayers. Saul cannot sleep for worry. In the darkest part of the night, he pictures his mother in the starring role of each of the bits of news he has heard. A whole village forced to dig its own grave and then lined up at the fresh earth edge and shot. Children sick, sweating together in work camps. Typhus and influenza spreading through the smaller-and-smaller Jewish ghettos like fire through haystacks. Men standing naked in the snow until their shivering slows and their eyes soften; their gold teeth collected for mantels and windowsills. Trains slicing across the tattered flesh of Poland, Austria, Hungary. It is inconceivable to be alive, to sleep on sheets, to close the door of his room behind him each morning, to drink coffee in the sun. Saul cannot decide whether he wishes he were there. There is something torturous about the filtered rumors on which he sustains himself, even as he is comforted by imagining his mother alive somewhere — anywhere. When he is sleeping his mouth sometimes forms the words of the Friday blessings. *Baruch atah Adonai,* he whispers. *Blessed are You.* While he is awake he will not speak to God, or cannot reconcile the idea of God and the sickness tormenting Europe. *God isn't so simple,* he knows his mother would say. But his mother isn't there to say it.

Whether or not Saul's body would have survived that winter alone, it is almost certain that his mind and soul would have been worse for wear. But thankfully, Joey Colicchio appears again in the middle of February, this time at the front door of Saul's boardinghouse. People in Europe are dying, swaths of them knocked down like dominoes, whole towns simply erased. The Family men are expecting a bigger tide of immigrants than ever to begin throwing themselves at the mercy of the Atlantic Ocean and Western bureaucracy.

The human instinct for survival kicks in when we least expect it. Desperate for some change, Saul accepts the job.

When Joey gets home from hiring Saul, Rosa, who is cooking, cleaning, and circling Frankie like a hawk to make sure she does her homework, kisses his cheek. Joey reaches for her with both hands, circles her waist, steers her toward him with palms on the back of her rib cage, growls down for her mouth with his mouth. But Rosa spins away, swats him with the back of her hand. "Dinner in ten," she says. Joey, feeling cold where he had hoped to wrap Rosa into his arms, into himself, kisses Frankie on the top of the head. "Papa, my hair," Frankie says, shrugging him away.

Down the hall, Sofia is sitting at her desk, chin propped up on her hand, hair glinting in a circle of lamplight. Joey imagines Sofia, four years old, running to him when he got home. Six, and sitting on his lap when they ran out of chairs at dinner, eating his olives when she thinks he isn't looking and then grinning up at him, maniacal, bright as lightning.

Sofia, eight, hand on the back of small Antonia, who has collapsed into sobs at their kitchen table for the second time that week. Sofia, half her attention on the grief of her friend, and half watching Joey's face the way a hawk watches a vole twitch, hundreds of feet below on the earth. *I know what you did.*

*All I've wanted is to make life easier for you,* Joey wants to say to Sofia. But Carlo's face surfaces in his mind. That, and the heart-swell of power. The perfection of control. *Liar,* says his memory.

Sofia at fourteen, glaring at him, fearless, as he and Rosa and Frankie left for church. She was always his girl.

*Go to her,* he commands himself. Nothing moves.

Sofia, seventeen, cannot feel her papa's desperation, and cannot connect to herself at four, six, eight, fourteen. Seventeen is an abyss: she feels divorced from her past selves, with their clearer heartbreaks. And the future — so close now the walls of the present buckle under its weight — is still a swirling panic. Sofia feels alone. She feels disconnected.

And when she sees Saul Grossman for the first time across a Sunday dinner table, she decides in an instant what she needs to tie herself back to the earth.

Saul is thin and dark-eyed. Close-shaven. Sofia watches him eat. He mixes everything together, small bits of beans and meat and cured lemon rind and sweet melon all in one bite. He chews carefully.

Sofia knees Antonia under the table. "Do you know who that is?"

Antonia looks. "I haven't seen him before," she says. *I can ask Paolo,* she almost says. It would slip out so easily. She turns her attention back to her plate.

"I heard my parents talking," Sofia says. "My father hired a Jew, from Germany. Does he look like a Jew to you?"

"I don't know, Sofia," says Antonia. Impatience hardens the ends of her words. Sofia will fall into infatuation now, like she always does. She will be in love by next week.

"I think he does," says Sofia. Saul is quiet across the table, observant. He listens with both eyes and both hands as Joey talks to him about business, as Rosa offers him third helpings of everything. "I never imagined falling for someone who works for my papa."

Antonia does not roll her eyes and tell Sofia that *falling* for anyone she has only seen for ten seconds from across a dinner table would be silly.

Paolo, like all of Joey's men, is invited to dinner every week. He stays in Manhattan with his own family because Antonia doesn't think she could pretend not to know him for three hours. *There's an easy solution to that, Tonia,* Paolo says. Antonia presses her lips together. Paolo wants her to tell her mother about them. He wants her to say she will marry him. They argued over coffee, and Paolo left his to cool sadly on the table. He looked disappointed, and angry, and outside he threw up his hands and said, *I don't know if I can do this anymore,* and walked away, and Antonia stood aching on the sidewalk alone. She has pictured him all week, nestled in the loud, fragrant recesses of his apartment, surrounded by his family. In her own bed she threatens to float up away from the mattress and dissolve into the night air.

"Antonia?"

"Sorry," says Antonia. *This is a perfect moment,* she tells herself. *Tell her. What do you think will happen?* But she says, "I don't know, I guess you just meet who you meet."

"I guess," says Sofia. And then, "I shouldn't have asked you, should I," which even Sofia knows is mean, but which she cannot help, because she feels mean, now: out of control, curdled. Inside herself she feels something small wither, something that had wanted to grow toward Antonia. Whatever it was disintegrates. *People change,* she tells herself.

She turns her attention to Saul, who has soft curls and could use a haircut. She watches for the rest of the meal. She sees how he holds a napkin, a glass of water, another man's hand in greeting, so delicately the things he touches seem holy. Sofia wants to be held like that. Like a glass of water. Like a library book. Like a pair of folded socks.

Next to Sofia, Antonia argues with herself in silent agony. *Say it,* Antonia tells herself. *Spit it out.* But the desert stretching itself along her tongue and down her throat is too dry.

After Antonia goes home, Sofia sits on her bed and tells herself, *you are not allowed to do this.* It has never worked for her before. She lists forbidden things that she has done: skipping class to sit swinging her legs on a park bench in the sun. Winking at the construction workers who tip their helmets to her and purse their lips. Once, telling her parents that she would watch Frankie, but spending the whole time in her room, and letting Frankie get into the bathtub alone. Buying the brassiere her mama *wouldn't be caught dead buying for my daughter,* with the scalloped lace edges and the modern cut. Walking alone from Canal to Fourteenth, shoulders thrust back, head high.

Down the hall, Saul Grossman has lingered to speak with her father. The doors to the parlor echo as they shut; the evening air thickens. Sofia Colicchio, skin all abuzz, ecstatic with curiosity in her bedroom.

■ ■ ■ ■

Antonia stalks home, carrying a plate of leftovers for Lina. Her anger is a red-hot coal, a condensed and burning thing. She slams the front door of the apartment harder than she means to, and not being a dish-thrower or an insult-hurler, decides to make tea. The water boils and Antonia pours it into a pot; the leaves soften and spread. And as the tea runs golden through the strainer into her mamma's cup, Antonia gets angrier and angrier.

She is angry with Paolo for giving her this awful ultimatum. She is angry with Sofia, for falling into infatuation over eggplant and sausage, for living so fully in her own affections. For saying, *I shouldn't have asked you,* so casually, as though there were no depths to Antonia that Sofia could not reach in and scoop up and comb her fingers through. She is angry with her mother, for giving her life to regret and sadness. Mostly, Antonia is angry with herself. For being unable to summon the courage to be her whole self in front of the people who love her most, and for refusing to show a man who has been nothing but kind and warm and giving that she loves him back. For looking happiness in the eye and telling it, *I'm not ready.*

Antonia puts her mamma's teacup on a tray. She drops a lump of sugar in and stirs it. "Mamma," she calls. "I made you some tea." She turns the oven on its lowest setting and puts Lina's plate in to warm up.

Lina shuffles in, wearing a robe and slippers. Her hair is wispy and tangled from resting against the back of the couch. She grips the back of her chair with long fingers. Her nails are cracked and the skin around them bleached. "You got home later than usual," Lina says.

"Mamma, I'm in love," Antonia says, and then claps her hand over her mouth, and then takes the hand away because more words are coming, quickly, in a small flood, "with a man. A Family man. His name is Paolo."

Lina looks at her daughter like she would study a painting, or a faraway vista. Antonia stands with her feet apart on the floor as though she is steadying herself for a fistfight, but her hands tremble and her face is empty of blood and her hair swirls in chaos around her head. Antonia has been taller than her mother for years, but she seems to shrink and cower now.

Lina is not bad. She is maybe weak, or lost. And as she looks at her daughter —

171

her beautiful, intelligent, suddenly grown-up daughter — she remembers the morning Antonia was born. It was in this corner, where the table is — she and Antonia are staring at one another over the spot where, almost eighteen years ago, she found herself locked inside a pain much bigger than herself. She knelt under the weight of it, knocked to all fours, and when she looked at her daughter for the first time, and Antonia opened her wet brown eyes and looked back — there it was. *I've got you,* she promised her tiny daughter. And also, *thank you.*

Lina is suspended, suddenly, barely balancing along the thread of her own life. *Where,* this memory asks Lina, *did that warrior woman go?* And Lina does not want to hear this question, for she has long ago decided that helplessness and a slow shrinking-away are the only solutions to the deluge of pain life has delivered her. *I do not want to fight,* she has decided. And she has not. She has let herself be swallowed: her body is small, her inhales consume less oxygen. She makes as few decisions as possible. She tries her best not to leave any traces of herself — no footprints in the mud of anyone's memory. But the memory of her baby girl looking at her — in trust, in love, in mystery — swirls in the air around them and tells Lina, *it's time. Here is your daughter. She is all grown up, and she is scared to tell you that she has fallen in love, because you have not mothered her in ten years. All you ever wanted was for her to live a life absent of fear, and you have failed. You have forced her to take care of you, to mourn for you, to live for you. You have asked her to propagate your prejudices. You are the weight dragging her away from happiness.*

Antonia stands, scared and defiant and un-mothered.

And Lina realizes she has not succeeded in disappearing. Here in front of her is the tangible evidence of her failure.

She is unspeakably sorry. She is filled with remorse that threatens to burst her open. She will not run away this time. She will not ask her daughter to hold her hand.

"Tell me about him," she says to Antonia. *Let me be your mamma again.*


Antonia calls Sofia the night after she tells her mamma about Paolo because really, nothing scares her anymore, and Sofia listens as Antonia says *I'm in love* and Sofia notices a small rancid place weighing her heart down as she listens, but she says *I'm so happy for you* and hangs up the phone

173

and is alone in her bedroom with her rotten heart and her flimsy fantasies.

Sofia develops a habit of lingering outside the parlor door, eavesdropping on Paolo and Saul as they work. It is this way she has learned that Saul is from Berlin, where he got the neatly articulated ends of his words and the quiet *ja* that sometimes slips out as he is listening to someone else speak. She has internalized his schedule by listening to him describe the rounds he makes of boardinghouses and hotels, unfathomably foreign neighborhoods like Borough Park and parts of the Lower East Side so low and so east they could be mistaken for water, for the crumbling edge of the island itself. She has seen Paolo checking off names on a long list, passing neatly wrapped packages that she has learned contain valuable forgeries for wealthy European Jews willing to pay for a new life. And she has seen her father, lurking in the room like a conscience, weighing stacks of bills with a practiced hand and kissing Paolo and Saul before they leave.

Sofia understands both the Family and Germany like a nightmare she can only partially remember — something sinister in both of them, her belly and throat are sure

— but she chooses to feel comforted by the sound of Saul and Paolo and her papa, plotting in their baritones, working against a vague and unnameable evil. They cannot all three be on the wrong side.

The day Paolo comes to dinner at her apartment, Antonia spends the afternoon cleaning. There is not much that can be done about the shabbiness of the sofa, the sunken spot that belies Lina's favorite place to sit, the browning throw rugs in the kitchen and living room. But Antonia shines the mirrors and countertops until they gleam. She makes dinner and the apartment fills with steam and fragrance, warm garlic and the fresh spice of lemons. She hounds Lina until Lina showers, dresses, pulls her hair away from her face. Lina looks almost normal, Antonia thinks. *Almost like a real mother.* Antonia shakes her head to rid it of that ugliness. Things between her and Lina have been good since their first tentative conversation about Paolo. Antonia believes Lina wants her to be happy. But Lina is strange, and getting stranger: women have begun sneaking in and out of the living room to visit with her when Lina thinks Antonia is asleep. Lina is charting her own course. Antonia might admire this, but there is a part of her that is still too angry. She doesn't trust Lina to shower before company comes over, or to give advice about wedding details. She doesn't trust Lina to stay in the real world for long enough to have dinner with her fiancé, and so Antonia spends the day cleaning and cooking, one suspicious eye trained on Lina, who wants to be trusted, but who cannot bear the inconvenience of making herself presentable for company, or eating at a pre-arranged time, rather than whenever she decides she is hungry.

The women visiting Lina came at the maga's suggestion. It is, after all, the maga's job to consider the unasked question, which in Lina's case had to do with how to move forward once you know there is no path that can guarantee against pain and disappointment. And so now there is the candle burning in Lina's window, the women slipping in her front door after Antonia has left for Sunday dinner. The women want a conversation over upturned tarocchi cards, or they want to hear the words Lina whispers to each full moon. The women come back again and again. And they pay her enough that Lina is planning to quit the laundry when Antonia gets married. Gone will be her chapped hands, cracks extending painfully down the pads of her fingers, no matter how much olive oil she rubs into them. She will never need to abide by the ticking of a clock again.

She will be done letting fear control her. And if Antonia wants to put herself in terror's way, Lina cannot stop her. No one would have been able to stop Lina, when she married Carlo. The inevitability of pain — the way love makes certain aches inescapable — used to wake Lina, heart pounding, terror coursing through her, every night.

*No longer,* she thinks, as her daughter's fiancé comes knocking at her door, that Family-slick hair, those irresistible high cheekbones, the toothy smile, one end of his mouth turned up so everything is a joke, everything is sex, everything is tension and energy and charm. Exuding that ignorant youngman confidence, that certainty that the world will roll out before him like a red carpet, that rejection of mortality. *You've never felt fragile,* Lina thinks as she shakes his hand, as he inclines his head, warmly, as she beckons him in, as Antonia stands looking back and forth, from her fiancé to her mother. Lina understands the power of fear, now: it brings into sharp focus that which is most important. *You've never been hurt,* she thinks, smiling at Paolo.

As for Paolo, he will not remember the food or the conversation of this evening. He will remember the glow of Antonia, bending over a dish. The way Antonia makes sure her mamma has everything on her plate before serving herself. The incandescence of her face as she looks at him, the strength in her set jaw, her determination breaking in waves over Paolo and Lina as they eat. *This is someone to build with,* Paolo thinks. *This is someone to care for. This is someone who will care for me.*

Two weeks later, on a Thursday evening in April, Sofia hears the doorbell and leaps away from her studying, which she was doing half-heartedly anyway. She hopes it is Saul, and it is — she hears him greet her mamma. The smoothness of his voice and steps echoing down the hall.

Toward her. He's walking toward her.

Sofia watches Saul from behind her cracked-open bedroom door. There is a way he has of just moving that shows Sofia he takes care of people. There are secrets vying for space behind his hooded eyes, a dark downturn of his mouth when he doesn't want to answer a question that causes Sofia to gasp for air. Her heart thuds, resonating wildly around her chest, threatening to jump out of her mouth. Everything pounds, from her face to her fingertips to her jellied legs. He's three feet away from her. He's going to open the bathroom door.

"Hello," says Sofia. He looks up. They are standing face-to-face, Sofia hiding halfway behind her cracked-open bedroom door and Saul, one hand on the bathroom door already, eyes quizzical, looking right at Sofia.

"Hello," he says.

And then something in Sofia erupts. And she is reaching out her hand and she is grasping a handful of his shirt and pulling him forward, and his eyes widen in mild surprise as Sofia tilts her face toward him and kisses him, damp and breathy, messy and fast.

She pulls away and looks at his face. Sofia has kissed enough boys to know they should look astounded after she pulls away. They should look amazed at their luck.

Saul is smiling, but he doesn't look astounded. He looks like he's about to laugh. "Sofia, right?" he says.

For an agonizing second, Sofia believes that her humiliation will be so powerful she will burrow down into the earth. She shuts her eyes and wills her body to sink directly through the floor.

When she opens her eyes Saul is still in

front of her. "I'm sorry," she stammers. "I'm so —"

"It's okay," he says, and the way he says it makes Sofia feel like it might, after all, be okay. "I have a meeting with your father," he says. "I should —"

"Go," she says. "Go."

That night Sofia tosses and turns in a pool of nervous sweat, hair slick against her damp neck, sheets alternately boiling and then freezing. *What will I say to you,* she wonders, *if I see you again?*

She doesn't have to wonder long. Sofia spends a restless Saturday staring out her bedroom window but Saul arrives early on Sunday, before Sofia's extended family, before the group of three to five uncles, Vito or Nico or Bugs, something like that, each of them, before their wives, who Sofia used to think were the height of glamour but lately whose acrylic nails and carefully curled hair and over-perfumed necks Sofia finds exhausting, trite, boring: this is, of course, a reflection of Sofia's own boredom, her own exhaustion, her own unanswered questions. There are only two months of high school left, and then nothingness.

Antonia isn't coming; she's in Manhattan with Paolo's family again, and Sofia is relieved she will not have to navigate Antonia's knowing glance, the way she understands everything Sofia is thinking without Sofia saying a thing. It is draining to watch Antonia's life spring forward in carefully constructed leaps. It makes Sofia feel like she is doing everything wrong.

The radio is on in the kitchen and Rosa is sifting powdered sugar over tarts and hazelnut cookies and there is the big pot, full of boiling water on the stove. Sofia is rolling out dough on the counter, breathing out each time she pushes the rolling pin away from herself, and Frankie is next to her, mincing onions and rolling stacks of basil leaves into thin tubes to slice them into ribbons. Sofia's hair has escaped into a dusty, floured cloud around her head, and there are stinging onion tears dripping from the corners of her eyes when she hears a voice ask, "Are you sure there's nothing I can do to help in here?"

Sofia shoves so hard with the rolling pin that her stretch of dough breaks in half and slips flatly off the counter and comes to rest at the feet of Saul, who has just walked in, who has just offered to help cook, if Sofia's ears are working properly. He picks the dough up and hands it to her, and it is covered in bits of onion skin and herb stem that have slipped onto the floor. Rosa snatches the dough from Sofia's hands and says something like *never get all this out in time,* and begins to tweeze the bread crumbs and chili flakes off of the once-velvety pasta dough. "Sorry, Mamma," mutters Sofia. And then she looks at Saul and before she can stop herself says, "I think you've helped enough," and Saul looks stricken, and retreats into the living room. Sofia's stomach lurches. *What's wrong with you?* she berates herself. *Why are you like this?*

"That one's a little odd, don't you think?" asks Rosa. "Offering to cook?"

"Sofia likes him," says Frankie. "Look how red her face is."

"I do not!" Sofia nearly shouts. Frankie is still shorter than Sofia, but she meets Sofia's angry face with a fearless, almost undetectable wink. Sofia wants to throttle her.

"I think he's Jewish," says Rosa, as though that settled that. Rosa knows he is Jewish, but this is her way: to present facts as questions. And, Sofia thinks, rolling out the unruined half of the ravioli dough, to present herself as a question. Rosa knows more than everyone in any room combined, but you'd never know it from the way she speaks. *Offering to cook?* There is something simpering about Rosa's tone, something that makes Sofia want to take a wrecking ball to her family home. *I think he's Jewish* — as if everyone else in the room will also adhere to whatever invisible, unbreakable rule Rosa invokes. Sofia spends the rest of the afternoon fuming, trying not to meet Frankie's probing eyes.

Later, when Sofia has washed her face and hands and changed out of her apron and smoothed down her hair, she slips into the living room to find Frankie squeezing herself into the empty chair beside Rosa. "There's one over there," Frankie says, nodding toward the chair across from Saul, who is sipping wine and wearing a brown vest and round glasses and whose hair is curling into his face so that Sofia wants desperately to run her fingers across his forehead and brush it away.

"Frankie, please," says Sofia to Frankie, who turns placidly away as if she does not hear Sofia.

So Sofia finds herself sliding down into the chair at the end of the table, across from Saul, who looks up and says, "Hello again."

"Hi," says Sofia, and then looks down at her plate. *Try talking to him, this time,* says the Antonia in her head, but Sofia finds that every last thought she's ever had has vanished, that the inside of her brain echoes like an empty marble corridor.

"I'm sorry about before," says Saul. Someone passes him a basket of hot garlic bread. Sofia's stomach growls so loudly she's sure Saul heard it. Steam fogs up his glasses.

"No," she says. "I'm sorry. I shouldn't have been so —" Sofia loses the words in her mouth; fills it with bread instead.

"I don't know how things work here, yet," says Saul. His accent is faint but trips over his tongue just slightly enough that Sofia cannot help but hang on to his every word. "I like to cook, but I think that's not my place."

Sofia laughs. "It's definitely not," she says. "I don't love to cook, but I'm stuck with it."

"Too bad we can't trade," Saul says. He passes her a dish of meatballs.

Sofia smiles, and something melts in the air between them. "Where did you learn to cook?" she asks.

"My mother," says Saul. "It was just us, so I helped her."

"Your mother — she's still in — Germany?"

"Berlin," says Saul. "I think." He is suddenly very focused on spearing a green bean.

"You don't know?"

"It's impossible to know. The Nazis. It's very bad there." But there is a shortness to his voice Sofia hadn't noticed before, and she feels like she is intruding.

"I'm sorry," she says. Saul meets her eyes, and suddenly the two of them have accessed something much bigger than the politics of Sunday dinner. There is a real world out there, with real consequences, she thinks. A world where people don't know where their mothers are. A world where everyone's biggest concern isn't whether a man offered to cook.

And then Bugs or Vito calls for Saul, and he turns away from Sofia, and she wonders if she imagined the whole conversation. "Sofia," calls Rosa, "will you pass that dish, please," and Sofia stands and brings the dish of garlic bread to the other end of the table, where Rosa sits across from Joey and Pop, who reaches into the dish and fishes out the best piece of bread without even looking at it, or Sofia. Suddenly Sofia feels very much tethered to the world she already knows. She glances down the table and Saul appears to be deep in conversation. Vito chucks him on the arm and the two of them laugh. Frankie is talking to Rosa, and Nonna, and to a woman Sofia thinks is

Bugs's wife. The four of them appear completely engrossed. Sofia is alone again.

But later that night, Sofia is drying dishes. Rosa has stepped out of the kitchen to go to the bathroom, and Nonna has left with Pops already, taking her eagle eyes with her. No one is watching as Saul moves quietly through the doorway of the kitchen and stands so close to Sofia she can smell him, so close the hairs on her arms and the back of her neck strain up toward him. "See you next week," he says.

Inside Sofia there is boiling, thick blood. There are rushing rapids pumping through her veins, against her hot cheeks, her fingertips, the eyes of her knees. Change thrumming itself close to the surface of her skin, threatening to burst through at every moment.

■ ■ ■ ■

# Book Three

## 1941–1942

■ ■ ■ ■

Paolo loves Antonia with a desperation that wakes him in the night and surprises him with its vehemence. When he is with her, he can feel the atoms in his body coalescing, straining, conspiring to be closer to her. When he is not with her, he is drawn by the string of his obsession, woven closer to her person. Paolo's fixation has started to express itself in sleeplessness. He lies awake staring at the cracked paint on the ceiling of his bedroom and feels something writhe under his salted skin.

Before Antonia, Paolo's fantasies of an adult life were all in black and white. He was a product of rough and winding tenements, where spit-swears and playground brawls transitioned into a crude adulthood. Life was about survival — of polio and measles, of violence perpetrated by the dregs of the Five Points gangs and the bigger, meaner school bullies, of factory work that left heads spinning and fingertips bleeding. Pleasure was taken haphazardly and without thought for consequences or continuation. It was meat served outside of Sunday supper, or whiskey tossed burning down an exhausted throat, or the soft bed of a loose woman. Just enough of them escaped and came back for holidays, telling stories of success as Broadway producers or bankers, that the rest of them were able to sleep at night, secure in the knowledge that hard work paid off; that the American dream was alive and well. Paolo's mother didn't stand for nonsense and that included *fantastical daydreaming* — she had raised her sons to work hard and take comfort in the little things. *This supper,* she would say. *The most beautiful radishes!* And then she would glare and raise her eyebrows and say, *if you're lucky, a good woman.*

As a child, Paolo did not think of women except as elements of a successful adult life: a good job, a good woman, a good home. He wanted desperately to follow his mother's advice, but also transcend it; wanted a neater, more orderly, more sensible home than the chaotic whirlwind of his childhood apartment. Wanted to be known, on the street, under his own name, instead of being lumped in with the passel of Luigio boys: *You're the smallest one, aren't you? The littlest?*

His thoughts of Antonia are all in color. His fantasies of present and future so wrapped up together he does not always know if he loves the Antonia in front of him or the Antonia fifteen years in the future in his head. But Paolo is twenty-one years old, and everything is still happening all at once, and he thinks he understands how he has been made, and what motivates him. The way his mother can reduce him to the barest, most desperate version of himself with just a word. The way he wakes aching from the tips of his toes to the webbing between his fingers with unfinished thoughts of Antonia, opening the door to a home they share, which is full of light, full of grand and unblemished furniture. Antonia, opening the door to a back bedroom. Antonia, opening the buttons on her dress. Opening her mouth. Swallowing him whole.

In July, Antonia dreams she has shown up for her first day of university. She enters an ivy-covered building and walks into her kindergarten classroom. The other students laugh at her as she tries to squeeze herself into a child-size desk. Maria Panzini leans to whisper to her neighbor behind a hooded hand and Antonia knows it is about her. *I've always wanted to come here,* she tells herself. *It will get better.*

Antonia wakes shivering, though the heavy midsummer air sits thickly in her bedroom. She wraps a sheet around herself and tiptoes into the living room and folds herself into the space softened by Lina's body on the couch. She is overcome by gratitude that she will not live in this apartment forever.

Antonia has done a good job of convincing herself that marriage — that the life she is carefully constructing with Paolo — is what she wants. Paolo wants something different than the world he was brought up in, too. For him, that change is the Family — which Antonia had always thought she needed to escape in order to move forward. But Paolo is sure of himself. He's a dreamer, like she is, but he's careful, measured, constructive. Paolo has a plan. He's saving his wages for an apartment, for furniture, for bedding. They will be married next spring. Paolo's future is full of clean rooms, of well-behaved children, of warmth and security. Antonia has adopted it as her own.

When she brings up classes at university with Paolo, he looks distracted, confused. He cannot fit the idea of Antonia working toward a degree into his future fantasy, but

192

he loves her. *He loves me.* He wants her to be happy. He will try, he says, to figure it out. *We'll figure it out.*

Like Paolo, Saul cannot sleep at all during the summer of 1941. He walks and walks and thinks of women. He spends the dark hours winding his way up and down the length of Manhattan, moving until his legs buzz with fatigue and then retreating into the steamy subway, the air of which is thick and helps him to keep his head attached to his body. Some nights he is ecstatic with thoughts of Sofia. When Saul is with Sofia, the terror that bitters his tongue and twists his stomach is reduced to nothing. Sofia makes him feel like he is standing on his own feet. He has become infatuated by her smell and her strength; by the ways she is tangible and surprising; by the honey of her laugh and the earth he can smell in her hair.

Other nights, his longing for his mother feels like a beast walking beside him down the gaslit avenues.

After high school ends, Sofia spends a week sitting aimlessly in her room, caught in a breathless sort of freedom that feels empty and insubstantial and overwhelming. The rest of her life — which until June had been no more than a surreal abstraction — asks her to think in lengths of time she had never conceived of. It paints every little decision she thinks of making in lurid shades of permanence. "You could consider university, you know," said Frankie, peering in around the door to Sofia's bedroom to find Sofia flipping through the same magazine for the third time, or staring aimlessly out the window. "You'll meet someone soon," said her mother. Sofia doesn't want to go to university, where she would spend years more being told what was right and wrong. And she doesn't want to meet someone. Someone other than Saul, that is, and he will never satisfy her family's requirements for "meeting someone." They will never get married. They will never have children. Saul's name will never come first on cards addressed to both of them; they will not be bound together by church or culture or anything but their own web of secrets and lies and love. This makes their time together irresistible. It makes it possible for Sofia, who has always felt a vague dread at the thought of marriage and children, to fall madly into obsession with Saul, who is safe, who doesn't threaten Sofia's independence. Sofia is beginning to understand contradiction: how it is possible to want something more than anything and not want it at the same time, how sometimes the impossibility of a dream is what makes it attractive.

Sofia is borne along by her new secret. She and Saul cross paths in the hallway; there is something magnetic about them, something molten. They clasp hands in doorways; they walk together around the block, quickly; they speak directly into one another's mouths, pouring sentences out like liquid, cresting a wave that is all animal addiction, all exhale.

Sofia and Saul pass notes when he comes to her house. They arrange meetings in other neighborhoods. They duck into small restaurants and try foods from places they have only ever seen on maps: Morocco, Greece, Malaya. Saul doesn't know which are the bad neighborhoods and he doesn't treat Sofia like she's fragile. They walk as far west as they can without stepping into the Hudson, and as the sun sets they watch the lights come on in New Jersey and Times Square and they find themselves on an island, an impenetrably dark patch of industrial wasteland at the edge of the world.

With Saul, Sofia feels there is room for her. Saul asks Sofia who she is, who she wants to be, and there is never the threat of disappointment, of Sofia not fitting into a preordained space. *I think I want to be power-ful, like my father,* she says to Saul, *but I will never do it the way he does it.* She does not know what she will do but she understands that it will be *something.* As the summer passes, Saul is on her mind more and more often, despite her resolve that they are only having fun, only breaking rules.

Saul, who is in love with Sofia despite it being unbearable to fall in love when you have lost your country and your family, understands contradictions. He understands standing in the presence of something impossible. And Saul begins to feel like he is coming out of a long hibernation, a lifetime of winter, the soft thump of his heartbeat speeding up as Sofia grows warmer and warmer in front of him, bath-ing him in heat. He begins to understand the value of sensation, the burning necessity of the present. Where once he had lived in memories, in speculation, in profound worry, Saul begins to claw his way toward his life as it unfolds in each moment.

In the fall, Sofia and Antonia do not start school again, for the first time in their memory. September yawns open and they fall in headfirst. They feel themselves borne along in the river of their lives. They are rushing toward what feels like a cliff, staring down a waterfall over which there is only marriage and children, sensible dresses, the business of running a home. They wage separate, silent battles with themselves: what they want; what will happen regardless of what they want. Love, they realize, is something that might happen regardless of whether they want it. They cannot tell whether it is the river itself or a life raft. They have to readjust how they thought it would be.

Joey Colicchio has been working too hard. He has been overextending himself, stretching himself taut between the world where he is a parent to two girls with long legs and discerning eyes, and the world where he is violence personified, the terror in the room, the reason men wake sweating in the night. In both worlds, his very best is demanded, taken from him, drawn out. In both worlds, he is the center. The beating heart.

Joey had imagined that the wartime smuggling operation he had spearheaded would relieve him of some of the guilt that sits like a rock in his intestines. He had imagined that enabling other families to feed off of the sizzling, decadent, fat-bellied American dream would help him to justify the relative opulence of his own lifestyle, compared to so many of the families he knows. Joey wants to believe he pays his men as much as he can. He wants to believe he uses violence as sparingly as possible.

But some part of Joey knows this is untrue. *You chose this life,* he remembers. There would have been less violence in the bricklayers' union, if he had kept quiet and paid his dues. He would have perpetrated less fear if he had stayed in his parents' house until he was married, brought ten or twelve grandchildren into a tenement hovel. He would have disintegrated into mud next to his father in the graveyard. *Dust to dust.* Joey finds himself wondering whether he is a good man.

Rosa stopped looking to Lina for comfort years ago, but recently — Sofia disappearing all day, secretive and defensive about her plans, Frankie bursting into flames at the smallest provocation, Joey rarely home and restless when he is there — she has found herself picturing, in the quiet hours of the night, padding next door in slippers and her robe and sinking into the familiar old rhythm.

She knows this is impossible. Lina has turned into a spectacle, a cautionary tale. Aside from her brothers, from the wives that show up each Sunday, Rosa is left to muddle through her weeks alone. And just like she always does, Rosa understands this. She knows why it is so. She understands the structures that make it necessary.

Still, Rosa stays up nights and pictures what it would be like. To shut the creaking door of her apartment and tiptoe through the halls and out onto the street and to find her way up the dark staircase of Lina and Antonia's building, where Lina might hug her and say, *I was hoping you might come.* And where, if they were lucky, they would know once again where their daughters were, and if the daughters were asleep yet.

On December 7, Pearl Harbor is bombed. Nothing is spared. The war, which had been someone else's problem, a faraway tragedy, something unapproachable, enters the houses of Americans. It fastens its hands around their throats. It forces them to look it in the face.

Sofia escapes her house, where her parents are mired in adult worry, a kind of depression that makes her feel like the ground underneath her feet is quicksand. They don't know what to do. They don't know what will happen. She takes a taxi to Manhattan. She watches the metal cables of the Brooklyn Bridge zip by and remembers being four, on her way to Sunday dinner.

Nestled in the lap of her father, the bosom of certainty. How can she focus herself? How can she decide to do anything in a world that is crumbling from the foundation up?

Sofia meets Saul under cover of a dark downtown cinema. The picture has already started when she shuffles in next to him, so she greets him by way of a hand on his shoulder and presses her body toward his in the dark. He offers her a half-empty box of popcorn and she is suddenly ravenous. She scoops up handfuls at a time and lets the salt collect under her fingernails and the grease soak into her skin. Sofia snakes an arm around Saul's elbow and leans her head against his shoulder. She can feel the bones of his arm, the long lanky way he extends out from his heart. He is solid and sure and breathing. Something in Sofia settles. Something opens.

After the film, Saul and Sofia wander through the tree-lined paths of Washington Square Park, trying their best not to look like good targets for pickpockets. They stop in a dingy artists' bar on MacDougal and Saul buys them half pints of dark beer, which they drink standing, leaning together at a tall corner table. Sofia likes the light and foolhardy feeling it gives her and drinks another while Saul nurses a cigarette. She makes conversation about the movie; she makes up stories about the other patrons (a mistress, the woman with the too-tight dress and the carefully arranged curls; a journalist, notebooks in tow, twisting a wedding band around his finger, who doesn't want to go home yet; an artist, who moved out of her parents' home in New Jersey and has only milk crates for furniture). She fills the empty space in their conversation, all the while thinking about the bones of Saul's arms, the jut of his knuckles against the skin, his dancing dreaming eyelashes. Inside of Sofia, the thing that has yawned open paces back and forth. It is hungry. Saul is quiet; his eyes look through her.

"What are you thinking about?" she asks, and Saul opens his eyes wider and focuses on her, as though he has forgotten where he is. He makes a twisted face; an inside joke, one he throws over the shoulders of men he is talking to when Sofia is standing just outside the room, watching. *I'm right here,* is what that face is supposed to say. *But I would rather be just over there, with you.*

"Nothing," he says, which is what he says when he is thinking about his family, and Germany, and the layers of unspeakable mystery surrounding his life in Europe.

Sofia reaches for Saul's hand, and he takes it, but his gaze stays neutral, focused somewhere above her shoulder. She doesn't know where he goes, but she wishes he would come back.

"You're somewhere else," she says.

"I'm right here," he says. He isn't, though. And Sofia, who often falls back into her own thoughts when her conversations with Saul reach this impasse, sets her mouth and puts her hand on Saul's chest. "Tell me," she says.

"You haven't seen the news?" asks Saul.

"Of course I have," she says.

"Well, I'm —" Saul stops. He shrugs. "I suppose I'm thinking about that, then."

"I suppose I'm trying not to," says Sofia. She is thinking about Saul's hands, about bubbles rising to the top of a glass of beer.

"I suppose," says Saul, "I can't help it."

"Fine," says Sofia. She wants to be enough for Saul. She wants her presence to draw him up and out. She wants to see herself do this, and feel like maybe she is good, after all; like there is not empty space ahead of her where a path should be. "Maybe I should go," she says. It would comfort her to comfort him.

"Sofia," says Saul, and there is an urgency Sofia does not recognize in his voice, "do

203

you even care that the world is falling apart? They think thousands of people died yesterday. And it's war, so the result of people dying will be more people dying. And each of those people is part of something. They have mothers, they have sons —" Saul breaks off abruptly. A pink flush has risen in his cheeks and his eyes are bright and animated.

"Of course I care," says Sofia. "But I came here to escape my family, to see you, and you are acting just like them, and there is nothing I can do to reach you, like there is nothing I can do to reach anyone, to do anything. I can't just feel so helpless, Saul. And I could go home, but my mamma would hand me a — a — a *sock* to knit, and I don't think knitting a sock is helpful!"

"Okay," says Saul. "Okay." Patrons at other tables are watching them out of the corners of their eyes. Saul nods toward the door and he and Sofia sidle out of the bar and onto the icy street. "I think you're right," says Saul.

"What?" Sofia has steeled herself for a fight.

"This worrying — it doesn't help. I just feel guilty."

Sofia has pent-up energy now, angry anxious breath, adrenaline pumping. But she has not been offered a fight, and she does not know how to resolve it without letting it out, without screaming into the weak and wavering winter sun, without destroying everything in her path. "There's nothing for you to feel guilty about," she snaps, harsher than she meant.

"What kind of son wouldn't feel guilty for abandoning his mother?"

"You didn't abandon her," Sofia says.

"But I did," says Saul. The simplicity of that threatens to pull tears from Sofia's throat. The two of them are hobbling down MacDougal to Bleecker. They are leaning in toward one another for warmth. Fingers of December air tunnel into their coats. The agony of being helpless rises in Sofia again, rakes her throat with its claws.

When Saul tries to turn right, toward Sixth Ave, where Sofia will hail a cab to Brooklyn, she stops him.

"I have an idea," she says, but her words get lost in the layers of her scarf and Saul has to lean close and ask her to repeat herself. "Take me home with you," she says into his ear. Her breath is hot and then freezes on his earlobe.

For the rest of his life, Saul will recall the moment he nodded and said *okay* and pushed his face into Sofia's scarf and hair to kiss her and put his arm around her shoulders. He will be able to taste the metallic freeze in the air, and to feel, as though it is right there, the urgency of Sofia's body leaning toward his. He will be able to imagine his life as it seemed to him in this moment: stretching out before him and filled with infinite pleasures. Sofia was always the only one who could reach down into the depths of his preoccupation with things he could not control and bring him back up to the surface. *Take me home with you,* she said, and the ice on his earlobe reminded him he was alive, and standing on his own two feet with a girl he loved in New York City.

"Okay," he says, and they begin to walk east, shivering with cold and anticipation and both of them quiet, shuffling along in the tide of commuters going home.

Later that night, Sofia lies in the unfamiliarity of Saul's narrow boardinghouse bed. Saul is asleep. She feels anonymous and powerful: a timeless woman, part of a ritual much bigger than herself. Moonlight shines in through the window and makes lurid shadows on the wall. There is a tree that grows and shrinks, distorted in the wind, and the unnaturally stretched-out bodies and small heads of pedestrians pass across the ceiling in a surreal parade.

Sofia believes in God the way a child believes its parents will know if it breaks a rule. She is curious, and a bit resentful, but God, like all big structures against which Sofia finds meaning in asserting her independence, is omnipresent in her world. God consists of the ritual Masses she stopped going to as a teenager, just to see if it would make a difference; of insalata di mare and baccala on Christmas Eve; of crossing herself as naturally as she breathes when she passes a cathedral. God is in the smells of her mamma's cooking. God, in the waistband of her skirt, the one that feels like it asks too-personal questions of her hip bones but lifts her up and smooths her out and makes her the focal point of every man she passes on the street. It occurs to Sofia, just before she falls asleep, to wonder if God knows she is naked and unmarried in a Jewish man's bed.

She wakes up in the gray predawn, and considers the shift of her bare body against Saul's sheets. *What have I done?* For all her posturing, Sofia has never crossed a line as thick as this one.

She stands up and wraps a shirt around herself and carefully eases open the door of Saul's room. The bathroom is a fifteen-foot walk down a creaky hall she is absolutely not allowed to be in, and she tiptoes along the wall, hoping for mercy from the ancient floorboards. She locks the door and peers at her face in the spotted mirror, wondering if anyone will be able to tell. She looks the same, but a bit pale from sleeping too little. She splashes icy water over her face and lowers herself to the toilet, which is cold enough to stop her breath in her throat.

In Saul's room, thighs still stinging and heart pounding, Sofia climbs back into bed and stares at the ceiling. She cannot decide if she feels more or less whole. She isn't sure whether she has been successful in drawing Saul into the present. The fear that she has not been enough chokes her. That she has not really changed anything — really, everything is the same — blinds her. She struggles for air, for light.

Next to her, Saul stirs. Sofia turns her head to look at him. She has never seen the features of his face so slack. His exhales whistle softly and Sofia finds she is uncomfortable to know this; it feels too personal. She feels frozen now. She wants to spring from the bed, to sprint down the icy Lower East Side street as dawn surges, to pound and thrash against something bigger than herself as light cracks the morning city open like an egg.

Sofia, in bed, claps a hand over her mouth to keep from weeping. All her life, she had been told this would change her. How disappointing to break the biggest rule she could and be left inside the same skin.

She leaves Saul's room with a vague sense of disease, with a disappointment bordering on disgust. Not at Saul — Sofia smiles at him as she leaves his room; he asks if she is okay; she lies — who is always kind, and in whose eyes Sofia has ruined nothing, has given away nothing, has betrayed no confidence. Sofia is disgusted by the lies she has been told about her own body. She trusts no one. She holds her arms slightly away from her body in the cab on the way home. She gets out at the corner and peers up into the curtained windows of the houses on her block, which all look like they are watching her. *I was just at Antonia's,* she says, to her furious and terrified mother, to her curious and shrewd sister. *I just fell asleep. I'm sorry. I know, Mamma. I'm sorry.* In the bathroom, Sofia undresses and turns the water on full-blast and stands in the shower until her skin shines with heat.

She forces herself to look in the mirror once the steam clears. She looks the same.

She doesn't feel broken, or damaged. She doesn't feel hurt. Rosa hadn't taken one look at her and asked, *what have you done?*

*Every rule you've ever learned,* Sofia realizes, *is a lie.*

And then the tears that have been building since she stood on the corner of Bleecker and MacDougal with Saul finally spill down Sofia's cheeks. And as she hugs a towel over her body in the bathroom and weeps, it seems to Sofia that the world has finally turned completely inside out.

But Rosa is of course wondering what has come over Sofia, who has spent all summer and fall sneaking away, avoiding her family. She knows, the way you can know something you don't want to know, that Sofia didn't fall asleep at Antonia's, because she knows, of course she knows, that Sofia and Antonia aren't as close now as they have sometimes been, that they are both preoccupied with the business of being almost adults, of figuring out what that will look like. Antonia has a fiancé, that beautiful boy from Manhattan, and Rosa is as happy for Antonia as she can be while desperately wishing Sofia would meet someone, too, that Sofia would take her ferocious energy and focus it toward a recognizable life. And

Rosa doesn't know where Sofia was the night before, but she knows Sofia is lying.

Sofia doesn't see Saul until the next Sunday dinner, where he hardly meets her eyes out of nervousness that Joey Colicchio will take one look at him and know what he has done. This suits Sofia, who spent the week moping in her room, and who isn't sure what she would say to Saul, even if she were given the chance. The magnitude of what they have done is like a concrete wall between them. The next week is Christmas, and then there is New Year's, and then the first weeks of 1942 are unusually busy for Joey and his team, and Saul keeps strange hours and Sofia goes on walks around the perimeter of her neighborhood, bundled in furs, wind whipping tears down her face as she turns every corner. So they don't run into one another, and neither of them picks up the phone. *What's gotten into you?* asks Rosa. *You seem stranger than usual,* says Frankie.

Sofia is stranger than usual. She doesn't recognize herself. And so Sofia finds herself sitting on her bed, willing herself to call Antonia. It is the middle of February. Antonia is planning her wedding, and it is all she can talk about. Sofia doesn't want to call her. But there is no one else who can help, so she is staring at the phone. She is commanding herself to pick it up. *Dial the number.*

Sofia knows there is nothing to be done, but she is sure Antonia will know what to do. Or rather: Sofia is sure that in Antonia's eyes, she will feel like herself again.

She picks up the phone. She says, "I need to come over."

"Are you sure?"

Sofia nods, hands in her lap. She is sitting on Antonia's bed, in Antonia's musty apartment, familiar as an old coat. Her knees are touching Antonia's knees. "I'm sure. I mean, I'm as sure as . . . it's been two and a half months, Antonia. I spent every morning in January kneeling on the bathroom floor." She shrugs. "I'm sure."

"But . . ." Antonia sits now, quietly next to Sofia, in reverence of the crisis at hand. "How?"

Sofia raises her eyebrows.

"I mean, I know *how*. I guess . . . when? No, I know when." Antonia is silent for a moment, and then asks, "Where?"

"In his room, in December."

"Wow. Sofia, wow!"

"I know," says Sofia.

"You're not married," says Antonia.

"I know," says Sofia.

213

"Oh, Sofia, he's Jewish!"

"I know." Sofia turns to look at Antonia, and her features are small and scared inside her big, white face. "My parents don't even know that he and I — that we — my father works with him every day. Antonia, I think he'll kill him."

"I'm sure he won't," says Antonia, and puts her arm around Sofia's waist. She is not at all sure, but she knows that the immediacy, the permanence, and the incontrovertible existence of the third life in the room with them means that everything has to be okay. It has to work out. Sofia and Antonia, playing make-believe, had always assumed there was nothing they couldn't tackle together.

"I can come for supper," Antonia says. "Do you want to wait and tell them then?"

And there it is: Sofia feels herself, again. Energy courses through her. Her fingers flex, her toes tingle. *Thank God,* she thinks. And then she reaches across the bed and hugs Antonia, wraps Antonia against her chest, presses her face into Antonia's hair. "Thank you," she says. Antonia's hands are tangled up with her hands; Antonia's eyes are on her face. "But I think I have to be alone with them. It's the only way — I have to make them let me explain. If you're there it will be too obvious — here is our daughter, the fallen woman, next to her friend who's marrying the good Catholic boy, you know?" She does not know exactly what she will "explain" because the whole thing is murky to her, still, too — the steps that got her there, the way her life will change. But she is impatient now, ready to move. She has a plan. She has something she needs to do. The nervous energy threatens to drown her where she sits. She stands and turns to go. "Thanks," Sofia says, again. She walks out of Antonia's room.

"Sofia," calls Antonia.

"Yeah?"

"Does Saul know?"

"No," says Sofia, from near the front door of Antonia's apartment.

Sometimes when they are alone Antonia wishes, fervently, silently, that Paolo would cross the expanse of sofa or table between them and seize her around the waist and peel the blouse from her shoulders, the skirt from her thighs. In the halfway space before she falls asleep, she can imagine the weight of his body; she fills with hot honey.

How thin the line is, Antonia realizes. How insubstantial the space between imagining and asking.

How easy it almost seems to cross over.

Sofia cannot bring herself to be sorry, but she is scared.

Some nights she lies awake and imagines hiding it. She spends sleepless hours designing baggy blouses, jackets with huge cowls, skirts that balloon out around her waist.

Sometimes she pictures herself and Saul and their baby, living wild in a cabin in the woods, or carrying tents on their backs like Indians. Saul would hunt for deer and she would gather acorns for flour and oysters to roast in the coals of their fires. They would dress their child in woven grasses. They would sleep curled into one another under the stars.

She fantasizes that her mother will embrace Saul and cry, and her father will clap him on the back and look at Sofia and be stern, but proud. They will plan a big wedding — outside, to be in plain view of both of their Gods, and Sofia will drape herself in jewels and silk and they will dance until sunrise.

She worries she will end up alone, baby strapped to her leaking breasts by an old scarf, hunting for pennies in the gutter.

She imagines it growing, but she can feel nothing.

She tells Saul first. He has not heard from his mother since the summer of 1941. He has not been alone in a room with Sofia since the night she spent with him in December. It is not in his nature to be angry with her for avoiding him. *What can I do,* he asks her. She does not look pregnant, and it is hard for Saul to comprehend what he is being told. *What do you need.* Sofia doesn't need anything. If she stands and does nothing, she will still grow a human being inside her body. But she is happier than she would have imagined to be with Saul. He kisses her and something in Sofia blooms upward, something is hot and waiting, something has been dreaming of this moment. She grabs fistfuls of his shirt and pulls.

She invites Saul to dinner without telling her mamma, which she knows will send Rosa into an anxious spiral. But Sofia can't figure out how to tell Rosa and Joey that Saul is coming without telling them why, and Saul wanted to be there. *It's my responsibility too,* he says, with the very serious crease between his brows. The problem had turned into an "it"; had been shared; had been named, and so it had been called into

217

being, into the world with them. Sofia gets into a cab and watches Saul walk away, scratching a nervous circle into the back of his head. Something about his slow steps makes her weepy, lumps like laughter she has to swallow down. *You love him,* a voice in her head says. *You didn't expect it, but you do.* It sounds like Frankie. *Shut up,* Sofia responds. She turns her head forward. The cab moves toward Brooklyn.

Saul shows up at the Colicchio apartment early and Rosa is wiping her hands on a dishrag as she says, "Joey will be out in a minute." He thanks her, because there is no way to tell her, *actually, I am here for dinner.* Luckily Sofia hears him enter, because she pops her head into the living room and says, "Mamma's making meatballs. Would you stay?" and Rosa, after a shrewd look at Sofia, says, "Yes, of course, we wouldn't hear of you going out in the cold, come," and offers Saul a glass of wine, and sneaks down the hall to whisper with Joey. Sofia and Saul hear Joey say, "No, no meeting," and they look at one another in furtive silence.

When dinner is served Sofia and Frankie and Saul and Joey and Rosa sit around the table in silence for a moment, staring at their untouched plates as the steam rises in

218

curling columns toward the ceiling. They are all lit from the top down by the overhead bulb and from the inside out by the candles on the table. It is Frankie who eats first and eases them out of their silence.

Only Sofia finishes her plate: she is ravenous; every space within her cries out to be filled.

And then there comes a moment where everyone has paused, where the candles still flicker and the attention at the table moves and comes to rest on Sofia, and on Saul. And Sofia wipes her mouth with her napkin and laces her fingers together and her voice creaks open.

"Mamma," she says. "Papa." She looks at each of them, and then back to the middle of the table, where the serving dishes are still half-full. And she thinks of how Antonia might say this, might talk about the relationship she and Saul had built, the subtle ways they have learned to care for one another, the surprise of it all. And then she says, "Saul and I are going to have a baby," which is as abrupt, as tactless, as unlike Antonia, as anything she could imagine.

Frankie gasps, and then grins: this will be something momentous, and she knows she will be both a spectator and, somehow, implicated. This is juicy. This is unheard of.

Rosa says, "Don't say that. What in Heaven would possess you to say something like that," but before she has finished her sentence she realizes Sofia is not making it up, and she falls silent and then turns to Joey and says, "Say something!"

Joey does not say anything.

"Sofia, this is absurd," says Rosa. "He's not Catholic. What are you thinking? How can you build a life this way? Where will your child go to school? What will you do on Christmas? Why aren't you answering me, Sofia, say something!" Rosa's panic rises like a bird trapped in the room, flapping in chaos against the furniture, the windows.

"I don't know, Mamma!" says Sofia. And her voice is loud, too, and it is clear, and everyone looks back at Sofia, back to where her center of gravity has pulled them all into orbit. "We didn't plan this. We didn't plan — I didn't mean to fall in love with him. But, Mamma, he's interesting, and he's kind, and he loves me, and I don't care if he isn't Catholic or if we're doing things out of order. I don't care!"

"Giuseppe Colicchio," Rosa says, turning on Joey, "unstick your damn tongue! Talk to your daughter!"

But Joey's eyes are on Saul. His face is

unreadable. His gaze is a needle, pinning Saul where he sits in his chair, like a specimen on a corkboard. He is silent for a moment, and when his voice comes it is clear and calm.

"You will get married," Joey says. "I'm going to speak to Father Alonso and he will perform the ceremony even though you" — he looks at Saul — "are not Catholic. Well, you can become Catholic. It will be a special favor to me. To us. You can take the name Colicchio. I'll arrange for it to be no problem."

Saul is on his best behavior, and as such feels himself smiling and nodding at Joey's words before their meaning organizes itself in his brain. He understands that Sofia's mother is smiling; that Sofia herself looks happy, or at least surprised. He hears Joey Colicchio tell him he is to give up his name, his language, and his heritage. He understands he is being given something immense in return. "Thank you," he hears himself say. *Thank you?*

"Papa, I," begins Sofia. *Papa, thank you for not killing the man I love. Papa, I can't bear to see you looking at me with a sad face anymore. Papa, it's been years — when did I stop being your girl?*

*Papa, you can't possibly expect Saul to give*

*up everything.*

"Papa, this is crazy." But it is not Sofia who has spoken; it is Frankie, her neat frame next to Rosa on one side of the table. Her bright eyes alight.

"This is not a discussion," says Joey, automatically, almost before he registers that he is talking to Frankie, his smallest baby. Frankie, who was born after four miscarriages and had to be sliced out of her mother as the sun rose, who cried and cried the first months of her life, soothed by nothing, but who, once she grew accustomed to the world, found comfort in the tastes of new foods and the laughter of her sister and has hardly cried since. "This is not a discussion," Joey repeats.

"Of course it is," says Frankie. "This is unfair, Papa. You haven't even asked Sofia and Saul what they want." She says this matter-of-factly, like she says everything. The truth of it weighs down on all of them. No one has asked Sofia and Saul what they want.

Saul is overcome by the urge to say something amenable, like, *it's fine,* or, *really, I don't mind,* but he is silent. How can he know which moments he has control over the direction of his own life, and which moments he has no choice but to surrender to bigger forces? He is good at keeping his head above water; good at thriving in whatever unexpected circumstances he finds himself. But here, in the moment of decision, Saul realizes he does not know how to make the choices that will steer him in one direction or another.

"Enough!" says Joey, and for the first time his voice cracks slightly, out of his control. "This is not your affair. You will sit there and you will not speak. You will *not*. You will not make the impossible situation your sister has put this family in any worse. You will not question my judgment. Is that clear." Frankie is silent. *"Is. That. Clear."*

But Frankie cannot stop herself. "This is ridiculous, Papa! People have rights. Women have —"

"Frankie, enough," says Rosa.

"But, Mamma —"

"That is enough."

"It's okay," says Sofia. She puts her hand on Frankie's knee. She keeps her eyes on her own lap and tells herself again, for emphasis, *it's okay.* She believes it. For the first time in months, *everything might be okay.*

There is what feels like an exhale — from each person in the room, from the room itself, from the very bones of New York —

as the Colicchio family makes itself into something new.

Saul is sent home with a foil-wrapped tin of leftovers.

By the time he gets there, he is so exhausted he can hardly lift his feet up the stairs. He draws the shades tight and stuffs two spare shirts along the cracks between the windowpanes. In bed, he wriggles his body around along the length of his icy sheets until he can feel his heartbeat quicken and the sheets start to warm up.

He counts his breaths — in, and out — and tries not to think about Sofia. He tries not to think about what it means that she is pregnant, and that his mother is missing, and that he will be a father in his new country. He feels swollen with a responsibility bigger than himself. And he feels guilty, too, because a part of him is relieved to accept Joey Colicchio's offer, to disappear completely into a new life.

Saul's eyes are heavy and his breath is slow and he is nearly asleep when the door of his room explodes open. He sits up in bed, heart beating in his head and chest and fingers, blinking furiously in the dark.

Before he can focus his eyes, Sofia's father has grabbed him by the collar of his shirt, picked him up, and pinned him against the wall. Saul's head slams against the brick and stars burst in front of his eyes. He can hardly draw a breath.

"I thought I could trust you," growls Joey Colicchio. "You sneaky sack of shit. How dare you."

"I didn't mean —" says Saul. His feet are barely touching the floor. Adrenaline courses through him like lightning.

"You didn't mean what?" There is whiskey on Joey's breath. "You didn't mean to ruin my daughter's life? You didn't mean to take the job I gave you? You didn't mean to set foot in this fucking country?" He looks right into Saul's face. "You bet your figlio di puttana Jewish ass you'll wish you didn't do any of those things."

Suddenly, Saul realizes he is looking at a different Joey Colicchio than the suave and charismatic man who sends him upstate or to the dock at Ellis Island to collect terrified German and Austrian and Hungarian refugees. The Joey Colicchio steaming in front of him, hands around his throat, is the murderer — the one who has watched men shit themselves and beg for their lives and has sent them sleeping into the Hudson with bricks tied to their ankles. Saul realizes that Joey could kill him. He might die.

"I love her," he says. "I know you don't believe that, but I do."

Joey Colicchio loosens his hold around Saul's neck. Saul crumples to the floor. Joey reaches into his back pocket and pulls out a pistol. He points it at Saul.

Saul stares down the barrel of his own mortality and wonders if maybe this is the way it's supposed to be. It would be so simple. For a moment, Saul considers the luxury of surrender with relief and gratitude.

"You love her," says Joey, without lowering the pistol. "You fucking love her?"

"I love her," says Saul. *They aren't bad last words,* he thinks.

"Stand up," says Joey, and gestures with the gun.

Saul stands. Joey levels the gun at Saul's chest. Saul closes his eyes.

"Open your eyes," says Joey.

Saul opens them.

"First rule of fatherhood," says Joey. "You don't get to die now. It's not about you."

When he gets home, Joey Colicchio pulls the pistol out of his jacket pocket and wraps it in muslin, slides it into his desk drawer.

Joey kisses Rosa. He peeks into Frankie's bedroom and tells her, "Lights out, now."

And then he turns down the hall to Sofia's room. She is brushing her hair and in her stark face Joey can see the baby he cradled in the hospital, the five-year-old he brought along to Manhattan meetings, the fourteen-year-old who stood, so mad she almost levitated, and told him — told *him*! — she wouldn't come with them to church. He doesn't know what to say, but he aches for her, so Joey clears his throat before entering his daughter's room. She looks up at him and he bends and cups Sofia's face in his hands. "La futura mamma," he says, like it is easy. And Sofia says, "Papa," softly, and Joey Colicchio folds her into his arms and for a moment is filled with unadulterated wonder.

Antonia marries Paolo as the winter air loses its sting. Lina sits tearless and erect in the frontmost pew, looking straight ahead. In the back of the church, Paolo's work associates line up neatly, and in a surreal coincidence, in order of height, like a matryoshka doll of criminals and smugglers. Lina can count the hairs on her head, so alert is her skin. So strong, her resolve not to acknowledge the Family men.

Joey walks Antonia down the aisle and is astonished that the little girl he watched learn to swim on a Long Island summer day is the capable, intelligent young woman he is giving away to be married. He nods as graciously as he can manage at Lina, but a nod cannot bridge twelve years of sorrow, the gaping vacuum between them where Carlo should be, the ways they have both evolved to survive.

Sofia and Saul do not sit together; they

are not married yet; Sofia has stuffed herself into her nicest dress, which zipped when she stood with her stomach sucked in but which now seems to accentuate the expansion of her belly. When she stands she looks perfectly normal but when she sits she spills over her waistband. She does not fit in her dress; does not fit in this wedding, where she sits with her mamma and Frankie and covers her midsection with Frankie's scarf. She does not fit with the women here; she cannot sit with the men. She is neither a child nor, truly, an adult. Sofia squirms. She can feel Saul's gaze from the back of the room, where he stands with the other Family men. In the back, in deference to Lina. Present, in deference to Paolo and Joey, to the connections that bind all of them. There is no easy way to untangle what is Family and what is family. There is no clean separation of professional from personal. Sofia understands more of this balance now, because of Saul. Saul is connected to a wider world, where a girl's anger at her father or frustration with her mother or adherence — or lack thereof! — to the rules is not the biggest thing. Where sometimes, Sofia is beginning to understand, you have to do things you wouldn't have expected to protect the people you love.

One of Paolo's brothers was taken by the draft in February. No one wants to sit in his seat; no one can bear either to mention or not to mention his name. He sends letters but is not allowed to tell his family where he is. Paolo's two other brothers wear matching suits, and their mamma flits like a butterfly among flowers between them, straightening their ties, reaching up to brush aside their stray curls. Moving as though her family is all there, as though one of her wings has not been torn off. Viviana Luigio is taking unexpected challenges one step at a time, and she is staying optimistic. She shares food and conversation with Paolo's new work associates because it is, she believes, the kind and magnanimous thing to do. She maintains hope she can convince Paolo to take a restaurant job her cousin is holding for him. That her sons will come home safe from every battle they fight.

Antonia feels hot and grateful, safety like a parachute carrying her along an inch or so off of the ground. She thanks Joey, and for only half a second feels faint with the realization that her own father isn't there, won't see her, would have loved to: Carlo Russo, a hand on her back as she drifted to sleep, would have loved to see his daughter commit her life to a man she loved. Or,

Antonia can tell herself this story: the breathless unfairness of not having Carlo also allows her to idealize him, to hold him up as the pinnacle of something she is constantly missing out on. *Love,* Antonia recites to herself, as she walks carefully through the sea of everyone she knows. *Honor.* She takes a breath. *Obey.*

Tonight Antonia and Paolo will go to a hotel in Downtown Brooklyn, the Grand Palace, where they will have a view over the East River. Tomorrow they will move into their own apartment. Paolo has been saving for rent and furniture all year. Antonia has picked out dishes, towels, bedside lamps. *So I didn't do it the way you wanted,* she says defiantly, imagining herself at fifteen, awestricken in the high school library. *I got us out, didn't I?* Last night was the final one she will ever spend in her childhood apartment.

They eat marinated red peppers and spinach ravioli with scalloped edges and trout with shriveled eyes and flesh of seaweed and lemon and river water. They all dance wildly; the sadnesses that always come to a family function are relegated to dark corners, to the bathroom line, to the side of the bar where they wait for their drinks. All night Antonia's face is hot with

231

food and wine and she watches Paolo, the boldness of his brows and lips and the half plum of his tongue; the jaunty tilted Homburg set just to shade one eye and then the other as he dances in the lowered light. After the reception, in the back of a powder-blue Cadillac, Antonia feels emboldened by four glasses of prosecco to run her fingers through the thick dark hair that escapes from under his hat brim, and he catches her fingers and pries open her fist so he can kiss the place where her middle finger meets her palm.

Sex makes Antonia feel like a wildcat, like a river. She finds herself kneeling on the edges of furniture, straining toward Paolo as he brushes his teeth, as he hammers a nail into the wall, as he opens the fridge and then meets her eyes across the room. She finds that she is spacious, that she is resilient, that she is flexible. Antonia is hungry as she runs a bar of soap over herself in the bathtub, as the water drips from the ends of her hair. She is surprised by the voracity of her own want; this tremulous, physical thing that comes from her body, that cannot be overthought.

She is pregnant almost immediately, and with each passing day feels less like an imposter in an adult world. She interlaces her fingers at night and squeezes the blood out of them in prayer. *Thank you, thank you, thank you.*

Sofia bakes and swells in the springtime sun.

Saul takes First Communion on a brilliantly blue May morning, body of Christ gluey on his tongue and the sour taste of wine lingering in the folds between his gums and his cheeks. Afterward, he holds the door of the church open for his pregnant fiancée and hopes his squinted, twisted face can be blamed on the bright sunlight outside. Because Sofia is who she is, she will not thank him for adopting her language and her holidays and her family's name. Because Saul is who he is, he will not ask her to.

They are married by a priest who comes to the Colicchio apartment on a Friday evening and leaves with a thick envelope of cash and less guilt than he would have expected. For a wedding present, Sofia's parents find them an apartment on Verona Street, situated carefully in the still-Italian area of Red Hook. Suspended on one side several blocks from Hamilton Ave, where the Irish kids who call themselves Creekies still throw punches, rocks, and sometimes knife blades at Italians who get too close, and on the other side, the old docks, where there are too many hollow-eyed desperate families who, Joey understands, would do anything to survive, the apartment is most importantly as far away as Joey can manage from the Red Hook Houses, where every day, it seems, new longshoremen and their families are pouring into the neighborhood like ants. Joey has his sights set on a town-house in Carroll Gardens: one of the modern ones, with brick walls and new plumbing and a front yard filled with flowers. He imagines Rosa presiding over one end of a long wooden dining table. He can picture Sofia and his grandchildren living on one floor, the sounds of small feet pounding the wood floors and laughter coming up through the radiator pipes. But in the meantime, he finds, for his daughter, a railroad apartment with two bedrooms and a kitchen and a sitting room all in a line.

Saul and Sofia move their things in before they are married so they can sleep there on their first night. Rosa packs them boxes of second-best dishes, the old stockpot with the small dent in it, and when they arrive and the door shuts behind them there is an awkward silence in the apartment until Saul says, *wait here,* and goes into the kitchen, and comes back with a drinking glass wrapped in a dishtowel. He puts it on the floor before Sofia and tells her to stomp on it. Sofia does not ask questions, but lifts her foot and slams it down, and as the glass crunches it is like a film is peeled back from her eyes. She is giddy. She wants to take the glasses down from the shelves and smash them all.

Sofia wakes sweating in the night and opens the bedroom window to let the sludgy air move around her like porridge. She turns to watch Saul sleep, the outlines of his face just visible in the gray city night. His brow furrows; words form and fade around the edges of his mouth. And it is now, while she is alone in the way one always is while watching someone else sleep, that something occurs to Sofia, something she has always known, but has never had the words for, or the courage to speak: it is possible she doesn't want to be a mother.

She considers the unshakable physicality of her baby, turning now, suspended above the bowl of her hips. Her doubt feels also like a tangible thing, twisting its way through the air and blooming around her like night-shade.

She cannot fall back asleep. Her eyes dry out and ache. In the morning, the doubt is still there. It has coiled around her night-stand and she can feel its scratchy leaves in the folds of her clothing.

"Don't," she says to Saul, as he snakes an arm around her belly. "Don't do that."

"Do you feel okay?" he asks.

"I'm fine." Her voice is a locked door.

"How about tonight I bring home Chinese?" Saul suggests. "You shouldn't have to cook."

"I said I'm fine," says Sofia, and walks to the bathroom.

After she closes the door, she stares at herself in the mirror. Her face is always bright lately, shiny with new blood and warm air. Her features look ordinary. *Are you bad?* she wonders. *Are you broken?*

In the kitchen, Saul has made a pot of tea. He has sliced bread for toast. He has set two eggs next to one another on the counter. "Boiled?" he asks Sofia as she comes out of the bathroom. Sofia wants to refuse herself food. She wants to feel the empty throb of her stomach until she figures out what is wrong with her. But hunger has taken on a new ferocity over the course of her pregnancy and Sofia finds herself unable to resist her primal needs: to pee, to sleep, to eat.

"Boiled," she responds, and sits at the table. It is still strange for her to sit in a kitchen that belongs to her, that smells like the food she and Saul eat, that is not presided over by her own mamma. It is strange to run out of olive oil, soap, bleach. Strange to wake up next to Saul every day. It makes her giddy; it makes her nervous. It feels like she is a child, playing house with Antonia. She has whiplash from the speed at which her life morphed into this adult shape. As her body stretches against the confines of her child's skin, Sofia wants, again and again, to be angry. Or else, she is joyous and bursting with energy, peppering kisses over the surface of Saul's chest and shoulders, making him late for work.

But Saul is unrelentingly kind. He makes room for her anger. He stays grounded when Sofia threatens to explode.

There is nothing tangible for Sofia to fight against.

And so she finds herself thinking about her words, swallowing down snappy comebacks and dissatisfactions that jar like rocks against one another in her throat. She finds herself choosing a gentleness she has never known before, conserving her energy.

At night, she curls into Saul's side like an animal making a nest.

It doesn't feel permanent. Sofia can no more see the rest of her life now than she could when she was fifteen. She considered a moment of panic at *until death us do part* but her death is impossible to imagine.

Saul toasts the bread and boils the eggs. He hands Sofia a plate with two slices of toast drizzled with honey, an egg still rolling in its hot shell. "I have to go in early, but I'll be back early." Sofia chews and nods. Saul kisses her on the cheek. He says, "I'll call about dinner."

"Thank you," says Sofia, but Saul doesn't hear her as he leaves.

The hours after Saul leaves for work stretch out in front of her and disappear into the distance. Sofia idles: forgetting to comb her hair, leaving her dishes in the sink. Standing limply in the living room, peering out the window. She is fourteen, raiding the fridge while her family is at Mass. Inside her body the baby she made with Saul is fluttering its hands and feet against her organs, tap-tapping like a branch against a window, like the wings of a moth against a screen door.

On the first Friday of July in 1942, as he does every first Friday of every month, Joey Colicchio dresses in his simplest and most expensive suit. He shaves, though it is afternoon and he already shaved once in the morning. He inhales the peppermint of his aftershave and checks his teeth for poppy seeds. He checks his breast pocket for the Fianzo envelope, and wipes his palms on his trousers before leaving the house.

Outside, Saul stands patiently on the sidewalk. His face is calm; it is one of the things Joey likes most about him. His face was calm in the heart of the bustling deli where Joey found him; and it is calm now, in long sleeves and pants on a July afternoon. "Thank you for meeting me," says Joey, kissing Saul on both cheeks. They get into a waiting car, which is idling on the street in front of Joey's building. Saul does not ask why; it is something else Joey likes about him. Saul trusts that he will learn what he needs to know when he needs to know it.

Joey is quiet for the ten-minute car ride to the waterfront. The driver is an old associate: someone he remembers from his early days with the Fianzos. He remembers standing with this man outside of an unmarked door at the ragged bottom of the Bowery, pursed lips and no eye contact as they waited for Tommy Fianzo to come back from a meeting. He took longer than they had expected, Joey remembers, but not so long that Joey and the other associate had had to go after him. Tommy had burst from the door with a wide smile and a half-moon of blood blooming from a cut on his cheek; he had been wiping slick red from his palms. He had handed Joey a bloody handkerchief and said, *andiamo*, jaunty, and the three of them had turned left and walked south for oysters, for chocolate fondue poured by women with stars for eyes and clouds for skin, for giddy, ecstatic consumption of every variety. Creation and destruction: they lived on the border; they played with sparks in rooms full of gunpowder. Tommy Fianzo, grinning maniacally as his cheek bled, as adrenaline ravaged all three of them, as the sun set, sinking bloody into the Hudson.

Joey tastes the memory of savagery on his tongue as the car arrives at the end of the docks. He nods to the driver in the rearview mirror, opens the door, and exhales into the wet blast of summer air. Saul follows.

They turn away from the river, where they can see men carrying lengths of pipe, sheets of wood, bags of concrete; some being loaded onto a barge and some being taken away. The ingredients for a city: for a blinding half-second, Joey can feel his own body, hands dusty and gripping under loads of iron, stone, wood.

Joey and Saul enter a crumbling building that overlooks the docks. It is blessedly cool; it is gray and looks like a Roman ruin, like it might fall down, or like it is half-finished, and it stands alone in the industrial wasteland and haphazard shacks at the western edge of Brooklyn.

Saul and Joey climb metal stairs to the third floor, and Joey knocks twice at an unmarked door. "Come in," a man says from inside. They enter.

Tommy Fianzo sits at a desk in the middle of the room, adding figures on scratch paper. He does not look up when they come in. He says, "You can put it on the table," and gestures with the tip of his pencil.

Joey tips his hat to the top of Tommy's head. Saul has never seen him act so deferent. Joey pulls a thick envelope out from an inner pocket in his suit and puts it on the desk near Tommy, gently, as if he is trying not to disturb the air in the room.

"It's full?" Tommy has still not looked at them.

"Of course," says Joey. He stands still for another moment, and then turns to leave. Saul twists to follow him.

"This is your Jewish friend?" asks Tommy Fianzo, as Saul and Joey hold the door open.

"This is Saul Colicchio," says Joey. "Sofia's husband."

Tommy stands and looks Saul in the eye. He stretches out a hand and Saul, quiet still, face unreadable, reaches forward to take it. "Pleasure to meet you," says Saul. "Sir."

"It's Signore," says Tommy. He turns his attention to Joey, and a slow smile begins to open across his face. "Eli Leibovich is going to shit himself when he hears about this." The Jewish boss with whom the Fianzos had had a casual rivalry for years was not known for taking what he saw as cultural defection lightly.

Joey gives Tommy a wry, twisted smile of his own. "I know," he says.

Back in the car, Joey turns to Saul and says, "You were great back there." Saul has said a total of one sentence since he met Joey. He has already learned that if he is quiet, he is told more. And that if he is told more, he has more power.

"Anytime," says Saul.

"That will be your job someday," says Joey.

"That envelope?" asks Saul.

"That relationship," says Joey.

Antonia spends the early weeks of her pregnancy developing a pattern by which she can measure time. Wednesdays with her mamma, where if Antonia is lucky, she can convince Lina to walk with her for half an hour in the sun, and where Lina has started slipping small dried beans and bundles of herbs into Antonia's pockets — *for fortune,* she says. *For strength.*

She spends Fridays at the butcher, the good vegetable shop, the bakery on Columbia with the softest bread.

Antonia cooks: big, lavish meals that strain their creaking dining table. Four courses just for the two of them. Paolo brings her flowers. He doodles on napkins in restaurants and brings her pictures with love notes written in his unmistakable handwriting. They are constantly presenting each other with gifts — *look, this meal; this clip for your hair.* Their home life is a choreographed waltz. Paolo is as quiet as Antonia except when he is frustrated or impatient and then he is explosive, rage boiling inside of him, and Antonia recognizes this energy from Sofia and knows how to soften it, how to soothe it.

On Sunday afternoons, Antonia goes to visit her mamma before dinner at the Colicchio apartment. Lina has draped herself so completely in long loose blouses and community legend that she is almost unrecognizable. Antonia regards Lina from a distance. There are moments she is sympathetic to her mamma, who has done what she needed to while surviving cataclysmic loss. But more often than not, Antonia feels separate from Lina. She feels judgmental. *If I were in your shoes,* she thinks, *I would have survived better. I would have parented better. I wouldn't have needed to become the neighborhood witch to move on.* Even Antonia's forgiveness of Lina is tinged with slight superiority, a *see what I can do despite everything.* She does not admit any envy of Lina's freedom, and she does not acknowledge, even to herself, how much she still craves Lina's attention, how weak-kneed her mamma's quiet voice can make her feel. But when Lina palms Antonia's belly, looking for her baby's kicking feet and pushing

245

hands, Antonia feels, like she did when she was five, as though she might expand and float away without Lina to hold her down.

She has only lived away from home for a matter of months but the still air inside her childhood home has already taken on the quality of something ancient, and more often than not Antonia finds herself grasping a doorjamb for stability, swallowing a lump in her throat, telling the smaller ghosts of herself that they will be okay.

In August, Sofia lets herself be cajoled into going to Mass with Antonia and Paolo. She knows Antonia is surprised she said yes. She almost never goes since she and Saul got married, and before that, she went only sporadically, when she didn't have the energy to argue with her parents or when Frankie convinced her.

The air inside is cool and dry. Sofia wedges her swollen ankles against the wood of the pew in front of them and leans her neck back and feels herself unhinge and soften against the hard bench. A lump rises in her throat. She takes a full breath, and another. The air smells like her childhood. It smells like sitting between her mamma and papa on the bench. It smells like restlessness, like play sparking along her arms and legs, like wanting to be grown up, like wanting to fly. It smells like knowing what she is fighting for: ten more minutes and she can burst out of the seat, home to Antonia, to Mars, to the great expanse of the Sahara Desert, to the horses she and Antonia will sit astride as the day grows older on her bedroom floor.

Antonia worries Sofia's pointer finger between her palms and feels unsettled. Sofia has been quiet for days, and Antonia does not know how to fill the gaps in their conversations. "Thank you for coming," she whispers.

Sofia offers a wan smile, and then, because she needs a distraction, plucks the Bible from its shelf in front of her. Its pages are impossibly thin and waxy, glossed with the oil from thousands of hands. She lets them slide through her fingers, catching phrases that run together and then disappear as soon as she reads them. She is seven years old, nestled in the space between Rosa and Joey. The whole world ripples out from the center of their family.

Suddenly Sofia, an adult woman at nineteen, and so pregnant she barely fits in the pew, cannot be there. She cannot sit next to Antonia. She cannot face the memory of her own old self. Sofia lets the Bible shut with a clap and stands up and begins, without breathing, to shimmy her way out of the pew.

"Sofia? Sofia!" Antonia stage-whispers and it echoes around them but Sofia is worried she will be sick and does not answer and presses her lips together. "Sofia!"

Sofia pushes against the crush of starched and perfumed Catholics. She bursts out into the street and sucks the noxious summer city air all the way down into her lungs over and over. She leans against the wall. The city spins. *You're stupid,* she realizes, and she is surprised it took her this long. She knew this could happen, and did it anyway. It was old knowledge, one of the first things she learned. *Anything could happen, Sofia,* says Rosa in her head. *Be careful.*

*Anything could happen, Mamma,* Sofia realizes. She is not invincible. She cannot go back in time and be less impulsive, less carefree. She cannot turn around and yell at her younger self, *the world will catch up with you!*

"Sofia!" Antonia is next to her, holding her hand, pressing her shoulder against Sofia's to avoid the crowd, and Sofia can smell her coffee and the heat from her iron and the must from the hall in her apartment building. Antonia is solid and regular and serene and once, just once, Sofia would like to be the even-tempered one and so she resolves to say nothing, to be okay by sheer force of will, to contain her monstrous, traitorous, unappreciative, heretical doubts and move on and be *happy,* and *normal,* like her friend, like her mother, like all mothers before her. She presses her mouth tight as a sewn seam and will not make eye contact with Antonia. Her determination feels flimsy.

Antonia walks Sofia home. She sits Sofia on the sofa and cups Sofia's white face in her hands. She tells Sofia silently, *if you are okay, I am okay.*

In the kitchen, Antonia boils water for tea, but when the kettle whistles she turns the burner off and reaches instead for a bottle of whiskey she knows is hidden in the cupboard above the sink. She pours two drinks, and tucks the bottle under her arm, and carries it all to the living room.

"Here," she says to Sofia, who silently takes the glass. Antonia sits next to her and feels bulbous and huge. Sofia's normally captivating gravitational field has shrunk to almost nothing; Antonia, used to ascertaining her own size and shape compared to Sofia, feels as though she might swell until she pops.

"I don't think I can do it," says Sofia, her voice small and wavering. There, of course: she feels better, she feels worse. She has not succeeded in keeping this small dark part of herself hidden.

"Do what?"

Sofia gestures at the globe of her belly. "I don't think I can do this."

Antonia is silent, but she wants to laugh. The two of them are swollen, rounded, peeing every three minutes, woken in the night by the incessant stretching and turning of their babies. Another reality is inconceivable. "I see," she says, so as to respond but not giggle, because the absurdity threatens to overwhelm her.

"No lecture?" asks Sofia.

"What do you mean?"

Sofia gulps at her drink. "No speech about how I *can* do it, how women have been doing it forever, how I'm strong and capable and loving and have the support of generations of nice Italian ladies who will, you know, swoop in and wash diapers and induct me into the eternal coalition of motherhood?"

Antonia raises her eyebrows. "You said it," she says.

Sofia rolls her eyes. "Look at me," she says, "I'm ridiculous." And she is, and she is exhausted. She is tired of fighting. She is tired of worrying.

"I'm in no position to judge," says Antonia, and wiggles her stockinged toes. "We look like popcorn, don't we."

Sofia snorts. "We're balloons in the Thanksgiving parade."

"We're the *Hindenburg*!" They laugh, and cannot catch their breath. They consider the improbability of growing other humans inside their bodies: that there is not room to laugh anymore, or to breathe deeply. There are four of them in the room.

"You can do it, you know," says Antonia. A small flame of fear singes the inside of her chest. If Sofia is afraid, Antonia is afraid.

"Tonia, I'm not sure — I'm not sure I want to." How astounding, Sofia thinks. To hear it echo in the room, like a gunshot.

Antonia does not tell Sofia, *well, it's a little too late for that.* Instead, she catches Sofia's hand in hers. "I want our babies to be like us," she says. "I want them to grow up together. I want them to have each other." She does not know what it is like to be scared of motherhood but fear itself is familiar to Antonia, who recognizes in quaking Sofia the silence that comes before either revolution or resignation. She has heard stories of women who leave their babies for Broadway or for Greyhound buses, women who do unspeakable things to avoid bringing their families shame. Antonia pictures herself, fifteen years older, burdened by children's bodies and Paolo's ironing and weighted down by the love of family, and she shivers at the possibility of Sofia not being there. *Want this,* she imagines screaming at Sofia. *Please want this with me.*

Sofia sees the narrowing light of her life, beckoning from the end of a long corridor. She looks at Antonia. *If you can see me, I must be here.*

*You can do anything if you decide to want it,* Antonia does not tell her.

■ ■ ■ ■

# Book Four

1942–1947

■ ■ ■ ■

As summer turns hot, deadly hot, and the asphalt softens and the buildings collect the sun so even through the night they radiate a thick warmth, Sofia and Antonia grow their babies and sweat rivers down their spines, in between their breasts. Antonia walks with a hand to her low back but Sofia refuses, standing up straight, as dignified as she can manage. They spend every moment together, like they did when they were children, only now they spend their days draped over furniture at one of their apartments, laughing as Saul and Paolo try to put together cribs. When Paolo and Saul take their hands from the fragile bassinette frame in Antonia's bedroom, the whole thing crumples to the ground. Paolo hops on one foot, swearing. Saul melts into a frustrated puddle and Sofia and Antonia weep with laughter. They feel each other's babies kicking. They tell each other secrets.

The raging war reminds them that they are impermanent, they are fragile, they are balancing on the surface tension of a giant ocean of catastrophe. The sky bends and contracts with madness. They feel desperately out of control. They cling to one another for balance, for reassurance. They all feel the weight of having been entrusted with something sacred, and the necessity of staying close together. They hold hands as they listen to the radio. They worry if they don't hear from one another for more than a day. They deliver bread and wine to one another's apartments, tracing well-worn paths along the blocks between their homes; the neighborhood becomes a map of their family. As they walk, they can picture themselves in relation to the others at every moment.

They trade weathered and folded recipes, briefcases, hairbrushes, casserole dishes, dog-eared paperbacks, wedding linens, loose change, throw pillows. The more of themselves they can leave with the others, the more real they all feel.

There is a time when the summer sun is at its peak where Antonia, Sofia, Saul, and Paolo seem to live in two apartments each: their belongings scattered evenly, their sleep interrupted often by the ring of buzzer or trill of telephone.

At night Antonia promises with a hand on her stomach that she will do a better job than her mamma did. *I'll take care of you, I'll take care of you,* she repeats as she falls asleep. Antonia makes lists. Glass bottles, stacked diapers, fresh knit hats in a row. A memory that is all sensation, all wordlessness, of Lina cradling her on the couch when she was a baby. *I'll take care of all of us.*

With her hands pressed to the cool brick at the head of the bed she shares with Saul, Sofia feels the same as she did when she was six, when she was eleven. She lets fear make a home in her throat, in her chest. It steals her air and chokes her. *I can't even take care of myself,* she prays. In response, the animal in her belly presses against her lungs.

Sofia wakes in the middle of the night. There is a low ache in her back that pulses in time with her breath. It rises and falls, spreading out across her hip bones and then receding to a bright point at the base of her spine.

She watches the long summer sun rise and

glow against the morning clouds. The room around her is painted with shadows. The pain grows. It stretches its arms around her belly and it holds her so she twists the bedsheet between her hands. She breathes. The pain crawls up her spine, around her hips, locks the bottom of her rib cage in its fierce hands. Exhale. The pain fades. The blood pumps in her fingers and face. Sofia, lover of big feelings, is not surprised by the beast of labor. She feels herself swell toward the dawn and then away. Sofia is made of a roaring heat. She breathes the sun over the horizon. And then she wakes Saul. "It's time," she tells him.

In a private room at the hospital, Sofia wishes she could have brought Antonia with her. She wishes she could smell her mamma's hair. She wishes she could kneel on the roof of her apartment building and howl. The room is all spinning figures in white, all stainless steel and well-intentioned bustle. Sofia feels small.

*Before you know it,* a nurse says to her, *you'll have a baby.*

There is the needle in her arm. There is the plastic mask descending over her face. Everything narrows to a point. It is impossibly dark.

■ ■ ■ ■

When Sofia becomes aware of her body again, she is wearing a thin cotton shift, not hers. The lights are so bright they hurt her eyes. She squints and tries to sit, only to feel a colossal unraveling inside herself. Movement will unspool her. Sofia sinks back into the crisp hospital pillows.

Soon a nurse brings a small bundle to her. Sofia tries again to sit up, but this time there is pain, immense, and a weakness that steals her breath, that collapses her. She doesn't like lying down, surrounded by strangers. She wants a mirror. Instead the nurse wedges a pillow behind Sofia's shoulders and hands her the smallest person Sofia has ever seen.

The baby is a real human the size of a winter squash. She has two eyes and two ears and a mouth with puckered lips. She has skin like clouds and thin soft fingernails. *She weighs seven pounds,* they tell Sofia. *We'll get your husband,* they tell Sofia. Sofia is left in the empty white room staring at a small womb-shaped animal, surrounded by the smell of wet flesh.

Julia is the name that comes to Sofia's mind; it is familiar but clean, like fresh

259

sheets or an open window. "It's just yours," she says, voice croaking, the first thing Sofia says to her daughter.

When newborn babies make eye contact they use their whole bodies to open their eyes and look at you and this is what Julia does now, she flexes her fingers and her feet and she purses her lips so she can open her eyes and stare at Sofia. Sofia stares back and she wills herself to be courageous. "What are we going to do?" she asks Julia. Her voice is jarring to her own ears.

Here in front of Sofia is incontrovertible evidence of her own power. No one had ever told her motherhood would be like this.

Look, look. Look what you have made.

Her whole family comes. It is not just Saul. Sofia is flushed with relief. She does not want to be alone. "I can give you ten minutes," the nurse says. "This really isn't the policy." Rosa and Frankie push past the nurse and drop to the bed, and then Sofia is in their arms and they are in hers, and Julia is lifted up and passed around in the cacophony of her family. And then Saul and Antonia and Paolo are there, and Antonia asks, "How was it?" and Sofia has to say, "I don't know," because all she can remember is waves crashing, the tide of herself, darkness, and she has no words for that, but she knows it is not what happened, really; she knows there is a part of Julia's arrival that she was not present for. And Saul asks, "Are you okay?" and Sofia says, "Yes," and she means it, she thinks she means it. Joey tucks a strand of Sofia's hair behind her ear. He presses the back of his hand to her forehead, like he did when Sofia was feverish as a child. He will tell Sofia later that Julia has his mother's nose. Sofia looks at the faces of her family and believes that she can do this.

It is a fleeting feeling, but it will sustain her. In the weeks ahead Sofia will have the presence of mind to surround herself with the people who make her feel most like herself. She will learn to swaddle Julia, to change her, to rock her. She will smell Julia's head and count her toes and stare at her in pure awe. Sofia will let herself be carried along by the changing current. She will feel fully. *Motherhood can be the adventure,* she will tell herself. *It can be something you love.*

Some mornings Antonia still wakes up with her fists clenched, remembering Robbie racing through her body like a train.

After he is born, she spends three weeks in bed on doctor's orders, trying not to think of the ways she has been turned inside out. She holds her mouth closed; holds her legs together. The doctor comes; a man with kindly small eyeglasses who stitches her where she has been ripped apart and tells her she will be fine, fine. Antonia nods when he says this, but she is sure as soon as she stands up she will split in half; her organs will come rushing down and land on the floor; her hair will fall out.

The days are long. Antonia is never alone.

Sofia comes, beaming, and kisses Antonia's forehead, and holds Julia, who is three months old and kicking, punching, grasping wildly, up to the small wicker basket where Robbie sleeps, his newborn features still pressed askew by the pressure of Antonia's body. Julia furrows her brow and reaches out with a round fist and pummels sleeping Robbie in the chest. He awakens with a betrayed expression and opens his mouth in silence for three full seconds before a cry emerges. Fall sunlight shines through the window and Sofia fairly glows. Sofia picks up Robbie and kisses him, passes him to Antonia to feed. Antonia tries not to weep. *Why isn't it this hard for you?* she imagines asking.

Paolo's mother comes, and wraps the baby tighter in his blanket. When she is leaving, she takes Paolo aside and says, *the only cure for those blues is to treat her normally. Stop treating her like a broken thing. She'll manage once she's back on her feet.* But Paolo, in reverence of the fragile and terrible and all-powerful force his wife has become, continues to bring Antonia hot and cold cloths, teas, broths; to insist that she keep her feet up, her eyes closed.

At night, though she is heavy with exhaustion, Antonia cannot sleep. Her body pulls her down, through the mattress, through the floor. Her eyes sting, but won't shut. Sandwiched between Paolo and Robbie breathing, she cries; her cheeks crack.

After Robbie was born, slickly ejected

from somewhere Antonia never knew existed in her own body, she clutched him to her chest, full of fear. She looked at his face and didn't know him. She grasped him with her hands, but they felt like stranger's hands. Robbie left a headprint of blood and white smear across her chest, and Antonia couldn't feel it. He opened his mouth and wailed, and she heard it, but faintly, like he was calling from some distance away.

When she stares down into his crib, Antonia still doesn't know him. She is blindsided by fear, by something like disappointment. *You wanted this,* she tells herself. But it is nothing like she imagined.

The doctor checks on her after two weeks. He tugs her stitches out one by one; tells her she is nearly healed. Antonia feels like a steak, scored with a knife where the salt will be rubbed in.

She hadn't considered it would be this physical. This consuming. This utterly erasing of everything she had been before. Her body is a wrecked ship's hull and she, whatever had been "she," was lost in a wide and dark sea.

During the day, Paolo and Lina and Sofia fold cotton diapers, scrub the stained wooden floor, sing to Robbie when he wails. Antonia's apartment is filled with the smells of laundry and chicken stock, drying herbs and antiseptic, baby shit and the metal of her own body healing. She tries not to inhale. When they bring Robbie to her, she holds him to her raw breast and turns her face to the wall.

Lina brings lavender tied in a bunch and boils cloves down to paste, to clear the air. She helps Antonia shower. Antonia sits in the tub with the hot water pounding against her back, her spine curved, her stretched and swollen belly resting between her legs. She leans against Lina like a child.

Sofia comes every day. She holds Julia and Robbie in her arms and hums them songs she suddenly remembers from her own childhood. She chatters to Antonia, swaying in the filtered winter sunlight coming through Antonia's bedroom window. She seems utterly carefree. Her voice always sounds to Antonia like it is echoing from very far away.

Paolo lies beside Antonia while she sleeps, and while she can't sleep, and while she feeds Robbie. He curls his body protectively around hers, but he stays on his own side, because she can't bear to be touched. For the first week, he hadn't been able to help himself from reaching for her, holding her hands in his hands, kissing her ears and her face. But she had leaked tears, muttered, *stop it, stop that, no,* and Paolo had retreated, circling their old marriage like a hungry animal making tracks around a carcass.

One night, Antonia wakes from a sudden, brief sleep, a sleep closer to unconsciousness than rest. She opens her eyes to see the looming shadows of her furniture. Across the room, Robbie is sleeping in his bassinet, which means Antonia has been asleep long enough for Paolo, who is sleeping next to her, to ease Robbie off of her chest and move him. She feels a wave of tenderness toward Paolo. *I'm so sorry,* she thinks, sensing the up and down of her husband's breath as he sleeps. There is no other sound but the white noise of faraway, all-night traffic. *I'm not good enough for you. I'm not good at this.* Their three children, their spacious future home, Antonia's rolled-up university diploma nestled against her chest with her children, in the picture she imagines taking someday. It all seems impossible. It seems further away than the moon. *You've failed,* she tells herself. She does not think she falls asleep again that night.

The winter passes this way.

When it snows, Paolo wraps Robbie in

blankets and stacks two knit hats on top of one another on his head and carries him outside. Robbie sneezes and blinks furiously as snow lands on his face, and Paolo carries him around and around the block for an hour.

On Christmas, Antonia is bundled into a dress; her hair is brushed. She sits through Mass; Robbie on Paolo's lap on one side of her and Sofia with Julia on the other. At dinner, she picks listlessly at her food.

Antonia spends the dark months germinating; a life sleeping, undetectable in a hard shell. All around her the days shorten and then begin to lengthen again. The old year slips into the new; all it takes is a second. Antonia avoids mirrors, so disappointed in herself she can't face her own reflection.

It's not how she thought it would be.

It's not how she thought it would be.

Sofia remembers this time as a haze of sleeplessness and fear. Antonia lay gray and small in her bed day after day and Sofia held Robbie, rocked him as he cried, learned his smell as well as she had gotten to know Julia's. Sofia remembers Paolo, helpless, running a hand through his dark hair and saying, *I gotta take a leak, I gotta take a walk, I gotta get out of here,* and grabbing his coat and going out to smoke, pacing in front of the building; and Sofia, crouching at the bedside, saying, *Tonia, I think he's hungry again,* and Antonia opening eyes like tunnels and saying, *okay,* automatic, empty. Sofia wants to pinch herself awake; this can't possibly be her life, Antonia's life. "She'll be perfectly healthy," says the doctor, washing his hands after depositing the small snarl of Antonia's old sutures into the kitchen trash can, and Sofia surprises herself by shouting "What is healthy? What is healthy? Do they make stitches for her mind, for her heart?" so loudly Robbie wakes with an angry scream. "I'm sorry," she says to the dumbfounded doctor, who has left the water running as he stares at Sofia. "I'm sorry." She turns to go pick up Robbie. Her heart hurts; her hands tingle.

But mostly, when she goes to Antonia's, Sofia is cheerful, as cheerful as she can manage. She tells Antonia about Julia's new facial expressions, about Joey's new hire, who is, *Tonia, you'll never guess, remember Marco DeLuca?* another neighborhood boy sucked into the inescapable vacuum of Family, and unbeknownst to Sofia, Marco has been hired to help Paolo, whose forgery business has evolved to include a print shop in Gowanus, a dressmaker on Thirty-Eighth, a warehouse of school supplies in Greenpoint, and who needs help running errands and managing his workload. All Sofia knows is Marco has turned up at Sunday dinner with a bottle of wine and his best shirt on; that he doffs his cap to Sofia's father the way he should; that he is possessed of a bigger, stronger body than Sofia would have imagined, given that her most salient memory of him is herself standing over his prone frame on the floor of their kindergarten classroom.

Antonia remembers Marco DeLuca. She remembers the wholeness of her own body, when she knew him. She remembers the day Sofia tripped him. Marco's face, horror-struck as he tried to reconcile the world he thought he knew with the unfamiliar and dangerous reality where a girl might hurt him, send him tumbling over his own feet, turn him upside down, break his tooth off at the root. And Antonia understands. She, too, is living through a nightmare in a world she thought she chose.

At night, Sofia prays. She doesn't ever remember praying before but it comes out of her like a flood. Every bit of restless and flammable energy Sofia has ever had, focused. *Please,* she prays. *Give her back to me.* She prays as she sanitizes Julia's bottles, as she waves to Saul when he leaves for work.

Prayer is an acknowledgment of fear, of that which cannot be controlled or contained or even understood. It is a surrender and an attack, all at once. *Please,* Sofia prays, thinking about Antonia, the darkness in her expression, the lifelessness in her breath. *I can't do this without you.*

But during the day Sofia understands that it is her job to fill Antonia's home with light, with space, with sun, and so she opens the shades and does not fall at Antonia's bedside to beg. She brings books; she turns the radio on so softly Antonia does not notice she is listening to something other than Robbie's disconsolate wails. She wipes the kitchen counters, humming like Rosa.

Paolo and Saul arrive each day after work, whenever they finish, so that Saul can take Sofia and Julia home. Each day Paolo asks Sofia, *is she better?* as though Antonia is broken, when nothing is wrong with Antonia. She is not broken; she is lost. Sofia runs out of ways to tell Paolo this, and it is one of the reasons she is grateful for Saul: he does not ask for progress to be chopped up into measurable pieces. *There are moments*

270

*she's there,* Sofia tells Saul. *She'll laugh, or she'll go for Robbie before I do when he cries. And then the next moment —* Sofia stops, because she is describing Saul too: the way his sadness can settle over him like a coat for a few days and then pass.

Saul understands. His mother hasn't written in over a year. And he has faith that the light of Sofia will be as much a balm to Antonia as it is to him. He slings an arm around Sofia and leans, as they walk, to kiss the top of Julia's head. And then he falls quiet, wondering about the language of Antonia's trauma. Wondering whether it is the same language he can speak so well. And wondering, though he is grateful every day for Sofia's relentless heat, what it would be like to sit with someone who understood.

One morning in February, Antonia wakes early from a dream of playing dress-up underwater with Sofia. Their hair and clothes floated around them and when Antonia looked down at her fingers she realized she was a child. She reached her hands out for Sofia and the two of them leaned away from one another, the circle of their arms holding them as they began to spin up toward the sun.

Paolo and Robbie are sleeping. It is dark;

only the faintest purpling of the light in their bedroom tells Antonia it is almost dawn. She pads into the living room and hears, as if for the first time that winter, the whisper of the radiator against the cold outside. She sits on the couch. She thinks about Sofia, who has come every day all winter to tell Antonia *you exist, you are here, you are in your body, you are in the world.* Sofia, who has her own new baby to take care of, her own marriage, but who has spent months with Antonia, watering her like a plant, waiting for her.

Antonia stifles a sob. She stifles a thousand sobs a day. But this one turns into a hiccup. A strange cough. A sound wants to come from the center of Antonia. She buries her face in a pillow.

It takes her several moments to realize she is laughing. The laugh tingles along her arms and legs. It reaches, thumping, into her throat. It settles in her belly, descends smoothly into the void where Robbie once lived, into the parts of Antonia she no longer looks at or touches, the parts that have betrayed her with their fragility, the ease with which they were destroyed.

And Antonia does not break. She laughs and her whole body moves quietly, as one piece, into the dawn.

There it is. Buzzing in the deepest pit of herself, resilient beyond measure, the very smallest bit of Antonia insisting itself back to life.

She begins going on walks: short ones, she promises Paolo, just around the block. Once she gets outside she walks as far as she likes, and tells Paolo she lost track of time. Antonia, who had been so hungry for the companionship and consistency of motherhood, finds that she is only strong enough to be a mother if she spends an hour a day completely alone. Young Antonia would have been disappointed: foolishly, of course, because young Antonia, sneaking off to Sunday Mass, knew well the power of keeping part of her life secret. But mamma Antonia is just grateful for survival, for sunlight, for the excitement of jumping away when a car splashes through a black and slushy puddle.

When she eats, Antonia's food has taste again. When she listens, and speaks, and looks, sounds and sights don't seem like they are stuck behind dirty, thick glass. The world, slowly, begins to make itself known to her. And Antonia, just as slowly, begins to remake herself as a part of it.

In March, Antonia walks all the way to

Sofia's apartment. Sofia opens the door and hugs her and then goes into the bathroom and gasps and shudders and heaves for air. She presses her palms, her forehead, against the closed bathroom door and for the first time in months she trusts that Antonia is on the other side.

By the time Robbie is five months old, Antonia has worked up the courage to look at her face in the mirror; to trace the contours of her new body with her hands.

And one ordinary afternoon in April, as the frost slides down from the trees and the earth begins to thaw out, Antonia picks Robbie up when he wakes from his nap and she feels the warm weight of him in her arms. He smiles, seeing her, his mouth stretching across toothless gums. Something in Antonia cracks. *I'm sorry,* she whispers to the sweet top of his head. And like Lina, so many years ago, *I'm ready to be your mamma.*

Now Antonia has settled lightly down into motherhood. Her days are punctuated by Robbie's small cries, by his uncontrollable belly laughter, by his simple, solvable needs.

With Robbie slung under one arm or braced against her shoulder, Antonia notices spring flush the city pink and green with a quality of attention she's never felt before. *See this,* she tells him, as he mouths along

274

her collarbone, or fans his fingers open and shut. *See all there is here?*

In spring of 1943, Joey signs the papers on a solid, four-story brownstone with a spacious front yard in Carroll Gardens. The war has made him, if not a rich man, a very comfortably situated one. Sofia and Saul and Julia move in to the first floor one frigid day, when the sky dumps snow in wet, sticky clumps which cling to coat collars and congeal in bootlaces and the folds of trousers.

Rosa wastes no time in her new kitchen. Sunday dinner had been too big for her Red Hook apartment for years. She invests in a long, sturdy table that runs like a canyon from one end of her dining room to the other. Even so, dinner has grown so much that folding chairs still have to be squeezed into tight places. Preparation regularly spills into Sofia's kitchen, where there are always pans of ravioli on the table, waiting to be boiled. Where the fridge is stuffed with twine-sealed bakery boxes and bottles of wine line the baseboard. A fog of tomato and meat floats out the windows of both Rosa's and Sofia's apartments. It fills the hallways of their building. It makes its way in fragrant tendrils down the street.

■ ■ ■ ■

Even after Antonia seems to have recovered, Sofia goes to Antonia's every day all summer. She is relieved the way the family member of anyone who has almost died is relieved: in no small part, *what would I have been without you,* a selfish and insistent wondering that has not lessened as Sofia observes herself in the mirror and in shop windows. She is stuck inside a disintegrating container. Her face is puffy and tired; her hair comes out in small slithering bunches when she runs her hands through it. She has stuffed herself back into her pre-baby girdles and hose, but her body resents being told how to breathe now. The fear that choked her when she was pregnant has changed; Sofia has developed a certain confidence in her own ability to care for Julia. She sleeps thinking of Julia, and wakes with the slightest hiccup in Julia's breath. Sofia knows where Julia is the way she knows she has arms; it's easy. Sofia loves Julia with her belly, with her hands; a hot love like a flame. But Sofia feels herself sinking into invisibility. She wants desperately to pull herself onto an alternate path. She is not the same as she was, and she is not the same as other mothers, and she mourns that, and she wakes hoping to see Antonia's face each morning. Antonia is a rudder, a root system, a time machine.

And so as the quietly rotting carpet of cherry blossoms below their feet is replaced above by waving rafts of lime-green leaves; as New Yorkers throw open their windows and let the life out of their stale winter apartments and begin to drape their court-yards in crisscrossing lines of laundry and the smell of their food and the timbre of their conversations bursts out into the air in waves; as the city begins, again, to feel full, Sofia Colicchio dresses her daughter, whose strong fat thighs and wildly waving arms threaten to burst the seams of any outfit, and together they walk the three blocks to Antonia's apartment.

A neighborhood can change drastically in just three blocks; so it is that Sofia and Julia walk from the carefully cultivated front gardens and brownstone smiles of historic Carroll Gardens to its shabbier tenement-style outskirts in mere minutes. Antonia and Paolo and Robbie live in an eight-unit red-brick building on Nelson Street. They have one bedroom in the front, the kitchen faces the rear, and there is a narrow second bedroom and a sitting room laid along the inside of the building like roe along the inside of a fish.

Sofia is breathless when she knocks, and sweating from carrying Julia.

"Tonia," she says, "I brought you a hungry child to feed." Antonia takes Julia and coos; moves aside to let Sofia in.

"Convenient," says Antonia, balancing Julia on her hip. "I was just sitting here hoping to feed a baby." She kisses Julia's palm. "A filthy baby! What, does your mamma not clean you? What is on these hands?"

Sofia is peeling off her hose, clips flapping against her thighs. She is hopping on one foot. "It's just mashed carrots, you should have heard her scream when I came at her hands with a washcloth. She needs to eat every two hours these days." She drops the hose to the floor, where they curl like snakeskins around her discarded shoes, and sighs. "It's hot already. It seems like yesterday I was sweating and pregnant. Now I'm sweating and a monster."

"You're not a monster," Antonia says automatically as she takes Julia to the kitchen sink to clean her hands. From the bedroom at the front of the house comes a wail, a siren call.

"I'll get him," says Sofia. While Antonia runs warm water in the sink and Julia leans in to splash it, Sofia walks the long hallway to the front room, where Robbie has woken up from his nap.

Robbie's hands are clasped around the wooden slats of his crib and he is pressing his face between them, waiting to be collected. He sniffs and stops crying at the sight of Sofia, sneaking in barefoot, grinning. "Bibi," she coos. "Has anyone ever not picked you up, when you needed it?" Robbie does not respond but he stretches his arms out to Sofia, throws his head back in warm release.

How easy it can feel, Sofia thinks. How simple it can be to slip into the role that is made for you. She and Antonia have the afternoon ahead of them. Paolo and Saul are out doing God-knows-what. And Antonia is healthy now, and Sofia is happy. Isn't she?

Robbie, tired of Sofia standing still, reaches out and clasps a healthy handful of her hair in his hand and pulls it. Sofia looks at him and remembers where she is and hears Antonia talking to Julia in the kitchen, and feels the insistent warming air through the open window. "Let's go find your mamma," she says to Robbie. It's what he has been hoping for the whole time.

Later that afternoon Robbie and Julia have

been fed and bathed and they have been convinced to take another nap, curled together in Robbie's crib. Sofia and Antonia have retreated into Antonia's bed with a bottle of white wine and they have thrown the window open so they are breathing in the thick green smell of new leaves and grass; someone's laundry; someone burning last year's charred meat off the grill before dinner. The late afternoon sun is rich and runs like maple syrup, pouring down into the room, and there is something lazy and delicious swelling up in Sofia and Antonia, who rely on these afternoons, each in her own way, for reassurance. Sofia likes that with Antonia, always with Antonia, she is herself. And Antonia likes this: that Sofia thinks there is a way they could be the same people they once were. Antonia, who has spent the winter deep-sea diving into the darkest, most formidable parts of her own consciousness. Antonia relishes Sofia's optimistic insistence that they can relax into selves that no longer exist.

The wine is a sloshing tablespoon in the bottom of the bottle and the room has darkened around Sofia and Antonia before they hear Paolo's key in the lock, and then he is there with Saul, flicking the kitchen light on, standing in the quiet evening apartment with two babies who, now that they have napped so late, will never go to bed on time, and two women who are laughing, laughing at something they will not explain. Saul slips out wordlessly to get pizza from Stefano's around the corner, where the service is abysmal and the hygiene a serious question but the pies are thin and crisp and dripping with cheese. Sofia and Antonia detangle themselves from the bed, from one another, from the dream of every late afternoon. Paolo is in the kitchen now, opening another bottle of wine, a red one an associate of Joey's gave him, from a family vineyard in the old country, and it was supposed to be saved for a special occasion, but Antonia doesn't remind him. She and Sofia will watch Paolo and Saul take off their coats and hats, greet their babies. They will accept scratchy kisses on the cheek.

Once in a while, Sofia and Antonia will catch one another's eye and wink, or grin. For although they are married — married! — it also seems like at any moment Rosa might burst in and tell them to keep it down, to go to bed. Though they are mothers, it is easy, when they are together, for Sofia and Antonia to feel the childlike elasticity that bound them together, that bound them to the wide world. And more often than not, when Sofia and Antonia make eye contact around their husbands, over their children, they both find themselves stifling laughter.

The first time Saul hurts someone, his daughter is two years old. Saul and Joey spend the evening in the back room of a bar near the Red Hook Houses. Joey has not told Saul why they are going, but has given him a length of iron pipe to lay against his thigh. *I don't want to hurt anyone,* Saul says. *I never want to hurt anyone,* Joey replies. The room is thick with cigar smoke and the smell of pomade, and a woman with cherries for lips brings Saul glass after glass of whiskey, which he tries to drink slowly or not at all but which, more often than not, he finds himself bringing to his lips to satisfy his restless need to do something, his worry that everyone in the room can hear the pounding of his heart, the clanking of the pipe he has concealed against his bones.

Saul doesn't know who started the fight, only that suddenly Joey has drawn himself up to his full height in unmistakable rage, and that one of the other men in the room has drawn a knife. It blinks and shines in the lamplight. *You don't have to do this,* says Joey. As a warning. *You've gotta be reasonable, then,* says the other man. And then Joey says, *Saul.* And the situation comes into unmistakable focus for Saul, who understands he is to draw the iron pipe from his pant leg and tap it lightly on the ground. Almost casually. *We can't afford this,* says the man. Whiskey swirls in Saul's brain and he is consumed by the echo of the pipe against the floor, by the oceanic sway of his own eyes and body as he struggles to stay on his feet. *It's tough out there,* agrees Joey. *It's why when we don't get paid on time, we can't take any shit.* Joey looks at Saul. The man across from them takes the opportunity to lunge forward, knife outstretched, eyes rolling in fear.

And easily, simply, as though he had always known how the evening would go, Saul raises the iron pipe up above his head and brings it crashing down against the other man's skull.

The man is knocked back against the wall, blood streaming from his nose and a gash across his cheek.

*You brought this on yourself,* says Joey. And then, *let's go.*

And Saul walks out behind Joey into the night, and eases into the waiting car, and watches the old gas streetlights flicker as they drive back to Joey's, and then to Paolo and Antonia's, where Julia and Robbie are sleeping with slack faces and long, heavy limbs, and where Sofia has gone to spend the evening. He says good night to Antonia, picks up Julia and kisses her head. She snuggles back into sleep against his chest. He carries her home, three blocks that feel longer in the icy fall air. Sofia shuts the door to Julia's bedroom after Saul eases her under her blankets, and they retreat into their own room.

As Saul feels himself drift away from the events of his evening, Sofia asks, "What were you doing tonight?"

Saul turns toward her. Sofia has propped herself up on one elbow and her hair hangs down over her chest toward her pillow. Her face glows in the lamplight. "Working," he says. He is confused; Sofia doesn't usually ask questions about his work, and he doesn't know how to answer. He doesn't want to answer.

Sofia is impatient. "I know," she says. "But working, where? Who with? What were you doing?"

"Just some — some routine stuff," says

Saul. "With Joey." And now his heart is racing, because it's as if Sofia knows that tonight was different, that tonight Saul crossed a line he cannot get back over. This is more an intellectual realization than anything else, because there is a blank space in his body where there should be regret, fear, empathy. Saul wants to go to sleep. He wants to dive into the place where Sofia's hair falls down over her collarbones, to fill his hands with her breasts and his chest with her breath until there is nothing left of himself.

"Fine," says Sofia. But she turns off the light and turns away from him, and Saul is left to stare at the ceiling.

It would be easy to tell himself that he was torn up over his actions: that the man he attacked, huddled on the floor, holding his face with shaking fingers, would haunt Saul's dreams. Or that to do his job, Saul has developed a finely tuned emotional system for separating his home life and his work life. Or that he was damaged in some fundamental way, and his violence was a reflection of the trauma of Germany, the helplessness of losing his religion and his culture.

It is harder to know what Saul is learning: that maybe violence just isn't as hard as it's made out to be. Maybe there is something human about it. Maybe it is easy.

Sofia hears Saul's breath stretch out as he slips into sleep. But Sofia lies awake, her eyes dry and the sheets heating up beneath her as she tosses and turns. She is not sure why she asked Saul about his work; she knows Family work is never discussed; she has always known this. She knows that her job as the wife of a Family man should be to provide a safe space, an alternative to the vague but perilous danger of leaving a man to his own thoughts. *This is not the way,* she tells herself, *to get what you want.*

And then, in an internal voice that sounds like Frankie, *what do you even want?*

Soon it is 1945. Sofia passes a sleepless winter. She is almost twenty-two years old. She begins waking up gasping for air, like there is an anvil crushing her chest. Each time, she stumbles to the kitchen and runs cold water and stares at the stream of it gushing out of the tap until her heartbeat returns to normal. She looks out the kitchen window and grips the edge of the sink and tries with all her might to remember what has frightened her out of sleep. But without fail, she lies awake for the rest of the night, heart upturned to her bedroom ceiling.

During the day Sofia cooks with Rosa. She takes walks with Antonia, and they watch as Julia and Robbie toddle in their snowsuits. She wipes counters and folds laundry. Saul works longer days, and comes home from God-knows-where talkative and hungry. He wraps Julia into his arms and tickles her and leans to kiss Sofia, who tries her best to bite her tongue: not to ask the questions that arise like hiccups, involuntary, one after another.

But at night, Sofia lies awake, dissatisfaction like water filling her lungs. She searches for air and finds none.

One crisp night in January, Sofia wakes, shaking and sweaty, and moves to the kitchen as a reflex: further from Saul and Julia, the better to find her way back to her body. Outside, the full moon shines, light like milk pooling down into the crisscross of laundry lines and scraggly backyard trees. Sofia heaves open the window in the kitchen and sticks her face out into the moonlit midnight.

Two weeks later, it happens again. This time, she tiptoes downstairs in her nightgown and stands on the stoop of her building, her hair swimming in the night air, her feet hardening against the frigid stairs.

Sofia has found she is living with hardly any concrete responsibilities, but innumerable unwritten expectations. The strange confined freedom of her new adult life suffocates her and makes her feel desperate, hysterical. She becomes short with Saul and Julia; she avoids Rosa's eyes. Sofia grows bitter, tasting vinegar at the back of her tongue as she scrubs scum out of the sink. It seems like Saul's life is moving and hers is settling into a rut. Rosa doesn't understand: she can't imagine not being satisfied with a pile of diapers and a child, a child whose overwhelming need for Sofia's attention, for her time, for her body, threatens to pull the whole house down brick by brick. Sofia holds back tears as she bathes Julia, as she hands a wooden block back and forth while Julia cackles, as she listens to the midday silence of her home while Julia sleeps, as she finds herself, more and more often, alone. She can't complain to Antonia. Antonia, who she almost lost. Antonia, who had risen to the occasion of motherhood like a phoenix, dusting off her near-death depression; Antonia with her ability to find something bigger in parenting than Sofia can imagine. Sofia has always known Antonia would be a better mother than she would. She has always known that.

It is February of 1945 when Sofia wakes gasping, and instead of standing furtively on the frozen stone steps of her building, folds herself silently into Saul's desk chair and begins to shuffle through the papers there.

It is March of 1945 when Sofia starts getting out of bed regularly to read through Saul's notes. There aren't many — times of day written down in a small nondescript notebook and a list of places that Sofia assumes correspond to the times of day. *Of course,* she realizes, *most of this would not be written down.* She is awake for the rest of the night. She knows, though it has never been explicitly talked about in her home or her parents', that Saul is useful for his language skills and his discretion. She knows they are rescuing European refugees, or helping them to get jobs, and homes, or at least helping them get off the boats and onto dry land. And once Sofia starts wondering in earnest about Saul's work, she cannot stop.

By the beginning of May — her third wedding anniversary with Saul — Sofia decides she wants a job.

"Why would you want to be a part of this?" asks Saul. They are eating expensive steaks under flickering candlelight. Sofia likes her meat bleeding on the plate, soft and red in the middle. She chews. Swallows.

"I know," says Sofia. "It's not what I expected either." She lifts another bite of meat to her mouth. "I'm bored, Saul," she says. Mouth full. "I need to do something. I need to be — someone. And it's not like if I don't do this job, it will go away." She takes a sip of wine. "It's not like you'll stop. It's not like you can stop. And I mean, you're helping people.

You're helping people."

Saul, who has barely touched his own food, stares down at the lake of butter in his baked potato. "We're helping some people," he says. "And that will stop when the war ends." *When the war ends,* he repeats to himself. It echoes in his head. The war will never end, it seems. And when it does, what will he have? Who will he be? What will be left of Saul, once he reaches the other side of the war that made him? Saul doesn't regret taking the job Joey Colicchio offered him. He loves Sofia. He loves Julia. (*And regret,* says a voice inside of him, a voice that sounds like what he remembers of his mother's voice, *isn't German.* A pause. She'd touch his chin or ruffle his hair. *Regret isn't Jewish.*) Saul isn't stupid, but he makes the

291

best of things. He adapts.

"Do you mean you wish you could do something else?" asks Sofia.

"This isn't what I imagined for myself," says Saul. Has he been fantasizing about driving west, or sailing east? About disappearing into the ever-changing tapestry of the wide world, and starting over? About throwing off the rules and expectations of Family life and becoming a painter or a historian or a pediatrician?

"What did you imagine?"

"I imagined sitting in the driver's seat of my own life," says Saul.

"So did I," says Sofia. "That's why I want this."

"You can't see everything you already have," says Saul. "You can't see that the world is laid out in front of you. You can't see that you have everything. Julia — your family." *Your life has been so easy,* he almost says.

"You can't see everything you have either." Sofia longs to walk out of her front door and have no one know where she is going. She longs to be watched, but not corralled, not limited, not contained. She longs to swing from the rudder that steers the world and change its direction. But she does not know how to say this to Saul without blaming him.

"I lost everything. How could you say that. I lost everything."

"You have us," said Sofia. "You have this job." And then, before she can stop herself, "Will that always be an excuse for everything that isn't the way you want it?"

She and Saul look at one another over the blood and butter remains of their dinner. There is surprise and reproach in Saul's eyes. "I would give anything," he says, carefully, "not to have this — *excuse.*"

"I want this," Sofia says, from her belly. "I want this."

The night ends in silence. Sofia and Saul curl away from one another in their bed.

The want grows inside Sofia like mold. First a little dot of it, inconspicuous, but before she knows it, it is everywhere.

Julia and Robbie hardly fit together in a pram any longer, but Antonia slides them in like cannelloni against one another and tucks a blanket around both of them. They are both tired, and their limp bodies and half-closed eyelids rock gently as Antonia walks.

It is May 9, 1945. The radio and the newspapers have announced that the war is won. But in three months, the United States will drop atomic bombs on Hiroshima and Nagasaki. Millions of people have already died: a faraway abstraction on most days, or, on the days Antonia lets herself expand out into the worlds around her, an unbelievable aching undercurrent. A whirring, gnashing, stone and razor-blade storm; a sickness rushing and wailing across the globe. It makes Antonia sick. It makes her sleepless. It makes her fearful, so she avoids the radio, even as she cannot help but glance at the front pages displayed in news-stands. She returns her focus to the children in front of her.

Julia and Robbie are slack-faced and sound asleep under a thin white rain of cherry blossoms. More pressing than war, today, is the fact that Sofia was supposed to pick up Julia an hour ago. She had exploded into Antonia's living room earlier, all smiles and laden with supplies for Julia, dripping with diapers and a change of clothes and promising, promising to be back by lunch, *just for a few hours, Tonia, I've just got to get some air, you know?* And Antonia had scooped Julia into her arms and smelled her squirming hard toddler head and said, *of course, Sof. We'll be fine here.*

And they are fine, she tells herself. Her day isn't much different with two children than it was with one, and they're sleeping now, and she has had time to wipe the jam from the floor and scoop the spilled rice from their lunch into the trash and brush her hair, and she has left a message for Sofia with Rosa that they are all going to Lina's for the afternoon.

Antonia and Paolo live at the very edge of Carroll Gardens, where the schools are improving but where, every weekday, they can hear the slam and shout of the highway construction.

Places Antonia knew as abandoned space or farmland when she was a child are buildings now. Canals have been dug and filled; the new highways stream through old Brooklyn, dividing Red Hook from Carroll Gardens with a kind of sanguine finality: *here*, they say, *this will be the bad neighborhood, and this will be the good.* At the construction site for the Brooklyn-Queens Expressway, Antonia ducks, crouching as though otherwise she will hit her head. The new highway will cut a deep gash through her old neighborhood. The Church of the Sacred Hearts of Jesus and Mary has already been demolished as part of what Robert Moses called *slum clearance.*

Julia and Robbie do not stir, even as Antonia navigates the pram over the cracked and neglected pavement endemic to Red Hook; even as she turns backward and thumps them stair by stair up to Lina's apartment. "Mamma," she says, as Lina opens the door, "the war is over."

"The war is never over," says Lina, and as she and Antonia look at one another they are both thinking of Carlo.

Antonia spends the afternoon at Lina's, where Julia and Robbie have to be watched every second so they don't pull glass jars down from shelves or dip their small fingers into hot candle wax. Lina is making jam, boiling Sicilian oranges in sugar, and the whole kitchen is filled with fragrant air. Antonia finds a set of wooden blocks for Julia and Robbie and then rolls up her sleeves and works with Lina, alternately dipping glass jars into a pot of boiling water and setting them to steam-dry on a towel on the counter with glances over her shoulder to make sure Julia and Robbie have not abandoned the blocks for electric sockets or haphazard bookshelves or tiny glass beads.

"The world seems so much more dangerous now," she says to Lina.

"Yes," says Lina, "because you're looking at it through his eyes and yours all at once."

"Were you scared?" Antonia asks. She still shivers, hot and cold hysterics, when she thinks of Lina after her father died: the way she would look at Antonia and see right through her; Lina's volatility, her fragile face.

"All the time," says Lina. "And I used to be ashamed of that."

"You're not anymore?" asks Antonia.

Lina swoops down and moves a lit candle out of Robbie's reach. "Fear is a tool," she says simply. "I have learned how to use it."

Inside Antonia's body she can feel herself,

in this very kitchen, at sixteen, the war just beginning, her life an outline, yet to be filled in. *Anything could have happened,* she thinks. The impossibility of ending up *here.* The strangeness of it. The luck and the tragedy.

Other people who were sixteen when the war began had their hands blown off; their faces burnt and twisted. Their mothers were killed by roving bands of soldiers, or their villages were ransacked. They escaped, like Saul, in the watery, mildewed holds of boats. They floated across the ocean away from everything they had ever known. They starved, their stomachs twisting in prayer, clenching at nothing. They died. Again and again, they died: the lives lost (lives! As vivid as Antonia's, as real) rattle Antonia's hands so she drops a jar onto the floor, where it splinters with a loud crack. She finds a broom.

*What do you have to show for yourself?* she wonders as she sweeps glass shards off the floor of her childhood apartment. Her hands have not been blown off. She has survived. The debt she owes fate seems too heavy to bear.

*Something,* thinks Antonia, *has to change.*

New York City spins along with the rest of

the world, but it is also an eddy in the river of the universe: turning and turning in its own current.

The city celebrates. The war is over, they tell each other. The war is over, they tell themselves, again and again. They look in the mirror and say, "The war is over," out loud. They make eye contact on the street; they almost smile; they do not go back to work on time after lunch; they forget where they live and walk, swinging briefcases and knocking into one another, saying, *excuse me, excuse me,* in a daze. It is as though all of New York has had one drink too many; the full-hearted wide-gestured open-mouthed buzz of a party at its zenith. All over the city, strangers find their hearts beating in time with one another. They look at other passengers on buses, at other diners in restaurants, at other commuters in elevators, and they think, *I know you.*

Paolo's brother was killed in France, when a chunk of shrapnel bounced off a building next to him and lodged itself in his chest. This is an open wound in his family. That the war is over, that the war is won, does nothing but illuminate the place Paolo's brother should have at the table. The hook where he should hang his coat. So Paolo is with his mamma; his two other brothers are there too; nothing can console her, nor will anything ever console her again. Her son's absence will be an aching, nauseating vertigo. The whole world is slanted now. There will be no body; she will not visit his grave. She says, *they were boys, they were just boys,* and Paolo puts a hand between her shoulder blades, soft, and as he does it he can feel himself clutching his mother at five years old, and nine, and twelve, and he knows she is right: he is a boy; his brother was just a boy.

Joey has kept a very expensive bottle of whiskey on hand for exactly this moment. He uncaps it and pours a generous drink and swallows, letting it heat him up and smooth him out. He feels a low tug of fear; his finances have been dependent on the war since it began. His family is comfortable now. They live in a better neighborhood, and there are children to think of. Joey Colicchio has never met a problem he could not solve. This, he knows, as he drinks again, from the bottle, will be no different.

Saul calls home before he eats lunch, but there is no answer. Sofia must not be home. Saul goes out for midday dim sum with three other guys who spend the meal clapping one another on the back and gesticulating with their chopsticks and laughing uproariously and nudging each other in the ribs, louder than everyone else in the restaurant. Their voices surround him and he feels dizzy and goes to the bathroom to splash water on his face and grip the edges of the sink and stare into the mirror. *The war is over,* he says to himself. But he does not know what parts of him will disappear now, and he is sure most of him will. What is left of Saul, without the war? What will he have to show for himself, once the war that made him turns into bland history? He can feel it happening already: his mother a memory, the metal and chalk taste of not eating or drinking enough fading, now that there is clean running water everywhere he goes. When Saul feels eyes on his back as he walks through the streets, it is his job to stay calm and authoritative. Inside of Saul, a Jewish child runs home as the sun sets, because the Berlin streets are not safe for him after dark.

Sofia sips Turkish coffee from a cup the size of her thumb and watches the door of the restaurant across the street for signs of Saul. She knows she is late to pick up Julia and she is surprised, still, to find herself here, shamelessly tailing her husband in broad daylight.

The coffee is sweet and strong and Sofia feels like she has been electrocuted. One of her feet bounces, two of her fingers tap against the table.

"Will you have something else, ma'am?" asks the waiter.

"No," she says. "Thank you." *Ma'am,* he says, again and again, in her head. *Something else, ma'am. Ma'am. Ma'am.*

The waiter leaves a check in a tin tray. Sofia drops her coins into the tray but her eyes stay glued to the restaurant, where she knows Saul has not come out yet.

Sofia doesn't know what she's expecting to happen. She's tailing Saul at his job, for what? Knowing what he does isn't going to change the fact that there's no way her husband and her father will ever let her in the door. Watching him clap other men on the back will do nothing but reinforce her understanding that the centuries of unspoken, unwritten, universally understood Family rules will not be bent because she is a little bored at home.

Then, knowing something is impossible has never stopped Sofia Colicchio from trying.

■ ■ ■ ■

Joey is sitting in his favorite armchair with his feet up when someone calls. He picks it up before the first ring is over. "Freddie."

"She's following him again, boss."

Joey sighs. He imagines having a simple daughter, one who didn't want to break every rule set down before her. "Where are they?"

"Lunch, boss. Chinatown." There's a pause. "Do you want me to . . . stop her?"

"Of course not," says Joey. "Don't be an idiot. Stay the fuck away from her." Some of your men are for strategy, he tells himself. Some are not.

"Sorry, boss."

"I'll deal with it. Just watch her until she gets in a cab," says Joey. "Make sure she gets home safe. Make sure she doesn't see you."

When Joey was a child, he sometimes imagined having a family. The woman he married looked like his mamma, and made the same chicken parmigiana, and hugged him, smelling like flour and roses, when he needed it. His children were small and rowdy, eight or ten of them like bumper cars around him. It was a happy chaos.

In his imagination, Joey never had an adult daughter. He never had any daughters at all. To ten-year-old Joey, there was nothing scarier than a girl. In his imagination, Giuseppe Colicchio certainly never had an out-of-control life-size firebrand threatening to topple his business and family to the ground. And while it's true that Sofia is the greatest pleasure of Joey's life, and that in his honest moments he is in awe of her determination, her perseverance, her absolute insistence upon being herself no matter what the circumstances, it is also true that Joey bristles when that determination is turned in his direction.

Joey taps his fingers on his desk in thought. Sofia doesn't know what she's doing, and if a goon with two brain cells like Freddie could tail her, so could anyone: your average overachieving newly minted police officer who hasn't learned better yet, or worse, Eli Leibovich's men, who are neither stupid nor newly minted, or worse than that, some Fianzo kid, a new guy wanting his bones, hoping to bag Sofia as a bargaining chip. As bragging rights. Sofia insists on risking her own life as well as the safety and security of his entire Family.

Something will have to be done.

When Sofia gets home that evening, a sleeping Julia in tow, there is a bouquet of roses waiting for her on the kitchen table and Saul is listening to the radio in the living room. *In Paris, victory celebrations are in full swing,* it says. Sofia points at the bouquet and raises her eyes at Saul to see if he knows what it is. "There's a card," he calls to her. And then, "And the war is over." *The young people are marching up and down the boulevards, singing and dancing and waving flags.*

Sofia looks at Saul. "The war is over," she says. She walks to the table and picks up the envelope there. "It's open," she says to Saul.

"Your dad gave me a heads-up," he replies. His face is strangely empty. Sofia lowers her eyes to the small card. It reads:

*Sof: It seems you might like a job. Ask and you shall receive. Love, Papa. PS: Stop tailing Saul.*

Sofia looks up at Saul. "He's going to let me work," she says. She grins. Sofia Colicchio, lamp-lit and triumphant.

"So it seems," says Saul. Joey had called him that afternoon. He had said, *you know our Sofia isn't exactly typical.* He had sighed, and then said, ruefully, *truthfully, she'll be better at this than either of us, if she decides to be.* And then there was quiet in the conversation, and Saul could feel the wind as the door beyond which other possibilities, other jobs, other lifestyles, existed slammed shut. No California, no Upper West Side. No painter, no pediatrician. So now Saul is staring down the barrel of the rest of his life. He is mourning something that would never have happened.

In Europe, Russian and American soldiers are firing their guns into the air in celebration. Nazi officers are slipping cyanide pills into the hands of their wives and loved ones. His mother is a breathing skeleton somewhere, or a pile of ash, and Saul has become unrecognizable to her. How will they find each other?

"You're mad," says Sofia. She doesn't want Saul to ruin this for her. She is almost angry. But there is also an insistent nagging, a genuine concern for Saul, whose shoulders are slumped in defeat.

Saul sits up and switches off the radio and lowers his face to his hands.

"Saul, what?" asks Sofia. She crosses the room and brings her hands to cover his. In her chest there is a small struggling bird that would have been elation and instead is a complicated disappointment.

"I'm not mad," says Saul.

"Okay, so?"

"It's hard to explain."

"Try," says Sofia, and it is a command.

"Well," says Saul. "I came here, and I was so alone. I've never been so alone. But then this job — it found me. And you — you *found* me. And the war was this monster in the background, this thing I was escaping. And then suddenly instead of being alone I was taking care of you, and Julia, and I was doing this job, and I was fighting against the war with everyone I picked up. And I didn't have time to think about everything I had given up, everything that had changed. It seemed to matter a little less what I had lost." Saul takes off his glasses and pinches the bridge of his nose between his thumb and forefinger. Sofia is silent. The silence presses down.

"But suddenly, today, the war is over. I am fighting against nothing. I'm escaping nothing. And you are — like you always do, you are just blasting into your life like dynamite through concrete. And suddenly I am here, and there's no reason for it. I could be anywhere now." Saul sits back into the sofa and feels himself sinking. *Blessed are You.* "I am on an absolute island, Sofia."

Over the course of their time together, Saul softens Sofia. It is one of the most monumental changes in her. She becomes the mistress of her own emotional topography. She learns to pause, to take in all the information. She can still react with fire, with tornado. But she is now able to control it. To sharpen it. To aim.

It is this softness and this aim which now compel Sofia to drop herself into Saul's lap and fill her arms with him, with his shoulders and the desperate hollow of his chest, with the brown curls that spring from his head. She fills her nose with his scent, with the spice of his aftershave and the yellow stench of cigarettes and sweat that collects in his shirt after he's been wearing it all day. And then Sofia fills her mouth with Saul, with his mouth and his breath, until the only sound in their apartment is an exhale, a collapse, and Sofia does not whisper *I need you here* but she feels need squeezing her like a muscle and she believes Saul does too.

Over the next week, Sofia meets with Joey alone several times. He pours her a glass of wine and shuts the parlor doors behind them. He sits, spread-kneed across from her, and he says, *it's time you learned some things about how this works.*

Sofia's first assignment is with Detective Leo Montague, who, Joey explains, has been willing to let certain things slide for many years. He got a cut of their profits as early as Prohibition, and he and Joey have achieved a tenuous mutual respect in their decades working together. He has been invaluable throughout the war. "But we aren't going to be making the same kind of money anymore," Joey says, "and that's a tricky thing to tell a man." Joey mentioned Leo might have to take a pay cut on the phone and Leo said, *whoa now, Colicchio, not sure I'm willing to do that.* And then he was quiet for a minute, and then he said, *don't forget, you need me.* And it had taken everything Joey had not to slam the phone down so hard it cracked. Joey could scare Leo into submission, but it would be possible for Leo to hurt Joey very badly in return. They could both lose. These things escalate quickly. "I think you'll be good at this," says Joey to Sofia. "You might not remember, but you spent every Sunday dinner sneaking around the table, trying to collect gossip, trying to understand everyone." Sofia remembers the thrill of conning her way into a tight-knit circle of women, into a smoky group of men.

So Sofia is to go to lunch with the detective, and she is to avoid the details of business with him, the limited outlines of which Joey has shared with her. She is to listen more than she talks. When she told Saul, gleeful, he got very quiet.

"It's perfect, Saul," Sofia says. "It's work, and it's exciting, and it's not dangerous."

"It's all connected," says Saul. "It's all dangerous."

But Sofia won't be deterred.

Sofia meets Detective Leo in a candlelit trattoria for a late lunch. Joey has told her what to order. "Eggplant parmisgiana," she says. "for me and for my friend here. Grazie." Her heart is pounding with excitement. She looks at Leo appraisingly. "It's the best here," she says, though in truth Joey has told her this is the meal Detective Leo loves, and they want him to be comfortable. *But, Papa,* she had asked Joey, *what do I* say *to him?* Joey had cupped her face with his two hands and said, *just be yourself.*

Detective Leo is in his late fifties with shocks of salt-and-pepper hair, ill-tamed, and thick square glasses. He reminds Sofia of what might happen if Saul put on twenty-five years, forty pounds, and a little American bravado.

"So you're the daughter?" he asks. "I think I met you once."

"You might have," says Sofia. She is wondering how to steer the conversation toward the Family without seeming like she is doing it. But Detective Leo dives right in as soon as their meals arrive.

"I respect your family, I really do," he says. "But I put myself at a lot of risk for you."

"Papa appreciates all your work," says Sofia.

"I know that," says Leo. He raises his eyes from his plate to Sofia and she realizes with a start that there is a flicker of fear there. Fear of her? "Please make sure he knows that I know that."

"Of course," says Sofia.

"It's just, a man of my age," says Detective Leo. "I'm five years away from my pension. If I'm going to rock the boat — if I'm going to break the rules — damn, excuse me, madam, but damn, this is a good eggplant parmesan." It's gloppy, Sofia thinks. The cheese is hardening over the flavorless filling like amber over an insect.

"It's delicious, isn't it," says Sofia.

"I've always trusted your papa," says Detective Leo.

"He trusts you too," says Sofia. "He's said the nicest things about you."

"Has he?" asks Detective Leo, and Sofia knows this was the right thing to say because Detective Leo looks tickled pink, a little rosy. "Well, that's very — that's nice of him — good man, Joey Colicchio." He trails off and takes another bite of food. "I have children, you know," he says. "They depend on me. I've been able to give them some extra — well, times have been hard."

"I understand," says Sofia. "I have a daughter myself. I would do anything for her, too."

"You have a daughter?" And here, Sofia can see, Detective Leo's eyes glance appraisingly at her waist. People often do this. They have to imagine Sofia pregnant in order to determine whether her child has ruined her. She keeps her face carefully blank. "Your papa," says Detective Leo, "did a real special thing, during the war, for people who needed it. People who were escaping something awful, you know, all that Nazi scum. Well, we showed them, didn't we. And I guess you might not understand this, but I just want some credit where credit's due. I have to advocate for myself." Detective Leo has finished inhaling his meal and sits back against his chair to regard Sofia through his thick dark glasses. There is a speck of tomato at the corner of his mouth. "Your old dad's an honorable man," he says, "so I think he'll understand where I'm coming from." And Sofia can see, now, clearly, what Leo needs.

"You know," she says, "I don't think he would have been able to run his business without you."

"Really?" asks Leo. "Well, I guess you need someone who knows the ins and outs." Leo takes a sip of water to disguise a slow smile, but Sofia sees it.

"Yes, certainly," says Sofia. "I know how much he values you."

"You can't just value someone, though," says Detective Leo. "You have to compensate them accordingly. You have to show them."

"I know my father knows that," says Sofia. "I think he's just doing what he can to take care of his family, and the families of everyone who works for him. He makes it seem easy, but it's a lot of responsibility."

"I understand that," says Leo. "When my precinct reorganized — well. I understand being saddled with responsibility over other people."

"I can tell," says Sofia.

"Joey Colicchio really is an honorable

313

man," Leo says, and for the first time in her adult life, Sofia can see a road stretched out in front of her, a path she wants to take. *This is the right thing for me,* she thinks, and she is so grateful she almost weeps at the table. *This is what I'm supposed to do.*

When Sofia returns home and Saul asks, *how was it?* she turns to him with light in her eyes and says, *it was easy.*

And she expects to fall sound asleep that night, but she finds herself staring at the midnight ceiling, and she cannot figure out what is keeping her awake. Was it Leo's face as they said goodbye, how he turned and scratched his head, so like Saul when he grapples with something wordless and gnarled? Was it Saul himself, who has only half-looked at her for days, who is gripped by a melancholy Sofia doesn't recognize, and wouldn't have expected, given that the war is over?

Sometime before she drifts off, Sofia remembers a school courtyard, and holding Antonia's hand. A cluster of girls on the other side of the windswept swingset and Sofia could tell they were all talking about her. *Your father is a murderer,* Maria Panzini said, matter-of-factly, as they waited in line to go back inside. Ice like concrete in Sofia's belly. Even in grade school, she had harbored some unspeakable desire to be *better* than the people around her. Has she succeeded now? Does she understand the price she'll pay? *It was easy,* her own voice echoes. It was like it was made for her.

Next to Sofia, Saul feigns sleep. For hours, he stares with half-mast eyes at the ticking clock.

At dinner on Sunday Joey raises a toast to Sofia and everyone cheers, Antonia and Paolo and Frankie, Pops, who is repeating stories lately and who might not understand what he is toasting, and even hawkeyed Nonna, even Rosa gives a tight smile, and Rosa's brother nods and Marco DeLuca and two other interchangeable new guys raise their glasses but look at Joey the whole time, instead of at Sofia. "Welcome," Joey says, warmly, and Sofia is too busy avoiding Antonia's eyes to notice that Joey is avoiding Rosa's, but Rosa finds Sofia washing dishes after dinner and begins to berate her with the fierceness of a thousand mammas: *Gussied up like you're for sale, this is disgraceful. You have a husband and a daughter, Sofia, what will Julia think, how will she grow up?* And Sofia, for the first time in her life, wants something more than she wants to argue with Rosa, and so she kisses her mamma and she says, *I'll be careful, Julia will be fine,* and she leaves Rosa sputtering in this kitchen, torn, as Rosa often is, between pride and horror.

The job becomes a part of her so that soon Sofia cannot ever remember not wanting it. She points her whole being toward the horizon of it, the glory of stepping out of the house and being seen.

While Saul is working late Julia is often at Antonia's house. This started as a way for Sofia to avoid talking to Rosa about her job, but it has become habit, lifeline. Sometimes Sofia comes with her, to stay up with Antonia past bedtime, conversation like a low sonata on the couch. Sometimes Sofia is elsewhere. When Sofia shuts the door to Antonia's house and walks away, she feels relief and joy and an anticipation that crawls like static under her skin. She does not think about Antonia, whose slightly pressed lips have been a moral barometer since Sofia learned to talk. She does not usually think about Julia. *Your Child,* people say to her, constantly, as though because Sofia Has A Child she has relinquished all claim to agency, as though Sofia needs reminding that the top of Julia's head smells like warm bread, as though Sofia isn't a better mother now, a fucking lioness. *My Child will never be made to feel guilty for existing the way she wants to,* Sofia thinks. And so she parents: when Julia wants to eat leftover pastry for breakfast, spongey cakes with chocolate ganache, thick cognac cream, Sofia opens the box and eats, too, with her hands. When Julia wants to skip her bath and crawl under her sheets with dirty feet and tangled hair, Sofia tucks her in. *So what,* she says to Rosa. *She's fine,* she says to Antonia, who finds an excuse to make bath time a part of any day Julia spends there.

Mostly, Sofia is a middleman; a calming draft prescribed to men who work for the Family when they begin to get nervous. This is something new Joey is trying. He imagines Carlo, and how things might have changed if Carlo could talk to a woman, someone young and professional and pretty who showed him how his job was connected to family, to the earth, without ever directly mentioning those things. Sometimes having a woman in the room can exacerbate tension. But there are many moments when Sofia can put a jumpy man at ease without saying a word.

Sofia doesn't mind. She is good at this — so good any objections she might have conceived of, objections to being used like a decoration, like the breathing equivalent of a stiff drink, fall to the wayside. She bursts out of bed each morning. When she gets home from her dinners, her drinks, her cappuccino-turned-glass-of-wine, she is bright-eyed and babbling, talking to Saul in tones loud enough to wake Julia, enamored with herself. *I changed him,* she thinks, she tells Saul, she whispers to herself in the bathroom mirror. *I made him different.* She doesn't think about whether she is changing men for the better, or in service of a mission she believes in. It is enough for Sofia that each man's intention appears to bend and shift as she speaks and moves. At the beginning of 1946 Joey pours her a glass of port and tells her he's going to have her start taking different meetings, and so when Sofia is not charming flighty Family men and nervous detectives, she is supervising shipments of wine, vinegar, aged and crumbling cheeses, and she is learning to set her mouth so no one asks her questions or gives her any shit, and she is feeling, each day, more and more powerful, more and more connected to the internal beating, not just of her own heart, but of the entire changing world.

With Antonia, Sofia is careful. She knows Antonia doesn't approve. But she cannot stop working, and she cannot lose Antonia.

They are bound together by so much now: their history, their families, their children, who sleep better if they are in the same room as one another. So Sofia's job is something that she and Antonia step around, examine silently, try to avoid.

And Antonia, who has softened into parenthood, into wifehood, into the role of best friend and babysitter and beloved aunt to Julia, does not say anything to Sofia. Antonia always takes Julia when Sofia shows up, dressed to the nines. She does not tell Sofia that the independence she boasts of stinks like Lina's job at the laundry. She is not certain, of course, that Sofia is doing any worse than she, Antonia, is — where is Antonia's independence, after all, her university certificate, her wraparound porch, her three children who have never heard of the Family, who will be doctors and explorers and farmers? She had a brief period of rebellion last year, when the war ended: she spent days and days looking up university schedules. She could have a degree if she took two night classes a week for six years. When she brought this to Paolo, he was angry. He told her there was enough change in their family with the end of the war. He didn't know what his job would look like, or if he would even have one. He didn't know what their finances would be like. His own family was in constant crisis, his mother refusing to get out of bed. *Everything is unstable,* he said. *I feel like the ground beneath my feet is already dissolving. The last time I felt so — was after Robbie was born, when you —* He hadn't finished, but had left Antonia to her own guilt about the last time she abandoned her family. *You know I want this for you,* he said as they went to bed. *You know it's just bad timing.*

So Antonia has thrown her whole self into motherhood, and in her efforts to be unlike Lina, unlike Sofia, she is there the instant Robbie wakes and she soothes him to sleep, a hand on his back every night. She tries to spare him any pain, any fear, any loss, and so she is constantly telling him she loves him, telling him to be careful, to look both ways, but rather than any common sense, Robbie develops a powerful need to have Antonia near him at all times, so they are rarely seen apart, except when Julia is there: Julia, in whose presence Robbie lights up, grows six inches taller; Julia, who sparks in Robbie something courageous and mischievous that draws him away from Antonia, that allows Antonia to rest, to come to terms with the toll her obsessive parenting is taking on her body, on her mind. Antonia would not call this the independence she once dreamed of but she had been unable, as a teenager, to imagine what loving two children would do to her, how completely she would want to give of herself, how difficult it would be to find balance. She is scared of her own need; she is exhausted; she wouldn't change it for the world but a small sense of self-preservation rears up in Antonia and reminds her of the months after Robbie was born, when she needed to walk alone, to clear her head, to come back to herself.

Antonia listens to Paolo when he complains that his post-war job has become droll and tedious, that the craft of falsified documents and the tedium of bookkeeping are incomparable, incompatible. She does not tell him how relieved she is that he is out of the line of fire, or as far away from it as he can be. She takes careful stock of her life and decides that each of its challenges is worth it, that each of its joys is indispensable, and in this way she reasons away Paolo's new sullenness and Sofia's new flightiness and the gnawing feeling that she is putting herself last, letting herself go unfinished. Most of the time she manages to feel full, full, full of love.

Soon 1946 is over. Sofia throws a party

for New Year's Eve. She dresses in sequins and Antonia feels like they are teenagers, sneaking out to a dance. Rosa and Joey beg out after midnight and take Julia and Robbie to sleep in their apartment but Sofia and Antonia and Saul and Paolo and a couple of guys Saul and Paolo work with climb up onto the roof and watch their breath puff in frozen clouds up into the starless city sky, up into the fresh new year.

In March, Antonia is watching Robbie and Julia. They are napping: faces utterly slack; hair plastered against their foreheads. Robbie is as enamored of Julia as Antonia was of Sofia but he is messier than Antonia was; he is more sensitive; he bruises easily. And Julia, too, seems messier than her mother, less focused, but just as big, just as loud, just as hot. She digs her hands into every patch of dirt she finds. Antonia is thankful they are sleeping.

Earlier that day Antonia had walked in on a wrestling match on the floor of her bedroom. *What exactly is happening in here?* She had hissed. *I'm a Fianzo!* Robbie had said to her. His face had been bright and upturned; he loved to tell her things, to bring her into his world. His arms were always reaching out for her. *A what?* Antonia had asked. Cold dread. Robbie drew himself up to his full height and raised his arms. *Wooooouuurrrghhh!* he growled. *I'll get you, Fianzo,* shouted Julia. She tackled him. Legs went everywhere. A water glass fell off of a bedside table and shattered. *Enough, enough!* said Antonia. She lifted Robbie and Julia away from the glass one by one. *Go, now!* And Robbie had gone: dejected, worried. He never wants Antonia to be upset.

Antonia had breathed a shaky exhale and shut the door. She lives in constant fear of becoming her own mother — *they killed your grandfather!* she imagines saying in a moment of panic — but then she wouldn't be the parent anymore; she would be making decisions for her own self-satisfaction. Antonia has made her peace with the mother her mother is able to be. But she does not want to become her.

She thinks, also, of the Fianzos themselves: their putrid cigars; the slick of their shoes and hair. She is grateful that her son thinks of them as monsters, and she is deeply disappointed: since he was born, Antonia has done her best to shelter him from the tragedy and terror in her own childhood. *You've failed,* she thinks.

Antonia is rarely surprised, any longer, by

the depth and fierceness of her love for Julia. It's not true what they say about blood being thicker than water. So she is grateful to have Julia sleeping soundly in her son's bedroom, and she tries not to dwell on Sofia, who showed up earlier and begged Antonia to take Julia, *just for a couple hours.* And Antonia always opens the door. She always kisses Sofia's cheeks and tells her to go, and she puts a hand on Julia's hair, and she tries to focus on the absolute ocean of her love for both of them, rather than on Julia's face, which crumples just slightly as Sofia leaves, like the top of a cake falling as it cools.

As she watches Julia and Robbie sleep, Antonia feels an internal keening: a primal, physical tug from her low belly that turns to quick tears before she is conscious of the feeling. She would like to cover their bodies with her body. She would like to cut off her arms and legs one by one and feed herself to the children sleeping in her apartment. She has just turned twenty-four.

Antonia misses Carlo. The mourning comes in waves. Robbie has Carlo's nose, the set of his eyes. As she sees him more and more often in her son, Antonia finally understands that something has been stolen from her. Something irreplaceable. She does not know what to do with this feeling, so she cleans her home, reminding herself of Lina, scrubbing at wooden floors that were stained long before their family lived in the apartment. *There is nothing to be done about this.* So she stays awake and dreams, or sleeps dreamlessly, restlessly, wondering about the alternate possible versions of her own life. What she has control over, what she's missed her chance at, and what will happen regardless of anything she decides.

She imagines being able to melt into molten anger like Sofia. How comforting, to direct a stream of fire in every direction. How final, to condense what is desperation and love and nostalgia into rage. Antonia imagines that rage would feel like action. It would feel like forward motion.

She feels so still.

Now if they stand shoulder to shoulder with other Family men, Paolo and Saul are indistinguishable from the old hands around them. This time four years ago they were so green they leaked sap; they were bright and awkward; a half-step behind. But father-hood has added gravity to both of their silhouettes; experience has written lines on their faces, and as 1947 passes, Paolo and Saul find themselves steeped in routine.

When the war ended, the job changed. Somehow, and against all of his intention, Paolo has ended up in a mostly-for-show office on Nevins Street, where he spends his days tapping pen against paper and coming up with business ideas that range from dog grooming for aging Upper East Side socialites to intercepting ocean liners and hustling the passengers out of a few bucks in return for a tour of the city. For an hour a day, he alters the books that let the Family pay taxes without disclosing where their money comes from; Luigio Travel does a hefty business. At the end of the week, he turns his notebooks over to Joey and says, *I think I've got some good ones here, boss.* And Joey, out of pity or generosity, continues to pay Paolo the same as he did when Paolo was an indispensable forger during the war. And so Paolo fights a never-ending and vicious battle between the part of himself who is comforted and relieved to sink into the same set of tasks week after week, and the part of himself who dreamed of something bigger. Who thought it, whatever it was, would feel like more, when he got there.

During the day, now, Saul waits outside cafés while Joey takes meetings, or he is paired with an older Uncle, and asked to remind someone of their debt, which usually means punching the indebted man in the jaw a couple of times and asking about his children; occasionally twisting a wrist or brandishing a switchblade and threatening the loss of a finger.

Saul misses the ferry ride to Ellis Island, the soft German he could speak to reassure the families he was meeting, the ease with which he could help them. *Speak English, not German,* he would tell them. *They'll spell your surname wrong. Let them. Don't cough. Stand up straight.* Now that it's over, Saul wonders why his interaction with those families ended where it did: at the other side of the Ellis Island ferry, as he handed them brown paper packets filled with falsified degrees and resumes and letters of recommendation with which they could start over as Americans. He wonders who they were: families so desperate they paid their weight in gold for a few false documents and a promise; once, a teenage girl, alone, who told him her family had sold their jewelry for her ticket. *When will they be able to come?* she asked, and Saul had said, *don't cough or touch your face when you get to the front of the line. Use only the first syllable of your surname.* Weeks passed when he told this to four families, nine. *Why didn't you run after them, beg them to ask their relatives about your mother, kiss the hands that had touched European soil?* Love for a place that wants you dead is an evolving beast.

With the end of the war, though, came the end of that job. And soon Saul found himself immersed in what anyone would call the scrap work of paid goons. Now his levelheaded stare, his impeccable work ethic, and his ability to close the door behind his face and fit in anywhere, while answering no questions, are all qualities that make him an intimidating and efficient errand runner.

There are moments, small ones, mere slivers of seconds, when Saul wonders how he ended up in his life. When he imagines being eight, spread prone on the floor of a house his mother was cleaning, reading a comic or staring out the window into the filtered, old-fashioned European sunlight, or walking along the River Spree, tossing bread crusts to ducks. It is impossible for him to reconcile the world through the eyes of himself as a boy with the world he lives in now. Impossible, that his mother is gone and that he lives in America and that he is married into a family that feels like home, some days, and like a prison, others. And in those moments of impossibility Saul considers the steps he would have to take to get himself back to a recognizable life: leave his wife, leave his child, hitch a ride across the seething ocean to a home that, by all reports, no longer exists. Leave the Brooklyn streets, so familiar to Saul they could be the lines carved into his own palm. *Still,* he thinks, some days, *the alternative is staying.* Staying in a world where feeding his family means menacing others'. A world where he comes home and washes other men's blood from his knuckles before dinner. Saul understands luck. He understands that given the slightest twist of fate, he could have lived a thousand different lives — some more lucky, some less.

Sofia has settled in to her role as The Boss's Daughter, a term a couple of the men used pejoratively under their breaths to describe her when she started but which is now for all intents and purposes a term of endearment, earned over the year and a half her father's men have watched her stand her ground against men much bigger than her, men who have the unpredictability engendered by desperation and fear. *My father won't like to hear that,* she tells indebted shopkeepers, importers, restaurateurs, a policeman hoping to get off the Family payroll. Or more recently, *my husband is a kind man, but I imagine this will test his limits.* Sofia has mastered the blank face and imperturbable tone of her father, of Saul. She has added a red lip. She has added her own flair. She is touted as psychological weaponry. *You're just a woman,* someone might say, a politician who paid for discretion, for protection. Yes, Sofia would respond. *I'm a messenger.*

Sofia hardly remembers her resistance to this job. This job, which she now knows, the way Saul and Paolo know, is a lifeline. Instead she thrives on a diet of adrenaline and performance. She feels like she has been standing in the dark, watching outside a bright room her whole life, and now she is standing inside, bathed in light. There is always a man or two with a pistol outside the door of her meetings. Her father didn't offer her the danger he offers the men. But Sofia never needs the backup. She has found that the very specter of the Family is enough. She has realized that Joey and Saul and Paolo, while formidable at work, all draw from the well of mystery and folklore surrounding their occupation. The very idea of them is enough to clear a path down the sidewalk, a space at the bar. Sofia drinks from the well. She finds that until this moment, she has been parched.

*I*, Sofia would say, *am a best-case scenario, for you.*

The summer they are nearly five, Julia and Robbie get the chicken pox at the same time and Saul and Sofia and Julia come to stay at the Luigio apartment, where for five days and nights Julia and Robbie have to be watched so they don't scratch each other and where Antonia and Paolo and Saul and Sofia can relive a sort of pre-child utopia, their lives and possessions and sleeping schedules interchangeable and magic. In the mornings Sofia distracts the feverish, stir-crazy animals who have replaced Julia and Robbie, and Saul makes breakfast: elaborate concoctions of eggs and leftovers, caramel-ized bacon, muffins fresh and filled with fruit and bits of chocolate. *Turkey with Swiss,* he sometimes thinks, doling out scrambled eggs. *Tongue with mustard.*

On the morning of the third day Saul is sautéing onions when Antonia walks into the kitchen. "Sofia had to run out," she says.

"Again."

Saul nods. And then he notices that Antonia, who is sitting at the kitchen table, chewing on a crust of bread, looks unmistakably melancholic. "Is something bothering you?" he asks.

"It's — well, it's Julia," says Antonia. She trails off. Saul can hear her chewing. "She reminds me of myself, lately. Just a kid, looking for a home, feeling lonely, missing — well, you're here, but missing my papa. Trying not to miss him. And — never mind."

"And what?" Saul is concentrating.

"And not having, necessarily, the mamma I needed, when I needed her." Antonia is quiet. She watches Saul's back, the shoulder blades moving through his sweater as he stirs.

Years ago, Saul asked Sofia what happened to Antonia's father. It was early in their courtship and he was distracted by her hands in his, the way the busy sidewalk seemed to clear for them to walk, and her smell: like soil or like lilac, something he wanted to eat, to choke on, to drown in. So when she said *a tragedy,* he accepted that as the whole answer. But as Saul looks at Antonia, he realizes there is a hole in his understanding of the sorrows that shaped

334

her. A specter, standing in the kitchen, watching him cook. He has not learned what he needs to know, when he needs to know it. "Antonia," he asks, carefully, "what really happened to your papa?"

Antonia's face goes gray and green. "You don't know," she says.

The air in the kitchen grows close, thick, rancid with the secret. Saul realizes he is holding his breath. "I know some of it," he says.

Antonia peers down the hall to make sure Julia and Robbie are still nowhere to be seen. "Do you know that Joey meets with a man called Tommy Fianzo every month?" she asks.

"I do," says Saul. He is taken to that meeting every month. Someday, he will go on his own. He has not asked why the meeting happens. He has been, he realizes, too trusting. This is something he has thought about a lot over the last year. Saul left his home, left his family, transplanted himself to the fertile soil of someone else's life. He is a breathing transformation. But in other ways, Saul is beginning to understand that he has let his life happen to him. How much has he let go of? How much is he overlooking?

"Joey used to work for Tommy," says Antonia. "Joey was best friends with my papa, Carlo. They were all friends." Antonia can feel her face heating up, but her hands and feet are freezing. It is as though her body itself does not know how to speak this secret out loud.

"I know that," says Saul. "Sofia told me — years ago. She said they were friends. She said he disappeared."

"No," says Antonia. "My papa decided he didn't want to work for the Family anymore. But it doesn't work that way. So Tommy Fianzo had him killed. In a way, I guess, disappeared. We never found out what happened to him. Joey couldn't work for him anymore after that. They made some kind of agreement. Joey pays him; they work separately."

Sofia had lied to him? Saul can picture her face as she told him. *A tragedy,* she had said, and shrugged. *A mystery.* She had lied to him.

"It broke my mamma. For years, she was — like an empty shell. I'm not saying that is what Sofia is like, of course. But from my perspective, as a child, I never had the mamma I expected. I never knew what I could depend on her for. And that changed me."

When Antonia finishes speaking, her mouth retreats into a small thin line and her face looks bare, defiant.

The aftermath echoes.

Before he realizes what he is doing, Saul is halfway across the kitchen to clasp Antonia's hands in his, to bury his face in her hair. He stops himself mid-step. There is an unspoken boundary there.

In Antonia's mind, she steps across the kitchen to meet Saul halfway. They embrace: her face against his sweater, the branches of his arms a hollow to hide in.

Saul cannot sleep that night. He turns over and over on the mattress Antonia and Paolo have laid out for him and Sofia on the living room floor. Antonia and Paolo are sleeping in their own room, the door cracked open. Julia and Robbie are asleep in Robbie's room. Above Saul, there is a crack winding out from the light fixture in the center of the ceiling. All is quiet.

He cannot stop thinking about Antonia's papa. He understands the violence inherent in the work he does. He perpetrates that violence. But how could they have killed one of their own? How could they have deprived Antonia of a father? How could Joey Colicchio have gone on afterward? It was the pragmatic thing to do — Saul understands this. It was the path of least conflict, least bloodshed, least upheaval. But how, Saul wonders, could Joey have dragged himself out of bed every day, knowing his best friend had been killed — *no,* he reminds himself, *disappeared, they don't say killed* — and how could Joey dress, and leave his home, and stand up all day under the crushing weight of knowing what had happened to Carlo — what he had done to Carlo? This is why Sofia had lied, he realizes. She had known Saul would have to do his job either way. She didn't want him to change the way he thought of Joey.

"Sofia," Saul whispers finally, unable to stand the snarl of his own thoughts any longer. *"Sofia?"*

Sofia turns. She has been sound asleep. "What," she murmurs. Saul is overcome with tenderness for her sleep-creased face, the way one of her arms reaches for him, unfolding from beneath the sheets. Her hand moving against his shoulder raises quick goosebumps. Saul sighs. He doesn't want to ruin her night, her rest. But he is bursting with unanswerable questions.

"Sofia, Antonia told me how her papa died today." Saul is whispering as quietly as he can. He has no interest in anyone else overhearing.

Sofia raises herself up on one elbow. "I

told you that, didn't I?"

Saul shakes his head. Sofia can do this: half asleep, she can make it so that he doesn't even remember whether she lied or not. "You just told me he disappeared," he says. "You didn't tell me why."

"I'm sorry," she says. "I guess I was protecting her."

"You were protecting *Joey,*" Saul says, more bitterness than he intended stealing into his voice.

"He's my father," says Sofia.

"How can we keep doing this?" asks Saul.

"Doing what?" And as Sofia squints through dry midnight eyes at Saul, a familiar sense of purpose steals over her like silk. Sofia Colicchio, talking a nervous Family man down.

"He wanted to leave, so they *killed* him? They left his daughter and his wife alone? How did Antonia marry Paolo, knowing what happened to her papa? How can you work for Joey? How can I?" Saul's whisper gets louder as he talks. It's inconceivable, to be in a world that is so very tangled up.

"Shh," says Sofia. "Julia and Robbie will hear you." She pauses. She is good at this when she is talking to a stranger, but she doesn't think Saul will be impressed by her batting eyelashes, her honeyed voice. She has no choice but to tell him what she really thinks. "I don't have the answers to all of your questions. When you say it like that, it doesn't make sense, does it? And you know how many questions I have. You know I can't ever keep my mouth shut. This 'don't talk about it' thing that my parents do — that my mamma always did — that doesn't work for me."

"So how can you —" begins Saul, but Sofia shakes her head.

"Family isn't so simple," says Sofia, and Saul can hear his mother's voice, telling him that God isn't so simple, and he can taste the darkened mildewed air in the ship on the way to America. "I used to think my papa was a god. And then eventually, I began to understand more of what went on, and I was so angry. Antonia's papa — Carlo was his name, Uncle Carlo — had *disappeared,* and we were all pretending like everything was fine, like it hadn't happened. I was angry at my parents all the time; I was angry at Antonia, even, angry at her for being okay when something so wrong had happened. And then you came, and it was like I learned that violence and war can result in something good, in love, even, which I think is what I had been learning my whole life."

"So it's my fault?" Saul finds himself angry. His whisper becomes a hiss. "I barely escaped a war with my life and you're telling me that's why you understand the value of violence? You would have left if not for me?"

"No," says Sofia, "of course not. But you helped me to understand that things are not all good or all bad. Because of war we have Julia. Because of violence Antonia and Paolo have Robbie. I can see both sides when I'm working. The people we help. I can see the good and the bad."

"You go out to dinner," says Saul, before he can help himself. "You don't see the violence."

Sofia's mouth becomes a thin line. "I was raised in it," she says icily. "And there is no changing what has happened already. So, you've decided you have a moral objection to the way things work. Do you propose we leave? Explain to Julia that she can never see Nonno or Nonna or Aunt Tonia or Uncle Paoli or Bibi again and flee and start over somewhere, and you can get a job bagging groceries and I can take care of Julia all on my own, and we can just worry for the rest of our lives that someday they would find us and you would disappear too? Because you would, eventually. They wouldn't spare you because of me." Sofia is whispering, too, but her words fill Saul's ears; they drown out everything else. "Do you think that would cause less pain than staying?"

Saul stares at the crack in the ceiling until he can hear Sofia's breaths even out again, and then he creeps off the mattress and into the kitchen, where he begins an elaborate breakfast, moving quietly so as not to wake anyone else before dawn.

Julia is the first one up. She stretches her limbs and drags her blanket into the living room, where Sofia is asleep alone. She crawls into the hollow where Saul's body had tossed for most of the night and presses herself against her mamma's back. When Saul next peeks into the living room he sees the heads of his daughter and wife lined up on the same pillow. Julia opens her eyes and says *Papa,* which is a command and a prayer and a pure, unfettered cry of love, and Saul opens his arms for her, imagines slicing himself open down the middle and enveloping Julia with every power of protection he has.

Antonia is not unhappy in her marriage.

There are many days she has everything she can imagine.

342

Those days Paolo gets home early enough that she is not run ragged and he is not so grouchy he spends the evening raging monotonously about how much use he could be in a different position. And she does not think about her papa, and she does not wonder if she made the right choice, and her mamma's voice saying *don't speak to anyone with slicked-back hair* does not echo in her mind.

Those days her baking turns out and she feels connected to Robbie, who still needs her desperately, from a wordless place in his small body, and who hangs and drags and claws against her until she lets him in, which some days she feels open and strong enough to do and which some days she is sure will destroy her. But some days Robbie practices his letters and they walk to the park and they joke with one another, and Antonia can see in his flawless face the man who will emerge, strong and sweet like his father, like his grandfather.

Those days she reads, in the patch of light that pours like liquid gold into their kitchen from ten to eleven in the morning as the sun passes overhead. She comes back to herself as the shadow of the next building over crosses onto her page and she feels exquisitely raw and preternaturally strong in those moments.

Those days she calls Sofia and Sofia is home, and she might go over there with Robbie, and drink coffee or wine with Sofia, and watch the sticks of dynamite that have replaced their children go spinning and spinning around the apartment, and she and Sofia might have an hour where because they are together, they can access themselves as children, and they can imagine themselves as old women. *Paolo thinks maybe when Robbie starts school full-time, I might look into classes at the college,* Antonia says. And so when Sofia responds, *I am hoping to be able to take on more work, then,* Antonia is having such a good day she does not respond, *you leave Julia with me so often it's as though she's in school already.* And as they leave, Antonia might be able to catch Julia and hold her close and smell her and look in her eyes and see Sofia flashing around their crinkled corners when Julia squeals and tries to get away.

Those days she starts dinner on time and the kitchen is filled with steam and spice, and Paolo rumbles in as she's chopping and slides his hands around her and pushes his face through her hair to her neck, and Antonia leans into his weight and feels warm electricity pulse down from Paolo's mouth through the center of her body.

A different life does not enter Antonia's thoughts.

But of course, the veil between different lives is thin. The alternate path is there. It is creeping up on Antonia; it is catching her scent. And soon, she won't be able to escape it.

The pox have faded almost completely from Julia's and Robbie's legs and Saul finds himself uncharacteristically restless on the fifth day of their seclusion in Antonia and Paolo's apartment, so in the afternoon he takes a walk. Paolo has gone to his office and Antonia and Sofia are curled together on the couch like tightly furled leaves and Julia and Robbie are wreaking quiet havoc in Robbie's room.

Saul turns left as he exits Paolo and Antonia's apartment and walks toward the water. It is one of his privileges: to walk where he wants without fear. Most everyone knows who he works for.

Saul feels the car before he sees it, coasting behind him as he walks. The hairs on the back of his neck and his forearms quiver. He does not turn around: the subtle dance of power in this neighborhood forbids him from acknowledging the car. He dares the driver to interrupt him; to ask for his time; to figure out whether to start with *excuse me* or *Mr. Colicchio* or *please pardon the intrusion, but* — but just then, someone from the car says, "Saul, right?" which is not what Saul was expecting, but which he can use to his advantage, assuming, as always, that there is an advantage to be had and lost in every conversation.

"That depends on who's asking," says Saul. He does not turn around; will not bend himself to look through the sliver of car window that has been rolled open.

"My name is Eli Leibovich. I think it's time you and I had a little chat."

Saul stops. He is surprised. He has lost any advantage he may ever have had in this interaction. He looks at the car, which rolls to a stop next to him. The door opens. Eli Leibovich is a little younger than Joey, with a dark strong brow and a mouth that turns slightly downward as he looks up at Saul. There are deep lines carved into his cheeks, from frowning and from laughing. He looks as though he has a lot to say.

"Get in," says Eli Leibovich. "My wife is making lunch."

Saul has learned about Eli Leibovich the same way he learned every other piece of relevant information for his job: by keeping his mouth shut and listening; by spending his sleepless hours connecting one small scrap of information to another; by replaying conversations.

In this way he has come to know that Eli Leibovich is the son of Lithuanian immigrants who fled the Russian Empire's increasingly anti-Semitic policies just before the new century. Eli himself was born in a ragged tenement building on Orchard Street. His mother bore ten children, six of whom survived to adulthood, and told fortunes to make ends meet. His father had been a physician in Lithuania. In New York, Eli Leibovich's father became a foreman in a garment factory. Eli was raised in the bloody belly of the Lower East Side, in a rear-facing three-room apartment with a shared bath. He decided, like so many before him, that he could use the skills he needed to survive there in more effective ways.

By 1940, Eli Leibovich was the coordinator of a citywide gambling syndicate. His games had high buy-ins and high payouts and invitations were widely sought after. Like in any gambling enterprise worth its chips, the house always won. Sometimes, after participants had been plied with snacks so salty they couldn't help but drink too much, the house won by a lot. And the consequences for being unable to pay a bill at a Leibovich game could be deadly.

Saul once heard a story about a man who showed up after Leibovich sharks got ahold of him with no skin on one of his arms.

In the old country before Eli Leibovich's parents fled for America, bouncing down a dirt road in a hidden compartment of a horse-drawn cart, Russian Orthodox authorities had stood by and watched while Jewish babies from a nearby village were torn limb from limb. They learned it is possible to tear a baby.

Violence was spawned with human beings in the primordial stew. It makes us less human, and yet.

Eli Leibovich lives with his wife and two daughters in a sprawling apartment overlooking the south curve of Prospect Park. It is lined with parquet floors; it is bordered by grand old windows, thick glass running down in the frames. One of the daughters takes Saul's coat; the other offers him a drink. Saul demurs, but Eli walks into the room just then, and claps Saul on the back as though they are good friends and says, "Come now, we're celebrating," and so Saul finds himself sitting with a cognac-heavy sidecar in the parlor, where the windows afford a panoramic view of the park to the north, and west, toward Manhattan. He feels hyper-aware of his posture, his skin; he tries to plaster a neutral expression onto his face but worries his nerves betray him.

Saul has never been to a meeting like this: unplanned, unannounced, not condoned by Joey or any other high-ranking boss. It is so forbidden it has never been expressly forbidden; so inconceivable no one has conceived of warning Saul against it. It is treachery, treason. Saul knows this. But curiosity races through him as he sits and sips his drink. He excuses himself to call Antonia's and tell his family he got caught up with work. *Back before dinner, I think,* he says.

Saul compliments the view; the drink; the subsequent meal: pickled beets and brisket, new potatoes immortalized in caramel schmaltz — he feels dizzy, but the room around him is in sharp focus. He is a child in flashes; each bite transports him and he can smell woodsmoke, bitter Berlin air, the musty inside of his school knapsack. His mother's skirt, unfolding around him. He feels the transition from Fianzo hostility to Leibovich hospitality like whiplash. His head spins.

After lunch, Eli brandishes two thick and fragrant cigars and he and Saul retire to a study at the end of the hall. The walls are lined with books; the desk stacked with papers.

"Thank you for coming," says Eli. His face is impossible to parse. Saul nods. "I've been interested in you for a while."

"Oh?" says Saul.

"Of course. A man of your — history. A man of my — cultural background. We've been working on opposite sides of this thing, haven't we? And I just can't make sense of that."

"Begging your pardon," says Saul, tiptoeing through a field of land mines, "but have we been opposed?" If he remains neutral, there is a way out of this trap: he can always tell Joey he was gathering information. *It was unplanned, boss,* he will say, *but I thought I might learn something useful.* His hands are sweating.

"If we aren't united," says Eli, "what are we?" Saul opens his mouth to answer and Eli stops him with a wave of his hand. "As much as I love to argue semantics, Saul, that isn't why I asked you here today. I wanted to offer you a job."

"I have a job," says Saul. Deep in his chest, some small hope or want begins to stir. Some unmentionable dissatisfaction yawns open.

"I'm offering you your culture back," says Eli. "Do you have a job and a full heart? A job and a sense of connection to where you come from? We take vacations, here. We have a summer house in the Hudson Valley. We come together for food, for birth, for death." Eli puffs at his cigar and blows two perfect smoke rings into the air of the study. "I'm offering you a fresh start," he says. "I'm offering you a family."

"I appreciate that," says Saul. "I know my situation isn't — traditional. But I have a job, and I have a family now."

Eli stands. Outside, the sun has stationed directly over Manhattan. Prospect Park is dressed in velvet light. "I understand that you feel some loyalty to the family of your wife, of your child. I respect that. I don't want to interfere with that. I just want you." Eli looks at Saul warmly, kindly. "I won't ask you to do anything that interferes with Joey's business. I wouldn't do that. It's the Fianzo Family I'm after. I shouldn't tell you that, but I trust you. I can tell I trust you. I can tell you're exactly what I need." Saul says nothing, but he wants very badly to trust Eli Leibovich in return. "It's getting late," Eli says, suddenly. "You should be getting back," he says. "Your wife isn't much for cooking, is she? Your daughter, she'll be getting hungry? And your work — it's consuming, lately. You aren't treated like family there. And you aren't sure how you fit into it all."

Saul is still silent. He remembers that when he was a child the Hitler youth often blackened his eyes, knocked his new hat into the gutter; once, held him down and smeared bacon rinds across his lips and called him *pig, pig, Unnütze Esser.* Useless eater. He was hungry; after they left, he licked the bacon from his face. It tasted of salt and his own blood from where his lips had pressed viciously against his teeth. After these encounters his mother would press him to her, wipe his face, squeeze him like she wanted to put him back inside her own body.

Saul pictures Tommy Fianzo Jr. looking at him like he is dirt. He pictures Sofia, sneaking out before he wakes up; Julia, spreading dirt from her shoes over his living room floor, unaware the way only a child can be willfully, infuriatingly unaware. He knows that his *job* is built on a bloodstained foundation, on the disappearance of Antonia's father, on the misery of the very people it sustains. And for a black hole moment, a sucking shaking earth-shattering instant, Saul wonders what he means when he says he has a family.

"Saul, when you decide you want to come home, give me a call."

Before he can blink, Saul finds himself standing in the late afternoon breeze. Cars zoom past him, hoping to beat rush hour. A thousand strangers going to a thousand different homes. *And do you have jobs?* Saul wonders, the incomprehensible diversity of lives around him, buzzing. *And do you have families?*

Saul calls Eli the next day and tells him he'll take the job. As he hangs up he feels elation bubble up within him. He turns out of the phone booth and faces the street and shouts, "HA!" surprising himself and a dusty family of pigeons.

Saul is making his own choices. He is making his own home. He finally feels like he is moving.

Of course, Saul cannot open the door and also control what comes in. So he exposes himself to the wide world of possibility. So danger scents him out, and, hungry, begins to stalk.

# BOOK FIVE

1947–1948

Saul spends the fall of 1947 living a breathless double life. He is a father to Julia, an employee and a son to Joey. He is a husband to Sofia. And every other Thursday at nine in the evening, when he stands on an otherwise unremarkable street corner in South Brooklyn and calls Eli, he is a traitor.

Eli is warm toward Saul, and kind, and speaks in a subtle cadence Saul would never have associated with home until home was taken from him. He speaks like the men at temple, bobbing their heads and asking after each other's families; in the next breath, arguing loudly. He speaks like the butcher with the best prices, the baker with the best rugelach, the super who used to change lightbulbs that were too high for Saul's mother to reach. When Eli laughs, Saul feels a bit of himself return, a small shred of soul he hadn't known was missing, and doesn't know how he lived without.

Taking Eli's offer had felt like medicine to Saul, who had become viscerally aware of everything he had given up or lost along the way to adulthood and who couldn't, no matter how he searched, find his way to a world in which he belonged completely. He assumed that everyone around him belonged completely to their worlds; that they felt no sadness, no shadow life they could have lived moving alongside them, and never a sense of homelessness inside their own homes, inside their own skins. His own world felt scarce in comparison.

And all Eli had wanted was information.

The Fianzo Family had long controlled the Red Hook docks, where they were beneficiaries of a cut of anything unloaded there. Saul was startled to learn this included the Colicchio imports — olive oil and wine, the finest cheeses, things that were forbidden during the war and remained prohibitively expensive to import via legitimate channels after the war was over. The docks also gave the Fianzo Family easy access to shipping channels, allowing them to get anyone or anything they wanted in or out of New York. After World War I, the Fianzos had been quietly renowned for their gunrunning operation. The docks allowed them to conceal crates of army surplus artillery on their way to somewhere else. The docks allowed them to spirit Lorenzo Fianzo, Tommy Sr.'s brother, back to Sicily when the Bureau of Investigation caught on. The docks gave the Fianzos steady income, as the unions designed to protect the longshoremen became incubators for corruption and extortion.

Eli Leibovich wanted control of those docks.

Saul started paying more attention to his and Joey's monthly meetings with Tommy Fianzo. On his way into the building he would count the men he saw posted casually around — two smoking outside the front, one standing in front of Tommy's office door. Once he got home he would scribble down every detail he could remember. *Different men in front this week but same guard in front of T.F.'s door. Office window has clear view west but obstructed by stack of shipping crates to the southwest.* If occasionally a flicker of guilt arose — Joey's face, offering Saul wisdom, a job, his daughter's hand in marriage; or Sofia, wide-eyed and beaming on the day Julia was born; or Julia herself, the warm, savage heart of her, exploding across the living room to hug Saul when he got home — Saul tamped it down, reminding himself that the Fianzos

359

were villains for the Colicchio Family too. *I'm helping them.* He can almost convince himself.

Of course, Saul's new side job doesn't just put him at risk. It risks destabilizing the peace Joey Colicchio has upheld since 1930. It risks starting a lethal turf war between Eli Leibovich and the Sicilian Families. It risks the very lives of everyone Saul loves.

Each month, Eli Leibovich receives Saul's scraps of information warmly, invites him for supper. At first, Saul declined; it felt unsafe, it felt disloyal. But curiosity and Eli's genuine charm won out. Eli's mother, who now lives in her own wing of Eli's sprawling apartment, hugged Saul the first time she met him. *A beautiful boy,* she called him, and Saul blanched and felt his heart and his stomach switch places; such was the power of being hugged by a mother who shares some inarticulable spirit with his own mother.

How simple family seems, from the outside. How desperate Saul becomes about the state of his own.

At home, Saul has started picking fights. Small ones, about Sofia's work hours. Julia's puzzles and playing cards, crusted in sugar or snot, abandoned on the living room rug. *Why can't we eat together like a normal family?* he asks one evening, sharp and dismayed. Julia, reading at the table as she balances steamed carrot slices on her fork, and Sofia, who has just run in, late again, look at Saul in surprise. *Sorry,* they say, which is unusual, because both of them are fighters, and Saul wonders what is so unstable about him that he has surprised them into apology. *I made chicken,* he says, by way of explanation. *It gets cold.*

Tonight, when Saul reaches the pay phone, he very consciously stands up straight and strides into the stall and pulls the sliding door shut behind him. The booth smells like hot trash and concrete. Saul pulls out his handkerchief and wipes the earpiece of the phone before sliding his dimes into the slot and dialing.

"Eli Leibovich," Eli says as he answers.

"It's me," says Saul.

"Saul! Right on time. Any news?"

"Nothing much this month. I'm sorry. You know, I'm not even sure they have plans for expansion right now." Saul can feel his usefulness ebbing. There is little he can pass along to Eli, other than the small details he can catalogue as he walks up the stairs to the Fianzo office and then back down.

"Everyone has plans for expansion, Saul," says Eli. "It's human nature." And then, "Tell you what: meet me for a drink this evening."

Saul is due at home. Sofia will notice if he's gone, and she might mention it to Rosa, or Joey. She might mention it to Antonia, who might mention it to Paolo, whose friendship with Saul has deteriorated over the last year along with his mental health and his own marriage. Paolo, who wanted so much more than his desk job.

"Saul?"

"I'm sorry, I can't this evening," says Saul. "My family."

"Your family," Eli repeats. "And how are they, your family?"

Saul doesn't like talking about his family with Eli. He compartmentalizes. "They're well," he says.

Eli can sense his reticence. "Call anytime," he says. Eli's warmth is a weapon. The kinder his voice, the more severe the consequences.

Saul hangs up, sweating.

*Everyone has plans for expansion,* says Eli, over and over again in Saul's head as Saul walks home. *It's human nature.*

*Is it?* Saul wonders. All he wants is to shrink into the places in his life where he

362

feels at home. All he wants is for those places to coexist.

When Robbie starts school, Antonia decides if she is ever going to go back to school herself she is going to have to take it into her own hands. So she hatches a plan: Monday and Wednesday mornings, after she has dropped Robbie off and Paolo has left for work, Antonia packs herself a snack and a notebook and a sweater, for it is always freezing in the library, and sneaks furtively out of her apartment and down the street, as if someone might stop her.

She still has no money for extracurriculars but the memory of reading Antigone in high school has come back to her like a long-lost friend and she has begun reading the classics section systematically. She sits curled into a chair like a snail into its shell in one of the vast, echoing stone reading rooms on the third floor and from nine in the morning to twelve noon, Antonia loses herself in the drama and heartache of another time entirely. Aeschylus and Euripides. Aristotle and Ovid.

Soon, Antonia finds *Metamorphoses,* a greasy, dog-eared copy that she becomes in thrall to almost immediately. Where teenage Antonia held on to stories of principle, of the great unfairnesses perpetrated by those in power, mamma Antonia prays to stories of evolution, stories that promise that no one is born into their final shape. She mouths words to herself, tasting them as they bounce along the tongue. She wonders if she herself has the capacity for change.

When she walks home in the early afternoon, Antonia is buoyant, the combined joy of exercising her brain and the adrenaline of keeping a new secret propelling her along. Of course, she knows in some way that this is a stopgap, something she made up to pass the time, to distract herself. She can see the concrete ways that the people around her have changed: Sofia, with her job; Lina, who has now built such a loyal clientele that she often sits with visiting women from dawn to dusk. Even Frankie, once small enough to balance with Antonia on one chair like a teddy bear, has begun saving money to move out of her parents' home. She cuts neighborhood ladies' hair and they forget she is only sixteen; her self-assurance is so contagious. Her face so poised.

*It's just us,* thinks Antonia. She and Paolo and Robbie. *It's just us who are standing still.*

The phone rings as Saul is finishing breakfast. Sofia is already gone, having kissed Julia's forehead and whispered to Saul, *my mamma can take her to school,* and then rather than kissing Saul, too, brandishing the bottoms of her shoes in a wave before disappearing in a cloud of Soir de Paris. Saul picks up the phone.

It is Joey. He is brief, but he asks Saul for a meeting.

The room where Saul has been told to wait for Joey is small and dark and smells like salted meat. There are two chairs, both soft brown leather that have seen better days, and there is an aged folding card table with an espresso machine and cups balanced precariously on one side. From the one dirty window a saturated afternoon light streams in, illuminating generations' worth of dust dancing in the air. On the ground floor, just below, is a sandwich shop, the din of which rustles up through the floor.

Saul sits in the room, accompanied only by his own curiosity about why he is here. He has gotten very good at waiting. At trusting; at holding himself still. He does this at work, when he has been given a job but not a reason for it; he does it at home, when Sofia is taken by a nameless rage or curiosity or joy but has not explained it to him.

He does it every other Thursday night, now, when he waits for Eli to pick up the phone. He did it, once, on a boat, rocking creakily from Europe to America, where the only thing he knew was that nothing was known.

Joey is late. When he pushes open the door Saul stands to shake his hand, to kiss the air next to his cheek.

"Ciao, buddy," says Joey, "I couldn't get here any sooner, did you get a coffee? That machine is dusty but it makes a perfect espresso." As he talks, Joey fills the espresso maker; tamps down the mound of fragrant ground coffee; gestures to see if Saul would like one.

"I'm fine, boss," says Saul. He is relaxing almost in spite of himself, that trademark Colicchio charm warming him up and weighing him down.

Joey turns around, holding two tiny espresso cups between his thumb and forefinger as though he hadn't heard that Saul didn't want any. He hands one to Saul, and settles himself into the other chair in the room. "Okay, alright. I'm ready. Saul. How's it going?"

Saul is afraid to speak. This is the flipside of working for Eli. His moments with Joey — especially alone — are terrifying. At any moment, Joey could reveal that he knows what Saul has been up to. Never mind that Eli has kept his promise — Saul hasn't been asked to give him any information on Joey. Saul knows it would make no difference. "It's going fine, boss," he says.

"Sofia? Julia?"

"They're good. They're great." Joey and Rosa had supper with them two nights ago. Joey had talked to Sofia just the night before, appearing in the doorway of their home like a specter to ask her if she could be at a restaurant on Sackett this morning to facilitate the delivery of some top-shelf olive oil.

"Good." Joey chuckles. "It's been good for Rosa, for us, to have you so close. There's been a lot of good lately. Sofia — you might have complicated feelings about it, Saul, and trust me, I understand, but Sofia has been a real asset for us." Joey pauses. "Does she seem happy to you?"

Saul thinks of Sofia, coming in late, leaving early. The flush of her cheeks when she tells him how she told off Mario Bruno, the new guy who thought since she was a woman she wouldn't notice him sneaking bottles of wine out of their delivery last week. *You should have seen his face. I just went over and said, "Is there something wrong with those?" He put the bottles back so fast it was like they had grown teeth. I thought he'd never get his jaw off the ground.*

"She seems happy," says Saul. A little relief. This doesn't seem like it is leading to a conversation about the ways Saul has betrayed all of them.

"That's good," says Joey. "That's better for all of us." Sofia's work is a problem Joey has solved. He regards the situation with detached satisfaction. He has had many arguments with Rosa, who cannot believe her daughter is letting herself be degraded — first by the dinners, and then by the shipments, *surrounded by gangsters and guns, Joey, what are you thinking?* These outbursts are followed by hours of silence, the dinner plates slammed on the table, the stony *yes, of course* in response to his *I think I know what I'm doing here.*

"I agree," says Saul. He sits back, leaning carefully against the dusty, wheezing old armchair. He sips his espresso and tells himself he will learn what he needs to know when he needs to know it. He tries to calm his heart.

"So listen," Joey says. "Things have not been going so well."

Saul does not react, or thinks he does not react. "How so, boss?"

"Well, I'm not alone here. You've seen how

368

things are going. Ever since the war we've been flailing a little, Saul. You've seen this. It is not Prohibition anymore. The days of champagne fountains and rivers of cash are over. There is more and more competition — Eli Leibovich, as I'm sure you know, would love nothing more than to edge us out of Red Hook. And he's getting more powerful, you know, he might be able to do it." Joey pauses. Saul shivers. Eli has promised him he does not want that. "And as you know," continues Joey, "we have extra expenses. The Fianzos have not, well. They have not lowered the rate of their percentage. That's an obligation we have." Joey looks down into his half-empty coffee cup, and Saul, on the edge of his seat, cannot tell whether he is being strung along like catgut on a violin or whether he is witnessing a genuine moment of vulnerability. "We have not quite found our stride," says Joey. "And I still command a certain respect. But that is increasingly not enough."

Saul leans forward and his chair creaks sadly in protest. "How can I help?"

Joey smiles, cat eyes sparkling, and leans forward in his own chair. "How would you feel about getting a promotion?"

Saul is silent. He wonders wryly how many people are offered as many jobs as he has been offered in his lifetime; how many of those offers, like these, weren't really offers, but incomprehensible moves in a life-size game of chess. "A promotion," he says, tasting it, buying himself some time.

"We need a change," says Joey. "I'm not stepping down, but I am looking for someone to take on some of my responsibilities. To share in the work, but also to shake up some of the old ways. If Sofia was my son, well. It might be different."

"And you want me to help?" asks Saul.

"I want you to be my number two," says Joey. "Officially. I want you to take some of my meetings, handle some of my conflicts, come up with some ideas for me. The monthly Fianzo meeting, to start — you've been coming along with me, you can do that yourself. I'll manage some of the big-scale things — and Sofia's work, I imagine it would be uncomfortable for you to do that, so I'll do it.

"I'm sure you've noticed we've spent a lot of time together lately. In some ways, you're already doing the job. But appearances mean a lot in this business." Joey is silent. He drains the espresso and puts the cup and saucer back on the table next to him. Then he interlaces his fingers and sighs, and Saul realizes that Joey looks tired, that in the curve of his spine and the heaviness of his facial features there is a profound exhaustion. "You're a more powerful tool than you realize, Saul. You disturb what people consider to be the natural order of things. I didn't always think that was the right strategy, but a lot has changed."

It would feel strange to say *thank you,* so Saul says nothing.

There is a thick silence between them. Saul doesn't know how to react.

"What do you think?" Joey asks.

Saul thinks. He thinks of Julia, running to hug him when he gets home, the voracity of her own desires the only thing she can comprehend or act on. He thinks of Sofia, opening her eyes in the morning and smiling at him, the clear light of her laugh, the magma of her rage. He thinks of his mother, whose name was never included on any of the death camp lists, whose house was leveled in the early years of the war, whom no one ever heard from again, and whom Saul has been unable to mourn, the way you are able to mourn someone who is gone, and so instead, whose absence Saul feels like a searing flame, a wrenching thing, a knot in his stomach, his heart, his head, constant. He thinks of the war that destroyed him and dumped him on a foreign shore. He was looking for family when he told Eli he'd join him. But he betrayed a family to do it.

"I can't," he tells Joey.

"Well, you're going to have to explain why," Joey says.

Saul feels suddenly that he might cry, and the thought of that is so reprehensible that he presses his mouth shut and closes his throat and digs one of his fingernails into the soft skin of his palm until the urge passes. "I appreciate everything you've done for me," he says. "I can't even begin to thank you for giving me this — this family. But I can't participate in any more wars. I can't — the violence, Joey, I can't do it." In his heart of hearts, of course, Saul knows that the violence doesn't bother him as much as it should. But he feels guilty. How can he accept a promotion from a man whose trust he has betrayed?

Joey nods. The air in the room is silent, heavy, waiting. "Do you know the story of my parents, before they brought me here?"

"No," says Saul. "Well — I know you were a baby."

"My father was an orchardist," says Joey. "He grew oranges and lemons. He loved those fucking trees. My whole life, he complained about the citrus in America." Joey picks up his cup, realizes it is empty.

Turns back to Saul. "I'm trying to cut back. So, my father grew oranges and lemons. When he was a boy, they kept the fruit on the island, or they shipped it to Rome. They traded boxes of fruit with neighbors who grew figs, or eggs, or chicory. They traded for fish, or they brought fruit in a cart to a small local market.

"But then," Joey continues, "after the unification of Italy, the rest of the world discovered the oranges, the lemons. And suddenly, they needed boxes of lemons on ships all around the world, to prevent scurvy. They needed to marinate their meat; they needed lemonade, they needed to eat oranges all winter. The price of oranges went up. The demand went up. And no one in Sicily could afford them anymore. My father's father had to ship his oranges out on a schedule, boxed and packaged. He wasn't making much more money, but there were new middlemen, who would jack the prices up when ships came to port, or during holiday seasons. All over the world, people were eating Sicilian fruit. And it was in such high demand that it started to be stolen. My grandfather would wake in the morning and trees that had been dripping with fruit the night before would be empty, stripped of all their fruit and even their leaves. Their branches would be broken; the earth around them would be destroyed. This was happening to farmers all over the island.

"Can you guess what happened next?" asks Joey.

Saul shakes his head.

"Yes, you can. But I'll tell you. A new market emerged. People who offered to protect orange and lemon groves, for a cut of the profits. Networks of citrus body-guards, if you will. It was usually peaceful, but there were people — would-be thieves, mostly — who were hurt, even killed, in that time.

"Our profession has gotten a bad reputa-tion," says Joey. "And to be sure, it has changed. We are not renegade orange sol-diers anymore. There are ways we have been corrupted. There are people — there are people I have hurt, Saul, who I wish I had not. But I applaud the men who guarded those orange groves. They saved the liveli-hoods of whole families. They allowed children to come into the world, and old people to be cared for. They defended small farmers against the conflict and violence and desperation caused by powerful and faraway leaders. They took care of their own, rather than trusting the government to do it.

"You're right, Saul, that war is a cancer. It is an ugly stain on the earth. It is the expression of deep human cowardice and fear. It is the whims of men in power, men who have rarely earned that power, sending children to fight their petty conflicts. It is the adult version of fort-building, pitting people against one another. They made Italy out of separate peoples, told us to speak one language, expected us to defend their borders for them. They made up those borders. They make up all borders.

"I know that you lost your home. I know that you lost your mamma. Saul, I am so sorry that happened to you." Joey pauses. Saul is breathless and rapt. He can see his whole life running like a river from one end of his brain to the other. His mother, bending to hold his face.

"This is your choice, Saul. But please hear me when I tell you. I would never ask you to fight a war. I am asking you to be a part of a family. To build something, not to destroy it. To protect our oranges." Saul cannot speak, but he overflows with gratitude toward this man, who has acted so like a father toward him. Who has, he realizes, taken Saul in, and who must have faced extreme opposition from his own community. Saul has always blamed Joey for taking his culture from him. He has never understood the magnitude of what he has been given in return.

Joey stands. He puts a small brown paper bag on the table. He nods to Saul, and presses his lips together. He says, "Let me know what you can, when you can. And please, pass this along to Sofia. I've kept it for her." And then he walks out of the room, the door closing behind him like a sigh.

Saul already knows he will say yes. His head is buzzing; the afternoon light is beaming through the dusty window in otherworldly planes; the air fairly echoes, as though it remembers Joey's booming voice.

Saul stands and walks to the table, wobbling like he has been at sea.

There is a note pinned to the outside of the brown paper bag. It says, *Sofia: I think I always knew this was for you.*

Saul unfolds the top of the bag and peers inside.

Sitting at the bottom, naked as a baby, is a gleaming pearl-handled revolver.

Later that day, Antonia is on her knees at the edge of the bathtub, trying to scrub out a dark ring while Robbie makes a mess in the kitchen, when she hears a door slam and then Paolo shout, "He's being groomed, Tonia." His angry footsteps cross the short expanse of their home. Paolo swings open the bathroom door and Antonia looks up at him with one eye. "Did you hear me?"

"I heard you," she says. She had just that morning read about Famine, whose thinness and pallor and utter vacancy nonetheless inspired in others an insatiable hunger. There is something Paolo hungers for, uncontrollably; some bit of Antonia's attention she cannot find within herself to give him. *Her belly, no more an indication of where a belly might be found.*

"Saul just called me at the office to tell me that Joey is making him his right-hand man. He's being groomed to take over." Paolo sits on the edge of the toilet and puts his face in his hands. "I thought it might be me. I thought my life was headed toward something more."

"Paolo." Antonia wants to say more than this. She can tell Paolo is waiting for something reassuring, that he is expecting her to make him bigger by giving him a small piece of herself. But she cannot give him any more, because she is feeling a wave of powerful disappointment. Their home, which is small and more chaotic than either of them had wanted, seems to shrink in on Paolo and Antonia in their bathroom.

Escape seems impossible. Antonia has no more words to give Paolo. No more of her self. *Just as the sea receives from round the world its rivers, and is never satisfied . . . all his eating only left him empty.*

"I wanted more than this," Paolo says, gesturing at the bathroom, its peeling paint, its thumping pipes. "I wanted to give you more than this."

"I'm happy," says Antonia. This is automatic, but it will quell the questions Paolo and Antonia do not want to ask one another. Questions like, *how did we get here?* And more importantly, *how do we get out?* And, terrifyingly, *can we do it together?* There is a crash from the kitchen. "Look, can you go check on Robbie? Can we do this later?" Paolo stands and walks out of the bathroom. Antonia wrings the rag between her fingers until they chafe.

A week later Antonia wakes with her skin aching against her nightgown. She knows she's pregnant even before she stumbles to the bathroom. She kneels on the tile floor with the side of her face against the porcelain of her bathtub and counts days. She had been careful — as careful as she could be — since Robbie was born. *What would be so bad about another baby?* Paolo has asked her as she turns away from him, saying, *not this week.*

*What would be so bad about another baby?* Antonia asks herself now. From the other end of the apartment she can hear Robbie stirring. Paolo has already left for the office — he goes earlier and earlier, as if he can escape his desk duties by overachieving.

When she has controlled herself Antonia stands and walks into the kitchen to make Robbie breakfast. He pads down the hall after her, black hair pressed into an architectural post-sleep sculpture. He wraps a proprietary arm around the low point of her hip bone, leans his head against her. "Mamma," he says. "Hi, baby," Antonia replies.

Five years ago she lay holding him — the same person, somehow, but nine pounds and wailing, reaching, a small packaged parcel of unending, absolute need. Antonia remembers settling Robbie to her breast and shutting her eyes, trying to be somewhere else. Trying to be someone else. Sure she couldn't feed Robbie when she was just an aching cavern of need herself.

Antonia puts a hand to her belly and feels fear like ice water trickling down her spine.

The idea of a raw egg makes her queasy and she slathers jam on toast for Robbie, who settles into his chair at the kitchen table with a comic book. "School starts soon," Antonia says to Robbie. He nods. He swings his feet against the floor, scuffing it like Sofia used to do. While he eats, Antonia calls Sofia.

Sofia and Antonia carve the afternoon out of their regular lives to spend together, just the two of them.

They don't do this often anymore, so there is a moment it is strained: the conversation dragging behind them, each of them flicking her eyes up to the clock behind the deli counter. They are eating pastrami sandwiches downtown.

"How did you find this place, again?" Antonia asks.

"Saul used to *work* here," replies Sofia. "He took me here once before we got married. He says they make the best pastrami in the city."

Antonia's mouth is full. She nods. There is something fluttering in her heart; she has not told Sofia the reason for their lunch. She feels rebellious, like drinking martinis all day, like being late to pick up Robbie from school, like shucking off her responsibilities, one by one like corn husks, until her glistening insides are exposed to the sun. She suggested *downtown;* she is wearing slacks, which bunch uncomfortably in her lap and which, she realizes, as the pastrami fills her up like a water balloon held over the mouth of a fire hydrant, might not have been practical for this particular lunch spot.

"Can you imagine?" Sofia says, looking around. "If Papa hadn't given him a job, Saul could still be working here."

Antonia swallows; she has been preoccupied by this exact thought experiment

381

lately: what if, could have been. She looks back and sees her life as a series of branching paths; she is obsessed with wondering what would have happened if she had taken another. If she had saved up and gone to university. If she had gotten pregnant before she was married. If she had never found her way back to her mamma. If her papa had never been killed. If she had never married Paolo. If she hadn't messed up her days last month. Inside her belly she imagines something growing. She imagines herself disintegrating. *Stupid,* she tells herself.

"What's wrong?" Sofia asks.

"Nothing," says Antonia. "How's work."

Work is exhilarating. It demands all of Sofia's focus. It helps her feel out into the edges of her skin, little electric jolts from head to toe. "It's the same," says Sofia. She is careful. Antonia is not outwardly judgmental but there was an awkward year between them when Sofia started and she wants badly to have it all: her friendship, her family, her Family. She finds herself being tactful, which she has never done before.

"And Julia?"

Julia is obsessed with bugs. She skins her knees; she collects moths in a jar. She flips through old copies of *National Geographic* sitting upside down on the sofa, so her hair hangs down to the floor and her feet kick absentmindedly near the headrests. Rosa is scandalized; her meager efforts not to show it only serve to accentuate the purse of her lips, the small disparaging shake of her head. "Julia is like a wild animal," says Sofia. Julia still burrows into Sofia and Saul's bed some nights, though she is always gone by the time they wake up. "She's amazing," says Sofia, though she is torn, as she always is, between the world in which Julia needs Sofia and the world in which Sofia needs herself. This is something Sofia has never been able to navigate smoothly, so she oscillates: coming home after Julia is asleep every night for a week and then taking her to Coney Island for the day, snapping at Julia about something small and then buying her the stuffed animal, the ice cream for dinner. Sofia marvels at Julia, but she is scared constantly: that she will lose herself in the love she feels, or that Julia will not reciprocate it and Sofia will have thrown her love into a void. She knows in her heart of hearts that working has not made her a worse parent; still, there are only so many unwritten expectations one can defy before questioning one's own instincts.

"How's Robbie?"

Robbie is sensitive. He is creative and full

of love, but he is unstable in a way Antonia has never been unstable. He has not inherited Antonia's even keel; he has her self-awareness, her expanding and generous consciousness for everything around her, but he has Paolo's misery when things don't go smoothly. The smallest setback can derail him. She feels like the heart of her family, the only thing holding it together.

"Tonia?"

"He's fine," says Antonia.

Silence descends. Antonia and Sofia chew their sandwiches. Antonia can feel herself shrinking under Sofia's gaze, even as inside of her, cells divide, and she grows.

"How long before you have to be back for Robbie?" asks Sofia, and if Antonia wasn't otherwise distracted this question would send her into fury: Julia and Robbie go to the same school; they get home at the same time. Sofia has abdicated the realm of normal motherhood, of responsibility, of knowing what's in the fridge, where the lost shoe is, which comb won't yank the hair out as it brushes.

"I'm pregnant," is what Antonia says in response.

Now Sofia puts down her sandwich. "Tonia, congratulations," she says. She is warm and expansive. She wants Antonia to be happy.

Antonia begins to cry. She holds her napkin to her face and shakes, as quietly as she can.

"Tonia," says Sofia, quietly now, urgently, "what is it."

Antonia stops crying by sheer force of will. She holds her brimming eyes as still as possible and opens her sandwich to tear a piece of pastrami into thin strips. She watches the pink juice well up.

"Tonia," says Sofia.

"Do you remember how this went, last time?" asks Antonia.

"I remember," says Sofia.

"I'm worried I'll disappear this time," says Antonia.

"You won't," says Sofia.

"I've been worried for months," says Antonia.

"Worried," repeats Sofia.

"I've been worried, I guess, that I've made all the wrong choices."

"What choices?"

"I should have gone to university." Antonia dips pastrami in mustard.

"You still could," says Sofia.

"I'm worried — I'm worried I shouldn't have married — so young. I'm worried there were other options, and I didn't even consider them. And now I can't. Consider them."

"Of course you can," says Sofia, and then, "What kind of options?" She is unnerved. Antonia, the metronome of Sofia's world, seems to be rocking faster and faster.

"My mamma never wanted me to marry into the Family," says Antonia. "And she's so — she just does things at exactly her own speed now, have you noticed that?"

"Yes," says Sofia. And then, quietly, "I really admire her."

"I don't, usually!" says Antonia, stomping her foot on the floor so hard the plates jump in their trays on the table. She looks around; lowers her voice. "I don't. I think I would be lonely. There are things to do in the world, and I want to do them." Antonia pauses. She can feel her heart racing. She can feel her mouth moving, faster than her thoughts. "But I don't know if I thought this life through. You know since Saul was promoted Paolo won't be, for years now? Change happens slowly. And I'm happy. I'm fortunate. I'm fortunate. But we've been in that apartment for a long time." Antonia chews on her straw. "Even Frankie works, you know."

Sofia nods. "I know," she says. She hadn't

thought about the ripple effects of Saul's promotion, the way it would bloom out away from their small family. Saul works longer hours, now, and Julia spends more evenings with Rosa or Antonia. Sofia keeps a gun in the drawer of her nightstand, now. Saul handed it to her in a nondescript paper bag and Sofia accepted it as her birthright. It was easy, to take on power that had until recently been inconceivable. When she feels small or overwhelmed she opens the drawer to look at it: the muscle of its trigger, the flesh of its handle. Knowing it is there makes Sofia feel powerful, a warmth washing up her thighs and down her spine. She realizes, sitting across from Antonia, that maybe the power she has is power that was taken away from other people.

Antonia stares past Sofia's shoulder. "I don't know what to do, Sof. I'm worried I was so surprised someone loved me that I missed out on — on — on everything!" Antonia tastes acid at the back of her mouth; her vision swims. Antonia is not a shouter; she is not a blurter-out of strange sad things. She is a thinker, a muser, a thoughtful deliberator. She is shaking with disappointment; with a fear that what she has just shouted in the deli is *true*.

And now something different rises in

Sofia, something she tries to push away before it has a name, but which is insistent, and strengthens quickly. How often has she shrunk herself in front of Antonia, because she has some sixth sense that Antonia disapproves of what she is doing? How frequently does she pretend not to love her work as much as she does, or subtly not mention it in front of Antonia? At what point did the tact Sofia tries to employ to keep her relationship with Antonia peaceful become its own kind of box she does not fit into? Sofia raises her face away from her drink, brow in a knot, elbows on the table. "Tonia," she begins. And then she stops, to make sure she wants to say what she is about to say, and then she takes a breath and says, "No one is stopping you from doing any of these things but yourself."

There is silence at their table. And then Antonia says, "You might be right," and this makes Sofia feel cruel and harsh: she had expected icy eyes, a *you don't understand.* "But it doesn't feel that way."

"Do you love Paolo?" asks Sofia. And the way she asks it makes Antonia feel like she could answer yes or no and either would be okay. Sofia asks as if *do you love your husband* is a question like any other.

"I love him," says Antonia. She pushes her

thumb into the seedy center of half a dill pickle, making a mushy fingerprint. "But our house is quiet, Sof. I love him, but he's not happy. I never thought I'd end up in an unhappy house, but I feel like I've been in one my whole life, now." The sadness of hearing this out loud rounds Antonia's shoulders; her face fills up; her eyes brim over. "I should have married out of the Family," she says. "I should have listened to my mamma."

Sofia reaches across the table to hold Antonia's hands. "Sometimes," she says, "I think about what it would have been like if I had never become a mother." Antonia looks up at her. *If I can see you, I must be here.* "But it doesn't mean I don't want to be one, Tonia. It doesn't mean I can't do other things." *If you can see me, I must be here.*

"I should have gone to Egypt," says Antonia. "I should have lived on top of a mountain somewhere. Do you remember Mr. Monaghan? That game we used to play, spinning the globe?"

Sofia nods.

"I play it in my head," says Antonia. "When I feel lost, or restless. I spin a globe and think about where I might go."

■ ■ ■ ■

No one has asked Sofia when her second baby is coming in a long time, and for this, she is grateful. They are scared of her, or they don't think she's a good parent, or both. She's ascended into a strange in-between world: she's stayed well within the bounds of the Family, but has moved out of the realm of women, so people don't know how to interact with her. The girls she went to school with have turned into stiff-nosed women. Sofia passes them on the street, in the market. They are all on their second or fifth baby. The wives of the men who come to Sunday dinner are always pregnant.

Sometimes Sofia remembers how she felt the morning Julia was born, before she left for the hospital. The way she knew — she *knew* — she could ride the waves of her labor all the way to the top of the world. The power of that, and the simultaneous powerlessness of motherhood, the way she can love Julia and have no control over Julia's happiness, the way she is reduced to a voiceless decoration once people know she is a parent, even though she contains everything needed to build a world from nothing. There are days she's sure of herself, sure of her choices, confident that she can point herself in any direction. But in the car back to Brooklyn, Antonia silent in the backseat next to her, Sofia is overcome by a sudden rush of despair.

And Sofia feels a small flicker of fear, thinking about Antonia having another baby. She almost didn't come back from the last one.

Late at night, Antonia turns to her side and cranes her neck to look out the window at the head of her bed. She stretches out an arm and presses her hand against the brick wall there. The wall presses back, cool, alive. Antonia shuts her eyes and she imagines being five, feeling for Sofia on the other side of their shared wall. Tonight she feels she might be the only person for a thousand miles; not even Sofia can help her. The cavern of surprise loneliness, unexpected disappointment, sucks her in and spreads out around her, blacking out all the light. *If you can see me,* she prays, *I must be here.*

But out in the dark, Antonia knows, Sofia is doing God-knows-what. With God-knows-whom. For God-knows-how-long.

It is October in Red Hook, and Saul is leaving his Fianzo meeting, driving his feet into the metal of the stairwell. He bursts outside and lets the door crash shut behind him; the sound echoes back up the building and out over the water, as though he has slammed the door on Red Hook itself, on New York, on the rules of this strange world in which he finds himself.

Saul has been taking these monthly meetings alone since July. But today, as though Tommy Fianzo had coordinated his transition with Joey's, Saul met with Tommy Fianzo Jr. *I'll waste no time,* he had begun, smirk crawling like a centipede across his face, *I'm going to be doing things differently than my father did. He was comfortable with you running things. I'm not.* Tommy Fianzo Jr., with his slick-greased hair and his grease-slick nose; with his thick Fianzo fingers like sausages, pulling violently at the laid slices of capocollo on a plate on his desk; his mouth like purple worms; like viscera; the red wine stains in circles on the table. Saul didn't touch his own wine; he took a certain satisfaction in refusing the ceremonial trappings of congenial meetings; he could assert, at least, that he was no fool.

Tommy Fianzo Jr. had looked at Saul like a dirty thing. Saul had swallowed the salt and bile of being unable to say what he so longed to say. With anyone else, he would have scoffed, said, *your comfort is not my concern.* But he is sobered by the seriousness of this feud; he is quiet with disbelief that Joey never found a way out of this atrophied and bloodstained relationship.

*I'll be watching you, my Jewish friend,* Tommy Fianzo Jr. had said, before taking Saul's meticulously filled envelope and tossing it in a drawer, pointedly careless. *Very fucking carefully.*

"I'll walk," Saul says to his driver. The driver tips his hat; his ride rolls slowly away. Saul turns north, to walk under the new highway. The line between Red Hook and Carroll Gardens buzzes now; it hums with construction, with transition; it vibrates the very core of South Brooklyn.

Managing two jobs is taking a toll on Saul.

He worries constantly. He jumps in public, thinking that every shred of overheard conversation is his name, that every wallet withdrawn from a suit pocket is the gun that will reveal he has been found out.

Saul doesn't know what to do.

Sometimes, when he is talking to Eli, he brings up the bounds of their relationship, carefully, trying to ascertain how long Eli imagines their partnership lasting. *Someday,* he says. *Eventually.* And once, *of course, won't always be sustainable.* Eli has not so much as shrugged in response, has not ever inclined his head as Saul dances around the question: *how will I get out of this?* Saul could infer that Eli has no plans to let him go, but he is hopeful, or stubborn, or desperate.

During the winter, as 1947 slips into 1948, Saul and Sofia alternate between short, vicious arguments and a manic kind of attraction to one another. Both stop them in their tracks, make them late for work. Saul wonders if it is the energy of the secrets he is keeping — if working for both Eli Leibovich and Joey has managed to make him conductive, if his marriage has become an electrical current.

He knows it can't last forever.

As the days grow colder, Antonia grows larger and larger. She eats ravenously. She sleeps ten hours a night. Robbie is late to school twice. Antonia gets a second alarm clock, but no bigger clothes. There are angry red lines across her belly and back at the end of the day.

Antonia fits herself into her old life for as long as she can. She sucks her stomach in. Her fear tangles itself amongst the buttons and zippers she begins to strain against. She stops going to the library to read after she vomits into a trash can, unable to make it to the women's bathroom. This is a small failure, one she lines up with her others. Where did she think she was going, truly: a housewife spending mornings at a public library? What a flimsy way of convincing herself she was changing. Not unlike Lina, reading to avoid the ways her life was still bound to the Family that destroyed her. Antonia feels desperate, some days, and resigned, others.

When she lies down to sleep at night, her heart beats furiously against her chest. She is transported into visceral memories of the months after Robbie was born. It is a time in her life she has carefully contained: an aberration, a cautionary tale. But she remembers now. Every time Antonia shuts her eyes, she remembers pain, holding herself together so she could pee without splitting down the middle. The months she knew the world was there but could not make herself a part of it, like there was an impenetrable film suffocating her. The fear she felt at being in the same room as everyone she loved, but also, a thousand miles away.

When Antonia told Paolo she was pregnant, he took her in his arms and cried, and then he promised to be more grateful, less ornery, less dissatisfied with his job, with his lot. He stays like this all winter, telling her to put her feet up, not to lift that, *Robbie, for God's sake don't torture your mother.* So there are moments of perfect joy, when Antonia can imagine she is twenty, and marrying a beautiful man, and planning to have three babies and live in a spacious and bright home, which somehow, in her imagination, always smells like the ocean.

But when Antonia dreams, Carlo stands just out of her reach with his back to her. They are at the seashore. The water is still and opaque; it is both the end of the world and the source. Carlo walks away from Antonia toward the water. She screams *Papa* at the top of her lungs. He doesn't turn around. *Papa, Papa.* Antonia rages. Her feet are stuck in the sand; she is too weak to pull them out, to go in after her papa. She watches as Carlo disappears into the sea.

When she wakes from these dreams she is angry. With herself, because Antonia often directs her frustration inward. But also, with Paolo. This is something she won't explain to him. *I'm angry because you got me pregnant* is a shameful sentiment, and Antonia cannot voice it. But Paolo knows. He can see the way Antonia shields herself from him, the way she holds herself slightly more erect in any room he enters. He is kinder in response, but he also works longer hours, lingering at the office, calling Joey to ask for extra tasks.

And so the rift deepens. The winter wind strengthens. The dark, cold months pass. And the valence of Antonia and Paolo's divide takes on a certain seriousness. They begin to forget their way back to one another.

Robbie knows all of this without actually knowing it. He can feel that there is a deep and deadly chasm in any room both of his parents are in. It is populated by silence and apathy. Later in his life, Robbie will know this was a dark time in his household because he will retain almost no memories of his mother while she was pregnant. He's old enough to notice it, and he is sensitive, so he feels it. But in his memory, this year will be blank.

For everyone else, it will be unforgettable.

Robbie and Julia know exactly what their family business consists of but not how it is accomplished. Their families, of course, would like to keep it that way for as long as possible. But as they hurtle toward their sixth birthdays they notice what seems like more closed doors than usual. More late-night whispers in the walls of their homes, as their fathers shuffle quietly back and forth, planning. Plotting.

Curiosity grows in Robbie and Julia, beanstalks of it sprouting in their stomachs and pushing up and out of their mouths. *Where are you going, Papa?* Julia asks Saul as he leaves on a Thursday night. *The Empire State Building,* Saul responds. He is distracted. Julia loves the Empire State Building. *You're not,* she says. *What are you doing?* Saul adjusts the collar of his shirt in the hallway mirror. *It's too late for you to be up, Jules,* he says. *Should I ask Nonna to come read you a story?* And then, *I love you.* And then Saul is gone, and in the click of the front door shutting Julia finds she is hungry, and frightened. Information might have fed her.

Julia cannot sleep that night. She twists and turns so she sweats damp spots into every inch of her bedsheets.

Robbie, gifted with slightly more stealth than Julia, creeps along the middle rooms of his apartment. His papa came home from work and shut the bedroom door and his mamma is in there now, too, the low hum of her voice against the sharp crackle of his. *Stuck here,* Robbie hears. *Half-assed . . . legacy.* And then nothing, and then, *Minchia!* which if Robbie said, his mamma would chase him around the apartment with a bar of Ivory soap to wash his mouth. And then his mamma's syrup, the tone she uses to calm Robbie down too. And then footsteps. Robbie flees to the kitchen table and has to pretend he has been practicing writing the alphabet the whole time. His mamma comes into the kitchen, where she braces a hand against her back and holds herself up against the counter with the other. She breathes, *shhhh,* a loud soothing sigh. The bigger she gets, the more inaccessible she seems to him.

Robbie promised to tell Julia if he learns anything but he goes to bed instead, because he has a small sickening feeling that there is something cracking in his family, some foundational beam that until recently had held them all up, held them together. That night he listens to his papa snoring and pictures himself falling deeper and deeper into his bed with every one of Paolo's rolling exhales. Deeper and deeper until he falls through the mattress. Robbie sinks through the floor. He buries himself in the ground itself.

Spring passes in a flash. Antonia grows. She spends the first truly hot day of summer irritated and alone. She watches Robbie through the front window as he leaves for school and then tries and fails to focus on tidying the house, on balancing the checkbook, on reading, on making a grocery list. She casts tasks aside one by one. She curls into herself like a wave.

Antonia is not surprised when, after a haphazard lunch of toast, her stomach tightens like a vise and she barely makes it to the bathroom in time to throw it up. She is not surprised when she feels a low ache thrumming through her. She calls Lina, but there is no answer. She calls Sofia, who must be working, and then she takes a taxi to the hospital.

*In Antonia's twilight dream she is standing at the edge of the ocean. Carlo is a few paces ahead of her. The water swells toward them and then away, like the whole world is being rocked to sleep. Antonia cannot see Carlo's whole face; it will not come into focus. But she can see the lines on Carlo's hands, the five o'clock shadow darkening his jaw, the way the muscles of his back ripple as he steadies himself against the wind. Papa, she says, I'm scared.*

*Here, he says, but he doesn't move. Take this.*

*Antonia steps forward. The cold water closes over her ankles. When Antonia looks down at her outstretched palms she is holding a pearl-handled gun.*

Paolo and Antonia name their new baby Enzo, after Paolo's brother who died in the war. Antonia weeps for the whole first week after he is born: poring over his dark brown eyes, his long thin fingers, which are like Robbie's, like Paolo's. She weeps in gratitude that her body has stayed whole, the jagged scar from Robbie's birth still intact, the inside of her body in and the baby out, the miracle of that exchange. She weeps as they leave the hospital, as they settle in at home. She weeps and she knows Paolo doesn't understand, knows she is pushing him away, knows he is scared, but she does not yet have the energy to call him back to her. She weeps, and she comes back to herself. She weeps in relief, because it is exhausting to be terrified for nine months, because it is exhausting to spend your life scared, your whole life since the morning your papa disappeared, really, but now you are an adult with two children, two perfectly formed human people that you made, and you know, the way some knowledge is given from above or outside, somewhere external and eternal, you know that it is time.

Take the gun.

Walk into the water.

Almost two weeks pass. Saul and Sofia and Julia spend every moment at Antonia and Paolo's apartment. They rock Enzo and teach Robbie how to hold his brother. Julia watches from a darkened corner, fascinated but uncharacteristically cautious, almost fearful. The seven of them are as happy as they've ever been.

On Friday, Saul leaves in the early afternoon for his Fianzo meeting.

He escapes each of these meetings as quickly as he can, but they stain the first Friday of each month like grease, like wine, like blood. The sweetness of his new nephew fills him with loathing toward Tommy Fianzo Jr., who never misses a chance to belittle Saul, to make Saul feel small in the hopes of making himself feel more important. Saul could use his growing family as motivation to be more patient with Tommy Jr. But he doesn't. Today, instead, he gets careless.

As Saul shoves the front door open like a battering ram, a slip of paper dislodges itself from his pocket. It falls like an autumn leaf down toward the ground. As Saul stalks off toward his waiting ride, the slip of paper lands on the burning asphalt. Saul doesn't notice as he walks away. His pocket does not feel empty on the drive home.

*2 guards today,* the paper says. *Summer busy for F's. Shipping season? Winter is quieter.*

Tommy Fianzo Jr.'s doorman reaches down and picks up the sheet of paper. He mouths the words on it as he deciphers Saul's handwriting.

"Get the boss down here," he says once he reads it.

■ ■ ■ ■

In her apartment in Red Hook, Lina wakes with a jump, as though someone has shaken her. She has taken a nap because she has been spending nights wide-eyed and sweating, some deep internal disturbance keeping her from dreaming. When she slips into shallow sleep at night she wakes half an hour later, her skin slick and icy.

With her eyes closed, Lina can feel a crackling in the air, an omen of change sneaking along the floorboards. Vines of it winding their way up and down the banisters. Something big is coming.

Two days later, Sofia is sweating in her kitchen.

It's not true that Sofia isn't much for cooking. She doesn't know that Eli said this about her, but she knows it's whispered about in the neighborhood shops. Groups of mothers stop their conversations when Sofia approaches with her shopping basket. *Trying something new?* they might ask. *Just some staples,* Sofia responds, as haughtily as she can while weighed down by flour, tomatoes, eggs, garlic.

Sofia knows her mamma's recipes the way she knows the rhythm of a Sunday Mass. Just because she doesn't use them every day doesn't mean they aren't there.

By sense-memory, she unrolls the flank steak. It curls slightly, the blood and muscle of it contracting on her counter. It smells like coins. She takes a mallet and pounds it until it lies flat. It will be lined with speckled sliced mortadella, a layer of wilted spinach, and a mixture of basil, parsley, pine nuts, and parmesan. It will be rolled up and simmered in wine, tomatoes, and bay. All the windows in the house are open, lazy fans pushing the hot kitchen air around. Sofia's hair is plastered to the back of her neck

The front door clicks. It's not Saul, who is late. It's Antonia, holding the small bundle of baby Enzo in one arm and a shopping bag in the other. "Christ, Tonia, you gave birth two weeks ago, what are you doing shopping?" Sofia asks. She wraps Antonia in her arms and then unwraps Enzo from his bundle of blankets and kisses him. "It's a thousand degrees out, and you have him in all these blankets!"

Sofia hopes her voice is cheery but not saccharine; she examines Antonia as closely as she can. Antonia looks exhausted, but her hair is clean. Her eyes meet Sofia's. *She seems okay,* Sofia thinks. "Are you okay?" she asks Antonia.

"I am," says Antonia. She is almost giddy. She is sleepless and aching still, but she is so surprised she survived her second birth that she's been cheerful, almost bubbly. Robbie has had to squirm away from her grasping hands; Paolo wonders where his mild-mannered, brooding wife has gone.

Antonia is superwoman. Antonia can do anything. "I'm going to ask your mamma about the seafood." Antonia leaves Sofia singing to Enzo in the hallway.

Sofia can just sense Robbie, sprinting off into the recesses of the apartment to find Julia. She looks down into Enzo's liquid brown eyes, his wrinkled face. "Is your mamma okay?" Sofia asks him. Enzo does not answer.

Sofia hears a key in the lock and she hopes it is Saul this time.

And then she hears a door slam.

Saul knew showing at dinner would cause a stir but not showing would be an even bigger problem and so he is standing in his front hall, wincing as he brushes his curls away from his eyes, as he shrugs off the trappings of his briefcase, his shoes. The house smells like meat and spices and his mouth waters. He hasn't eaten in hours.

"Paolo, is that you?" comes Antonia's voice. "Paolo, I asked you to meet me at the house this afternoon, did you forget?" She is walking toward Saul, who has the impulse to turn toward the wall. Instead he freezes, and so when Antonia turns into the entryway she is face-to-face with Saul, whose eye has been blackened and whose lip has been purpled and swollen. Antonia steps backward in shock. "What happened to you?" she says. Small teardrops of blood litter the front of his shirt. He does not speak. He hasn't seen himself.

Antonia reaches a hand out and hovers it alongside Saul's face, afraid to touch him, and unable to stop herself. "Let me get you some ice," she says.

"Oh, my God." Sofia is standing in the doorway to the kitchen, Enzo in the crook of her elbow. "Oh my God, Saul!"

Saul raises his eyes to meet Sofia's. "I'm okay," he says to her.

"What happened to you?" Sofia has dropped a dishtowel, stained with steak juice and tomato and crusted with small fluttering garlic skins, onto the floor.

"Sofia, the kids," says Antonia. She shepherds Saul into the bedroom. They shut the door. Antonia's heart has started tapping out a quick jazz on the inside of her rib cage. She and Paolo have attained a tenuous peace. They are polite and gracious toward one another. Paolo promised this morning that he would meet her at their apartment before dinner. He promised they'd take a cab together. He promised she wouldn't have to shuttle two kids and her own swelled-up self to Sunday dinner by herself. But he never showed. He didn't answer the phone at his office. And Antonia had to herd Robbie and carry Enzo and ease her aching body into a taxi on her own. She had to choke down a fearful lump, the same one that rises whenever there might be *trouble,* whenever *something might have happened.*

Anything, Antonia knows, could happen. She feels stupid to have forgotten that. The moment you stop worrying is the moment trouble begins.

And if there is trouble, she wants to look Paolo in the eyes while he tells her. Antonia expands outside herself, feeling out for her family, counting Robbie with Julia in her room, Enzo with his half-mast sleepy eyes in Sofia's arms. Robbie and Enzo are here. Where is Paolo. The beat inside Antonia's body quickens.

Antonia takes Enzo from Sofia and slips out of the bedroom to get ice and Saul sits heavily on his bed. Sofia kneels on the floor in front of him to look at his face and says in a low voice, "Tell me what happened."

And Saul raises his eyes to meet Sofia's and says, "I can't."

Sofia laughs. Her husband has come home bleeding and beaten. He will tell her why. "Don't be ridiculous."

Sofia's hands are framing the sides of Saul's face. Saul reaches up to cover them with his own, which are crusted with dried smears of black blood. "I love you," he says.

Sofia begins to heat up. Frustration and disbelief knot at her temples and her vision shadows. "Don't patronize me," she says through gritted teeth. "Tell me what happened, Saul, why won't you tell me?" God, it feels so good to be angry. There is fear licking like a small flame at Sofia's heart and there is a yet-unnamed apprehension racing around the room and Sofia stands and she lets it all be flattened by the avalanche of her anger. "What the fuck happened to you, Saul?"

"Sofia, Sofia," says Antonia. She has slipped into the room without Sofia noticing. "The kids."

"I have to get cleaned up," says Saul. He stands and flexes his hands. "I promise, I'm fine." He unbuttons the top button of his shirt and opens the bedroom door. "Everything is going to be okay."

Sofia and Antonia sit on Sofia's bed until they hear the shower run.

"It will be okay," Antonia says. She repeats it to herself. *It will be okay.*

"It already isn't," says Sofia. Antonia and Sofia look at one another solemnly, two girls

411

playing dress-up in the skins of women. "Did you see him? That wouldn't have happened if everything was okay."

Does Antonia have a half-formed memory of Carlo, stepping down the creaky inn hall on the night he disappeared, stopping to lift the sweaty curls from her face as she slept? Does she hold it somewhere wordless, as the moment her own fallibility became inescapable? There is nothing that cannot fall apart.

She holds Sofia's hand. "It will be. It will."

Saul lets the bathroom fill with steam and sits on the toilet, fully clothed.

It was only two days ago that he went to his Fianzo meeting. It feels like ten years. Saul's thoughts scatter. Solutions appear and then dissipate like mirages.

Saul stands to undress. He steels himself: he cannot tell Sofia what happened. He has to face the family at dinner. He is scared: a fear that skips his brain and moves straight into his body and blood. Trembling the muscles, tightening the breath.

Paolo doesn't show for dinner. Antonia sits where she can watch the doorway, which yawns open as each neighbor, each Uncle, arrives. Each time someone who is not

Paolo walks in, Antonia feels a vise squeezing her heart tighter and tighter. *Where's Paolo?* asks Rosa. *Oh, he got caught up,* says Antonia.

*I'm sorry.* Rosa knows she is lying; Rosa wraps an arm around Antonia's shoulders and squeezes; Rosa smells like flour and jasmine, like orange rinds and parsley, and Antonia would like to curl up in her lap and be rocked to sleep. Instead she smiles and says *thank you, thank you,* as one by one people come to stroke Enzo's cheeks, to smile at him, to lean with their breath and their overflowing blessings too close to Antonia, too close to her until she feels she might explode. She might scream.

She stays quiet. She says, *thank you.*

Sofia has powdered her face and re-lined her lips and gritted her teeth. She has stifled all of her fear. She has turned it into anger, she has turned it into a uranium core. She has climbed upstairs with trays of ravioli, with the braciole sitting in its own fragrant juices. She has opened bottles of wine for Rosa and laughed at a small joke Frankie made. Sofia is a china plate. Any hairline fracture could shatter her.

Saul manages to laugh off his injuries (*last time I deal with business after I drink a bottle of wine at lunch, am I right, boss?*) but Julia says *but, Papa, what what what HAPPENED to you* loudly enough to draw the attention of everyone in the room and Joey stays disarmingly quiet and Saul feels his lies all pounding at the windows, the ceiling, the front doors, trying to get in.

Antonia makes it through the cleanup and the goodbyes and she hugs Sofia tight and says, "We'll figure all of this out in the morning, okay? I will call you in the morning," and then she leaves, accepting Saul's offer to have his driver take her home. As she is being driven away it occurs to Antonia that her husband is missing, and Sofia's is right there, right there where she can see and touch him. In the back of the car she stares through the space between the two front seats and holds Enzo close to her and squeezes Robbie by the hand until he squirms away. *Mamma, Mamma. That's too tight.*

When they arrive home, Antonia stands still at the bottom of the stairs to her building until Robbie says, *Mamma, come on,* and then she moves, one leaden leg after another. The windows in her apartment are blank, black. Darkened. Paolo isn't there.

Antonia puts her boys to bed with shaking hands. She feels herself settling into a role

414

she knows all too well: *petty criminal missing, idiot wife surprised.* Antonia and Paolo have been drifting apart, neither of them possessing the energy to pull themselves back together. Antonia's body remembers the rattle of Paolo's key in the lock. The way a part of her would tense, steeling herself against the fug of depression, the moody cloud Paolo would surely drag through her living room. Antonia prays for Paolo's key in the lock now. She remembers it and she wills it to happen. The rattle of metal in metal. Antonia's want pulls goosebumps up out of her skin, but there is only silence outside the front door of her apartment.

She pictures Paolo's feet sunk into a bucket of hardening concrete, his body dragged through the far reaches of Canarsie, dumped flailing off the Belt Parkway into Long Island Sound. She pictures Paolo tied to a chair, swollen, beaten, while a faceless Fianzo brandishes bloodstained garden shears. Antonia spirals into panic. *Mamma, are you crying?* Robbie asks, as Antonia, a warm hand on his back, soothes him into sleep. *No, caro mio,* Antonia responds. She turns her face away. She hums an old song.

When Enzo and Robbie are both breathing deeply, evenly, their dreams inaccessible to watchful Antonia, she tiptoes into the living room and folds herself into the couch. Deep inside of Antonia, her organs are shifting back to their original places. The parts of her that carried a human being are shrinking, throbbing smaller and smaller so soon it will be impossible to imagine that anyone else ever lived inside her body. It will also be impossible to imagine that she had ever been alone. She clutches a small pillow and feels herself strain against it with every inhale. Somewhere, a clock ticks.

After dinner all it takes is a quick jerk of the head and Saul follows Joey into his study.

Rosa watches them go, and then tries to return to the cleanup. But she cannot focus: of course she can't. She shuts her eyes and feels out into the wide world for Antonia's fear, for Sofia's, for Julia's. She realizes that Antonia and Sofia will have to face whatever catastrophe is unfolding on their own.

Saul finds his hands are trembling.

The study has achy French doors which Joey shuts now, so the end-of-dinner din sounds like it is coming from a different world. Joey hands Saul a drink, which Saul grips until his fingertips go white. Joey runs a hand through his salt-and-pepper hair, as if he is trying to rake up a solution to whatever catastrophe Saul has wrought.

"You're in trouble," says Joey.

"I'm fixing it," says Saul. He is twenty-three and he is promising Joey he loves Sofia. "I can handle it."

"I've retired," says Joey. "I will take your word for it."

"Thank you," says Saul.

"But I need you to promise me something."

"Anything."

Joey crosses his arms. "I once told you that you don't get to die when you're a father," he says.

"I remember," says Saul.

"I lied," says Joey. "If you have to choose between you and them —"

"I know," says Saul.

"I trust you can get yourself out of whatever predicament you've found yourself in," says Joey. "But, Saul, if it comes down to it."

"I know," says Saul.

"Promise me."

"I promise," says Saul.

How can anyone move forward when their lives are increasingly full of ghosts that demand their time and attention? The ghost of Carlo, who haunts them all, and the ghosts of their former selves, the exoskeletons they all try to shed and bury, to lock in a closet, to repurpose. Their houses are full to bursting.

Paolo is sitting on a bench in the middle of the pedestrian overpass on the Brooklyn Bridge as the sun rises. He hasn't been awake for a full sunrise in a long time. It is cloudy; it is as cool as New York ever gets in July; as still. There are thick, heavy thunderstorms predicted for this week, Paolo remembers. He read that in the newspaper, nine hundred years ago when he sat at a kitchen table for breakfast with Robbie and Antonia, with Enzo, this new person.

Paolo is sure he is tired, but he doesn't

feel it: the achy limbs, the scratchy, sticky eyes. If he is still enough, he feels like he is shimmering, detaching from his body. As the air thickens Paolo feels himself as something insubstantial and disconnected from the world. Later he will admire the power of this: to have an essential core, something unchanged by the chaos around him. To be a self, battered and bolstered by the tides of time.

Below him, cars begin to speed across the bridge. Big trucks with cargo for grocers and furniture and bags of concrete rumble over the East River. Commuters file across, jostling for space, honking. Paolo can feel his back begin to sweat against the wooden bench. He should have called home last night, he realizes. Antonia will be furious. She'll be disappointed. Antonia is so often disappointed in Paolo. He never intended to be the kind of man that would cause such regular, small-scale domestic depression. *You are not the man I thought you were,* he says to himself.

The sky has darkened as the sun has risen, the pronunciation of morning thunderheads against the horizon becoming sinister. Green and gray. Paolo stands. It's a long walk home, and he wonders if he will make it before it rains.

■ ■ ■ ■

It is the first dawn after the longest night of Sofia's life.

Saul had taken Sofia aside after dinner, whispered *I'm sorry, I'm so sorry* into her ear and *I promise you'll be okay, it will be okay.* He disappeared through the front door of Rosa and Joey's apartment like he was never there. Sofia's rage was made of panic, of fear, of a hollow, bitter, wrung-out stomach. Joey hugged her and said *put Julia to bed,* and wouldn't engage with her, wouldn't fight, wouldn't tell her what was wrong. *Saul's good at what he does,* Joey said. Sofia felt sure she would feel better if someone would tell her why Saul had been hurt. *I know he's good,* she said to Joey, desperate. *So am I.* Nothing. Her want, so powerful it rose from her body and filled the room and gnashed its teeth and roared, had no effect on Saul, on Joey, on the big universal machinations guiding all of them.

So Sofia took Julia by the hand and the two of them walked the stairs back to their own apartment. Julia had hidden in the kitchen with Robbie during dinner, their play whispered, their legs crossed and sweating together. Julia curls her fingers around

420

Sofia's and walks in Sofia's shadow, as close as she can, as if she might disappear into Sofia's body. *Why won't Papa tell us what's going on,* asked Julia, but it was more of a statement: asking questions is how Julia knows to participate in collective worry. What Julia wants is more nebulous: not to know what's happening, necessarily, but rather, not to wonder. To have the people she loves laid out in front of her like candies to choose from.

Last night Sofia supervised toothbrushing and as she leaned against the bathroom doorway and watched Julia watch herself in the mirror she realized, perhaps for the first time, how much she had missed. The night-time rituals, the place Julia hangs her bathrobe. Which elbow she likes her bear tucked in when — usually Saul, sometimes Rosa — smooths the covers over her before she goes to sleep. And even though Saul was in trouble and Joey was keeping secrets from her and Paolo — Paolo jumped into her head, an apparition — Paolo never showed at dinner, did he, and Antonia must be frantic — Sofia found herself laughing with her daughter. Tucking Julia's hair behind her ears and pressing a palm to her forehead.

When she left Julia, Sofia couldn't sleep.

She lay in her clothes on the bed and accepted that she would feel the whole night pass her by. Her anger became white-hot. She blamed Saul for stealing her sleep and her youth. She did this with her whole self. She scanned the room for something to destroy. There was a glass of water on Saul's nightstand. She wanted to stomp on it. She wanted to slam it on the ground. She wanted to throw it against the wall. But Julia was just in the next room. Sofia opened her nightstand drawer to look at the gun there. What use is a gun? What use can a small body of steel and stone possibly be against the tides of time, the suffocating maw of tradition, the withholding of information? Sofia slammed the drawer shut. She climbed back in bed with a raging heart.

She didn't sleep. But sometime in the middle of the night Sofia woke with the thick air pressing down. She eased herself out of bed and tiptoed into the living room to sit at Saul's desk. *How things have changed,* she thought. How young she was, when she first did this, sneaking away from baby Julia and Saul to imagine what it would be like to live for herself. How much she has learned since then.

Sofia sat up straighter. Yes: how much she has learned. She is not the idealistic newlywed, not the untried new mother. She is no one to push around.

Sofia opens each of the drawers in Saul's desk in turn. The last is locked. She narrows her eyes, slides her hand into the drawer pull and yanks so fast and so hard that anyone awake might have thought there was a crack of thunder. The drawer splinters. Inside are small notebooks. Sofia is opening them before she realizes what she is doing. She is scanning pages covered in Saul's quick scrawl. *T.F. alone, though last time he said he'd bring Jr. this month. Apparently Jr. not as enthused by the opportunity to meet me. One guard, the big one w/nine fingers who spends all his time smoking. T.F. says things might change now that Joey's not in charge, now that he's stepping down.*

If this was a journal, Sofia thinks, or a record for Joey, it wouldn't be locked away. What could Saul have been doing that he needed to hide from his family?

And then Sofia begins, like anyone would, to replay moments from the last year. *Why can't we sit together like a real family?* Saul had been touchy, angry, sure of what a real family would do. Implying, Sofia realizes, that he didn't have one. *He has been unhappy,* she realizes. *And I have not been listening.*

There is a phone number written on the first page of the notebook Sofia is holding. She picks up the phone on Saul's desk and dials.

"Whoever is waking me up for the second fucking time tonight had better have a good fucking reason," says a male voice on the other end.

"Who is this?" asks Sofia. She asks with the same certainty she had once asked Joey *why*. She asks, and she expects an answer. She calls it out of thin air; she demands it.

"Ma'am," says the voice on the phone, "I think you might have the wrong number." It is softened, now. It is off guard.

"I can assure you," says Sofia, "I do not. Who are you?"

"My name is Eli," says Eli Leibovich, "but I am certain you've dialed —" Sofia doesn't hear the rest of what he says, because she has put the phone on the table. There is only one Eli whose number Saul would need to lock in a drawer. The way Saul has gotten into trouble becomes crystal clear.

Like she is in a dream, Sofia leaves the phone buzzing off its hook and floats downstairs to stand on her porch in the night air. As a child, she was scared of Lina's helplessness, the way a part of her disappeared when Carlo did.

The part of Sofia that lives in Saul will disappear if Saul does, but Sofia, standing in her nightgown in the warm predawn air, is not going to let that happen.

As daylight grays the sky it reveals a building which stands alone at the edge of the Red Hook dockyard. It is a Monday, so the longshoremen are arriving in quiet pairs, with their lunch pails and their thermoses of coffee. The building looks like it must once have been grand, but soon the sky will be light enough that the cracks and missing chunks in the façade will all be revealed.

If the longshoremen look closely, they can see something strange there. Something like a specter, a fairy tale. Something about which their mothers would have said, *don't get too close.*

*Did you see?* one might ask the others. *No,* the others will reply. It's best not to see.

But some of them will be sure they saw her. Lying in wait: a barefoot woman with wild hair, sitting on the steps to the building as dawn brims over.

Antonia wakes with a shooting pain running from the crown of her head down the side of her neck. *Serves you right,* she thinks, getting up from the floor of Robbie's bedroom, *for sleeping.* And then: *where is Paolo.*

Antonia pads into the kitchen on soft feet. Her boys are sleeping, still as windless water. Paolo is not in the kitchen; he is not in the living room.

When Antonia was a teenager, she resented Lina for reminding her, again and again, about the pitfalls of Family life. Her mamma felt she married into a trap. Antonia can feel the metal teeth biting into her own leg now.

*I should have listened to you, Mamma,* Antonia thinks as she sits on the stool near the phone in the kitchen. She hovers her hand above the phone. She wills Paolo to call. Antonia's worry has settled down into the throbbing of her neck, her back. It sits like lead in her intestines.

And then the phone rings.

Antonia answers before the first trill dies down. "Paolo." A prayer.

"It's Saul."

"Saul." Antonia's neck twinges. Her hips are connected to the top of her head by a live wire of pain.

"Sofia didn't answer. Have you talked to her?"

426

"Saul, what is going on? Where is Paolo?"

"I don't know," says Saul. "I'm sorry. But, Antonia, I can't reach Sofia. I've been calling all morning."

Antonia's boys are still asleep. She can feel them through the walls. Somewhere, something rumbles: thunder, or her own self. Antonia grips the phone. "Did you try downstairs?"

"I don't want to worry Rosa and Joey unless I have to," Saul says.

"Saul, why don't you go home? Go check on her? Where are you?"

"Just keep them safe," says Saul. "Just tell them how much I love them."

"Saul, please," says Antonia. "Don't do anything stupid."

"I'm not, Tonia. I promise."

"Saul," says Antonia. "Are you going to be okay?" She does not say, *I promised Sofia.*

"Everything will be fine," says Saul. There is a click. He is gone.

Antonia hangs up the phone. The silence buzzes. It crackles. It slams.

No — the front door slams. "Antonia?" Paolo.

The first thing Antonia thinks when she sees Paolo is that he looks like shit. His eyes are bloodshot and his shirt is untucked and dirty. His face is stubbled in rough black

427

patches and he looks unsteady on his feet. She crosses the kitchen in two steps and hugs him, wraps herself around him, and the second thing she thinks is *thank you.* "What happened to you?" she asks, which feels wildly insufficient. And then, "Saul just called. He doesn't sound okay. We have to help him."

"Did he tell you what happened?" asks Paolo.

"No," says Antonia. "But he's hurt. He won't tell us who —"

"It was me," says Paolo.

"You?"

"Sit down," says Paolo. "I need to make some coffee."

Antonia sits.

Paolo tells her that on Sunday morning he got a call. "Which is yesterday, I guess. I'm having trouble keeping track," he says. It was Tommy Fianzo Jr. "He wanted me to meet him. I refused." Paolo is pouring espresso grounds into the pot. He is tamping them down with careful fingers. "He said I would meet him if I knew what was good for me." Paolo shrugs. "I agreed." Paolo does not tell Antonia that part of him relished being the one who got the call, the one who would be in danger, the one with the information, for once, the power. But she knows.

"I met him at his office," says Paolo. "He told me Saul's been working for Eli Leibovich."

"That's impossible," says Antonia.

"I know," says Paolo. "That's what I told him. But he insisted. He said Saul dropped a piece of paper as he was leaving their meeting the other day. It had details about the Fianzo dock operation written on it. Fianzo connected the dots. I didn't believe him until he showed me the paper. You know how Saul does that strange thing with his A's. It was his writing. And, Tonia, Leibovich has been after those docks for years. There's no other answer." The espresso is wailing on the stove. Paolo turns it off and pours it into two cups. He hands one to Antonia. "He told me they're going to get rid of Saul. He's been looking for an excuse." Paolo clenches the kitchen counter. His knuckles are white. "He knows our sons' names."

"Of course he does," says Antonia. "But he has to be lying."

"He offered me a job. He said — if I take care of Saul — if I take care of Saul for them, they'll take me on. Give me the promotion I never got here." Paolo runs a hand through his hair in a very good imitation of Joey. "So I went to find Saul."

"You hurt him?"

"I confronted him."

"And he told you he didn't do it." Antonia says this loudly, but the truth is starting to whisper in through the windows.

"He admitted to all of it," says Paolo. "He apologized. He said he's been trying to think of a way out for months."

"There's no way out," says Antonia. *This is not happening.* The walls contract and expand around her, the way walls always do when an old world is being exchanged for a new one.

"I told him they offered me a job in return for taking care of him," says Paolo. "He said he would understand. He said, *do it.*" Paolo puts his empty cup down on the counter. "I punched him. I couldn't help myself. I hit him again." Paolo begins to cry. "I hit him over and over again, Tonia, and he wouldn't fight back, he wouldn't do anything. Of course I wouldn't do it. He's family. He's a part of us. I could never — does he think I could do that?"

Antonia is at the center of a storm. It is calm and quiet there. "Sofia's missing," she says. And then she crosses the kitchen. She buries herself in Paolo's chest. She feels her heart thumping against his ribs.

■ ■ ■ ■

Saul is calm as he hangs up the phone. He hasn't slept in long enough that his swollen lip and blackened eye are singing, his whole body throbbing.

In the middle of the night, after Saul had arrived in Paolo's office, which seemed to him as good a hiding spot as any, he called Eli Leibovich. He asked for help. And he was refused.

*I have to think about my family,* said Eli. *I have to play a longer game.* Eli would not protect Saul. He would not defend Saul. Saul put family on the line for a man who was not, in the end, anything more than a work acquaintance with a familiar accent. And now Tommy Fianzo Jr. will not rest until Saul is gone.

Saul thinks about his wife. He thinks about his daughter. He aches to be tangled under them, Sofia and Julia on either side of his chest, sleeping. Every moment of his life until this moment is washed in gold. Saul realizes how utterly alive he has always been. How full of self his skin. How full of breath his lungs.

Saul wonders what it would be like to be Paolo. To be born into a family that raised you. To have a father. To work each day behind a desk, to go home on time.

And like it did when he was twenty-one, rocking empty-stomached in the bottom of a boat to America, a wave of will, of survival itself, swells toward Saul. *Fight,* his nature tells him. *Fight,* from his lungs. *Fight,* the incessant beating of blinking.

Saul closes his eyes.

He thinks about his mother. *Mama,* he tells her. *Mama, I think I'll see you soon.*

He thinks about Sofia. She will be okay no matter what happens to him. She is a force of nature. *If you have to choose,* Joey says in his head. Saul knows what he will choose.

Outside people look at the purple sky and pray for rain. The air is thick as water. It hurts to breathe.

It is mid-morning, and Lina Russo is drinking tea when there is a knock on the door.

The knock comes again. Lina sets her tea on its coaster.

There is sadness in the air of her apartment. This is the price for emotional caretaking: the sadness of others lingers. But this particular sadness, Lina realizes, as she shuffles to open the door, is new.

It comes from Paolo and Antonia, who are standing on her doorstep like children. Robbie hovers behind them; Enzo is asleep in the crook of Paolo's elbow. Paolo's head is hung like an old tulip on the stalk of his body; from Antonia there emanates a desperate kind of strength; the tightrope balance of staying upright.

"Mamma," says Antonia, "can we talk to you?" Her face is grave; drawn; Lina can see small, stern Antonia as a child, quiet and measured, doing her homework or folding her clothes, building a foundation around herself.

Lina pulls them inside, hugs Paolo, kisses Antonia, says, "Tea?"

Antonia says, "Sure."

Lina takes another look at them and says, "Gin?"

Paolo meets her eyes for the first time. There is a wry smile there. "Better," he says.

Lina beckons to them from the kitchen, holding three clear glasses with an inch of gin and an ice cube and a lemon slice each. She passes Robbie a cookie and he sidles quietly out of the room. "Come, sit," she says. Paolo and Antonia sit across from her at the kitchen table. The apartment smells of earth, as though Lina has been growing mushrooms in corners, letting moss sprout on walls.

"You have something to tell me," Lina says.

"We need help," says Antonia. "But, Mamma — you won't like it." She is struck through by an icy rod of fear: how carefully she has constructed her relationship with her mamma around not having conversations like the one she has come here to have. But there is no one else who will be honest with them.

Paolo has thought of a thousand ways to

begin this conversation. "When Carlo," he begins, and then stops.

Lina has raised an eyebrow. She can hear her late husband's name now. "Yes," she says.

"When Carlo wanted — to get out." As Paolo speaks he drapes the name of his wife's father over his tongue, holding it out to Lina like an offering, entering himself into a tragedy which has never been named explicitly but which sits at every dinner with them, follows Robbie out the door on his way to school, hunching Antonia's shoulders as she sits on the side of their bed to brush her hair at night. The work Antonia must have had to do to love him all these years strikes Paolo like a bag of cement to the chest.

"Yes."

"What did he do?"

"Well," says Lina. She leans back in her chair. She raises her drink to her lips. "My husband," and here she tips the drink to the sky, a toast, "didn't do a very good job, getting out. So. Why do you bring this up?" She looks at Antonia, whose face is a map. And Lina understands.

"It's Saul, Mamma," says Antonia. The words bloom in the air around them like tea leaves; they settle. "Saul has been working

435

for Eli Leibovich. He's been sneaking —"

Lina waves a hand. The same mess. The same men, getting themselves into inescapable trouble without thinking how they are going to get themselves out.

"I never thought it would be Saul," she says, looking straight at Paolo. Paolo stares at his glass. He tries not to take it personally.

"Sofia is missing," says Antonia.

Lina smiles. "How do you know that?"

"I can feel it, Mamma," says Antonia. "I can just —" She doesn't know how she knows, really, except that when Saul told her he couldn't reach Sofia something clicked into place, something caught flame.

"Well," says Lina, "she might not be missing. She might just be solving the problem." This feels oblique even for Lina because *what,* thinks Antonia, *could Sofia do?* Even Sofia would not be able to solve this inherited problem, this problem every woman who enters into a Family family knows she might someday face.

"I don't know what you mean," says Antonia.

Lina looks at Antonia and Paolo. "You know there is nothing you can do. That's why you came, right? So that I could tell you there is nothing you can do. You are out

436

of options. Saul has made his choices, and he will suffer. We will all suffer," she says.

"Mamma," Antonia says, but then falls silent.

Lina drains her cup. "Because there is nothing you can do — there is no right choice — there is no way to get out of this unscathed — there is also no reason for you not to fight for him." The air in the apartment sits, waiting.

Lina leans forward to look at Antonia. "Don't let him do to her what your papa did to us. You fight for him. You use everything you have."

When Sofia and Antonia were nine years old, they made a blood oath. This is what they called it.

It happened one evening when Antonia slept over at Sofia's house. Antonia was supposed to sleep on the floor, on a nest Rosa made for her near Sofia's bed. But every time she slept over, Rosa would come in to wake them and find Sofia and Antonia with their brown limbs tangled together in Sofia's bed.

On this particular evening they had gone to bed early because it was November, and the city had gone dark and quiet earlier than they were used to, and Rosa had served steaming bowls of soup that made them sleepy. Sofia was in the middle of a ghost story about a sailor forever looking for his missing foot when her hand, idly tapping along her bedframe, came upon a loose nail. *Tonia, look,* she said, working it out of the wood. It gleamed in the lamplight when she held it up.

Without speaking, Sofia sat up, and Antonia did too.

Sofia took the nail and aimed it at the soft skin of her open palm. She dragged it across her hand, eyes narrowed. She had to do it twice to get the blood. She passed the nail to Antonia, who with held breath scored her own palm. Sofia and Antonia stared at the blood in their palms until they both had thick drops balancing there, and then they pressed their palms together. Each of them prayed for the blood of the other to mix with her own. Each of them imagined she could feel it: just the one glistening drop of it, spreading out inside of her. Giving her strength.

The next morning it could all have been a dream, but for the rusted crust both Sofia and Antonia carried with them to the bathroom tap. For a week they had sore hands where the nail, not made for slicing through girlflesh, had bruised as it entered.

And for that whole week, they each hid their hands from their mammas, and from their teachers at school. On Sunday, they avoided looking at one another for the whole meal because they were both sure they would burst into laughter, the kind of hysteria that betrays a kept secret. *What's wrong with you two?* asked Rosa. *Nothing,* they chorused. *Nothing, we're fine.*

Before Antonia left, she met Sofia's eyes, just once. She was standing by the front door of Sofia's apartment, and Rosa was going to walk her home, because it's never safe for girls to be out alone after dark. Sofia smiled at her friend. And Antonia winked. Inside each of them, the blood of the other rushed.

And they knew they weren't just fine.

They were immortal.

Julia wakes in her parents' bed, alone. The sun is high and she wonders if it is a school holiday. When she cannot find Sofia or Saul in the apartment, Julia walks upstairs and knocks on the door to Nonna's. She is not afraid.

At Antonia and Paolo's insistence, Lina squeezes herself into a cab with them, Robbie, and baby Enzo, and together they ride to the Colicchio brownstone in Carroll Gardens.

Rosa is there, sitting on the couch, mending socks. Rosa can of course afford to just buy new socks, but she is nervous and unhappy today. It is not totally out of character for Sofia to leave without telling anyone and forget Julia entirely — Rosa, after all, is right upstairs. But there was something so solemn in Julia's eyes this morning. And Saul has not come home.

Rosa has not asked Joey for answers, but she knows what's going on. And she has fed her granddaughter, mended seven socks, baked bread from her mother's recipe, scrubbed the tile in the bathroom until it shines. Now Rosa looks up to see her family in her living room: Antonia, holding her baby; Robbie, who runs off to find Julia; Paolo, his eyes darting from Antonia to Rosa to Lina. And Lina. Standing in a cloud of fragrance: orange rind and deep must.

"Sorry for barging in." It is Antonia. Her face is calm. *She is a good mother,* Rosa thinks. Little Antonia. "But something is wrong. Sofia and Saul are — well, we have to find them." In her mind's eye, she puts a hand to the wall that separates her bedroom from Sofia's. *I'm coming,* she tells her. Antonia sets her jaw. She shifts Enzo from one shoulder to another. And then quiet Antonia raises her voice. "Uncle Joey!" Lina and Rosa and Paolo all drop their jaws in shock. There is no answer from the study. Antonia stomps her foot. She opens her mouth. She bellows: "UNCLE JOEY!"

Joey comes stumbling out from his study, straightening his shirt, blinking like a rat thrust into sunlight. "Is someone shouting?" he asks. And then he sees Antonia.

"Uncle Joey," she asks him, quietly now,

"where is Saul?"

Joey sighs. He looks at his family assembled in the living room — Rosa and Antonia and Paolo and Lina (Lina? When was the last time he saw her?). He can hear the sounds of Robbie and Julia and Frankie in Frankie's bedroom. "I'm sorry," he says. "I'm sorry about Saul."

Antonia has not taken her eyes off of him, has not relaxed her hands enough to let the blood return to her knuckles. Enzo sleeps against her shoulder. "Where is he?" she asks. And she asks like a command. She expects to be told.

"It's complicated," says Joey. "It's so — it's so complicated, Tonia, and I am so sorry. I never should have hired him. I take the blame for everything." What Joey wants, what he always wants, is to spare his family any pain. To take charge, to solve the problem, to be the dumping ground for everyone else's fear and anger for as long as it takes them to heal. He cannot believe he has found himself in this situation again: someone Joey loves is going to die. It is the only way Joey can protect his family. And it is Joey's fault.

"Uncle Joey, there is no *time* for sorry," says Antonia, urgency in the way she leans forward toward Joey as though she might take off. "We have to stop him, we have to help Sofia!"

"This is how we will help Sofia," says Joey sadly. "This is how it works."

Joey cannot know how tired Antonia is of being told how things work. So he is surprised when she flies at him, screaming. "There is no *how it works!* You decided! You decided *how it works* when my father died! You decided *how it works* when you hired Saul, when you promoted him, when you gave Sofia a job she loves more than her own —" And then Antonia stops, abruptly, because she can see that Julia and Robbie have crept up behind Joey and are hovering in the shadowed hallway, listening. Hearing everything. Learning how it works. Antonia controls herself with a great effort. "We are going to save Saul, and Sofia. We are going to fix this. You are going to tell us where he is. That will be *how it works.*"

Joey looks down at Antonia and feels a great surge of love. Antonia is so sure of herself he almost believes she can do it. All of his power will not prevent her from trying.

"Where are they?" Antonia asks again. Her voice is calm now.

But it is not Joey who speaks. It is Rosa. "The Fianzo dock building," Rosa says.

"You know where it is?"

"Of course I do," says Antonia, who has never been there, but who of course knows where it is. "I've been doing this my whole life."

A quiet settles over the room, the whole place vibrating in the wake of Antonia's storm. "I thought I'd go look for them, and you can stay with the kids," says Paolo to Antonia, but to all of them. He speaks to Antonia the way you'd speak to a nervous horse. Their reconciliation is predicated on catastrophe and he does not know if it will last. He still can't figure out what sea change the birth of Enzo has wrought; it is like he can't see Antonia, can't bring her into focus, can't fit all of her into his field of vision. One moment she is joyful; the next, she darkens away from him. One moment she is buying shrimp for Sunday dinner and the next she is screaming at Joey Colicchio. Paolo remembers how well he thought he could see Antonia before they were married. It occurs to him now to wonder whether he has ever really understood her.

"I'm coming," says Antonia. "Can the kids stay here?"

Rosa says *of course* or something to that effect; she wants to convey the absolutism

445

of her affirmation, *of course,* forever, all of the children, for as long as you want.

"You can't come," says Paolo; the idea of letting his wife go out to search for Sofia and Saul in a Fianzo stronghold is absurd.

Antonia does not respond, but hands Enzo to Lina, kisses his face, his curled hands, and everyone in the room can hear and feel the space between Antonia and Enzo echo and tear as Antonia stands and moves away. Antonia's face is all long anguished lines, all primal torment. Lina looks at Antonia and nods once, almost imperceptibly.

"Tonia, listen to me," says Paolo. "Let me go find them." And still, Antonia is silent. But when Paolo reaches out to touch her shoulder, to guide her back to reality, Antonia wheels around and emits a feral, choking snarl, something so animal Paolo flinches back away from her.

"Thank you," says Antonia to Rosa and Lina, and then she turns and walks out the front door.

Paolo stands for a moment, in shock or in reverence, in absolute silence, and then he looks at Lina and Rosa, at Enzo and Robbie, at Frankie and Julia, and at Joey. And because he has to, Paolo finds his voice. He says, "I have to go." He turns and walks out the front door of the Colicchio apartment.

The sun comes barging around the corner of the Fianzo building like a battering ram and almost immediately Sofia is sweating. Her underarms and the creases at her knees and elbows drip.

It feels like she has been waiting here for hours. For most people, the anticipation of confrontation would have dulled, but Sofia is not most people. She burns just as brightly now as she did when she left her apartment in the predawn light.

Sofia has been thinking about Saul, and she has been expecting to feel anger but she has been surprised to feel pride, instead. She can see how hard Saul has been working, and she realizes that part of what has attracted her so ferociously to him over the last months has been a sense that there is something he is keeping to himself. Something he is doing apart from her, apart from her family. Sofia has always been attracted to power, and this new thing that lives in Saul is power incarnate: he has been making choices. Fulfilling something. Saul has been forging his own path.

When a black car finally pulls up to the front of the building, she recognizes Tommy

Fianzo Jr. immediately. He has the same narrowed eyes he did as a mean little boy. The same smirk, which sits crookedly over his teeth, the same slightly too big for his face lips. He unfolds himself from the car and looks her over with the same disdain. "They told me you were working," he says to her. On the other side of the car, a man — a guard — shuts his own door. "They also told me you were smart." Sofia says nothing. "But here you are," Tommy Jr. says, "so I must have been given false information. Well. It's not the first time." Sofia can tell he is enjoying this. She keeps her face neutral.

"I thought we could have a conversation," she says.

"No harm in a simple conversation," says Tommy Jr. "Check her," he says, and then jerks his head. In one motion, the guard comes around Tommy's car toward Sofia. His hands are on her before she can think: they are rough and dispassionate, as though Sofia could be a bag of sand, a block of ice. He presses his fingers against her ribs, her calves, the small of her back. "She's clear," he says to Tommy Jr.

"Very well," says Tommy Jr. He gestures for Sofia to follow him upstairs.

The Fianzo office smells like stale meat,

something brown and sinister Sofia does not want to inhale too deeply. Tommy Fianzo Jr. offers her a seat before lighting a noxious cigar that clouds Sofia's eyesight and mind. She and Fianzo could be anywhere. They could be the last two people alive.

"I know what my husband has been doing," says Sofia. "And judging by the state of him, I assume you do too."

" 'The state of him'?" asks Tommy Jr. He leans forward, interested. "I haven't touched him, no." He raises a hand, anticipating Sofia's disbelief. "It's true! I would admit it if I had. And I'll admit I'm glad *someone* has."

"I'm sure you are," says Sofia. *Make him feel safe. Make him feel like it was his idea.* "I wanted to apologize for him."

"And what good do you think that will do?" asks Tommy Jr.

"I'm not focused on what it will do," says Sofia. "I just think you deserve an apology. You gave him a chance, and he betrayed you."

Tommy Jr. is looking for the trick. Finding none, he leans back slightly in his chair. "I've always been against outsiders," he says. "There's no way to do this right unless you were raised in it. And people — people thought it was the Jewish thing, and sure, you can't deny that they're — well, crafty — but I would have felt that way about anyone, anyone from outside.

You can't join in, here. You can't do it halfway."

"I know," says Sofia. "I know how it works."

"Then why," snarls Tommy Jr., impatient now, "are you here?"

"I have information I'd like to give you," says Sofia, "in exchange for my husband's safety."

Antonia and Paolo take a cab to the docks. They do not speak.

Antonia stares out the window at clouds so gray they are purple, a surreal darkening of the hot midday. She knows she can never again sit back while action unfolds around her. Terrible things happen to her family when she lets them out of her sight. And Antonia, who has always trusted in adulthood, in passing time, in the order she was told reigned, realizes now that nothing holds fast.

Everyone is just as wild and strange as she.

Everything just as unstable.

In Paolo's head, a war rages. His wife is in danger. His friends. His family. He wants to tell the driver to stop the car. He wants to

450

throw himself on top of Antonia, press her arms in close to her sides and shield her until the danger has passed. He wants to stop her, but he knows he cannot.

Tommy Fianzo Jr. has settled down behind his desk. There is no less scorn on his face but his expression has been brightened by blatant curiosity. "You have information?" he asks, and even Sofia can tell he is trying to keep his tone light; his day is shaping up to be much more exciting than he had thought it would.

"I have information you could use to your advantage," says Sofia. "But I have some conditions."

"It doesn't seem to me like you're in any position to bargain," says Tommy Jr.

Sofia keeps her face still. "I want to guarantee Saul's safety. You won't harm him. This whole thing will be behind us."

"You'd have to have pretty special information," says Tommy Jr.

"I can give you Eli Leibovich," says Sofia, "in exchange for Saul."

Tommy is both curious and frustrated. His father has not given him the autonomy that, say, Joey Colicchio gave to Saul. Tommy's work life is a long series of telephone calls to ask for permission and reports on his day

451

and bookkeeping he wishes he could outsource. Truthfully, he should tie the Colicchio woman to a chair and call his father. But he is just smart enough to know that having one up on Eli Leibovich would be huge — so huge, in fact, that maybe he would be rewarded with a little of the independence he craves. "How do I know you're telling the truth?" he asks.

"How do I know you won't kill Saul as soon as I give you what I have?" Sofia responds. "Trust." She shrugs. "Honor." And then, "It's what our fathers would have done."

"Tell me what you have," says Tommy Jr.

"Promise me," says Sofia, "that Saul will be unharmed."

"I won't touch the Jew," says Tommy.

Sofia reaches into a pocket and pulls out a fistful of small, wire-bound notebooks. "This is all of Saul's work for Eli," she says. "I think he wants these docks. If you use these carefully, I think you'll be able to stay one step ahead of him."

Tommy reaches for the notebooks greedily, his hands outstretched wide in unabashed desire.

Sofia stretches her hand out to give Tommy the notebooks, to start a war between Tommy Fianzo's Family and Eli's. To save her husband. Sofia can feel her heartbeat in her fingers, her toes, thumping through the building itself. Tommy raises his head to listen. He can hear it too. The clang of blood in Sofia's head sounds like feet hitting metal. And then the door to the office bursts open, and for the second time in as many days, Sofia gasps at the sight of Saul.

Saul's breath is heavy from running up the stairs. A pen falls from Tommy Fianzo Jr.'s desk to the ground. It is the most ordinary clatter in the world.

"Saul *Colicchio,*" says Tommy, with barely suppressed delight. "Just the traitorous bastard I was hoping to see." And then he has the nerve to look at Sofia, as if hoping for some praise. *Good line,* he might want her to say.

Sofia doesn't notice because she is looking at Saul, who is looking back at her. "I'm so sorry," he says, which is the most inadequate thing that has ever come out of his mouth. "I understand," she says, which is the most inadequate thing that has ever come out of hers.

"Against the wall," says Tommy Fianzo Jr., and it is not just inadequate, but unnecessary, because he is pointing a gun at

Sofia. "Let's all take a walk." And Sofia understands that whatever tenuous moment of understanding she might have been building toward with Tommy Fianzo Jr. has been lost, and with it, any hope she and Saul have of getting out of this unscathed. Of getting out of it at all.

The cab pulls up short a few blocks away from the docks. Next to Antonia in the backseat, Paolo takes her hand. "Please stay here," he begs her.

"I love you," she responds.

(Paolo and Antonia, seventeen years old, ran out of things to say halfway through their first date. Words seemed entirely insufficient.)

Antonia opens the car door and slips out. She begins to run, alone.

It is noon, but it looks like evening. The air smells like metal and engine oil, like every evening of Antonia's childhood, the kitchen window in Sofia's apartment open to the slow breeze coming off the East River. The way the air can smell like the ocean and the city all at once.

Antonia is alight with energy. The deepest parts of her have been pulled up to the surface of her skin.

And of course, Antonia is not alone. She

has Sofia with her. She has Carlo. And because she stopped upstairs in Sofia's apartment before getting in a cab, she has a gleaming, heavy, fully loaded pearl-handled pistol.

Paolo is running to catch up with Antonia. She is stealthy, quick, better at this than Paolo would have guessed, moving from dumpster to shipping container, sheltering herself.

In front of the Fianzo building there stands a guard. Antonia cannot see him from her vantage point behind a tall metal pylon. Paolo can see that when Antonia moves again, she will cross right into the guard's line of sight. He runs.

As a child, Paolo was scrappy. Three older brothers and the bloody path home from school had beaten into him the importance of self-defense, and defense of those you loved. Paolo was well-known in his neighborhood, and not just for his handwriting.

Paolo's fist connects with the Fianzo guard's face before the guard even has time to register that anyone is approaching. Paolo draws back his right fist again but then jabs viciously with his left, hitting just under the guard's rib cage. The soft flesh there collapses; the guard lets out a *whoosh* of breath. Paolo elbows him in the face. Something cracks. *I love you,* Paolo thinks, picturing Saul and Antonia. The Fianzo guard slips into a blissful unconsciousness. Paolo leaves the guard bruised and bloodied, draped over the concrete steps. He takes off after Antonia. *I love you,* he prays.

Antonia sticks to the shadows. She hopes Saul and Sofia will be there. She hopes they will not be there. She moves as slowly as she can bear, as quietly, as carefully as anyone ever has.

In the distance, toward the river, there is a small cloud of seagulls flapping and keening. Recently disturbed.

Sofia.

Antonia stands. She is at the edge of the ocean.

*Come on,* Carlo says.

Antonia is all storm, all clash and fury. The summer air is still but in her ears wind roars.

Sofia and Antonia, playing make-believe, once started a war in Sofia's bedroom. They vanquished the entire army. They were the only survivors.

Antonia can smell Sofia. She is close. There

is no time. There is less and less time every moment. Antonia must move impossibly fast. She must move backward in time.

Three figures are standing at the edge of the docks, the edge of the world. One is on his knees. One is holding a gun. One is Sofia.

Antonia can feel everything.

The wind comes now, little tendrils of it stirring trash and dust on the docks, making ripples on the water. The clouds cannot get darker but they do, somehow, sealing themselves to the edges of the sky so that rain is the only way out.

Antonia is running, with her jellied legs, with blood leaking down her thighs, with her deep soft new-mother skin, the darkness of her eyes.

"Hey!" Antonia shouts. The wind carries her voice. Tommy turns.

When she is twenty feet away from them Antonia stops and plants her feet and raises the gun. Tommy Fianzo Jr. has let his own gun swing down to his side in surprise. When he realizes Antonia has a weapon of her own he puts his hands up by his shoulders and says something like, *alright there, sweetheart, no need to do anything rash.*

Antonia tightens her finger toward the trigger.

"This won't end the way you want it," says Tommy Jr. Saul and Sofia are still, staring. Antonia is moving backward in time.

Eighteen years ago, Antonia knows, Carlo was walked up to the edge of these docks. He begged, didn't he, because he loved his life, because he didn't want to leave it. He imagined Antonia's face, Lina's arms, the ecstatic staccato of one day passing after another. He was absolutely animated, wasn't he, those last seconds his lungs drew breath. He was halfway through an inhale when the shot was fired. Antonia can picture it perfectly. Carlo's fervent wish to stay alive.

And a gunshot.

Death is indiscriminate. Death does not come knocking and ask who is least needed. It does not notice if you have a family; it does not care that you are one of the gears that turns the very world. Death does not take the slowest, the weakest, those separated from the pack. It reaches its hands into the heart. It pulls out something essential. It does not ask you to continue on, but you do anyway.

You cannot help it.

Sofia and Antonia hold on to one another as the wind picks up. It blows their clothes against their bodies. It cannot worm its way into their embrace. They are saying *thank you, thank you* and they are mourning everything and they are not just talking about this moment but their lives, their whole lives side by side, the incomprehensible blessing of it.

Behind them, Saul and Paolo stripping a sheet of plastic from a nearby pile of bricks. They will cover Tommy Fianzo Jr.'s body with it. They are already plotting how they can make this seem like an accident, like Eli's fault, like a casualty of conflict, rather than a catalyst for war.

Paolo and Saul turn to look at Sofia and Antonia. Every moment they are alive, they have more to lose.

Antonia pulls away from Sofia and looks down at her right hand.

The gun is nestled there; her finger still brushing the trigger. They are locked together now, it and she, part of something. They are at the beginning, and the end.

They are a choice, and they are the after-math.

Antonia moves her gaze out over the East River. Carlo is there. It is the first time Antonia has been able to picture his face since she was a child. He looks at Antonia. *All my life I've wanted you to see what I've become, Papa,* she tells him. He sees everything. He smiles. And then he disappears into the river.

"Thank you," says Sofia again. *If you can see me.*

*Thank you,* Antonia does not say, but Sofia hears it. *If I can see you.*

It begins to rain.

# ACKNOWLEDGMENTS

Before I was a writer, I was a reader. It's an incomparable privilege to contribute a volume to the libraries I love so much.

This would still be a Word document I kept open behind my other work without Dana Murphy, who loves this family like I do. I am in awe of the compassion, honesty, and thoughtfulness you put into your work, and I feel so lucky to do this alongside you. Thank you, my friend.

Tara Singh Carlson has nurtured the seed at the center of this book; it has grown bigger under her care than I ever imagined it could. Thank you for your bold vision and for the trust you put in me. Working with you has made me a better writer.

At Putnam, I'd also like to thank Ashley Di Dio, Bill Peabody, Janice Barral, Katy Riegel, Monica Cordova, Madeline Hopkins, Katie McKee, Nicole Biton, Brennin Cummings, Cassie Sublette, and formerly of Putnam, Helen O'Hare. It still amazes me that so many incredibly talented people have devoted their time, labor, and expertise to my story. Thank you for making such a beautiful book.

It is possible for me to draw a line from every book I have ever read to this one. Maybe this is less true in later books, but this is my first, and everything is in here. However, I owe a particular debt to *Christ in Concrete* by Pietro di Donato, to Kevin Baker's gorgeous New York fiction, to *The Godfather* by Mario Puzo, and of course, to *The Sopranos* — which is not a book, but whose richly realized characters helped me understand the importance of getting violence and love to coexist on the page. The paper "Origins of the Sicilian Mafia: The Market for Lemons" by Arcangelo Dimico, Alessia Isopi, and Ola Olsson provided direct inspiration for an important scene. Antonia would not have had the same translation of *Metamorphoses* as I do, but I am attached to my copy, translated by Charles Martin.

My remarkable network of family and friends served as emotional ballast, home base, personal chef, first reader. This wouldn't exist without any of you:

Mom, you are my North Star. I am of and

because of you.

Dad, thank you for teaching me to read, and to ROAR.

My brother, Adam, follows his heart; he always has; he gives me courage to do the same.

Nancy Veerhusen, Jana McAninch, Emma McAninch, and Violet Wernham expanded my understanding of family, and I am more loving, more empathetic, and smarter because of it; this book is better because of it.

I am immensely grateful to the Galison-Jones-Freymann clan. Mia and Sax, thank you for housing me the first fall I worked on this book in earnest. Thank you, along with Marion and Gerry, for sharing your family and its stories with me, and for telling me which is the best bagel place in New York. Carrie and Peter, thank you for letting me write in your Wellfleet house, which has solved every case of writer's block I've ever brought to it. Thank you all for giving this California girl an East Coast home.

Katie Henry has been my role model since I was sixteen; thank you for doing this first and answering all my panicked questions. I hope to move through the world with a fraction of your grace and humor. Rob, thank you for the tour of Arthur Avenue. Emily Beyda read an early draft when I didn't think I could write another word and gave me feedback that enabled me to keep going. Tessa Hartley housed me during that same nomad fall I began to really work on this; some of what's here was written on her porch in New Orleans. Ezra and Nick Paganelli are the official keepers of my soul and sanity; thank you for snack cake and sips and scaloppine, for Sunday dinners and shouting. All anyone needs to know about Alyssa May Gold is that despite living together when we were nineteen, she's still willing to be my friend. But on top of that, she is a force of nature, an incisive and feeling artist, and she has talked me down from countless emotional and creative ledges. My teachers Laura Slatkin and Christopher Trogan gave me many of the stories I love most, and a whole new language in which to consider them. Kathryn Grantham and the staff at Black Bird Bookstore have been an inimitable support as I edited; thank you for the privilege of spending my working days talking to people about books. And I would be remiss without thanking Fresh Direct the cat, without whose persistent weight on my feet I never would have been able to sit still long enough to finish even a single chapter.

I was not alone for any of this, even when

I was, technically, by myself. Sam, loving you is the honor of my life. If all I had been given was you, dayenu.

And reader, I cannot believe you are here. I am grateful and humbled. *Thank you* is wildly insufficient.

# ABOUT THE AUTHOR

**Naomi Krupitsky** was born in Berkeley, California, and attended NYU's Gallatin School of Individualized Study. She lives in San Francisco, but calls many places home. *The Family* is her first novel.

The employees of Thorndike Press hope you have enjoyed this Large Print book. All our Thorndike, Wheeler, and Kennebec Large Print titles are designed for easy reading, and all our books are made to last. Other Thorndike Press Large Print books are available at your library, through selected bookstores, or directly from us.

For information about titles, please call:
(800) 223-1244

or visit our website at:
gale.com/thorndike

To share your comments, please write:
Publisher
Thorndike Press
10 Water St., Suite 310
Waterville, ME 04901